TIME WALKER

EPISODE 2 OF THE WALKER SAGA

SHANNAN SINCLAIR

GNOSIS PRESS

INTRODUCTION

Dear Dream Walker,

In Episode 1 we talked about music being a basic tool for activating the brain centers, especially the lobes that house memory and recognition.

We can use music as a gateway, not only into our memories and history, but also to tap into our creativity and other dimensions. I provided links at the end of Dream Walker to music that helped me tap into the Signature Frequencies of the characters and relationships.

Because reading is already a portal into new worlds and experiences, I wanted to enhance that experience with music in Time Walker.

So throughout Episode 2, I have inserted music that sets tone and provides a signal line into and out of scenes. As a reader, you can chose skip these if it helps you stay in the story. If you'd like to take this story to a different level, the musical interludes provide a great place to pause from the words (one part of your brain), and into imagination (another part of your brain).

If you take that musical journey, I would love to hear your thoughts and feelings about it! Drop me a line at ShannanSinclair@gmail.com.

Catch you on the Astral~
Shannan Sinclair

TO TIME WALKERS EVERYWHERE

*"Sometimes nature guards her secrets with the unbreakable grip
of physical law. Sometimes the true nature of reality beckons
from just beyond the horizon."*
Brian Greene

$E=mc^2$

Albert Einstein

$4\ cps + 44\ cps = \infty$

Shannan Sinclair

OVERTURE

Ghosts 'n' Stuff ~ Deadmaus

ONE

THE BLACK VOID SUFFOCATED HER. Whether her eyes were open or closed, she couldn't tell. A persistent hush buzzed in her ears, and velocity pressed her hard against an unforgiving surface. Time and again, a hitch or a swerve heaved her to and fro. Total blindness, coupled with the erratic motion, gave her vertigo.

A cold sweat broke out first, then the bitter burn of bile filled her mouth. She swallowed it back down, her stomach lurching. Blood-red streaks of light strobed through her brain. Fiery explosions of orange and white flashed behind her eyeballs. An excruciating pain pierced her temporal lobes, and a clawing sensation scraped along the inside of her skull. The kaleidoscope intensified, pulsating in furious counterpoint to the mad scratching.

Come here, Poppet. I have some things to show you.

Aislen resisted the pull of the raspy voice in her head, terrified of where it would lead her, but a vise grabbed hold of her brain and began to squeeze. She tried to cling to the fading lucidity, but she was in a tug of war with something, someone, more powerful.

Come on, Poppet. It's very important.

The tenuous thread of consciousness snapped, and Aislen succumbed to the black.

TWO

SIGMUND SMELLED of skunk and sex. A sticky concoction of cheap eau de toilette, marijuana, sweat, and musk violated his nostrils. An occupational hazard: one could easily sniff out certain ways of making a living. Blood and raw meat clung to the butcher. Antiseptic, feces, and urine enveloped the doctor. Oil and metal coated the mechanic.

No matter how vigorously Sigmund scrubbed himself during his bath, the effluvia of the whorehouse ever wafted about him. Soap and water erased the Mary Jane, but nothing erased the cloying tang of flesh ground into fabric and skin. Even after draining and filling the tub three times, the stench lingered in the rising steam.

He gagged.

Yet at the same time, his scientific mind marveled at how easily the smallest scent—passing through two insignificant orifices—could vault him back through time.

The aroma of baking bread dropped him into his mother's arms, though he could recall nothing but yeast and milk rising from her chest.

The sharp savor of wet cement after rain transported him back to the Lebensborn, to the plump Fräuleins in crisp, white dresses who fussed over him like prized glass. They bathed, fed, and dressed him, tucked him into bed at night with stories. His favorite was the one about how his mother left him at the Lebensborn as a gift to the cause. They whispered that he was special, Himmler's chosen. *Aryan. Ideal. Superior.*

Even now, he relished the certainty of it: he had been born for greatness, marked out from the start. Power was his inheritance, his right.

Sigmund lathered harder, citrus soap fizzing across his pale skin. Orange and lemon rinds conjured their painted lips, bright eyes, and perfumed laughter. They were not unlike the whores he worked with now, except *those* women were eugenically valuable: flaxen-haired, blue-eyed jewels—perfect breeding vessels.

He remembered spying from the nursery, watching men in sable uniforms and shining knee-high boots, their red armbands glowing like hot coals, filing into the ballroom. One by one, the women paired off with them, vanishing behind doors. Giggles slipped into muffled cries. The air thickened with the scent of rutting and musk.

It always comes back around to sex. Sigmund thought. *Sex and death.*

He drained the claw tooth tub of its malodorous filth for the fourth time. Steam thinned into the air, carrying ghosts with it. The memory of the nursery soured: bellies swelling, bellies emptying, the endless wail of infants, and the stench of sour milk and shit. He remembered which ones were chosen—and which were not. A fat hand pressing down, silence replacing cries. Siggy slept peacefully after.

The weak existed to be culled; the strong to be refined. He had never doubted which he was.

Sigmund rinsed the last of the soapy lather off his pale skin, pulled the rubber plug, and watched as the water gathered into a vortex and slipped down the small dark hole. He sat back in the warm porcelain basin, letting his skin drip-dry.

A hard tap at the window jolted him from his reverie. Even though he knew it was only the glass readjusting from the balmy heat of the room back to the chill of the morning air outside, he still glanced over his shoulder. A wisp of fog slipped through the open gap between the pane and the sill. He watched it drift toward him, curling around the tub with unsettling precision, as if it had a will of its own.

Sigmund shrugged off the ridiculous notion and inhaled the cool filaments. He could make out the scent of the bay, a briny mixture of fish and iodine that reminded him of the snot and tears. Children again. Nordic boys and girls dragged from their homes, crying into the forests. Gunshots echoing. Not pheasant. Never pheasant.

The air stirred harder, a draught raising the hair on his bare arms. He half expected a Fräulein to appear, towel in hand, ready to scrub him dry. The thought aroused him—the memory of duty twisted into submission.

Then a door creaked from the floor below, and a sharp flare of irritation disrupted his arousal.

Astrid, fumbling as always. Her clumsiness both infuriated and excited him. Fear thickened the air from beneath the floorboards; he could feel her pulse through wood and plaster. He drank it in like wine. The idea of punishing her stoked his hunger. He fantasized about denying her food or bestowing one of his humiliating whippings upon her.

But the first hint of frying bacon whiffed its way into the room, and cast Sigmund back in time again. Back to his life after the Lebensborn, to his time at Auschwitz, and to Vater, the officer who fostered him.

It was with twisted pleasure that Sigmund remembered the smoke that clung to Vater's uniforms, not cooking smoke but human smoke—from the pits and furnaces that fed the Reich. Ever after, any scent of charred meat elicited a Pavlovian response. The phantosmia—exquisite and vile—aroused him.

Vater taught discipline with his hand. Three lessons every day: release your rage, remember your place, and prepare to command. The whippings were never a punishment. They were a coronation. He bent so that one day others would bend beneath him.

Sigmund had learned his lessons well. Astrid could attest to that. Vater would have been proud.

A clatter rang out from the kitchen below—Astrid dropping a utensil on the floor. The silence that followed was deafening, as though the house itself was holding its breath. Sigmund could feel Astrid standing below him through the floorboards. He could feel her listening for him. He could hear her heart race. A wave of her fear passed through the room, and all the hair on his body stood at attention. It was good that she was afraid; so very good. Excitement thrummed beneath his skin.

Sinking deeper into the empty tub, Sigmund allowed his mind to wander into more forbidden pleasures of his childhood memories. The heat of his passion was undamped by the chill of the porcelain. As he reached for himself, a loud percussion rocked the bathroom.

His first instinct was to rage against Astrid, but it wasn't her faltering in the kitchen this time. It was emanating from the mirror hanging above the bathroom sink. The air around him crackled with static, and Sigmund watched in amazement as the condensation on the mirror slowly frosted over into a thin film of ice.

What sort of phenomenon is this? He rose from the tub and moved closer to the mirror.

Peering into the rime, Sigmund saw a hazy fragment of his own reflection—only he barely recognized himself. The man in the mirror looked well beyond Sigmund's 32 years. The man in the mirror had hair more white than blonde, wispy and receding. The clear, bright blue eyes that normally looked back at Sigmund were grey—frosted over like the mirror itself.

Sigmund reached up and tried to wipe the disturbing distortion away. As he cleared away the frost, a figure stood in the reflection behind him. Immobilized, he continued to stare in the mirror as an apparition materialized at his back, a young woman with long, chestnut hair. The green in her eyes blazed at him—too sharp, too real.

"Who's there?" he shouted, whipping away from the reflection to confront the woman face to face.

With a loud whoosh, all the air was sucked out of the room. The window slammed shut with a crack, leaving Sigmund naked in silence, skin stippled with cold.

PRELUDE TO A DRIVE

The Chauffeur ~ Duran Duran

THREE

RAZE TOOK ONLY rural routes back to the city, the lost highways that led from the sleepy wasteland of the Central Valley to the lusty metropolis of San Francisco. He couldn't be too careful. Not only was the car he was driving hotter than hell, but there was also a woman bound and gagged in the passenger seat next to him. The last thing he needed was some CHiPie with a hero complex to come across them. He'd hate to have to kill someone over this clusterfuck.

But he would.

He had wasted precious time looking for the car. Raze wasn't a fool. He knew better than to use his personal vehicle for this mission. The 8 most definitely kept track of Raze as best they could. It was a given that they had a tracking device on his Audi.

He had wandered the pier for over thirty minutes, scanning for frequency emissions from cars with keyless ignitions that he could hotwire telekinetically. He rejected a dozen hybrids. There was no way he was going to kidnap someone in a Prius.

He finally happened upon this beauty. Only some spoiled

rich girl would have left a Mercedes SLS AMG parked on a waterlogged dock, exposed to the salty air of the Bay. With his left hand, he scanned its electrical system and honed in on its security frequency. With his right, he projected the coded frequency back into the circuitry. The doors unlocked, and the engine started. Raze threw the owner's chick-shit in a pile on the dock, hopped in, and sped off.

It was a sweet ride. Such a shame he'd have to torch it later. The 8 had ways of knowing where you'd been.

In the beginning, they had tried to implant nanotrackers to monitor him, but the mechanical bugs interfered with his frequency control, which limited his abilities during assignments. When Infinium's bioengineering subsidiary developed the first organic nanotracker, Raze was their first guinea pig. This time, however, the frequencies Raze channeled in and out of his body during his Travels cooked the bugs in his veins.

When The 8 finally allowed Raze to live off the corporation campus, they had Qi readers installed throughout his warehouse. The energy scanners were programmed to identify Raze's base signature frequency. Any frequency that didn't match his profile was identified as a "guest" and was tracked the whole time they were inside his house. This was a security measure to protect both Raze and his highly classified workspace, but Raze knew the Qis monitored his every move as well.

The Qis were going to be a problem. Especially since he was planning to stash his current "guest" there. He only had 50 more miles to figure out a way around them.

Aislen stirred beside him, the tape rasping against her skin.

The only other tracking option at The 8's disposal was having an operative assigned to him, a hound who could remotely view his activities and monitor his whereabouts. It was a huge waste of resources—Raze was a boring target in the physical world. He pretty much only drove from his warehouse in San Francisco to Infinium's headquarters in Palo Alto and back. The rest of his "Traveling" was 4D, and The 8 didn't have a hound good enough to track him in The Stratum—yet.

Even though Raze hadn't felt a hound around in months, he had still taken extra precautions for this mission. First, he made sure he was in constant motion. A hound couldn't hone in on a fast-moving target. Except for the nine seconds it took him to snatch the girl in the parking lot and restrain her in the getaway car, Raze had not stopped moving.

He had also set his watch to remind him to alter his signature frequency every three minutes. The constant fluctuation of his signature would make it impossible for any Viewer to pinpoint him on the grid. This was a trick he'd learned just yesterday from a 12-year-old.

These measures were probably unnecessary. Raze had never given The 8 any reason to suspect him of being a traitor.

Until tonight.

Was that what he was now? he wondered. *A traitor?*

Raze flexed his fingers against the wheel, knuckles whitening, and dismissed the thought. Absolutely not. He still had Infinium's interests at the forefront of his priorities. Everything that he'd learned tonight had the potential to make The 8 very, very happy. Raze had done good work.

First, he'd had a personal encounter with a rogue operative that The 8 had been hunting for over 24 years: Preston Reed.

Reed had once been Infinium's golden boy—the best of the best. Able to Travel beyond the Fourth, he brought back technologies that earned the company billions. But when Infinium pushed him into Control and Elimination ops, Reed refused... and vanished from the grid. The 8 had been scouring the planet for him ever since.

And tonight, Preston Reed had contacted Raze. Reached out to *him*, of all people. It was insane. Raze was the last person on Earth Reed should have trusted—and not only that, he'd asked him for help.

Raze should have refused. The request threatened everything he'd built for himself. But it could also pay off in ways he couldn't yet measure.

He cut a glance at the woman in the passenger seat. Aislen Walker—the daughter no one knew Reed had. The genetic link to Infinium's most wanted operative sat bound beside him. Oh, the things they could do with her.

This was going to be very good for the organization. Without a doubt. The 8 were going to be ecstatic with this little piece of asset he had acquired... when he got around to informing them.

It wasn't that he didn't plan on telling them.

He did.

Eventually.

He just needed a little time.

But before he briefed The 8 about Aislen—especially before he handed her over to them—he needed to figure out who *he* could trust, if anybody. Because over the past three days, Raze had discovered that nobody was really who or what they seemed.

Aislen Walker had been the first one to surprise him.

Raze looked at the woman again. Her head wobbled like a bobblehead as he sped through the winding hollows. Bound into the seat with some heavy-duty caution tape he'd found at the wharf, wearing an eye mask made from a black Wonderbra he found on the floorboard of the car, and some good, old duct tape plastered across her lips, she didn't look all that pretty anymore. But he definitely remembered what she looked like underneath his MacGyvered bindings.

He shook the image out of his mind. That was a distraction that could get him killed. He returned his attention to the stuttering yellow lines that snaked before him on the black asphalt and thought back to the first time he saw her instead, when she was covered in soot and reeked of fear—a more manageable vision.

Hard to believe that was only three days ago. On that morning, he'd been in *Demesne*, putting the finishing touches on the Parrish Project. His twelve-year-old Manchurian candidate, Blake Parrish, had already nailed phase one—putting a bullet through his father—and was seconds away from finishing phase two... ending himself... when Aislen Walker had the gall to gasp.

One breath.

And it fucked up everything.

Demesne was his baby. A controlled fourth-dimensional construct, carved out inside the bigger 4D plane Infinium, called The Stratum. Whenever Infinium's usual toys—mass manipulation, mind-control campaigns—failed, Raze stepped in. He lured subconscious minds into *Demesne*, jack them into his gaming interface, and do what he did best.

Nobody ever walked back out.

Until Aislen Walker stumbled in like she owned the place.

At first, Raze had thought she was just a harmless blip—an accidental astral tourist who'd taken a wrong turn in The Stratum. No big deal. He put a 4D round through her 4D skull and assumed she'd vanish like the rest. End of story.

Except it wasn't.

Because Aislen Walker wasn't harmless. She wasn't weak. She wasn't even close.

The meek little thing sitting beside him was a frequency bomb. Her oscillations tore *Demesne* apart when she deresonated, collapsing the whole construct like wet cardboard. And later, when she strolled into the psych ward, her voltage had blasted his astral body right out of Remote View. Sent him tumbling like a rookie.

He'd been wrong about her. Dead wrong.

And Raze didn't do wrong.

A few hours later, he learned his little puppet, Blake, wasn't really *his* puppet after all. It was Blake himself who'd confessed —that Ichiban had been inside his head from the start, teaching him tricks, showing him how to slip frequencies like a snake shedding skin.

Raze's jaw flexed as he sped through another hollow curve, the yellow lines stuttering beneath the tires.

At first, Raze suspected that Grant Parker had gotten hold of the boy. Parker dared to tell Raze to "watch his back," that he had found a new talent who could finally beat Raze at his game. So, of course, Raze thought that Parker was Ichiban and that Blake was his new protégé.

Mistake number two.

Raze should have known better. Parker didn't have the balls to do what Ichiban had done. Taking control of the mind of a 12-year-old kid and brutally murdering the kid's father? No. Parker never got his hands dirty like that.

No, Raze had jumped to conclusions, blinded by his own arrogance. He'd only scanned his immediate vicinity for threats, never imagining something from outside his sphere could interfere.

And that was mistake number three—one he hadn't noticed at all. Troy Kellen.

Parker, desperate to stay relevant so The 8 wouldn't "retire" him, had latched onto a solution in Troy Kellen. And Raze had never looked twice at the mild-mannered therapist who worked with Aislen at the hospital—never suspected he was Grant's new protégé. Too nice. Too pretty.

Kellen had a way about him, especially with women. Warm

and friendly, a Prince Charming straight out of some sappy rom-com or Grey's Anatomy. One look and the ladies melted. But it was all a farce. Underneath that magnetic charm, Mr. T was twisted and sadistic—everything Parker needed in a right-hand man. Parker could play the whiny bitch while his boy-wonder played it rough. They made the perfect couple.

Aislen was fooled, too. She was actually running *toward* him in the parking lot, like he was her rescuer, when he was more likely to slit her throat. Kellen had figured out there was something different about her. He knew who Ichiban was, knew Ichiban was looking for her. He just didn't know *why*. But thanks to Preston Reed, Raze knew. And if Kellen or Parker—or The 8—learned the truth, Aislen was done.

Kellen wasn't just a problem for Aislen. He was a problem for Raze. Kellen knew Raze had made contact with her and had been keeping it from The 8. Kellen had vowed that as soon as he uncovered her secret, he'd hand it over to The 8 himself. Which meant a death sentence for Raze.

Yeah, Kellen was his biggest threat right now. And if Raze thought he could get away with it, he'd have killed the bastard already. No hesitation. No doubt.

But doing that would send up red flags with The 8. No, Raze needed to flip the situation, turn it to his advantage—before Kellen beat him to the punch.

Aislen moaned and mumbled something under her breath. Her head was slumped forward as far as the restraints would allow. Her fingers were twitching, and a tremor worked its way up her arm. She had fallen asleep. And she was dreaming.

Raze wished he were dreaming right now. The fact that Aislen Walker was in the passenger seat next to him was a nightmare. It violated his personal code of ethics—not giving a shit. This was by far his worst mistake, and if he wasn't careful, it could end up being his last.

Raze had always prided himself on being in control. After years of playing everyone's bitch, he'd flipped the script and seized his own life. He'd popped smoke from the Nebraska shithole he never called home and clawed his way into a new reality.

He'd cut himself off from the virus of humanity, stripped out his weaknesses, and conquered the disease of emotion that clouded higher senses. With each demon he vanquished, his clarity sharpened, and his skills accelerated. He Traveled lighter, faster. It became effortless to pry open his targets' defenses and to bend them like toys. Controlling others was just the icing. Controlling himself—his own life—was the cake.

But now, Raze was in control of nothing, least of all himself. Every moment in Aislen Walker's presence—from *Demesne* to the hospital, from capturing her to channeling her frequency into his veins—had rewired him. His belief structures, his operating codes, every construct he'd built to keep the maggot life separate from his life, had started to unravel.

He was in *Demesne* when he realized the truth. He wasn't in control. He wasn't free. In building *Demesne*, he'd built his own prison. He was the real puppet—the pawn under the thumb of Grant Parker and The 8.

And when that truth hit, he came undone. The rage he'd buried deep surged up, and in a fit of fury, he turned on the only thing he still thought he controlled—*Demesne*—and tore it apart.

That's when Preston Reed showed up—walking straight through the wreckage into the heart of Infinium's territory to confront Raze. But instead of attacking, as Raze expected, Reed begged him... to help Aislen.

You are her only hope," Reed had said. "I can't stay close enough. I need you to protect her, Raziel. She won't survive without help."

Raze had scoffed. *Him?* Protect *her?* Reed had to be out of his mind. But the man pressed on.

"It isn't too late for you, Raziel. You've chosen the wrong path, and you know it—don't pretend you don't. You can keep selling your soul, clinging to scraps of power... or you can do the right thing for once."

Raze barked a laugh. "Spare me the sermon, Reed. You want me to believe there's such a thing as the right path? Newsflash: there isn't. There's only the one you carve yourself —and I already carved mine."

He turned to walk away—until Reed dropped the words that froze him in his tracks.

"That thing you call Ichiban? He's my grandfather. Aislen's great-grandfather."

The revelation sent Raze's mind reeling. He'd already guessed Parker and Kellen were scheming together, but Ichiban's identity and his obsession with Aislen had remained a mystery.

"Ichiban is really Sigmund Lange," Reed continued. "Founder of Infinium. The original Number One. He gathered eight of the most powerful people in industry to manifest his vision of controlling the world. But years ago, the others turned on him—locked him into a manufactured dementia so he couldn't expose them or strike back."

Raze thought of the Sanctum Sanctorum at Infinium head-quarters, of the single empty chair among the eight. A warning. A reminder of what happened to anyone who stepped out of line.

"How'd he break free from the option-lock?" Raze demanded.

"My grandfather created that lock. Getting around it was the easy part for him. But it didn't solve his need for a body. His body is failing. Too old. Too weak. So he hijacked your Blake—

used the boy's mind and body as a shell. But Blake is a temporary fix." Reed's gaze sharpened. "Lange intends to take revenge and reclaim his seat. For that, he needs a stronger vessel."

Raze's stomach dropped. "Aislen."

Reed nodded. "She's the one he wants. Their genetic link makes her the perfect host. He can overtake her cells almost as if they were his own." Reed's eyes blazed. "You need to protect her, Raziel."

"You actually think I care?" Raze sneered. "Lange, Ichiban, whatever name he's using—he can have her. Saves me the trouble of taking her out myself."

"Well then," Reed said at last, "if you won't do it for her— then you better do it for yourself."

Raze frowned. "How does protecting her help me?"

"Because if Sigmund Lange succeeds, he'll take back Infinium—and you are doomed."

Reed looked around at the burning ruins of *Demesne*, then back at Raze. "You don't want to help for the right reasons? Fine. Don't. Do it for the wrong ones, I don't care." He stepped forward, pressed his hand hard against Raze's chest. He didn't shout, but an energy of urgency traveled through his palm with a force that shattered Raze's last defenses. "But do it."

The charge was a command, not a plea. It reached deep inside of Raze, honed in on the last bastions of energetic fortresses he was clinging to, and sent them crumbling.

Raze's reaction was visceral. He snapped out of Theta with a single-minded focus: get to Aislen Walker. The repercussions of his actions didn't cross his mind, not as he hot-wired the Mercedes, not as he tracked her signature, not as he drove 100 miles per hour to the hospital to save her.

To kidnap her, he corrected himself, shaking himself out of the reverie. *Get it straight!*

But the image came anyway—her face smudged black with soot, eyes wide with shock. He shoved it away with a snarl. That wasn't saving. That was a mistake.

If he were saving Aislen Walker, it would mean he *was* a traitor. It would mean he was doing this for her. And if Grant or Kellen or The 8 suspected that, Raze was a dead man. No question. Raze needed to keep that focus. He was doing this for *himself*. Not Reed. Not Infinium. Most definitely not Aislen Walker. This was his last chance to regain control of his own life.

Aislen startled in the seat next to him. A scream, stifled by the thick tape across her mouth, rattled in her throat. She thrashed against the restraints, gasping for air, her nostrils opening and closing like the gills on a guppy just pulled from a pond.

If Raze didn't do something, she would suffocate. He downshifted his frequency, placed his palm on the center of her chest, and projected the vibration into her body. A trick he learned from her father. A breath caught in her lungs. Her heartbeat immediately decelerated, and she slowly relaxed back into her seat.

Suddenly, Raze knew exactly how he was going to get her past the Qi readers and into his house. It was a long shot, but it might work. The Bay Bridge was just ahead, its steady stream of orbed white lights creating a portal across the dark waters into the city. He jammed down the accelerator and launched the car through the toll plaza.

"We're almost there," he said, trying to keep her calm for the last couple of miles, but beneath the drone of the engine and rush of the road, Raze heard Aislen whimper.

FOUR

AISLEN SWOONED IN and out of consciousness, vacillating between a hazy fog and complete darkness. She couldn't pull in enough air, and her lungs were burning. She felt like she was drowning.

Beyond the darkness, Aislen felt a warm hand press against her chest. Her heart hammered hard against the unseen palm, but then it suddenly downshifted to a normal rhythm, and she felt her breath catch.

"We're almost there," a rough, male voice said from beside her. She could still feel the warmth from his hand on her chest.

Almost where? she thought, but slowly it all came back to her, and she went cold.

She was in a car... driving to who knows where... kidnapped by the man sitting beside her... the man who was probably going to kill her.

Aislen had awoken from one nightmare straight into another.

As the car accelerated, bits and pieces from the terrible dream floated around in her mind. She had been standing in a room heavy with steam. At first, she barely noticed the man in the tub—his pale skin and fair hair nearly blended into the porcelain. She would not have seen him at all if it weren't for the piercing blue eyes focused directly on her.

She tried to run, but an unseen force pinned her to the floor, holding her like iron to a magnet. The man lounged naked in the empty bathtub, watching her without a reaction, as though she wasn't really there. He leaned back, closed his eyes, and sighed.

Images raced through Aislen's mind in high-speed time-lapse. Women in particolored dresses dancing with what appeared to be Nazi soldiers. Children being dragged from their mothers by soldiers, their cries echoing like shrapnel through her skull. Shots cracked. Silence followed. The visions carried the nostalgia of memory, though none of them were hers.

She gasped—the force of her revulsion breaking her free from the grip that held her to the floor. She tried to make a run for it, but the unseen force pinned her in place.

Ah, ah, ah... you will see, the voice rasped against her ear, an icy hand forcing her gaze back toward the tub. *You will be a witness,* it growled inside her head.

Another memory slammed into her: a nurse drying off a small, towheaded boy as he stepped from the bath. The boy shifted, but what horrified Aislen was not his confusion—it was the way the man in the tub responded. His thoughts tangled shame with power, innocence with corruption, and she felt his hunger as though it were her own.

Aislen realized she was seeing this man's thoughts—his memories. As they played out in his mind, they ran amok through hers as well. Not only did she see the disturbing images, but she could also feel his feelings—how he felt powerful and in control. She could feel his excitement peaking.

The creak of a door opening from the floor below pulled both the man and Aislen out of his reverie. Aislen felt a flash of aggravation as the man began thinking about the person who had caused the disruption. She could see her—the young woman of his thoughts—no more than 17 or 18 years old, hair hanging in strings around her face as if she had not showered in days. Her pretty face was ashen with fear as she frantically worked in the kitchen.

With a peculiar omniscience, Aislen experienced the young woman's thoughts, too. *Father will hear me,* her mind whispered. Punishments flashed across Aislen's senses—denial, hunger, the lash of a belt.

Father? Was this man the girl's father? The idea repulsed Aislen, and she tried again to move toward the door, but she still had no control of her body.

Finally, another scene rose up: the towheaded boy being whipped by a soldier's hand. Pain and humiliation blurred with submission and perverse gratitude. Aislen could smell the acrid sting of scorched flesh, feel the twisted pride it evoked in the man whose memories she was trapped inside.

Revulsion broke her paralysis. She screamed, the sound wrenching her free of the phantom chains. She staggered back, turning away from the monster in the tub, desperate for escape—

And came face-to-face with a fogged mirror.

She expected to see her own reflection, of course. Instead, the mirror showed only steam, as though she weren't there at all —as though she were a ghost. Aislen leaned closer, desperate to find proof of her existence. The glass sizzled as if charged with electricity, then cracked loudly. The dew flash-froze into a thin sheet of ice.

The man stood up behind her, as shocked by the phenomenon as Aislen was. His pale silhouette stepped out of the tub and slowly moved toward her, closer and closer until he stood in the same space her ghost-presence occupied. Evil radiated from him the way heat bled off bathwater, and Aislen's heart froze solid, a mirror of the glass.

Then his reflection appeared in the mirror, where hers did not. But it was not the youthful blond she had seen in the tub. This version was aged—hair white as ice, eyes clouded with cataracts.

And Aislen knew him—old Mr. Lange. The man who had seized her in the hospital, pulling her into his lap with a strength that belied his age, forehead pressed to hers as though he could claw his way inside her skull. She remembered the sensation of scratching, of him trying to burrow into her mind.

"You want to help your bloodline, now don't you?" he had whispered, voice dripping with mockery as she fought to get away.

The words echoed again, coalescing into a new refrain in her head.

Sehen sie jetzt, Poppet? Verstehen sie, wer sie sind?

Do you see now, Poppet? Her mind translated the foreign tongue. *Do you understand who you are?*

Shock chilled her marrow. She looked back at the mirror.

Yes. Yes, she did.

Aislen understood that the man in this room was a younger version of Sigmund Lange.

She understood that Sigmund Lange was her great-grandfather.

She understood that Sigmund Lange was speaking now, inside her head.

The car suddenly screeched to a halt, slamming Aislen forward against the restraints and knocking her fully into the present. The engine sizzled and spit, then went silent as the man sitting next to her shut off the ignition. A half second later, there was a loud pop, and a rush of damp air flooded into the compartment. The man got out of the car, and the driver's side door sealed shut again.

Aislen sat alone in the car for a long time, the car ticking and clicking as it cooled, like a countdown to doom. She wondered what the man was doing—and worse, what he was thinking about doing.

The possibility of being rescued was vanishingly small. Her kidnapper would make sure of that. In the brief moment they were face to face, Aislen could see pure calculation and hard clarity in his eyes.

She knew that no amount of pleading, crying, or begging would move him. In fact, any play for sympathy would probably enrage him and only hasten her death. An uneasy shiver scampered through her stomach.

The door beside her suddenly popped open, and the man was immediately present. She could feel the heat of his breath on her face and the warmth of his hands as they moved quickly across her body, snapping loose the restraints. The tension that had been propping her up in the seat released, and she slumped forward, falling against him, which felt like falling against granite. The man grabbed her hard by the shoulders and shoved her back up.

"Do you want to die tonight?" he growled in a low voice.

Each word stabbed her in the gut. "No," she choked.

"Then you need to listen and do exactly as I say. Do you understand me?"

I'm going to die, her mind said, even though she heard her mouth whisper, "Yes."

The man coiled something around her wrists and cinched it tight. Then he reached an arm around her waist and scooped her up out of the car. He carried her effortlessly, like a sack of potatoes, for several minutes before setting her feet first on the ground.

"Stand here. Don't move. Don't speak. Got it?"

Aislen nodded, then listened as the hard tap of his heels quickly walked away from her, leaving her alone. The terror coursing through her body was electrifying. All of her senses were on fire. A drizzle in the air kissed her skin, setting all her hairs on end. It was laced with trace scents of wet wood, salt, and rotten fish, like she was near the ocean. But the ground she was standing on was hard, not pliant like grass or dirt, and the atmosphere around her hummed with the drone of traffic, not waves. In the distance, she could hear a siren wailing.

They were in a city! The man had brought her to a city! The thought gave her hope. She had thought for sure the man would have taken her someplace isolated to do whatever it was he had planned. The fact that he brought her into a city astounded her. There would be people around. She could scream! She could get someone's attention! She had a chance! But before she had time to orient herself further, she heard his footsteps returning, and she shrank inside.

"Come with me," the man said as he grabbed hold of her arm and yanked her toward him. His fingers dug painfully into her bicep as he pulled her along, but she dared not whimper. She stumbled unevenly beside him, trying to keep up as best she could. It must not have been good enough because his arm slipped around her waist again, and she was lifted and carried along as if she weighed nothing. The man didn't slow his stride in the slightest, practically running with her like that for what seemed like a mile.

Pressed up against him, Aislen could smell a faint tinge of clean skin mingled with the stronger scent of gasoline. The combination was strangely pleasant until she realized that she hadn't smelled the gasoline earlier, and the man had probably set fire to the car they were in. The scent quickly lost its appeal as another hope of being rescued was dashed.

The man stopped abruptly, flung her around, and set her back on the ground. Then he seized her by both shoulders and thrust her back against a wall.

"Pay attention," the man barked. He was louder now, so Aislen knew they were somewhere more private. "If you don't do exactly as I say—I mean, exactly—you will die. Understand?"

This is it, she thought to herself. *This is where he is going to kill me.*

Aislen nodded. She felt the heat of him move in closer to her, and she flinched in anticipation of a violent physical attack. But rather than touch her, she only heard him draw in a deep breath, then exhale it. A growl whispered through his throat.

He repeated this several times.

What was he waiting for? she thought.

"Match my breathing," he ordered.

Was he serious? Match his breathing? What kind of pervert was he? Aislen decided that if she wanted to live a little longer, it would be a good idea to do what he said, even if it didn't make sense. She began following his breathing pattern, inhaling when he did, holding it for a second, then breathing out long and slow. They repeated this over and over again, the man never touching her.

"Close your lips," he whispered slowly across a slow breath. "Exhale through your nose and match the sound that you hear in my throat."

It was getting creepier, this synchronized breathing, but Aislen did as she was told, mimicking his breathing pattern for several more minutes until she found herself growing relaxed and slipping into a serene trance. This was surprising, given the predicament she found herself in.

You've been able to create signal lines before, right? The man spoke again, but this time she heard him in her head, not her ears.

Aislen was startled by the telepathy and by the fact that he knew about signal lines. It was one of the things her father had shown her how to create. She stopped breathing and fell out of sync with him.

"Focus," he seethed out loud. His mouth was so close that his breath brushed across her face. She clenched her eyes under the blindfold.

Lock in, he said back inside her head. *You've got to be able to do this, or it's over!*

Okay, Aislen thought. *I'll try.*

No trying! Do it. Slip for one second, and it's the last second you get.

Aislen did what he said, tuning out everything else going on around her like her life depended on it because, in fact, it did. She focused on the rhythm of it, the ins and outs, the sounds, and the waves of it. She descended into the calm once more.

Unexpectedly, swirls of color began to fill her head, if you could call it color—it was actually the lack of color that stood out to Aislen. Varying shades of gray were threaded with veins of the blackest obsidian. Flecks of gold sparked in and out, interrupting the play between shadow and night.

You see that? the man asked.

Yes.

Good. Now, instead of creating a signal line with that energy, imagine it moving around you. Let it overtake your space —wear it like a cloak. Once you are wrapped in it, hold it there and don't let it go.

I mean it. His mental voice took on an insistent edge. *Do not lose hold of it for even a second. No matter what.*

Aislen didn't quite understand what he was asking her to do, but she hadn't understood her father's instructions about creating signal lines either, and she had been able to do that.

She concentrated on the kaleidoscope in her mind's eye and imagined wrapping herself up in it. An intoxicating swoon set her spinning for a moment, but then she felt something snap into place, and she instantly became clear and alert.

The man must have felt the shift, too, because he wrenched her off the wall, flipped her around, and pulled her back up against the front of his body. He felt as rock-solid as the wall she'd just been up against, only warmer, and she found herself falling into distraction.

Don't. You. Dare! The man's snarl stung her brain.

Aislen gasped, mentally grasped the energetic cloak, and pulled it closer. Sharp clarity snapped back in place.

Good. Stay right there, the man said, and suddenly they were on the move. They didn't have to go far this time, only a hundred feet, before they stopped again.

Aislen heard the grinding of a motor, and somewhere deep inside, she felt an inkling that she should be afraid, but swimming within the dark energy, she felt completely calm. It was an amazing relief. Her normal reaction would have been to allow her fears to overwhelm her. This utter indifference was a sanctuary. So much so that she opened herself up even more to the inky mist, allowing it to invade her space until she became one with it.

A montage of images began to flicker through her mind. Pictorial fragments juxtaposed and superimposed on each other in a speed-of-light composition. A small red tricycle sitting on a country road faded into an ocean where dolphins frolicked. A crashing wave dissolved into a messy bedroom and panned across a floor littered with dirty clothes and candy wrappers and walls pocked with holes. It was all so random and unfamiliar.

The man carried her forward, and the motor started again. Aislen could feel the change from being outside to inside. They were in a garage.

Steady now, the man telepathed. *It's do-or-die time.*

Aislen's inner coward tried to rear her frightened head again, but the hyper-calm suffocated it.

Another jumble of images appeared. This time, the faces of strangers, all men, approached and passed by her. One showed her that he had a rope twisted around his neck. Another pointed to his throat, slit open like a bloody smiley face. One had a knife embedded in his chest. One after another, they marched past—a thousand faces of death. At the end of the long, morbid line, one last man approached. The rhythm of his gait and the features of his face seemed familiar to Aislen. As he drew near, Aislen saw a single bullet hole in the center of his forehead. She recognized him. It was the man from the first of her strange dreams—the man she watched getting shot by his own son, Blake Parrish.

The havoc playing out in her mind should have stirred up dread and panic, but Aislen felt absolutely nothing: no fear, no sadness, only a placid apathy.

The man jostled her roughly from behind, snapping her out of the strange theater. He pushed her forward a few more steps, stopped again, and stood completely still. Aislen felt him holding his breath.

There was a loud beep followed by a series of clicking sounds.

"Alone," the man commanded, and there was another sequence of beeps and clicks.

He turned Aislen in a different direction and pushed her

forward again. They moved quickly, turning this way and that as though navigating labyrinthine halls. The man's footsteps rapped loudly on the floor and echoed off into the distance. Then he suddenly swept her off her feet and into his arms and began ascending what could only be a spiral staircase. They spun round and round, climbing higher and higher.

The gyration swept her mind off into another foreign scenery, and Aislen was standing in a dark room. Her eyes traveled up its stone walls until her head leaned all the way back and she found herself staring at a domed skylight of faceted glass. Embedded in the center of the crystal ceiling was an infinity symbol of gold with two platinum capital Is superimposed over the top of it.

She had seen that symbol before in the strange landscape of her first dream, in the alternate reality she'd come to learn was Demesne. An animation of the symbol had repeatedly looped on the arm patches adorning each of the soldiers' arms—including the arm of the man who was carrying her now.

She lowered her gaze and faced a seated line of men and women, eight of them, each sitting on a gold throne behind a massive table of glass illuminated by an eerie blue light. They glared down at her. The normal Aislen would have wet her pants being in front of such an intimidating group, but this Aislen felt composed and confident. It was nothing like her.

Aislen realized that just like in her vision of Mr. Lange in the bathtub, she was experiencing the thoughts, memories, and feelings of the man holding her. He not only had her in his grip physically, but he also held her mentally. Or maybe it was her holding him. That was what the cloak of dark energy really was —his energy.

The man stopped climbing and moved through a few more turns before stopping and holding still yet again. There was another beep and the sound of a door sliding open. Then they were going down a flight of stairs. With all the twisting and turning, ups and downs, and traveling in and out of visions, Aislen was thoroughly disoriented. Even if she could find the strength to fight the man and try to escape, there would be no way she could find her way out of the maze they had just gone through.

There was one more sound of a door opening, and the man finally set her down.

"Alpha 8," he commanded.

A soft glow of light pierced through the cracks in Aislen's blindfold, and light jazz began to play.

The man turned her around to face him, pulled apart the bindings on her wrists, then reached up and yanked the blindfold from her face.

Aislen tried to open her eyes, but even though the lighting was low, it was still blinding. The man was only a black shadow moving away from her to the other side of the room. There was a large door beside him, open into a gaping yet inviting darkness.

"Don't even think about it," he snarled over his shoulder as he began typing on a keyboard.

He knew her thoughts, too, apparently.

As her eyes adjusted, she could see that they were in a small laboratory. It reminded Aislen of a dentist's office, stark white and antiseptic, complete with a strange reclining chair in the middle of it. The lounge was suspended in the air without strings or a pedestal to hold it in place, floating like a magician's assistant. Besides the computer the man was working on, an enormous television screen hung on the wall. A pattern of gray, black, and gold that matched the abstract image Aislen was seeing in her mind circulated on the screen.

The television suddenly went blank.

"Hopefully, this will buy us a little time," the man said as he turned around to face her.

Aislen choked on her next breath. It was the first time outside of her dreams that she had seen him.

She'd have thought that her nightmare image of him would have been a gross exaggeration of reality, but no; in reality, he was downright supernatural. Dressed all in black, from the form-fitting long-sleeved shirt to the slacks to the shoes that he wore, every ripple of his imposing physique cut through the monotone of his clothing. His attire was just a shade lighter than the jet-black of his hair, which framed a chiseled face. The arctic blue of his eyes stood out in surreal contrast to the rest of his cimmerian presence.

His flawlessness was inhuman.

Her body jolted with a response she didn't understand—skin prickling, breath stuttering, a coil of heat tightening low in her belly. For a dizzying instant, she couldn't tell if it was terror or something worse. She crushed the thought before it could bloom. No. It was fear. It had to be.

He's a monster, Aislen thought.

The man's eyes narrowed at her, and a flash of anger passed across his face.

Aislen felt something inside her body rip away from her. The cloak of calm evaporated, and she was completely immersed once more in her familiar terror.

He took a step toward her, and Aislen jumped backward, losing her balance and falling into the chair behind her. Something slipped from the front pocket of her jeans and clanged loudly on the floor. She listened to the musical ting as it rolled across the concrete toward the man. Aislen watched helplessly as he bent down and picked up the labyrinth amulet.

She had forgotten all about the pendant. How could she? It was a gift from her father at their last meeting. Earlier, it had been screaming at her nonstop, first insisting that she go to the hospital to find Troy, but then trying to stop her. Its mixed messages had confused her, and finally, in frustration, she had ripped it from her neck and placed it in her pocket. Still, it harangued her. It stung her legs and held her back, keeping her from getting to Troy—to safety.

Yet once this man had her imprisoned in his car, it had gone silent, and she had not felt it stinging or vibrating since. Had she broken it? Why had it stopped talking to her?

"Where did you get this?" the man asked, examining it. He ran his thumb around the outer ring of it, then looked up at her, waiting for her answer.

Aislen didn't want to say. It was her only connection to her father, and he had told her not to talk about him to anyone—that he could be tracked down if she did. Even though she had failed to keep herself out of harm's way, the least she could do was protect him.

"It's nothing," she said, hoping she sounded convincing. "Just a family heirloom. It's worthless."

His eyes leveled at hers.

He already knows, she thought. *He's going to kill me.*

The man narrowed his eyes again, looking downright hateful. He marched across the room toward her, and Aislen cowered back into the chair.

The man leaned down and got into her face. "You're a liar."

The accusation stung. She had never been called a liar before. But she'd never really been a liar before. He stood back up, towering over her.

Aislen's heart stopped. *This is it. This is really it now.* She recoiled deeper into the recliner, curling her knees up against her chest as a final bastion of protection.

As the man watched her trying to protect herself, Aislen could see the muscles in his jaw clench and his fists balling up.

She waited for him to attack. But he didn't. He just looked at her. Something other than murderous rage passed over his face. Something resigned, even sad. But it evaporated in an instant.

"I have shit to do," he snapped. He slipped the amulet into his jacket pocket, turned his back on her, and walked toward the door.

"Theta 4," he commanded into the air, and the lights went out in response. The room was filled with a low hum and the sound of static.

As his dark silhouette stepped through the darker passageway of the door, a question bubbled up involuntarily.

"Who are you?"

The man stopped cold. Aislen sucked in her breath, expecting him to come back and really do her in.

"My name is Raziel," he growled as the door slid shut between them. The name burned into her like a brand, sealing her to him whether she wanted it or not.

FIVE

BWEEEEP! *Bweeeep! Bweeeep! Bweeeep!*

The high-pitched bleating griped on and off incessantly in his left ear. It had been going on for hours, and it was driving him nuts.

At first, he thought it was his alarm clock... until he remembered that he didn't own an alarm clock. Never had. Being raised on a ranch and having to wake up before the sun for chores had developed an inner body clock that automatically woke him up exactly when he needed to *for the rest of his life.* Which was kind of annoying now that he thought about it—he never could sleep in for shit.

Bweeeep! Bweeeep! Bweeeep! Bweeeep!

Maybe it was Tuesday, and the garbage man was picking up the trash in his alley.

But that would only make sense if the goddamn truck was stuck in perpetual reverse!

Mathis tried to open his eyes so he could locate the aural torture device, but a thick layer of eye-gunk had thoroughly superglued his eyelids together.

He tried to reach for the service revolver he kept on the nightstand next to his bed so he could shoot the fucking thing. But not only was his arm too heavy to lift, it was tied to something. No, something was literally buried into his flesh, and every time he attempted to move, there was a painful tugging in the crook of his elbow.

That sort of freaked him out, and he would have hollered like a little bitch, but his tongue was stuck to his soft palate with a spit-paste that tasted like butthole.

Bweeeep! Bweeeep! Bweeeep! Bweeeep!

God, what he wouldn't do for a brewski right now, the ice-cold nectar of heaven. The thought of it sounded so good, Mathis heard himself moan.

"Robert?"

What? Who's there? He had assumed he was alone. Had he gotten lucky last night and not freakin' remembered?

"Robert, are you awake?" The woman's voice was sweet and melodic, like heaven just on the other side of the infernal bweeeeping.

"Robert, can you hear me?" The voice was next to him now, tinged with worry. Familiar. He felt soft fingers brush lightly down his forearm and embrace his hand.

Sabine! The name registered, and he caught the flash of a memory of her beautiful face.

Mathis wanted to open his eyes to see her there, to ask her where he was and what was going on, but his head was swimming. This was the worst hangover ever! He couldn't even manage to articulate another grunt from his throat. He tried to squeeze her hand, to acknowledge and reassure her, but he couldn't get the message to his fingertips.

"Hello, Ms. Walker." A male voice interrupted his attempt at hand-to-hand communication with Sabine. This voice also sounded familiar—*too familiar.*

This voice made his stomach turn.

This voice needed to fucking die.

"Hello," Sabine said. It was obvious that she recognized the man, too. She sounded warm, almost relieved. "It's Troy, right?"

"Yes, ma'am. That's right."

Troy? Who's Troy? Mathis scoured through mush, trying to put a face to the name, trying to understand why he wanted to kill this motherfucker.

Mathis listened as slow footsteps moved closer to them. He tried to shout out a warning—to tell Sabine to get the hell outta there—but he was paralyzed.

"How is he doing?" The man was right beside Sabine now. "Has he woken up at all? Has he said anything?"

None of your goddamn business! Mathis yelled impotently through his forehead.

Sabine sighed. "No. Not yet, unfortunately."

"Yeah? That's too bad," this *Troy* said, but Mathis had the distinct feeling that *Troy* really was perfectly fine with the fact that Mathis hadn't woken up yet.

"I'm just so relieved that he's going to be okay," Sabine continued. "The officer said that if he hadn't been able to call me, and if I hadn't called 911 when I did, he might not have made it."

What? He had called her? He might not have made it? What the hell was goin' on?

"That is very fortunate for him."

Nope. This guy was only *trying* to sound supportive. His voice was dripping with kindness, but Mathis could tell it was affected; something sinister lurked beneath the words.

Mathis tried again with all his might to figure out where he knew this man from—where Sabine would know him from—but his memory was too cloudy.

"Yes, very fortunate," Sabine said, squeezing Mathis's hand

again. There was a moment of silence between Sabine and this Troy, punctuated by the agonizing bleating sound.

"Here, let me take care of that for you," the man said. A spark of recognition peeked through the brain stew, and a memory burst into his mind: *"Here, let me take care of that for you,"* followed by an automatic weapon spraying electric blue bullets into two soldiers.

The shrill squeal stopped.

"Works for me. Does that work for you?" Troy asked.

Another recollection overcame Mathis.

"Works for me. Does that work for you?" A voice, *that* voice, had said those exact words to Mathis after the two soldiers exploded into a gory spray of blood and guts. Mathis turned around in his mind's eye to confront the voice and came face to face with a nubby, green troll whose eyes bulged out from his skull.

Dookie! It was Dookie! From the Demesne!

It all came back to him. He had gone back into that stupid game. He should've left it alone, but he had to solve the Parrish murder and find out why this "Ichiban" wanted Aislen.

Just as Mathis had pulled a ragtag clan together and was making decent progress, Dookie showed up, whining for a lift. Mathis let him tag along—he needed the firepower—but by the Sixth Octave, the little troll turned on him, vaporizing the newbies and shoving a gun in Mathis's face.

"My hero!" Sabine exclaimed, back in reality. "That machine has been going off nonstop all night. It was driving me crazy. Seriously, thank you."

My hero, my ass! Mathis thought.

"No problem," Troy said. He was standing beside Sabine again. Mathis felt his gut clench. He wished his fist could, too, so he could pummel this asshole.

"So, Ms. Walker," Troy started again, his tone still reeking with false friendliness. "I was wondering if Aislen was around here somewhere?"

"What? Oh, no! She left hours ago. She said she was going to meet you at the hospital. Something about helping you move that little boy, what's his name? Blake?"

"Yeah, that was the plan... but she didn't show up. I thought maybe we crossed paths somewhere along the way and missed each other."

"Must have, because it's like her not to do something she said she was going to do. She didn't come back here, though."

"Hmmm, that's too bad. I really wanted to take her there. It's a very special place."

Moving Blake... meeting at the hospital... the puzzle was coming together, but at the mention of a "special place," Mathis swooned back into a stupor, back into the jungles of Octave 6. Ichiban was about to take him to the "special place" in the game.

Only when they got there, it wasn't paradise—it was a wasteland.

Fed up, Mathis had ripped the game visors off his face and thrown them on the ground. He should have found himself back in the comfort of his own home, but he was still standing in the desert, the visors disintegrating into the red earth.

Then Ichiban had waved his hand across the sky, and right before Mathis' eyes, the desert completely transformed into a ruined metropolis. It was the same cityscape that had been frozen on the bloody television screen in the Parrish house the night of the murder.

Mathis tried to demand answers, "What does Aislen Walker have to do with the murder of Scott Parrish?"

The question sent Ichiban sideways—*literally*. His neck snapped, nearly breaking in half, and the panicked cry of a boy shouted, "*What happened to my dad!?*"

And that's when Mathis knew: somehow, Blake Parrish was inside of Ichiban, and he had no idea that his dad was dead.

Everything had suddenly spun out of control. Dookie appeared, demanding answers. And then, out of nowhere, a man materialized from the crackling air—black-clad, eyes burning with unnatural blue fire.

Both Ichiban and Dookie knew him. Ichiban vanished from the desert. Dookie confronted the guy.

"Raziel, I can explain everything. But let me take care of this guy first." Then the fucking hobgoblin turned his massive ray gun on him. "Sayonara, Sergeant."

As blue bullets flew toward Mathis, white-hot electricity burst from Raziel's palms, colliding with Dookie's fire. The clash nearly stopped them, but a residual charge hit Mathis dead center.

He fell to the ground, his heart seizing and offbeat. As he struggled to breathe, Raziel knelt beside him, placing one hand on his chest and one on his head.

"Go now," the man whispered, and everything went black.

"I have no idea where Aislen might be," Sabine said from outside his dream of dying. The remaining images disintegrated like everything in the game, like ash blowing away. He clawed to hold onto Blake's voice, Raziel's eyes—*don't forget!*

"I thought she might have come back here to be with you," the fuckwit next to Sabine was saying.

The need to pulverize this guy began pulling Mathis to consciousness faster. He tried to grab as much as he could from the dream before it was gone for good. *Blake's voice. Inside Ichiban. The man in black. Those eyes. Raziel.*

"I'm sure you're right. Aislen would have definitely come back here when she didn't find you at the hospital." Sabine sounded very concerned now, and a need to protect her stirred

Mathis out of the memory. Though the ache in his chest remained, the last of the dream vanished.

"I'm sure it's nothing to worry about, Ms. Walker," Dookie said. "But would you do me a favor?"

"Sure, Troy. Anything."

The lightbulb finally lit. Troy *Kellen!* Aislen's co-worker! And the therapist who had treated Blake Parrish for his video game addiction! Of course! He knew all the secrets of the game. He knew all the ins and outs of the Parrish murder. He also knew who Ichiban was and that Ichiban was after Aislen.

From the sound of it, Troy was after Aislen himself. And it definitely wasn't because he was a friend.

But if Aislen wasn't with Troy... and she wasn't here with her mom... *where was she?*

"If Aislen comes back here tonight, could you have her call me right away?" Troy said. "We need to get together as soon as possible."

"Will do," Sabine agreed. "As soon as I see her, I'll have her call you."

"Thanks a lot. You have a good night. And I hope he gets better real soon," Troy said, patting Mathis on the chest.

Mathis wanted to roar to life, play a little game of payback with this fucker, and interrogate him with his fist. But a heavy lethargy was pulling him down. All his body wanted him to do was sleep. Mathis tried to resist its alluring pull, listening to the click of Troy's shoes dissipating down the hall.

Sabine squeezed Mathis's hand. "Something doesn't seem right about that, Robert. If he hasn't seen Aislen, how did he know we were here?"

Call Juckson now! Mathis tried screaming. He could feel his sticky lips peel apart and open and shut, but only static filled his ears.

"Shhhhhhhhh." Her whisper crackled like static in his

skull. "Just rest, Robert." She smoothed a cool hand across his forehead, sending him into a glissade down the mountain of consciousness.

"Everything will be all right," she said.

Mathis knew damn well it wouldn't.

SIX

AISLEN CURLED up in the strange chair, looking into the dark space where her captor had stood. A million questions peppered her mind, and her emotions roiled.

Who was this man, Raziel?

For sure, the most evil man alive.

What kind of name is that?

Of course, that couldn't be his real name. He wouldn't give her that.

But why not? If he was planning to kill her?

Unless he wasn't planning to kill her.

But why kidnap her if he wasn't going to kill her?

Aislen noticed that the chair she was in, although it looked sterile and institutional, was extremely comfortable. So comfortable, she felt like she was floating, suspended in the air. The darkness was dense. She seemed to be floating in a black hole, its heavy energy magnetizing all her questions, confusion, and fear, drawing them away, calming her mind and body.

A memory of her father and their last visit together drifted into her mind. She was surrounded by an infinite blanket of stars, hovering in a bubble in space. He was standing before her, weaving a three-dimensional hologram in the air between them, talking about the nature of reality.

"Reality only *appears* three-dimensional, but you are *more* than three-dimensional," he said. The abstract words had spun incomprehensibly around her head.

She could see her father now, drawing sweeping spirals of sterling light, layering and intertwining them. He had flattened the hologram in the palm of his hands and formed it into the labyrinth pendant, and then he placed it around her neck on a chain.

Listen to it carefully, for it will guide your way. And someday—I pray—it will guide you back to me.

She heard his words again and understood. The pendant was some kind of map—a guidance system that could help her find her way back to her father, wherever he was hiding.

Then he said goodbye, and she floated away in space, away from him, waking up on the floor of her bedroom with the necklace still around her. Somehow, she had brought it with her from the dream into reality. She had forgotten about it until it fell from her pocket.

And now her captor, this *Raziel*, had it.

Despair washed over her, pulling her out of calm lucidity and back up into anxiety. Aislen was no match for this man. She didn't know where she was or how to get out of this place. Overwhelmed, she buried herself deeper into the chair. The deeper she sank, the more it adjusted, catching every muscle before it could tense again, shifting at each breath as though it already knew her shape. It didn't feel like furniture. It felt like a design.

Aislen reached into her pocket again, finding the fine silver chain and fastening it around her neck. She would find a way to get the pendant back, then find a way to escape, then find her way back to her father and home.

The chain and the chair were a small comfort in the thick darkness, and she found herself relaxing despite her fears.

The hum recalibrated when she exhaled, cycling through frequencies until it found the one that bypassed her fear. The longer she lay there, the deeper she fell into it, and the noise became something more.

It became the wind, a lullaby that calmed her anxiety. Then it became the ocean, languid waves rolling in and slipping away, massaging her senses, hypnotizing her overthinking mind. She felt all the tension drain from her body.

Her body betrayed her first—the heaviness in her limbs, the slackening jaw—while her mind thrashed, unwilling to yield. She shook her head, trying to rattle the fog loose. 'Stay awake,' she whispered, clawing for panic as if fear could anchor her. But the rhythm of the room only pressed harder, stripping her of even that weapon.

The last thought she had before darkness closed in was that she hadn't chosen this.

SEVEN

RAZE SAT HEAVILY on the edge of his bed. Exasperation escaped from his body, half sigh, half groan.

What did the hicks in his hometown used to say? Up Shit Creek without a paddle?

Yeah, that about summed it up.

Although his idea of having Aislen match his base signature to get past the Qi readers had worked brilliantly, locking her in The Womb was not a good idea at all. It was an unsustainable solution for all the obvious reasons—lack of food, water, and toilet facilities. But there was a bigger issue: Raze had given her a key—the key to the whole house—and the key to him.

For Aislen to conceal her energy field from the readers, Raze had let her in, and not just superficially. He'd buried her in. *Deep.*

He had felt her in there, riffling through buried memories and stirring up the sediment of his psyche. He could feel a shadow of her in there still, like an echo bouncing faintly through a canyon. It put him in a very vulnerable position, being *that* connected to her.

Before tonight, he'd had the option to disappear if need be. Even Infinium hadn't touched upon or captured those darkest frequencies. If he'd ever needed to hide, like Preston had, those unmapped energies could have cloaked him.

But now Aislen had been there. If she was adept enough, and Raze was certain she had that potential, she could tap back in. They were intrinsically connected now.

Even worse, Aislen had seen the truth of him—she knew him for what he was. And she had called him "monster." The assessment angered him. That he cared what she thought angered him even more. Nobody's opinion of him had ever mattered before. In fact, he relished the disgust and fear his presence invoked in others. But the fact that her opinion of him was so low, and the look of fear and disgust that had passed over her face, disturbed him. He had never had remorse for any of his actions. Remorse was a product of morality, morality a paradigm for sheep, and Raze had severed the connections between action and conscience long ago.

But it mattered tonight. Because she thought it. A new feeling had seeded itself in his gut. Shame.

He hated the word, hated the heat it spread in his chest, hated that it came from her.

"Who are you?" she'd asked.

That was a good question.

Who am I? It had always been an easy answer: *your worst nightmare.*

But that wasn't his answer. He'd given her his name. He could have used his gaming moniker, Craze, but why? She already had access to everything about him. Knowing his name wouldn't make it any worse. And at least if she called him Raziel, she wouldn't be calling him Monster.

Raze wished he could go back in time and rearrange the sequence of events that had led him to this place, to having ever crossed paths with Aislen Walker. Being in her presence had rewired him in a way he did not understand—in a way he did not like. He was uncomfortable. His skein didn't fit over the new truth of him. He wanted to go back to being who he was and doing what he did and not giving a damn about any of it.

But that was impossible. The third dimension ran on a fixed timeline. If there were cracks in that law, he hadn't found them. So this was where he was now.

Raze thought of her lying in The Womb below and pulled her trinket out of his pocket.

He traced his finger around the glimmering spiral maze, from the tip of the thin molten metal path where it began, then back and forth around the loops. The pendant was definitely a gift from her father. He could feel a trace of Preston Reed's energy emanating from it. He could also feel it broadcasting several distinct signal lines. When his finger brushed across one of the embedded stones, the vibration of the amulet changed. Raze could feel a distinct tone, a unique signal line, in each jewel.

Over and over, he traced the path, ruby to tourmaline, citrine to emerald, topaz to amethyst to sapphire to diamond, until it stopped in the center on a stone that was unlike anything he had seen before. It wasn't a color; it was beyond all colors, like every color all in one.

Raze put the amulet back in his pocket. The amulet wasn't for him. It was for Aislen. But maybe if he decoded it, he could help Aislen faster. And the faster she could learn how to take care of herself in the new reality she found herself in, the faster she could be out of his life, and Raze could get back to his.

He checked the clock. 3:33. He had just enough time for a power nap before his next task in this fiasco: taking on The 8.

He needed to slow down the wheel that was turning toward his inevitable destruction. If he did this right, maybe he could turn it back in his favor. Maybe he could become his old self again.

EIGHT

SIGMUND STOOD before the full-length mirror, trying to admire himself. He'd never gotten used to the casualness of white-collar work clothes, preferring the thick, scratchy wool of a uniform instead. He felt coarse and uncouth. He didn't recognize himself looking so unimportant.

Muted shuffling noises rose through the floorboards beneath his feet as Astrid continued her work in the kitchen, desperate to complete his meal and clean up before he made his appearance.

Sigmund smiled at himself in the mirror. Her distress brought him such pleasure. He shifted his weight, left foot to right, agitating the floorboards just to torment her. It had the desired effect. The energy from the kitchen became frantic, like a kicked anthill.

Smiling, he returned attention to his reflection and was immediately deflated. The first signs of imperfection mocked him. He reached up to rearrange his hair, smoothing the pale locks from the back of his scalp toward his forehead and then to the left, carefully working to conceal the beginnings of a receding hairline.

He stepped back to reassess. Not much better. What did it matter anyway? He worked with whores and drug addicts. He was a god amongst them. He was more than presentable for the night's festivities.

Remembering the evening's agenda galvanized him, and he turned from his disappointing reflection and headed for the bedroom door.

He could hear that Astrid wasn't done. She should have been tucked away in her basement hideaway by now. That was the rule.

By God, he should march down there, grab her by the grubby head, and drag her into the basement, but he didn't have the time for that. He was on the brink of something huge at work. It would have to wait. He'd make her pay double later.

Sigmund slowly pulled the door open, creating a creak loud enough for Astrid to hear. He moved toward the landing, then deliberately stepped down onto the sweet spot of the top step. It popped under the pressure.

He almost laughed out loud at the sound of Astrid scurrying toward the basement. He stood on the top step a moment longer, relishing the surge of power he felt at having so much control of her.

Her rush sent a zephyr up the stairwell. A whirlwind spun around him. He inhaled the scent of ham and toast in it.

And also something foreign—something sweet and fresh— *that didn't belong in his house.*

A chill tickled his skin, and the apparitional waif he had seen earlier in the bathroom mirror crossed his mind. It was like she was circling him in the breeze. The presence stopped beside him, palpable in the nothingness, yet Sigmund still searched the empty space, expecting to catch a glimpse of her.

"Go away," he whispered out loud, trying to shake off this figment of his imagination. Phantasms belonged in his laboratory, taunting his test subjects, not in his home, haunting him. Sigmund felt his ears pop, and the air around him felt hollow again.

The basement door clicked shut below, and Sigmund continued down the staircase toward the kitchen. He paused at the basement door for a moment to savor the fear radiating through the wood. Astrid was just on the other side. He could feel her there, holding her breath, petrified that he would open the door and escort her down into her chambers.

She would wait there for hours if she had to. She would only dare move once he pulled the chair away from the table. One step as he pulled the chair underneath him, and its legs squealed against the linoleum. Then another when his knife scraped across the plate as he cut his ham. And another, when his spoon tickled the porcelain of his teacup. The rest, quiet as a snowflake, as he enjoyed his breakfast.

Sigmund knew. He knew her every move.

He sighed with satisfaction. It was tempting to play this little game for a while longer, but he needed his breakfast. It was Tuesday, after all.

He moved to the table and examined the spread laid out before him. The setting was immaculate, everything precisely in place as he required. He was surprised that Astrid had managed it. He settled into the chair and picked up the copy of the *San Francisco Chronicle* carefully placed to the right side of his plate. He glanced at the front page.

The Viet Cong had launched rockets into Saigon. A hurricane was poised off Florida, and five people were missing at sea. A Seattle dentist died while saving his children from freezing to death by barricading them in a cave with his body. The presidential primary elections were being held today.

Normally, he would read the front section in depth, looking for events and details that validated his experiments, but he didn't have the time today. His best test subject would be at the brothel soon. It was *tomorrow's* paper that would have what Sigmund was looking for. He tossed the paper on the floor, giving Astrid something else to clean up when he left.

As he began to eat, he heard the springs of Astrid's bed squeak from the basement. She was far too noisy today. Was she trying to distract him? Trying to tempt him? Any other afternoon, Sigmund would not let the opportunity pass, and he would enter the basement.

But not today. Another day.

He popped the yolk into his mouth and imagined Astrid sitting on the edge of her bed, hands cinched in her lap, toes barely touching the floor, right knee quivering as she tried desperately to dispel the hum of terror coursing through her body. The whispers under her breath as she prayed to a God she didn't even know existed.

Because God didn't exist for her.

Only Sigmund did.

He took a deep breath, savoring the delicious tension building up inside him. It would be enough to sustain him. He had a big night ahead. Thomas Reed would be arriving at the lab soon, and Sigmund would be there.

With renewed enthusiasm, he removed himself from the table, leaving a narrow slice of ham and the other half of the hard-boiled egg on the plate for Astrid. He had to keep the pet alive.

He retrieved his jacket from the hall tree, picked up his briefcase off the floor, and stepped out the front door into the late afternoon sunlight.

∞

"ÖFFNE DEINE AUGEN, POPPET."

The old man's rasp startled her awake.

Aislen opened her eyes and found that she was standing, not lying down. A wild vortex of energy was swirling around her, and she could feel a panic so intense it turned her insides out.

A young blonde woman dashed past her. Aislen recognized her immediately. She was in *that* house again. This time in the kitchen, with the girl.

Aislen wasn't awake at all. She was back in the dream, a dream she had no desire to be in. The last time had been disturbing enough.

Ahhhh, you realize you are in the dream, Lange's voice hummed in her ear. *Well done. That's the first step to everything.*

It also meant that she could escape—by waking up. Aislen closed her eyes again and tried to will herself awake.

"*Nicht so schnell! Ich habe dir hier noch viel mehr zu zeigen.*"

Again, she understood him perfectly.

"*Not so fast! I have so much more to show you here.*"

Aislen's skin crawled, and her eyes were forced open. The young woman flashed past her again.

"*Astrid,*" Lange hissed. "*Ihr Name ist Astrid.*"

The terror the girl was emitting made the room violently turbulent, and Aislen was swept up by it, pulled into her wake. Without volition, Aislen followed her as she carefully set a plate on the dinette and made sure the silverware was aligned evenly. Aislen was then whisked down the hall, out the front door, down the steps to pick up a newspaper, then back. Aislen watched as Astrid carefully unfolded the newspaper and arranged it beside the plate of food: the *San Francisco Chronicle.*

"Dies war ein wichtiger Tag."

This was an important day.

Aislen looked at the date on the newspaper: Tuesday, June 4, 1968.

Was she really back in time? And why was this day important?

"It was the day it all began!" Lange declared in her head. She could feel his sense of pride and excitement.

Aislen heard a door creak open upstairs. Astrid heard it too and scrambled, hiding a dirty frying pan in a cupboard under the sink and wiping debris off the counter into a napkin that she shoved into her dress pocket.

There was another loud crack of wood as someone stepped onto the stairway, and the girl bolted toward an open door behind the table. Her chaos threw Aislen into a tailspin. Her ethereal body, lighter than air, was carried off by the rush of energy.

Unable to control her own movements, Aislen was thrown back down the hallway, then lifted off the ground. She watched helplessly as stair steps passed beneath her. She was lifted higher and higher until she was sent into a tailspin around a man in a dress shirt and slacks—it was the younger version of Mr. Lange, standing at the top of the stairs.

The spinning stopped abruptly.

I don't want to be here, Aislen thought.

You must be here, Lange seethed back.

The young Sigmund slowly turned his head toward her. Aislen's breath caught in her chest. There was no way he could see her, right? Not if she wasn't really there.

This is me, Lange whispered in her head.

I know, she thought back, trying to will herself away—will herself *awake.*

The younger Lange searched the space where she stood; she could feel the gaze boring into her, though he couldn't actually see her there.

This is the moment I knew you were real. I just wasn't ready for you... yet.

A chill crawled down her spine.

Young Sigmund glared into her eyes, and though he really didn't see, he knew.

"Go away," he snarled. The words reverberated inside her chest, the magnetic hold snapped, and Aislen slipped deeper into a tunnel of darkness.

NINE

SIGMUND CAUGHT a taxi at the Main Post of the Presidio and had it drop him off just outside of Golden Gate Park. It was one of those rare, mild afternoons in the city, and a brisk walk the last part of the way would help him clear his mind.

A hazy fog began to set in as he passed Hippie Hill, a mixture of the evening marine layer and the sweet smog of marijuana that always hung low in this part of town. It drifted from cafés, apartments, and the parks, escaping like exhaust from the lips of barefoot hippies frolicking along his route.

Sigmund frowned as the first layer of skunk settled through his clothes and onto his skin. Bathing was useless.

Today is Tuesday, he reminded himself, to quell the anger at the assault on his sanitized body. He panted shallowly as he quickened his pace toward Haight Street.

A waif blithely passed by, giving him a sly smile. Her flowing skirt pressed against her thighs in the breeze. Her long, red hair dangled in curls around her shoulders and framed her face. Her eyes met his, a vivid green with sparks of fire. The scent of fresh flowers and vanilla enveloped him.

Was it *her* again? That ghost of a girl who had been haunting him all day?

She passed by him and smiled. Her lithe body kept moving in the opposite direction, but her essence slipped in around him and shadowed him as he continued down the street. Sigmund refrained from turning around to catch her following him. He knew it was only his imagination. He could not allow himself to get caught up in the same type of delusions that his test subjects often succumbed to.

He quickened his pace even more. His laboratory was only a block away. He could see it. The 19th-century Queen Anne row house, subtle in its blue-gray gingerbread, was nestled between more flamboyant, painted ladies of buttercup yellow and periwinkle. If he could just get inside, he could shake the apparition and focus on his evening properly.

Sigmund bypassed the doorbell and used his key. He stepped into the dimly lit parlor and shut the door quickly behind him. Although the hippie chick had not actually followed him, he felt as if he had locked the ethereal version of the waif on the porch.

Leaning against the door, he allowed his eyes to adjust to the parlor.

Lamps draped with red scarves bled their color across the parlor, where cheap perfume and cigarette smoke hung heavy. A handful of girls in nylon nighties pawed at nervous johns, some too timid to move, others already half-drugged. The array of human product here was not dazzling. These are not first-rate whores. They are on the cheap. Government rate. Literally. But they knew their job.

"Good afternoon, Mister Sigmund," Candy purred. He choked back bile. None of them tempted him—their very presence disgusted him, which was good. He had no interest in distraction. Only the work.

He made his way past the parlor and up the mahogany staircase with a slight spring in his step. Today was Tuesday. It was usually a slow day for the brothel, but Sigmund's favorite lab rat, Thomas Reed, always visited on Tuesdays.

Sigmund worked his way down the hall toward the main observation room, where Misty would bring Thomas when he arrived. The rowhouse was divided into four poorly constructed apartments. Between units, the closets and unused restrooms had been made into makeshift observation rooms, each equipped with a table, chair, and one-way glass. Sigmund could move between the various observation rooms as the girls brought in his lab rats.

He had been involved with several MKUltra projects in the past, one for the US Army, one in Las Vegas, and one in Texas near the Mexican border. But this was his very own. His expertise in manipulation tactics, learned first-hand from Vater, had impressed his American superiors. His successful results had earned him this assignment: Operation Midnight Climax. And OMC had surpassed every other project funded by the CIA.

San Francisco was the perfect place to set up shop. It was outside the norm in every way, especially since the beginning of the psychedelic heyday, which they called the Summer of Love. Timothy Leary, the flowers-in-hair spokesperson for irresponsible excess, had called all fringe, intergalactic beings to "turn on, tune in, and drop out." And Sigmund had no problem persuading the CIA to capitalize on the craze and set up a faux brothel here.

In the spirit of "Don't beat them, join them," Sigmund embedded with the hippies and hid in the counterculture. The clients were naturally less conventional. They let their guard down easily, tried his drugs, and readily experimented with deviant sexual acts.

It was not Sigmund's goal to exploit a subject's suppressed

appetites. All subjects became uninhibited enough to stray into the fringe sexually. It was not unusual for them to allow themselves to be spanked, penetrated, peed on, or even defecated on. But this was not what Sigmund was looking for. The gold mine lay in what the subject could be manipulated into doing–things that would usually be completely *unthinkable* to them.

The chime at the front door rang. Sigmund glanced at his watch. 9 o'clock. Thomas was always on time.

Sigmund took his seat in the room connected to #6. He had about an hour to prepare. Unlocking his briefcase, he pulled out four pens–two blue and two red. The blue was to document Thomas's idle chit-chat with Misty as the drugs took effect. The red was for when he started hallucinating. He always had an extra of each color. If one ran out, Sigmund could change pens without missing a transmission. He used another key to open a hidden compartment in the briefcase and pulled out a notebook labeled "Thomas Reed – DOB: June 10, 1948."

Sigmund browsed through the file on his lap while he waited for Misty to prep his subject. Like a good scientist, Sigmund had meticulously documented Thomas's behaviors and conversations over the past year.

During an engagement with Viet Cong militants in the Tay Ninh Province, Thomas had been grazed by a bullet. Though the bullet was deflected by his helmet, it rattled his skull enough that he lost consciousness. Because everything else about the soldier was perfectly healthy, Thomas was sent back into the field after a short rehabilitation. But a severe, near-constant headache plagued him, and visions of light blinded him at unpredictable moments. Perplexed, Army doctors finally sent Thomas back to the States to be evaluated by the Presidio doctors and to investigate whether he was malingering to get relieved of duty. If they had believed he was, he would have been sent back for another tour. But their findings were inconclusive, so they sent him to Sigmund and Operation Midnight Climax, where they could still reap some benefit out of their investment.

While most johns came to the brothel to fuck, Thomas was addicted to the magic. He was one of the few who came for the tablets of acid the brothel dropped for free. He wanted to talk, then sleep, then talk some more; things he wasn't doing outside the walls of the brothel. It was what he spoke of that was unique and that interested Sigmund.

Thomas would sit in the parlor and wait for Misty to make him a cocktail. He always chose Misty, the oldest, least attractive whore in the brothel. Her qualities of listening were what Thomas sought out. A therapist in a threadbare robe and crotchless fishnets.

While the US government was the real madame of this house, Misty was hired to act the part. She took care of the busier girls, playing confidante, peacemaker, and cashier. She knew very little about Sigmund's research but was paid well enough not to care.

Misty would mix Thomas his cocktail, usually laced with LSD, but tonight she had instructions to make him a straight drink and ply him with BZ instead. Sigmund wanted to up the ante on what Thomas might reveal tonight. BZ was a super-hallucinogen, which was why Sigmund had been itchy with excitement all day. Thomas was going to trip hard tonight.

It was hard to say who was more addicted to these journeys, Thomas or Sigmund. Thomas realized something unusual was happening. He understood what he was doing, and seeing was incredible, even frightening. But he didn't know that he was being watched from a little room behind the large picture frame mirror on the east wall of room #6. Only Sigmund and Misty knew that.

He didn't know that his trips were being documented and validated or that he was being used.

Thomas never truly fell asleep during sessions. He only drifted into a semi-conscious stupor. Relaxed, but coherent. And then he'd take his trip. In his drug-induced state, he spoke of places and situations as though he was there, witnessing them firsthand. At first, Sigmund thought Thomas was the dullest of all his test subjects. His other lab rats spoke of demons and angels or had conversations with the headless, limbless charred corpses that haunted their recent memories of Vietnam.

Initially, Thomas's hallucinations seemed boring by comparison.

The first time Sigmund realized something was different about Thomas was on January 24th. He opened the log to Tuesday, January 23, 1968, perusing through his transcribed shorthand.

2100 Thomas Reed arrives

2326 Assistant escorts Mr. Reed into room #6

2334 Assistant gets Mr. Reed comfortable. Asks him if he wants services. He says no, per usual.

2351 Thomas mumbles about a ship. A commander orders men to positions.

2356 Distressed: "There's a warship advancing, patrol boats coming fast. We've hoisted our flag."

0006 "Two MiGs! What the hell is going on?!" He kicks at the air. Misty grounds him softly.

0013 "They're firing... torpedoes!"

0013 "We're incinerating documents, destroying equipment."

0049 He whispers, "We've been captured. Blindfolded. Ribs broken."

SIGMUND HAD LEFT the lab that morning in a terrible mood. He remembered marching up to the house, feeling the need to take his aggression out on Astrid, when he noticed that the *Chronicle* was already on the porch. Something about it made him stop and pick it up.

Even folded, he could see the headline: N. Korea Hijacks US Ship.

Astrid evaporated from his thoughts, and he sat on the porch to read the article.

A Navy intelligence vessel engaged in a surveillance mission off the North Korean coast was chased down by North Korean patrol boats. The North Koreans intercepted, opened fire, and captured the vessel.

The news article that morning made no mention of the crew being held hostage. But Sigmund knew, knew that Thomas had seen the whole thing!

It was incredible.

And that was just the beginning.

On March 12, Thomas witnessed a rampage in the village of My Lai, Vietnam. He described American soldiers going berserk, killing domestic animals, unarmed men, and elderly women. He described the CO, Lt. Calley, obliterating infants like a maniac. Thomas Reed's vision lasted for three hours, his longest trip yet, until finally an American helicopter landed between the rampaging company and the fleeing villagers, stopping the carnage.

The next morning, when there was no mention of it in the paper, Sigmund thought it must have been a flashback from Thomas's own time in country. But then, it actually happened... *four days later*.

The CIA was calling it a successful MKUltra experiment, but the Army was covering the whole event up. The public still had no idea that it had even happened.

Then, on April 2nd, another jackpot. Sigmund flipped through his log to find it.

TUESDAY, April 2, 1968

2100 Thomas Reed arrives

2318 Assistant escorts Mr. Reed into room #6

2322 Assistant gets Mr. Reed comfortable. Asks him if he wants services. He says no, per usual.

2338 Thomas' fingers twitch, leg jerks, he appears to be asleep.

2344 Thomas speaking, voice affected,

"...difficult days ahead... doesn't matter with me now. I've been to the mountaintop...

He's allowed me to go up to the mountain...

2348 "I've seen the Promised Land... I may not get there with you... But I want you to know... tonight... that we... as a people... will get to the promised land."

2356 Long silence.

0001 "There's a motel across the street. The sign says Lorraine."

0012 "He's there. He's on the balcony. He's leaning over the railing."

0013 "He's turning to leave."

0014 "He's shot. He's shot. Oh my God, he's been shot in the face."

Assistant: Time check. "I'm here. You're all right."

0016 "Someone is yelling from the balcony, 'Dr. King has been shot!"

0020 Silence.

0045 Still silence.

0052 "They killed The Dreamer."

SIGMUND KNEW Thomas was talking about Dr. Martin Luther King, Jr. Everyone had heard his "I Have a Dream" speech. He was inspiring people, galvanizing them into action regarding civil rights. He was also making enemies, enemies who would want him dead. But on April 2nd, Dr. King was not dead. And he was not dead on April 3rd. It wasn't until the afternoon of April 5th, 1968, that Sigmund was able to confirm that his assassination had taken place in Memphis.

Sigmund had been keeping these premonitory visions to himself. His project was proving to be far more successful than the past three, and Thomas was turning out to be Sigmund's legitimate star. A bigger picture was beginning to form, a vision for what all this could mean and what Sigmund could ultimately do. Each session with Thomas provided a goldmine of information that added credibility to Sigmund's résumé and could be used to line Sigmund's own pockets.

Sigmund turned the log pages to a clean sheet. Even if tonight was a bust, the BZ should make things very interesting. In blue pen, he titled the page.

TUESDAY, June 4, 1968

2100 Thomas Reed arrives

Sigmund looks up from the notebook as Misty escorts Thomas through the door.

2203 Assistant escorts Mr. Reed into room #6.

Hello, Thomas. What will you have for me today?

∞

IT IS SO easy to dance when everything is so incredibly beautiful: the sky such a brilliant blue, the air sweet and sour with the essence of the city, the streets filled with happy people sharing nothing but love for each other. She dances barefoot in the cool, wet grass, then along the warm sidewalk of Haight Street. She sashays through the music playing from one transistor radio in the park and into the music of another playing around the corner.

A crisp breeze billows up her skirt. It feels delicious caressing her warm thighs. And this skirt! What an intoxicating kaleidoscope of patchwork fabric! How it sways and dances right along with you! Makes you feel like a princess! If only she could pull it apart and devour each patch like a bright piece of candy and be one with its pure color.

Well, well, well, who's this?

She feels the man before she can actually see him. His life force projects out in front of him, full of purpose, commanding her attention. *What a turn on!*

As he draws closer, she is ready with a smile that says, *I am willing to play if you are.*

My, what light golden hair you have, Sir.

She adds a little more sway to her hips and lifts on her tippy toes to dance a little as he passes. He turns his head ever so slightly as she slips beside him.

My, what blue, blue eyes—

Aislen tripped backward, spinning frantically away from the young Mr. Lange. As she gained control of herself, she watched the girl dance past him on the sidewalk, still smiling slyly at her target.

Had she just been that girl? Aislen could feel that, yes, she definitely had. It wasn't like watching anymore—it was like borrowing a body, sliding into a space that wasn't hers. She hadn't meant to do it, and she had no idea how she'd slipped back out.

Aislen was helplessly caught up in another vortex of energy now, following reluctantly behind Sigmund. He was walking briskly past a row of Victorian houses, painted in bright, gaudy colors similar to the bohemian girl's dress. Like a magnet, she was dragged along by his forceful energy as he marched up the stairs of a drab, gray house, unlocked the door, and escaped inside, slamming the door in her face.

It's just another dream, she told herself, grateful for the realization. She didn't feel old Lange in her head anymore, either, and she sighed with relief. She did not want to be around that man in any form. His thoughts and feelings were extremely alarming.

Aislen tried to will herself awake again, out of this new dream state, but she still felt weighed down. Instead of Lange pulling her down like an undertow, it was as though she lay under a heavy sheath that she could not lift or break through.

She gave up and looked around the porch. An old rocking chair sat in the sunlight, occupied by a spiced orange tabby. He was lounging in the fading warmth of the setting sun, busily grooming himself, lick-lick-licking his legs and rubbing his head with a paw. Aislen had always wanted a cat and thought how awesome it would be to *be* a cat. What a life! Lying around, sleeping during the day, being served your meals, and being pampered.

It had been so easy being the bohemian girl in the street; why not try being a cat? Was that how this worked? She only had to want it badly enough, and she was there? The thought both thrilled and terrified her.

She walked over, shrank herself down, and stepped inside the kitty's space. How warm and comfortable! It is a whole new level of being relaxed. He is languid and carefree, very similar to how the stoned girl had felt. His purring hums around her from all sides, relaxing her even more, and the licking feels scratchy and calming at the same time.

Footsteps on the sidewalk startled her awake, and Aislen pounced out of the cat back onto the porch. A man was coming up the pathway. There was something very familiar about him. Was it the way he walked? The way he carried himself? He was wearing army green fatigue pants and a denim jacket. Waves of dirty brown hair came down to his collar and were tucked behind his ears. He looked up to where she stood on the porch, and it nearly took her breath away. *Dad.* The man standing below looked almost exactly like her father, only his hair was darker and longer, and he looked a bit younger.

He stood at the bottom of the stairs staring up at her, but Aislen realized he wasn't actually seeing her. He was stalling— he didn't want to be here either.

Aislen felt a sudden urge to be this man. If she could do it with the girl and the cat, why not? She slipped down the stairs and slid into the man's space, hitchhiking within his energy field. Maybe she could find out who he was and why he looked like her father.

TEN

IT'S ALWAYS HERE that he hesitates–here at the bottom of the stairs. Shame and anxiety wait for him at the top.

When he was first sent here, he thought he was going to another psychologist to analyze his sanity... or lack of it. After a shitload of tests, the Army determined that he didn't have any permanent brain damage, but there was still no explanation for the blinding headaches and visions of light.

That first night, when the woman opened the door in a see-through robe, her figure tired, her skin mapped with age, Thomas thought that maybe it was the Army that was nuts, not him. Did they think that getting laid by a prostitute was the miraculous cure he needed?

He was obviously at the wrong address, but as he turned on his heel to leave, the woman called out to him, "No, no dear, you are in the right place. Come on in. We know how to help you."

Thomas was so desperate for relief, he'd try anything, so against his moral judgment, he followed her inside.

The woman had led him to the parlor and asked him if she could make him a drink. He accepted. If anything could clear his head, it was Jack Daniel's. Then she sat with him on the worn, velvet love seat—not too close. She knew to keep her distance. Her name was Misty, and she told him that she was there just for him.

The drink relaxed him, probably more than he was used to, and to his surprise, he started to talk. At first, it was just idle chit-chat, but it felt so good to finally communicate with someone who wasn't judging him. After all, who was she to judge? He lost track of time, and at some point, Misty took his hand and led him up the stairs.

He doesn't remember the details of that night. He doesn't remember if they had sex or not. All he remembers is waking up the next morning and Misty leading him to the door. She told him he could come back anytime, that services were on the house.

It was his first walk of shame back to the barracks.

He had no intention of going back. But after a while, the headaches wore him down, and he eventually sought out the bliss he'd felt briefly within the walls of the brothel. Soon, his visits became a weekly addiction.

His headaches stopped. The blinding lights dimmed. His nightmares at home subsided. And now, here he is again.

Thomas pulls a cigarette out of his pocket, lights it, and reaches down to pet the orange tabby brushing up against his legs. Cigarettes and cats are all a person should need. They shouldn't need what he is here for.

He looks back up at the brothel door. While it had been a bastion of bliss for several months, it's now a different kind of monster. In exchange for the headaches and blinding light, the brothel had started giving him visions of greater magnitude.

In the beginning, the visions had been random—some frightening, some absurd. But then they started coming true. A ship hijacked. A village slaughtered. Even Dr. King's assassination, exactly as Thomas had seen it days before it happened. Each one left him more shaken, more certain he wasn't just imagining things.

Thomas had stayed away from the brothel for weeks, but the questions haunted him—worse than any headache he'd ever endured.

Thomas throws the spent cigarette onto the ground and wills his feet to climb the stairs. He forces himself to press the doorbell before he can chicken out, and he waits, awash in shame and fear of the unknown.

What would his mother think of him? Visiting a whorehouse? What would she think of her delusional son?

Stiletto heels click across the hardwood floor behind the door, and the shame and fear are displaced by strange relief. Like Pavlov's dog, Thomas emotionally salivates for what lies beyond. Because he needs this place. He needs Misty. He needs her magic potion to help him make sense out of what is taking place inside his mind.

The door unlatches.

"Hello, Thomas. We've been waiting for you."

∞

AISLEN STEPPED out of the man as he entered the foyer. She didn't want to go inside. Sigmund was in there, and Aislen had a sick feeling that something bad was going to happen.

But this man, this Thomas, he was what was important

about today. He was why Lange wanted her here. And he had dreams like her–dreams that weren't really dreams. He was a Walker, traveling like she does, and he was just as lost and confused. Aislen felt an irresistible need to understand him, no matter what her great-grandfather had planned.

Before Misty shut the door on her, Aislen slipped back into his space.

∞

WHILE MISTY MAKES HIM A DRINK, Thomas finds a space on the couch. He passes the time watching the other guests make their selections for the evening, while in reality, the girls are making their selections for them.

Misty doesn't take long. She is back quickly, drink in hand. She's made more of an effort tonight, her hair freshly done like he's her first client of the evening, a robe over her cheap lingerie.

She hands him the drink, then slides seductively onto the davenport next to him.

Thomas slams the whiskey. The sooner he gets into it, the better he will feel.

"So, honey, I only made you a straight cocktail tonight." She looks up through her lashes as she breaks the news.

Thomas pulls the empty glass from his lips. "Why would you do that?"

"Well, I was wondering if you'd like to try something a little different. A little stronger perhaps."

Thomas hesitates. "Um, I don't know about that. The other stuff is pretty powerful. I don't think I need anything stronger."

Misty puts what is supposed to be a reassuring hand on his thigh. "I know, baby. That's why I was thinking this might be better. Maybe something stronger would be more relaxing for you... more controllable."

Thomas weighs this. "What is it?"

Misty draws her finger up his thigh. It makes him uncomfortable, but the whiskey is already dulling the edges, so he doesn't stop her.

"They call it Buzz. All the boys who have tried it like it so much better than the sugar. Really mellow. Really deep."

She draws her finger back down and circles his knee. She usually doesn't touch him; it is an unspoken agreement, not what he is here for, but he doesn't protest. He'd become used to her presence over the past year, had felt her nearby in his visions, heard her like an angel calming him during the terror.

She moves her finger up to his hand and slowly traces it up his arm.

"The other boys have said the visions are way more pleasant, that they can control them better... that they can leave when they want."

This sounds appealing, having more control. And if the drug is stronger, maybe he can finally prove they aren't meaningless visions–that he isn't really crazy.

Misty circles a fingertip on his shoulder. "And the boys say they don't feel as sick to their stomach because you don't drink it. It's just a little shot in the arm."

Thomas grabs her hand and puts it down in her lap. "No shots. No needles."

"Okay, okay." She raises her hands in meek surrender. "I understand. But there is another way. You can inhale it... you know, like laughing gas. Just a quick puff. Would you like to try that?"

Thomas considers this. The opportunity to get the answers

he wants is very tempting, although trying something new is not. If he had never come here, he'd never have had the vision in the first place. To up the ante is risky. But Thomas needs to end this once and for all. If this doesn't clarify his situation, he is done. Never coming back. It is his last visit, one way or another.

"Okay. I'll try it."

A look passes across Misty's face, a mixture of uncertainty and relief. Thomas almost changes his mind.

No. Let's be done with this.

Misty stands up and takes him by the hand. "Follow me."

Thomas follows her up the stairs, noticing the peeling wallpaper and the frayed carpet. Usually, he'd be stoned by now. He'd never noticed these details before. The hallway at the top of the stairs has several doors. More doors than Thomas expected. Misty shows him into room #6.

There is the bed and Misty's chair. There is a canister next to the bed that had never been there before, a steel canister with an oxygen mask. The mirror on the wall seems more conspicuous tonight. Before, it blended in with the surroundings. Now, it looks strategic.

The room doesn't seem like a brothel; it feels like a doctor's examining room.

Thomas drops Misty's hand.

"Wait a minute." It is coming together now. This is a part of it. He should have known better. None of this was ever to help him. He's a guinea pig. How could he have been so naive?

"It's all right, baby. I'll take care of you. You want answers, right? You want to know what's happening to you? Let me help."

Thomas is torn. Part of him wants to turn and run out the door as fast as he can. But part of him has to know... has to know what is happening.

Reluctantly, he moves to the side of the bed.

"Take off your shoes so you can be more comfortable."

Thomas does as she told, on automatic pilot now, trapped by his need, a slave to his destiny. Misty places the mask over his face.

"This is just oxygen, honey. It will help. Just sit back and relax. The Buzz will be administered through the oxygen."

Thomas' heart begins to race. He's gone too far. This is all a mistake. Yet, whoever is running this operation, if the Army knows what is really happening, then maybe they know what they are doing. Maybe this will help. He'll make sure to ask questions after.

The oxygen comes on, a gentle hiss. Thomas leans back against the pillows and closes his eyes.

At some point, Misty touches his hand. "Would you like some water? Or orange juice, hon?"

Thomas opened his eyes.

Has he been asleep already?

He feels as if he has.

Is it over?

He'd felt nothing.

He nodded his head. He is starving.

"Just relax, I'll be right back."

Misty leaves the room. And Thomas closes his eyes.

Misty touches his hand. "How are you doing, love?"

Thomas opens his eyes.

Why won't she let him sleep?

The mask is off.

Misty is in a chair next to the bed. She looks tired. There is a table there now, with a half-empty glass of juice. Thomas doesn't remember drinking the juice. Has he really been asleep? But he'd just lain down.

He looks around the room, feeling a bit dizzy, motion sickness like the bed is floating on water. He feels the familiar fade of reality and slips into a gauzy space. The mirror on the wall is beginning to melt, and the sinews holding matter together start snapping.

Thomas feels his heart slow down. It thumps harder in his chest but only intermittently. That isn't how it usually works.

Misty senses something and touches his arm. "Close your eyes now, dear."

He closes his eyes, and his brain shatters into a thousand sparks of light.

He moves through a tunnel of white and gold rays at an incredible speed. He no longer knows where his body really is. He only feels the spinning of the light and a floating sensation. Thomas takes a deep breath, and the light opens up.

He is in a large room surrounded by a large crowd. As all the brightness dims, Thomas tries to orient himself. It reminds him of when he was in the church, but this is a ballroom. And like the church, this room is filled to capacity.

Red, white, and blue cloth swags are draped behind a podium across the wide stage in front of the crowd. Balloons cover the ceiling. The air is electric with excitement. A sign on the front of the podium reads "Los Angeles Ambassador Hotel." This means nothing to Thomas. Hanging askew below it, a smaller sign reads "Kennedy."

Thomas recognizes Bobby Kennedy standing behind the podium. His golden brown hair is parted on the side; a toothy, boyish grin spreads across his face.

"We are a great country, an unselfish country, and a compassionate country. And I intend to make that my basis for running in the period of the next few months," he tells the ecstatic crowd.

The scene is similar in look and zeal to his visions of Dr. King. Thomas had listened to King's speech, too, and the next night, King was dead. A sense of impending doom envelops him.

It is going to happen again. It isn't just a hunch or faint inkling; Thomas knows it with clear, unadulterated certainty. And it is going to happen tonight.

While Thomas couldn't stop it from happening to Dr. King, he feels sure he can stop it from happening to Robert Kennedy. He just has to get near enough to tell him.

Thomas starts moving through the crowd. Although it is packed solid with people, it is easy to get through them because he is a ghost.

Thomas makes his way to the end of the stage just as Kennedy is finishing his speech. As Kennedy and his entourage start moving in his direction, Thomas swoops in and steps in front of him.

"Sir, I have to tell you something," Thomas starts. Kennedy walks right through him, and the group follows, leaving the stage and completely ignoring his existence.

Thomas follows, circling back around Mr. Kennedy, "Please! I need to speak to you, it's important!" He yells louder, but still, no one flinches or reacts.

Of course they wouldn't! I have no voice! I'm not here! This is a hallucination!

Thomas feels helpless. There is a static charge of danger in the air that only he can feel. He follows the crowd out a side door through a service way and into the kitchen, catching up with Kennedy as he is signing a poster for a supporter. Thomas begins circling him, trying to generate enough energy to stir Kennedy into noticing, trying to make him stop and pay attention for just a moment.

And then he does stop. It worked! Thomas starts to warn him, but Kennedy turns his head away, reaching out to shake a supporter's hand. The young Mexican busboy is holding his hand when Thomas feels the energy shift behind him.

He swings around and is face-to-face with the gunman.

"Kennedy, you son of a bitch!" the man screams as he raises the gun.

"No!" Thomas screams, jumping in front of the weapon, trying to block the bullets.

The impact shoots through his chest, agony radiating through his body. His heart feels on fire with pain, beating wildly. As Thomas falls backwards, his heart races faster and faster, and he can no longer breathe. A blazing vortex opens up, and he falls into darkness.

∞

THE IMPACT of the bullets threw Aislen out of Thomas's body. She staggered backward and watched as Thomas's ghost disappeared from the dream, leaving her there alone.

Rigid in a pool of blood, arms splayed wide open, Robert Kennedy lay crucified on the kitchen floor. The young Mexican busboy dressed in a pure white smock knelt beside him. One breath ago, he was shaking a great man's hand; the next breath, he was cradling a dying man's head.

"Is everybody OK?" Kennedy asked the boy.

"Yes, everybody's OK," the boy assured him in a voice ragged with fear.

"Everything's going to be OK," the man said.

The boy took a rosary out of his pocket and placed it into the dying man's hand.

In shock, Aislen slipped out of the vision, following

Thomas into the dark portal and finding herself back at his bedside in the brothel.

Thomas was hyperventilating, clutching his chest, and gagging for air.

"Thomas!" Misty was starting to panic. "You're okay! Everything's going to be okay!"

"Kennedy! Kennedy is shot!" Thomas managed to say between gasps for air.

Aislen watched helplessly as Misty tried to calm Thomas down, but then he began convulsing, his eyes rolling back into his head.

Misty held his body to stop it from shaking.

"Mr. Lange!" she yelled. "Please help!"

The door to the room swung open, and Sigmund barged in, a storm of wrath carrying a large syringe. He was immediately upon Thomas with the syringe.

"No! Please don't!" Aislen yelled out involuntarily.

Sigmund stopped cold, whipping around to face her.

Aislen froze. He'd turned toward her. Not toward Thomas. Not Misty. Toward *her*.

He'd heard her.

That wasn't possible. She wasn't really here. She wasn't supposed to be anything more than a phantom, an accidental passenger. But the way his eyes pinned her—the recognition, the rage—told her she'd crossed a line she didn't understand.

Thomas stopped convulsing and lay still on the bed. Foam bubbled from his lips.

"Mr. Lange!" Misty pleaded. "Hurry! I think he's dead!"

Sigmund turned back toward Thomas, raised the syringe high above his head, pointing the needle at Thomas' chest.

"No!!!" Aislen cried out as Lange slammed the needle into his chest and injected its contents.

Sigmund stood up, eyes locked on her, advancing toward

her like a predator, until he was so close she could feel the venom in his breath.

"Get out!"

His hiss struck like a blow, an energetic shove that hurled her backward—out of the room and into a blazing vortex that swept her away.

PRELUDE TO A DECISION

Bad Wings ~ The Glitch Mob

ELEVEN

RAZE STOOD outside the massive steel doors that led into the Sanctum Sanctorum, collecting his thoughts before Qi'ing in.

He was late—deliberately. Keeping The 8 waiting was forbidden, but it was part of his plan. He welcomed their wrath. The more they threw at him, the better. He had one shot. If he failed, he wouldn't make it back out these doors.

At least Aislen would survive. Infinium would be at the warehouse immediately to deconstruct The Womb, and they would find her. But in that scenario, alive would be the only good thing about it. She'd wish she were dead.

Raze was as confident about this course of action as he was going to be. If it was his last breath of freedom, so be it. He placed his hand up toward the Qi reader and projected his signature frequency.

Nothing happened.

Either The 8 were pissed, and they were fucking with him.

He dropped his hand and took a deep breath. *They don't own me. I'll beat down these doors if I have to.*

Raze straightened his jacket, reset his posture, and raised his hand to the Qi reader.

Fuck. You. All. The doors slid open.

Raze paused a moment, then walked purposefully into the center of the large, circular boardroom. Bright sunshine beamed down through the stained glass dome ten stories above, projecting the II shadow onto the floor where he was to stand. He stood on top of the logo within the beam of light.

The 8 were in disarray. Numbers 7 and 5 were seated while the rest were gathered around in a heated discussion.

They turned in unison to glare at Raze.

"What is the meaning of this, Mr. Tanis?" snarled Number 7, the self-appointed speaker for the group. "You have some nerve calling an emergency session, then taking your sweet-ass time getting here."

One always stood at attention before The 8, but Raze crossed his hands behind his back and relaxed at parade rest. "I've been busy," Raze responded, sounding bored.

"*Busy?*" Number 7 spat at him. "Dare I remind you, Raziel, that the last time you were here, you were put on notice: to accomplish our objectives cleanly and succinctly after you failed to do so with the Parrish Project. Do you remember that conversation?"

"Yes, sir. I do."

"And you remember that you were advised of the consequences if you failed in your tasks?"

"Yes, sir. I do."

"Well, it doesn't take too much deduction for us to figure out that your call for an emergency session was not to share any good news with us."

"You are correct, sir."

A disgruntled rumble moved through the group. Raze soaked it in.

"So what exactly do you mean by that, Raziel? Would you care to fill us in?"

"Blake is alive."

The rumble grew deeper.

"The option-lock never worked."

An open-mouthed gasp came from Number 4.

"And *Demesne* has been compromised."

Though they maintained a calm exterior, the explosion of outrage rushed out toward him, a highly concentrated punch in the gut. Raze reeled it in, thirsty for more.

He continued. "I wish I could say that it was an easy fix, but it was irreparable."

Number 7 leaned forward on his throne. *"Was?"*

I'm glad you caught that, Raze thought to himself. He tried not to smile as he delivered his next blow.

"I destroyed it."

A temper scampered through the group: anger, disbelief, and a tinge of panic. They directed every drop of it his direction, and Raze soaked as much of it in as he could gather.

Number 6 was the first to start losing it. "What do you mean by destroyed? Do you mean gone? It no longer exists? Who gave you the authority to do that?" Each question was more shrill than the next, but Raze took it in calmly.

"I did."

"You did?" Number 3 growled. "Since when do you think you have the right to destroy Infinium property without our consent?"

"Since the moment I created it."

It was like a nuclear bomb of fury rose out of the collective. Outrage thundered around the chamber, a cacophony of accusations hurled his way—exactly as Raze had planned.

Number 7 slammed a hand down on the table, and the room snapped to silence. His voice cut cold, measured.

"Enough. Don't forget who owns you, Tanis. We can shut you down with a single directive. All your resources, your clearance, your operatives—gone. And if you still refuse? We option-lock you. Erased. Gone."

Raze tilted his head, almost amused. Months ago, that threat might've mattered. But option-locks hadn't held Sigmund. Why the hell would they hold him?

"Do it," he said, calm, almost bored. "Lock me, starve me, strip it all away. See how far that gets you while your empire bleeds out."

The fury that followed was delicious.

"Tanis! You have violated protocol! Displayed blatant insubordination! Destroyed classif—"

"Don't start with me."

Every voice shut at once.

"This is *your* fault." Raze scanned The 8, including them all in his condemnation.

"Excuse me!?" It was Number 7's turn to turn into a shrill bitch.

"Sit down!" Raze commanded. He pulled up some of their indignation and launched it back at them. "You have some nerve trying to pin your incompetence and lack of leadership on me. You—*all of you*—have failed as the command of this organization, while I have been the only one trying to save it and preserve its mission."

Several of The 8 had begun sputtering, but he rolled right over them.

"For years you have been training control operatives to hunt Preston Reed, trying to eliminate 'the end of the line.' But you kept valuable, necessary information from us, sabotaging our ability to do our job."

"What necessary information?" balked Number 7.

"Don't play dumb with me," Raze shot back, adding more

of their own fuel to the fire. "I am talking about Number 1. *Ichiban.* Your founder. The creator of all this and the creator of *you.*"

Number 3 sat down in his chair, visibly struck that Raze knew about Sigmund Lange. One down. Seven to go.

"He was a 'need to know' classification," Number 7 fired back.

"Well, actually... *I did.* Because he added a whole other layer to the clusterfuck we now find ourselves in. And there is even more shit you don't have any clue about."

"Grant Parker: requesting immediate, emergency access into The Sanctum," the Sanctum Sanctorum interrupted. She sounded just like The Womb: Siri with an attitude problem.

Right on time, Raze thought.

"Declined. When we are finished," barked Number 7.

"No. Please, allow him," interjected Raze. "I mean, why not? *He* was in the 'need to know' circle." He eyed The 8, daring them to contradict him. Number 4 dropped her eyes and slowly walked back to her chair. Number 6, no longer Ms. High and Mighty, glanced at Number 7 and then also walked back to her chair. Three down.

The others followed suit one by one, resetting their positions behind the table.

Number 7 glowered at Raze. "Access accepted for Grant Parker."

The steel doors slid open, and Grant stormed in, starting in on Raze before he was even in the room. "This man is a traitor!" he yelled, pointing his finger at Raze. Troy Kellen strolled casually in his mentor's wake. He glanced sideways at Raze, throwing him a smug smile.

"He has been undermining our company's mission, making decisions without authorization, and withholding critical information from you regarding Scott and Blake Parrish. *And* there has been a breach in The Stratum!" Grant was ready to run Raze over with the bus he was throwing him under, but Raze had already laid the road.

"Now that he's had his little tantrum, may I proceed?"

Number 7 shifted his attention back to Raze. "Proceed," he seethed.

"As I was saying." He glanced at Grant, then back to The 8. "There has always been more than one loose end in the form of Preston Reed. Now that I am aware of him, there is Sigmund Lange."

"That's impossible!" Grant exploded. "Sigmund Lange was option-locked and put in storage a long time ago. Troy here has been keeping an eye on him."

Raze looked back at Grant. "You're joking, right? Sigmund Lange was always capable of working his way out of an option-lock. He's the one who discovered the technique. Why couldn't he master it? And really, Mr. Kellen here might be a great thug in 3D, but you didn't think he was capable of keeping an eye on Lange's 4D activities, did you?"

Raze pointedly eyed Troy up and down, then looked back at Grant, "Really?" He turned back toward The 8.

"The point is, Troy here failed, and Sigmund Lange possessed Blake Parrish, trespassed into *Demesne* through Blake, and sabotaged the whole project.

"And he isn't even our biggest problem," Raze continued. "Because Preston Reed had a secret... a wee, little anomaly that goes by the name of Aislen Walker."

Grant tried to interject.

"Shut. Up," commanded Number 7, looking back at Raze. He sat up straighter and folded his hands, clearly trying to regain the upper hand. "Preston Reed never had contact with any women while he worked for his grandfather or Infinium Incorporated. And once he absconded, he never stayed in one place long enough... definitely not long enough to father a child. Whoever this Aislen Walker is, she cannot be his daughter." Number 7 sat back against his throne.

"Really? You sure about that? Because he sure as hell stayed in one place long enough to fuck someone. I mean, in your circle that only takes like, what, 3 minutes?"

"How dare you!" Number 7 was back out of his chair.

"No! How dare you!" Raze stepped out of the circle and marched toward the dais. "I stand for the values that this organization is based on. I created a place that allowed this organization to fulfill the mission of *your* elite class. I have given my life to that mission, and I fulfill that mission!

"And you." Raze pointed his finger at Number 7, then drew it around the table at each of them. "You allowed that man to exist. Your incompetence and lack of disclosure to me gave him an opportunity to create a line into The Stratum, to work his particular brand of magic, and to call in Aislen Walker, a blind, naïve outsider with the genetic potential to destroy us. And newsflash—that is what Sigmund Lange intends to do."

Raze could feel the shift from 2, 5, and 8. They visibly shrank in their chairs. Number 9 sat defiantly with his arms crossed, still not buying it. Number 7 wasn't going down without a fight.

"And just what makes you so sure about this, Raziel?" Number 7 said, still leaning over the dais, glaring down at him. "What makes you think that you have all the answers and we don't?"

He looked at each of The 8 before he looked back at Number 7, measuring his next words for maximum impact.

"Because Preston Reed paid me a visit. And told me *everything*."

Number 9 dropped his head to his chest.

"Preston Reed?" Number 7 was losing steam.

"Preston Reed." Raze turned his back on The 8 and walked toward Grant and Troy, rubbing his victory in with a knowing smile. "Apparently, Reed can do whatever the fuck he wants. He can just wander into The Stratum, confront a Control Operative, spill the beans about his daughter, and try to make a deal." Raze turned back to Number 7.

"What kind of deal?" 7 said, failing miserably at containing his seething rage.

"That we leave his daughter alone and stop Sigmund Lange."

"And why would we do that? How can that decrepit skinbag be any threat?"

"Because his energy *is* still strong, and his vengeance fuels it. He plans to take over his great-granddaughter's young, able body and utilize her genetically engineered skill sets. Then he will come back here and reascend to his rightful place." Raze looked at the throne. Its emptiness was potent. "And he will destroy every one of you if necessary."

The silence deepened as his words sank in.

"Well, why didn't you kill her then?" Troy's snarky voice chimed in from the back of the room.

All eyes looked to Troy and then back at Raze.

Raze turned and strolled toward Troy, enunciating every word as if speaking to an imbecile. "Because I'm not the fucking idiot around here. *I* don't leave loose, live wires hanging around. Killing Aislen still leaves a competent Sigmund Lange and a master, Preston Reed, out there. Killing Aislen will make them both very angry... angry with a target." He got face-to-face with Troy, eye-to-eye. "Eleven targets."

He let them do the math. They were all doomed.

He turned back to The 8. "I'm thinking we would all like to

tie up all these live wires, right? Finish it? Once and for all, so we can go about our business?

And they all fall down.

"What do you suggest?"

Raze resumed his position at parade rest.

"I propose we kidnap Aislen Walker. Then we use her as an energetic lure. We can eliminate Number 1, Preston Reed, and last but not least, Aislen Walker herself. Exterminate the whole lineage."

The 8 looked from one to another. One by one, they nodded their approval.

"Okay then," Number 7 said, looking at Grant. "Mr. Parker, take Mr. Kellen and prepare the test facilities for our guest... *personally*. No one is to know of this project. Mr. Tanis, you are directed to initiate the project. Kidnap Aislen Walker and bring her to the test facilities. Then notify us directly."

"I won't be doing that," Raze said, making them his bitch now. "Troy over there is going to do that. He's been wining and dining Ms. Walker for quite a while now. Isn't that right, Troy? You have quite a connection with her, wouldn't you say?"

Troy tried to defend himself. "Well, I didn't know who she *was!* She's just a dumb nurse..."

"She isn't as dumb as you think. Anyway, you were hired for your charm and good looks—you're bait—so you go ahead and hook her. That shit is beneath my skill set, and I need to prepare for the real work."

"Raziel's right," Number 7 said. "Mr. Kellen, if you have established a... how shall we say... a *friendship* with Ms. Walker, invite her on a date. Bring her here, and we will have Raziel handle the rest. Raziel, prepare yourself. And I am sure that my colleagues will agree, if you handle this situation for us, for Infinium Incorporated, we will make it *very* worth your while. You may go."

Raziel turned on his heel and strode toward the steel doors. Grant and Troy trailed after him, obedient as dogs. The doors sealed behind them in the antechamber, and Grant exploded.

"What the fuck, Troy? You've been sniffing around this girl this whole time—the one who could destroy us?"

Raze turned back, savoring the spectacle.

"You took your eyes off your duty for a distraction in heels?"

Raze slipped in, smooth as a blade. "To be fair, Grant... she is striking. And you know the weak cannot control their base instincts. What else did you expect?"

Troy glared at Raze like he wanted to rip his throat out.

Raze smiled. *Fat chance.*

Grant turned on Raze. "Fuck you, Raziel. I swear on all that is unholy, I will find a way to destroy you if it's the last thing I do!"

Raze looked down at him. "Good luck with that." Raze turned his back on both of them.

"Get to work," he threw over his shoulder as he walked out.

TWELVE

AISLEN DRIFTED IN A NOWHERE PLACE, an in-between with no form or structure, suspended in the air. With nothing to anchor her, she was unable to get her bearings. She could feel the weight of something holding her down and looked up.

A shimmering wave rippled above her like she was deep underwater. She swam toward it. As she moved closer to the shiny veneer, she could see it was part mirror, part window. Just beyond her reflection, another version of herself was lying far below, curled up in the arms of the sterile white chair, sound asleep.

She was still dreaming! But she was also right there! If she could just pop through the thin membrane, she could fall back into her body and wake up.

Aislen pushed against the reflective image of herself, stretching toward her body below, trying to extricate herself from the trap of the dream. Her body inched closer as she struggled with the mirror, feeling it pressed taut against her.

Almost there.

Just a little further.

Da bist du ja, Poppet!

His distinctive rasp rattled her concentration, and she was thrown back into the in-between.

Where have you been? I've been looking for you.

Aislen scoured the emptiness for the old man, but he wasn't there.

She felt a *tap tap tap* against her skull. *No, no, dear. I'm right here. But you shouldn't be running away from me like that. We have work to do.*

Aislen started feeling a tickle against her scalp like he was scratching her head with his spindly old man finger. She shook her head violently and turned to run away. She moved quickly, flying rather than running. She could feel the speed and the wind, though there was only the blank canvas around her, and she could not gauge how far she was traveling.

Young Sigmund appeared out of nowhere, stopping her like a brick wall. "I am not letting you get away this time," he said in Old Lange's voice. His phantom finger went to work on her skull again, scratching and digging, like a prisoner trying to spoon his way out through limestone prison walls... only Sigmund was trying to spoon his way *in*.

Aislen pushed herself back from the phantom.

"I've seen what you do. What you *did!*" she spat with disgust.

"Which part are you talking about, Poppet?" he said, encroaching upon her.

"To that poor man! The drugs! The visions!"

Sigmund cocked his head to the side. "Which young man would that be? There were so many, you know."

"Thomas!" she yelled, whacking at the worm digging at her head. "You killed him!"

"Ooooooooooh, you mean your *grandfather!*" Sigmund smiled as he let that information sink in.

Of course, it was her grandfather! That was why he reminded her of her dad.

"And he wasn't dead... *yet.* Do you think I was going to let that happen? Tsk tsk." Mr. Lange moved in closer to Aislen's face, his icy pale eyes boring into her. "You really need to get to know me better if this is going to work out between us."

The worm stopped boring into her skull, and he shoved Aislen backward.

∞

TAP TAP TAP. Sigmund hammered the final nail in his office wall. He picked up the large frame on his desk and carefully hung it on the nail, balancing it so that it was perfectly straight. He stepped back to admire the masterpiece. This was the moment it had all changed, the first jewel in what would be his crowning achievement.

Sigmund stepped back from the framed front page. June 5, 1968—Kennedy shot—was a jewel in his gallery, proof that his experiments produced truth. He wasn't collecting headlines for nostalgia; he was building product.

MKUltra was never madness to him. While the CIA saw chaos and corpses, Sigmund saw a blueprint. Visions could be standardized, triggered, repeated. Control wasn't theory anymore—it was protocol. And protocol could be packaged. *Sold.*

All he needed now was capital. Three more titans—media, telecom, defense—and his board would be complete. Then

Infinium Incorporated wouldn't be an idea. It would be a regime.

He toyed with the key to Thomas's shackles.

He wasn't happy about his new living arrangement. It was quite a step down from the Army barracks at The Presidio. Twenty-four steps down, to be exact. But he should have been grateful—at least he got the bed! And a servant.

Astrid, relegated to sleeping on the floor now, made sure he was fed, watered, and cared for. It didn't take much to get her to comply. Years of discipline had made that easy.

Thomas, on the other hand, was harder to break.

He really did not understand just how much Sigmund was protecting him. By hiding him in his basement, he was making sure the CIA didn't find out about him. The CIA had been busy lately. Their MKUltra experiments were producing a plethora of Manchurian candidates, and the body count was stacking up.

If Thomas opened his mouth to the wrong people about what he had seen... he'd end up one of the body count.

Sigmund wouldn't let that happen. Thomas was essential to his master plan. He had a gift! A gift that could be utilized to change the world.

Sigmund walked to the window of his new office. He was moving up in the world. The cityscape rolled out below him now, jagged gray steel and concrete bit hard against the senses, like teeth Sigmund would use to take his bite out of the world.

Then he turned his attention to the artwork that was also lying on his desk. The designer had gotten it just right: a perfect geometric reproduction of Bernoulli's lemniscate, which, in Sigmund's view, aesthetically represented the potential of infinity in a superior manner. You could hop on the continuum at any point and travel in uninhibited flow through time and space.

Except in Sigmund's logo, two golden I's pierced through the perfect infinity symbol. Infinium interrupted.

That was the whole purpose of his vision: to disrupt the cosmic order of things, control the material world, and all the people in it. Thomas and the successes of the MKUltra experiments had convinced Sigmund that it was possible to block the ultimate reality of the universe from the masses and utilize it for the benefit of the few—the elite—who had invested in his technology.

He lifted the logo off the table, admiring how the diffused sunlight glinted off the iridescent curves of the symbol, when a loud tap hit the window behind him. He turned to look, thinking a bird may have hit the glass, but was greeted by a refreshing breeze that told him it wasn't a wayward bird at all. It was *her*.

"Well, hello there," he said out loud. "It's been a while since you've been around."

The air went icy.

"Aww, don't be scared. I won't hurt you. Come in! Have a look around! See what you're helping me to create!"

The air grew colder as she moved through his office. He could sense her moving past the framed newspapers on the walls, the USS Pueblo, the MLK and RFK assassinations, and, hot off the presses today, November 12, 1969, the still unframed: My Lai. Twenty months after Thomas's vision—the final proof!

"Incredible, isn't it?"

The room was ice in response. To the faint of heart, photographs of the massacre would be horrifying. But to Sigmund, they were beautiful. They held promise.

"Come here, dear," he called to her. "Come look at what I'm doing." He coaxed the ghost his direction, and surprisingly, she bent to his will. He had to laugh at himself for being so afraid of her before when she'd appeared all those months ago during his morning bath. He'd thought he was going crazy. But now he realized, the girl wasn't a haunting. She was validation. Her appearance was evidence that his vision, his corporation, existed in the future! She was his harbinger of success.

"See! This is our symbol. It will be on everything: our building, our letterhead, our clothing. I envision a room buried deep in the earth with walls of stone and molten glass, and a tower reaching for the surface, for the light that shines through this logo in stained glass and pure gold."

He held it up and let it shimmer in the light again. The apparition moved away.

"Don't tell me you aren't impressed? You should be! You've helped me understand! Helped me see! Because of you, and Thomas of course, I understand the nature of reality, the nature of human existence, and the material world! I know how we can take advantage of all that now!"

Sigmund took a deep breath, inhaling the beauty and power of it.

The phone erupted on his desk. Sigmund looked at his watch. "Five minutes early. See! Everyone else understands. And they can't wait to be a part of it.

"Thanks for visiting, but I have work to do."

He snapped the air like a whip, chasing the ethereal waif back out the window from where she came. The office was warm again, but Sigmund stood grinning at the empty air. Even the ghosts had no choice but to bear witness to his empire.

THIRTEEN

AISLEN FELL out of the window of Sigmund's office. The windows reflecting the sun's glare strobed and streaked light as she kept falling toward the ground, though the ground didn't come. She kept falling through space, becoming nauseous from the velocity and g-forces until she couldn't take any more.

"Stop!" she cried out before she threw up.

Miraculously, she stopped, landing feet first on a slab of concrete. The air was dank and still. She caught her breath while her eyes adjusted to the lighting. She was standing at the bottom of a flight of wooden stairs, painted white but worn grey in the center from foot traffic. She heard footsteps at the top, shuffling, then clattering, someone working in the kitchen.

Aislen surveyed the room. The concrete seemed to press into her chest, though she had no chest, squeezing the air she couldn't breathe. There was a thin mattress on the floor near the shelves, with a grungy flat pillow and a neatly folded stack of blankets resting on top.

Did someone sleep there? It wasn't even fit for a dog.

"Who's there?"

Aislen nearly jumped out of her skin and looked toward the voice. Thomas was sitting up on a bed in the opposite corner, looking her direction. He *was* alive! Like Lange had said!

He was in the same clothes Aislen had seen him wearing in the brothel. His ankle was shackled to the metal frame of the bed. He'd been here for a while, a few weeks at least. Gaunt, unshaven, eyes wild—her father's eyes, but caged.

"Who's *there!?*" Thomas whispered gruffly, sounding a bit crazed.

The door at the top of the stairs creaked open, sending a slash of sunlight into the darkness and spotlighting Aislen. She looked down at herself, seeing only a snow of dust dancing in the beam. She was still in the dream, if she could even call it that anymore. Was it really a dream if you were actually in the past? She wasn't confused about where she was, only about *when* she was. Time felt like a trap.

Astrid appeared at the top of the stairs, carrying a tray with food. She walked into the cellar, and Astrid's body passed through hers. The girl's fear seared Aislen like static electricity. Sadness and guilt clung to her like damp clothes. Aislen shook herself, but it didn't come off.

Astrid walked to the bed and set the tray on it, bowing like a servant as she shuffled back to the mattress on the floor. She crouched down in a ball on the makeshift bed and watched Thomas watching her.

"Astrid, please," Thomas whispered. "Please... you can help me."

Astrid curled into a tighter ball.

"Astrid, help me get this chain off. We can cut it with something. Find a saw or a bolt cutter. Then I can get out and find help."

Astrid covered her eyes with her hands and put her face in her legs, shutting the only door she had.

"God damn it!" Thomas screamed, sweeping the tray and all its food off the bed. The crash tore through Aislen's ears like gunfire—glass, food, juice spraying across the cellar, spattering Astrid's hair.

Astrid looked up at Thomas, then at the mess, horrified. A thin cry sang from her, and fast as light she bound up the stairs, then back down with a broom and dust pan. She scurried around the room trying to gather up all the glass and food that she could.

Thomas watched for a while, then grumbled to himself, lying back down on the bed and turning his back to her frantic activity.

Astrid ascended and descended the stairs, carting away the destruction.

"Vater wird mich töten," Astrid repeated the worried mantra under her breath as she tried to mop up all the stains from the juice. "Father will kill me."

Aislen understood, but Thomas kept his back turned to her in oblivious apathy.

The dusky light of the basement grew darker as evening fell in the world above. Astrid was upstairs trying to wash the remaining evidence of the catastrophe away when suddenly there were footsteps. Astrid was at the top of the stairs in an instant, shutting the basement door behind her and quickly but ever so quietly descending into the darkness. She rushed back to her mattress and squatted into the tiniest of balls as a key turned in the lock and the front door opened.

There were the ominous footsteps of Sigmund Lange... and the drop of his briefcase by the door. There was the sound of the closet door opening and shutting as he hung his coat. There were the footsteps that stopped at the door at the top of the stairs, and the vacuum of his listening. Then there was the scrape of a chair across the floor that continued like nails on a chalkboard all the way back to the basement door.

Astrid let out a quiet thread of a whimper, hushing herself as Sigmund descended the staircase, thumping the kitchen chair behind him. He walked past Aislen in her dusty corner and stopped, looking over his shoulder, sensing her there, before continuing toward Thomas, who lay still, facing the wall on the bed.

"Wake up, Thomas! We have some catching up to do."

Thomas didn't move. His only way to protest.

"Thomas! We have to talk about Kennedy. You've had enough time to recuperate." Sigmund set the chair down and waited for Thomas to sit up and face him. But Thomas did not.

Sigmund marched to the bedside and kicked the metal frame several times. "Thomas Reed! Up and at 'em!"

When Sigmund set his foot back down, there was a loud crunch under his foot. He lifted it back up, bent down, and picked up the tiniest shard of glass lying on the floor. He stared at it, embedded in the tip of his finger, then turned his head slowly toward the little ball in the corner. He walked back to the chair.

"Astrid, come here."

Astrid knew not to tarry. The punishment would be worse if she did. She went to her father.

This got Thomas's attention, and he rolled over and sat up.

"Behind the chair, Astrid," Sigmund commanded.

"Mr. Lange," Thomas interrupted. "That is my fault. I lost my temper and threw the food at her."

Sigmund turned to Thomas and flicked the glass off his finger.

"No, *you* don't understand, Mr. Reed," Sigmund said as he circled the chair behind his daughter. "It is *always* Astrid's fault. You are my guest. It is her duty to keep you happy. And the sooner you cooperate, the sooner your situation will improve. And Thomas, by improve, I mean *vastly* improve. You have no idea the breakthrough your last trip was or the plans that I have, that you can be a part of."

Sigmund took Astrid's right hand and placed it on the back of the chair, opening her fingers so they weren't gripping the back.

"Astrid's only job is to keep you happy until you decide to stop being so stubborn. And she is apparently failing."

Sigmund picked up her left hand and placed it on the back of the chair, lifting her fingers one by one so they couldn't hold on. "Isn't that right, Poppet?"

"Ja, Vater," Astrid whispered.

Sigmund unbuckled his belt and slid it from his waistband.

"You see, Thomas? Disobedience earns the belt. That's a simple order."

He looked between Thomas and Astrid, the belt folding and unfolding like a sermon's punctuation.

These are not whims, Thomas. They are principles. Without them, all collapses into chaos." He pressed the belt flat against Astrid's trembling hands on the chair—"I will never permit collapse."

"Mr. Lange, please don't. Please. It's my fault. I'll do what you want; I'll talk. But don't hurt her."

Sigmund moved into a position behind Astrid and folded the belt in half.

"Well, Thomas, I am very pleased to hear that. And I am going to hold you to that, too. But let this be a lesson to you of what happens when you are not fulfilling your end of the bargain."

As Sigmund raised the belt, Aislen's whole body convulsed. The sound split through her like it landed on her own skin. She doubled over in a pain that wasn't hers, yet branded her ribs anyway.

∞

AISLEN WATCHED the cement floor as it faded into black, then into light again, night into day in mere seconds. Time surged so fast it tore her balance, like being pulled forward on invisible strings.

Each day, Astrid rose, worked, and fed Thomas. Thomas watched from the bed, remorse reeking from him.

It began as a small thing, Thomas reaching out and resting his hand on top of Astrid's. She jumped as if she had been set on fire and cowered back towards her isolated cushion.

"Astrid," Thomas said, raising his hand like he was trying to calm a frightened animal. "Please... I don't want to frighten you. I'm so sorry for all of this. For everything. So, so sorry."

Astrid slowly sank onto the mattress and pulled her knees up to her chest. She sat there peeking over her knees at Thomas for a long time.

Sigmund came down each evening, walking through Aislen then turning back, acknowledging her with a smile. He sat in the reminder chair, notebook in hand, interrogating Thomas. Thomas compliant. Astrid watching from the corner.

Another day, Astrid brought Thomas his food, and he rested his hand on hers again. Only this time she didn't flinch.

"Thank you, Astrid," he said, looking at her hand.

Her eyes, usually glued to the tray, glanced at his hand for a half-second before she slipped hers away and went back to her place.

Another day, Astrid watched Thomas finish his meal, retrieved his tray, and took it upstairs. But on this day, when she came back down, she was carrying a tub filled with soapy water and set it on the floor by Thomas' bed. Then she brought towels, scissors, a shaver, a comb, and finally a clean shirt.

"You can wash yourself and change," Astrid told Thomas. "I'm sorry, I don't have the key."

"You speak English?" Thomas was shocked.

"I know English." Astrid kept her eyes on the floor. "*Vater* only allows me to speak German."

"*Vater?*"

"Father."

"I see."

Astrid shuffled her feet awkwardly. "I'll give you privacy," she said, before making her way back to her mattress. She sat with her back to Thomas, put her face on her knees, and covered her arms around her face. Thomas looked at her back, confused by this type of privacy, but realized it was all they had. He set about washing himself as best he could, shackled to the bed. He trimmed his beard, soaped his face, and did the best he could at a clean shave. The water became a dingy soup, and he realized that he'd forgotten to wash his hair.

"Astrid, I'm sorry to ask this, but could I get some fresh water for my hair? I didn't do this in the right order."

Astrid turned to him and stopped, her face flushing with embarrassment. She dropped her head, rushed in to scoop up the tub, trying not to look at Thomas' half-naked form, before disappearing up the stairs.

"Jesus Christ," he muttered, wrapping a towel around his shoulders before she came back down.

"I'm sorry about that," he said when she returned. "I wasn't thinking." He looked up into her face, trying to catch her eye, but she avoided him by turning her head down and away.

"No. *I'm* sorry," she said. "I should have helped you. Hold this."

Astrid handed the tub to Thomas, then moved beside him, gently tilting his head over the water. Her fingers were clumsy at first, awkward, trembling, as though afraid of what even this small contact might cost her.

The first trickle slid down his scalp, cool against fevered skin. Thomas closed his eyes. Weeks of grime loosened beneath her touch, and for the first time since the basement, he felt human again. Not a prisoner. Not an experiment. Just a man.

Her soapy hands moved through his hair with a tentative care, each pass slower than it needed to be, as if she were memorizing the strands. A rivulet ran down the back of his neck, tracing his spine, and he shuddered.

Astrid avoided his eyes, watching the water cloud with dirt and hair, her face tight with restraint. But her hands betrayed her: gentler, lingering longer than duty required.

Thomas breathed in sharply, and for a moment neither of them moved. The damp silence between them felt heavier than chains.

Aislen's chest throbbed. She wanted to press her hands into Astrid's shoulders, tell her to keep going, that this small mercy mattered. Instead, she only shivered in the corner, watching tenderness bloom where only fear had lived.

When Astrid finished, she took the tub and carried it upstairs. Thomas watched her as she left, eyes wet, not from the water but from the first compassion and kindness he'd been shown in a long time. And coming from her, a girl who didn't even have a bed.

∞

ASTRID RETURNED, bearing fresh sheets.

"Let me cut your hair first," she said, picking up the comb and scissors. She combed out the tangles in his hair and cut the long locks to a more manageable length. When she was finished, she removed the sheets, swept up the hair, and put the clean sheets back on the bed for him. She disappeared up the stairs again.

Astrid was gone for a long time. When the familiar footsteps sounded at the front porch, she scurried back down and found her place on the mattress.

Sigmund sensed a difference right away, stopping midway down the stairs before descending the rest slowly and deliberately.

"Well, well, well, what have we here?" Sigmund said as he surveyed the new and improved Thomas. Thomas looked from Astrid's shrunken form to Sigmund, confused.

"Um, I've had a bath," Thomas answered.

"As I see," Sigmund responded. "As well as a shave, a haircut, a clean shirt, and clean sheets. You realize I am neither blind nor an imbecile, don't you, Thomas?"

"Yes, Mr. Lange, I didn't mean to suggest—"

"Astrid! Come here!" Sigmund yelled.

Thomas jumped at the show of rage. Astrid stood up calmly and walked to the chair. She placed her hands on the back without prompting. She knew what was coming... had known all along. A dawning realization came over Thomas' face. She had done this for Thomas on her own, without permission from her father, knowing the ramifications.

Sigmund whipped his belt off and marched toward Astrid.

"Wait!" cried Thomas. "Hold on! I asked her!"

"You what!?" Sigmund whipped back to Thomas.

"I asked her. I asked her for the water and soap. I felt like I needed to start being more presentable, more tolerable to be around... so we could continue our work."

"Is that so?" Sigmund was suspicious.

"Yes! I swear! She didn't want to! But you told her she had to do what I asked. She had to make me happy. So I told her to do it."

Sigmund's eyes narrowed at Thomas. "You realize that Astrid cannot lie to me, don't you?" Sigmund walked behind her. "Isn't that right, Poppet?" He looked down at Astrid's hands. They were already open, barely resting on the back of the chair.

"Ja, Vater," she said, resigned.

Sigmund looked back at Thomas, smiling. "You see, Mr. Reed. The punishment for disobedience is the belt. But the penalty for lying is far, far worse." He placed a hand on Astrid's hip, hitching her dress up a bit. "Isn't that also correct, Astrid?"

"Ja, Vater," Astrid said, her voice catching.

Sigmund's eyes narrowed, his hand coiling the belt like a serpent ready to strike. "So tell me, dear girl. Was this your idea? Or was it Mr. Reed's?"

Sigmund looked at Thomas, knowing what her answer would be.

The silence was suffocating. Astrid's fingers quivered on the chair back, but then—slowly—she lifted her gaze. For the first time, she met her father's eyes head-on.

"Er hat mich dazu," she said, voice steady as stone.

The words cracked through the basement like lightning.

Sigmund froze. The belt stilled in his fist. He searched her face, hunting for weakness, for the flinch he could exploit. But her eyes stayed on his, unwavering, even while her knees trembled. For the first time, it was he who lingered, uncertain.

Thomas's breath caught. He knew what she had done—

taken his crime onto herself, drawn the fire to her own back. She had just saved him, and it might cost her everything.

Even Aislen felt the jolt. The echo of Astrid's words rippled through her incorporeal chest, thudding like a heartbeat that wasn't hers. Courage. Defiance. For a second, she almost believed Astrid could shatter the chain between them all. Astrid had changed the rules.

∞

TIME RACED through two more days, stopping one morning.

Astrid set the tray down, her hands tight around its edges. She hesitated, then slipped a hand into her dress pocket.

When it emerged, something small gleamed against her palm.

"I shouldn't..." Her voice shook. "Vater left his coat. It was in the pocket. I—" She swallowed, refusing to meet his eyes. "If he finds out..."

She opened her palm fully, the iron glint catching what little light filtered down the stairs.

The key.

Not just a scrap of metal—it looked like it pulsed with consequence, radiant and terrible. A holy relic. A death sentence. A salvation.

Thomas froze. The air between them thickened, as if the basement itself were holding its breath.

He didn't reach for it right away. His hands hovered, trembling, as if he might profane it just by touching. "Astrid... you don't know what this means."

"I know what it means." For the first time, her gaze lifted to his—fragile, fierce. "I choose this."

She pressed the key into his palm, closing his fingers around it.

Thomas clutched the key to his chest like a relic, torn between awe and terror. "God help us," he whispered.

Thomas pulled his legs around and tried to stand up. But he was too weak from the weeks of inactivity, and he lost his balance. Astrid stepped in and helped him, supporting him while he shuffled across the floor.

"Help me back to the bed," he said when they reached the stairs.

"But you can go! You are free!"

"No. I am too weak right now. And I am not leaving you behind."

Astrid looked at him, unable to comprehend his reasons.

"Come on, now. Take me back."

Reluctantly, she took Thomas back to the bed, and he relocked the cuff.

That night, when Sigmund came down for his session, Thomas proposed a deal.

"Mr. Lange, a while back, you told me that my trips at the brothel had been a breakthrough for you, and it was something I could be a part of. Is that still the case?"

Sigmund looked up from the notepad and surveyed Thomas. "It could be something that we work out, provided that you are a willing participant in some more experiments. The BZ took you to a whole new level. If we continued with that, I could assure you that some changes could be made."

"Hmmm... I see. Well, I am willing to negotiate with you. I am willing to start now, in fact. But I have one condition."

Sigmund snorted. "Are you really in the position to be proposing conditions, Thomas?"

"Actually, I am."

Sigmund's eyes narrowed.

"Don't worry, I understand that I need to build your trust," Thomas continued. "But you have to give a little bit. I'm getting too weak being chained to this bed. I need some regular exercise. And some sunlight. And more meals. And I would like the ability to use a real bathroom."

"My, my, that's sure a lot of demands for someone in your position, Thomas."

"I know it seems that way. But I feel that if I am healthier, what I have been doing lately will improve."

That got Sigmund's attention. "What you've been doing lately? You mean two months ago at the brothel?"

"No, I mean last night. And the night before that. And the nights and nights before that."

"What! What do you mean?"

"Like I said, Mr. Lange. I am willing to negotiate for some basic improvements. And as I build your trust, I will expect a few more."

"I don't understand? You've had trips this whole time? Outside the lab? Why haven't you told me this?"

"First, you haven't asked. Second, you haven't earned it."

Sigmund grumbled. He did not like being in a weaker position.

"It isn't a weaker position, Sigmund," Thomas said, reading his mind. "It's a cooperative position. Similar to what you are negotiating with your future board members for Infinium Incorporated."

Sigmund dropped his pen on the floor.

∞

TIME RUSHED FORWARD. Thomas was unchained only at night when Sigmund was at the residence. He walked around the basement and did pushups while talking. Sigmund took copious notes. Another day, Sigmund came into the basement carrying a newspaper, clearly excited that it confirmed something Thomas had told him. After that, Thomas was allowed to be free while Sigmund was at his office, and he started helping Astrid with her chores.

One night, Thomas had a severe nightmare. He was tossing and turning so violently that instead of just watching from the corner, Astrid got up and went to his bedside. She laid her hands on his chest to calm him.

Thomas jolted awake, breathing heavily, staring into Astrid's eyes. Then he pulled her into his arms and held her. She didn't know what to do, but he wouldn't let her go, and after a time she relaxed in his arms and allowed him to comfort her, and himself.

The next night, Thomas watched Astrid sleeping on the floor. He called to her, she came to his bedside, and he moved over, offering her half the bed.

Astrid looked to the door above the stairs and back at Thomas, shaking her head. He reached up, took her hand, and pulled her gently to the bed. She lay down beside him. He kissed her hair, then her temple. He caressed her shoulder, down her arm. Astrid trembled but didn't pull away. Her body softened into his, yielding inch by inch, until the barrier between comfort and hunger dissolved. When morning came, the distance between them was gone.

Days blurred—shadows to light, working, sleeping, their bond deepening until love was undeniable.

One afternoon, Thomas was sitting on the bed writing notes on a pad. Sigmund hadn't come for a session three nights in a row because he had been working later at his office, so

Thomas had begun providing his information independently. He stopped writing and looked up at Astrid, standing at the shelves, stacking jars of preserves she had just made. He walked to her, turned her around, and swept the hair out of her eyes. He looked into them with love and conviction.

"I am going to take you away from here. I promise." He lifted her chin, caressing its shallow indent with his thumb, and kissed her.

As time rushed forward, there were too many close calls. Too many times, Sigmund arrived home, and Astrid had to scramble to dress and make it to her mattress before he opened the basement door.

Weeks—months—passed by with dizzying speed. When it finally stood still again, Thomas and Astrid were sleeping next to each other, legs and arms entangled, her head on his shoulder.

They were comfortable with each other now, comfortable in the routine.

Aislen heard Sigmund's familiar footsteps coming up the walkway. She looked to Thomas and Astrid, expecting Astrid to make a mad dash for her mattress on the floor.

But neither of them moved, both in a deep sleep.

The front door opened, then closed. Still, neither stirred.

"Astrid, wake up!" Aislen called from across the room. But, of course, there was no reaction.

The closet door opened, then closed. *It's late,* Aislen thought, *maybe he will just go to bed.*

She held her breath, listening to the tap, tap, tapping of his feet on the wood floor, willing him to go up the stairs. But the tap, tap, tapping moved toward the basement door.

Aislen willed herself to the bedside so she could stir the air, or move the bed, but she was frozen, her legs pumping slowly like they were stuck in molasses.

"Alpha 14," a voice sounded in the room. It wasn't Thomas or Sigmund.

The door opened at the top of the stairs, and Sigmund started descending.

Aislen looked to Thomas and Astrid, still sound asleep on their bed.

"Wake up!!!" Aislen screamed at the top of her lungs, but the only movement was the steady rise and fall of their breathing.

Sigmund stopped in front of her, turned to her, and smiled. He knew she was there; he always knew.

"Aislen! Wake up!" The voice cut sharp through her skull —urgent, commanding.

But Sigmund's lips didn't move. And it wasn't his voice in her head.

Sigmund turned toward the sleeping figures in the bed. Aislen watched helplessly as Astrid began to stir, sensing her father's presence.

Sigmund was on her in a second, grabbing her from the bed by her hair.

Aislen cried out, tried to run toward Sigmund, to stop him from hurting Astrid. But something had hold of her, wrapped around her like a straitjacket.

She watched helplessly as Sigmund ripped Astrid from the bed, her dress half-pulled, hair tangled from sleep. He flung her against the wall, exposing the secret she carried—the unmistakable curve of her belly.

Aislen's entire being splintered. The revelation detonated in her skull.

Sigmund noticed it too and charged toward his daughter again.

Astrid's terror slammed into Aislen's chest like her own heart had been seized. The basement tilted, warped, every surface vibrating with Astrid's fear until Aislen couldn't tell where her body ended and Astrid's began.

She screamed, tried to throw herself between them, but arms she couldn't see locked her down, firm and immovable.

Sigmund's hand arced toward Astrid—and in the flare of impact, the monstrous silhouette shattered into light.

Through it, blue eyes blazed at her. Raziel's hands held her shoulders. "Steady now. I got you."

The vortex snapped shut behind her like a door slamming, leaving only the echo of Astrid's terror in her bones.

FOURTEEN

A PERSISTENT TAP, tap, tapping pulled Sigmund unwillingly from the dream—just as it was getting to the best part!

He tried to hold on, to stay in the moment Aislen had abandoned when she slipped out. He squeezed his eyes tight and tried to go back into the same place: Astrid pressed against the wall, her thin body trembling, the curve of her belly betraying what she had tried to hide.

Sigmund's fingers tightened on her throat. "You think I wouldn't notice?" he hissed. The truth made his blood sing. Astrid's swollen belly wasn't a liability—*it was an opportunity.*

Thomas flew from the bed in a rage, thinking he could take Sigmund down, and got the unexpected blow of Sigmund's foot to his chest.

Sigmund had the advantage here. He was prepared. He knew what he would find. He'd seen the subtle looks, felt the shift in their connection, and had hatched his most brilliant idea ever.

Tap, tap, tapping was growing louder. The sharp odor of

bleach and bedpans, the sterile perfume of the dying, dragged him further into reality.

Not yet, God damn it! I am so close!!

He had stayed at work late that night, hoping he'd finally discover this. It was time—and if he'd waited any longer, it would have been too late.

Just as Sigmund had all the final pieces in place, ready to showcase Thomas's talents to The Board, Thomas had been pulling back, slowing down on the details of his nightly Travels. It was only a matter of time before Thomas would have persuaded Astrid to run off with him.

Thomas lunged again. Sigmund welcomed it.

He flicked open his father's knife, the steel catching the dim light. He pressed the blade to Astrid's belly, just hard enough to draw a sharp cry from her lips. Thomas froze, horror etched across his face.

"Don't even think about it," Sigmund said. "One wrong move, and I cut my way through her to the prize inside."

"You wouldn't!" Thomas gasped.

"I so would. I brought her into the world this way, I will take her out the same." He jabbed the sharp point into her flesh, and she cried out.

Thomas stopped, put both hands up, and stepped back.

Thomas was never a long-term solution for Sigmund's plans. He was too soft, too moral. *Weak.* He would never do what needed to be done. But a *child?* A child could be molded. Shaped. Controlled from birth in ways Thomas never could. And if the gifts were genetic...

Tap, tap, tapping was too loud, and he was almost there.

Sigmund threw an arm over his eyes to shut it out.

"Mr. Lange, please—" Thomas's voice cracked.

"Say goodbye, boy," Sigmund growled, relishing the

torment. "You're coming with me now. Your woman and your child belong to *me*."

Ah, the anguish on his face!

The tears that welled up in his eyes!

The ache in his throat as he whispered:

"Goodbye, Astrid."

It filled Sigmund with savage delight. The moment sealed it—Thomas broken, Astrid captive, the child destined for him. A specimen. A legacy. Not a son of Thomas at all, but his.

The *tap, tap, tapping* grew louder, pulling him away.

"No," Sigmund snarled, digging his nails deeper into Astrid's skin, desperate to stay. The dream dissolved like smoke, slipping from his grasp.

He opened his eyes to the dim light of the nursing home. His body lay heavy, useless, wrapped in its option-lock prison. His fingers twitched in sequence on the blanket, but with none of the power he had felt moments before.

The tapping continued—slow, deliberate—across the floor.

Sigmund turned his head. Not the nurse. Not the faceless aides who spoon-fed him slop.

It was Troy Kellen. His so-called "guard." Infinium's leash. The bastard walked with deliberate clicks of his polished shoes, a smug smile twisting his face as he loomed over the bed.

Tap. Tap. Tap.

"Good morning, Sigmund," Troy said, voice oily with satisfaction.

Sigmund glared up at him, fury boiling beneath the cage of his frail body. In his dreams, he still ruled. But here, in this husk, he was reminded of the truth: trapped, contained, watched.

For now.

FIFTEEN

"AHH, ah, ah, Aislen, stay with me now. C'mon. Stay with me." Raze lifted Aislen's limp body from the chair, holding her in one arm as he gently slapped her face a few times.

He ran his hand up and down her arm, trying to stimulate her blood flow and bring her back, but she had already slipped under.

This was his fault. He'd put her into Theta 4 to keep her calm, but it was too deep for too long, and the light jazz and mood lighting of Alpha 14 were not rousing enough to anchor her into consciousness.

"Beta 20," he told The Womb.

The Womb responded, increasing the lighting to 10,000 lux and 4000 kelvins. The jazz faded.

"Energize," he commanded.

The Womb promptly played a song engineered to emotionally and physiologically affect Aislen's brain.

"Aislen, c'mon now, wake up." Raze pressed his fingers across her temples and gently squeezed her shoulder.

She gasped for breath and opened her eyes. As the deep

sleep fell away, she realized just how close he was, the way he was holding her, how he was touching her, and her body went rigid.

"Hey, it's okay! I'm not going to hurt you," He pulled his hand back, palm open, proof he wasn't a threat. "We just need to get you good and awake. You were asleep too long. We have to sober you up."

He propped her up by herself and moved both hands up and down her arms and shoulders. Aislen stared at him wide-eyed.

"Do you think you can stand up? It would help."

She cocked her head to the side like she still didn't understand.

"C'mon, let's try to get up on your feet."

She came up shaky but managed, her gaze locked on him instead of the floor. When they reached the doorway, she froze, eyes on the warehouse's darkness. To Raze, it looked like she was already giving up.

"Okay, let's get you back to the chair."

Raze let go of her arms and let her turn back and walk on her own. He kept one hand on the small of her back to steady her. This wasn't a role he was used to, being helpful. A few days ago—hell, *this morning*—it would have been repugnant to him. But at this moment, it was natural. He *was* concerned. His life depended on her. He'd bought them some time, but she needed to get up to speed so they could figure out the best course of action.

Their fates were intertwined now. It was a fact that he had accepted when he faced The 8 and then lied to and manipulated them.

Aislen slid back into the chair, pulling her knees to her chest, eying him with suspicion.

Her silence was frustrating. Raze wasn't much of a talker—

in fact, this was the most he'd spoken to a stranger in weeks—but he was going to have to get her to communicate so they could make a plan that would keep them both alive. He was going to have to get her to trust him before his patience gave out.

"I'm going to get some OJ and water for you." Raze tried sounding more "nice," whatever "nice" was. But it sounded fake, like a kindergarten teacher at a parent/teacher conference.

She responded by hugging her legs tighter. She wasn't buying the compassionate Raziel schtick.

"Wait here a minute. I'll be right back," he said, as if she had a choice. Raze turned and left her in The Womb with the door open. Even if she tried, she wouldn't find a way out through the warehouse. And she was in no shape to run.

He returned with juice, water, and a blanket. She hadn't moved, though her eyes widened when she realized he'd actually left her alone.

He opened the juice and handed it to her. "Drink that now. It will get your blood sugar up." She took it and guzzled it down. She was dehydrated. It had been 12 hours since he'd snatched her from the hospital parking lot.

He opened the waters and set them next to the chair. "You can drink these while I'm getting food."

She stared at him in response. He couldn't read what she was thinking and finally gave up.

As he turned to leave, she found her voice. It was a whisper, but it was something.

"Is there a restroom in here?"

He'd forgotten about that part. He wasn't used to having a pet. Raze considered the options. The old Raze would've handed her a bucket. Instead, he offered his hand.

"Do you feel strong enough to walk up some stairs?"

She nodded.

"Do you still know my signature frequency?"

She nodded again.

"Okay, then match that and follow me."

She rose from the chaise and came to the doorway.

"Stay close. After this morning, they will be looking for discrepancies."

They synced frequencies and moved up the stairs.

"Shower. Jet." Raze commanded, and the shower roared on. Then, "Metal." And The Womb laid down some Metallica. Both would provide some masking interference.

"Quick," he told her, pushing the door open.

Yet another nod as she slipped around him and shut the door. She followed his orders and was back out quickly. He pulled her in behind him and back down the stairs to The Womb.

She returned to her position on the chaise, wrapping the blanket he brought around her.

"Better?" he asked once she was settled.

Again with the nodding.

Raze was exasperated now. "I need you to stay in here while I get food," the edge was back in his voice. "I bought us some time this morning, but I need you at 100 percent—sooner, rather than later. I'll figure something out for when I get back. So be ready."

No response.

Fuck it. He turned to leave. "Alpha 10."

The lighting faded back down, and the music shifted back to light jazz.

"Could you leave the lights up, please?"

Ahh! A voice. Raze assessed Aislen. She looked like a child afraid of the dark.

"Alpha 14," he commanded, and The Womb recalibrated. Aislen sighed with relief.

"Is everything okay?" he asked.

She winced.

Of course, everything wasn't okay. She was kidnapped and being held hostage.

"The dreams..." she whispered, as though if she mentioned them, they would hear her. "They've gotten worse."

The word hung between them. Dreams. He hated that word. Raze moved closer, kneeling to meet her eyes.

"First, they aren't dreams. You should call them what they are: a Viewing or Traveling. The sooner you address them for what they are, the sooner you can navigate them with control."

Aislen thought about that and nodded.

"Viewings do not bend to your will like dreams do," Raze continued. "You have to assert yourself in order to manipulate it. You have to approach them like reality."

She nodded again, "Like reality."

"Yes. *Reality*."

Aislen thought for a moment, then tentatively asked, "Is it possible to Travel back in time in this *reality*?"

His gut clenched. She shouldn't know about that. "You think you've been going back in time?"

Another nod, this time confident.

This was Level X territory—shit operatives didn't touch unless they were suicidal.

"Yes. It's possible. Backwards and forward. But risky, especially if you're new."

There was no sign of relief. In fact, she looked even more petrified.

Raze stood up. "We can talk about this more when I get back. Drink some water and try to relax. But stay awake! You've Traveled enough for today."

He left her sitting in The Womb, looking like a child waiting for the Boogeyman. Raze had a distinct feeling that *he* was no longer the worst nightmare she was having.

SIXTEEN

THE DOOR SLID shut behind him, and Aislen was left alone again in the strange laboratory.

He had changed. One person had left her in here the first time, and another, a completely different person, had come back; Dr. Jekyll into Mr. Hyde. And it wasn't just his demeanor that had shifted, but his signature frequency had, too. Aislen noticed it when she matched him before going upstairs. When they first got here, she felt a resonance with him, like they clicked into place when she matched him. But that didn't happen this time. He felt different; off.

While it should have been reassuring that the Raziel who was just in the room was legitimately concerned for her well-being, it was actually more disconcerting. Who would he be when he got back? If this were reality, it was shifting faster than her dreams.

Travels, she corrected herself. If she needed to call them what they were, that's the only thing they could be. She was definitely going to another place, and she was definitely going to another *time.*

She was seeing the past. She was seeing how it all began with her great-grandfather, Sigmund Lange, and his experiments. He had discovered Thomas Reed, then developed him.

When she'd been pulled out of the basement—out of the Viewing, as Raziel called it—Thomas and Astrid were in bed together, and Astrid was pregnant!

Aislen did the math. Astrid would be Aislen's grandmother... and if she had that baby... that baby would be her father!

Aislen realized she was seeing his history—her history—first-hand. Seeing how he came to be... how she came to be... how all of it, this situation, this place she was in, *Raziel*, came to be.

She had so many questions. She knew Raziel could explain, maybe even help, but that would mean she would have to trust him.

Aislen shuddered. How could she trust the man who had used a little boy, orchestrated a murder... who had hunted her down and kidnapped her? He was holding her captive like Sigmund had held Thomas.

But then she remembered his arms around her when she woke up, the fire as he rubbed her arms, the intensity in his eyes as he looked at her. The warmth of his hand lingered on her back, a brand she hadn't asked for. It terrified her that her body noticed him at all, as if her body hadn't gotten the message that he was the enemy.

She could take the chance and trust him. Or she could figure out a way to escape.

Aislen curled up in the chaise and pulled the blanket over her head. She didn't want to think about any of it. She wanted to block it all out, this reality and all the others.

She closed her eyes and let it all slip away.

SEVENTEEN

TROY KELLEN HOVERED OVER SIGMUND, a twisted smirk on his face.

"Mr. Lange, you've been a very bad boy. You've created a complete and utter mess of everything." Troy leaned down into his face, so close that Sigmund could smell the peppermint from his toothpaste. "You need to tell me where Aislen Walker is, Mr. Lange. And you need to tell me right *now*."

Sigmund's aged mouth worked itself, but even moving his tongue was a struggle. "She's mine," he managed to growl.

Troy reached his hand down to Sigmund's chest, grabbing the sheets and blankets and part of Sigmund's paper thin skin.

"She is not *yours*. And you will tell me where she is, or I will snap every fucking bone in your body until you do."

"She's Traveling," Sigmund rasped.

Troy's grip tightened. "Her *body*, you decrepit fool!"

"I don't know." Sigmund's tongue had loosened up, and he continued. "But you should help me... you should help me find her. If you bring her to me, I will make it very worth your while."

Troy scoffed. "*You* will make it worth *my* while, huh? You are delusional, old man. You are a dinosaur. You have no power here anymore. In fact, you are completely unnecessary. I don't give a fuck what Raziel says about eliminating all of you at once. He can go fuck himself, too. You have outlived your purpose, and I am sick of babysitting you."

Troy moved his hand up to Sigmund's throat and closed his grip around it.

There was a tap at the window and a knock on the hospital room door.

Troy instantly released his grip and stepped back, casually leaning against the wall as if he hadn't a care in the world.

As Nurse Rachel wheeled her med cart in, Sigmund noticed a slight movement at the window—a loosened fold of air that smelled of her. He knew it: she was here.

"Ashlyn! You came!" Sigmund barked, throat tearing with effort.

"Good afternoon, Mr. Lange! No. No Aislen today, I'm afraid. You get me today!" Rachel looked to Troy. "Well, good afternoon to you, too, Troy! I wasn't expecting you here!"

"Yeah, yeah... just making a few rounds this afternoon."

"Well, lucky me! Aislen is usually the one who gets all the pleasure of your company." Rachel winked at him, then turned her attention back to Sigmund. "Ok, Mr. Lange. It's time for your meds."

"I don't need meds!" Sigmund howled. "I need Ashlyn!"

"Aislen will be here in the morning, Mr. Lange. I will make sure she comes in for a visit."

Troy perked up. "She will?"

Rachel smiled slyly. "She's on the schedule tomorrow. Shouldn't you be asking her out by now?"

"It's coming along," Troy said with a knowing smile. "In

fact, I'd love to take her out tonight, but I can't get hold of her. You wouldn't know where she is, would you?"

"She's right here!!!" Sigmund was infuriated. He searched the room, trying to find her essence. "Ashlyn, please! I need you!"

Rachel moved to the side of the bed, white cup in hand. "Mr. Lange, I need you to calm down, or we are going to have to restrain you. Aislen will be here in the morning, and I will have her come in straight away. Now, let's take these meds; they will make you feel better."

"I don't need your stupid pills, you stupid cunt!" Sigmund swung his arm up, knocking the pills from her hand and hitting the side of her face in the process.

Rachel recoiled. "Mr. Lange! That's unacceptable! I'm sorry, but you'll have to be restrained if you are going to be combative. Troy, can you help me please?"

"Sure thing." Troy pulled up the restraints from his side of the bed as Rachel pulled them up from hers. "This is for your own good Mr. Lange," Troy said, masking the obvious pleasure of this turn of events. They strapped his arms down and then moved to the foot of the bed, strapping each of his ankles.

Rachel moved back to the cart and prepared an injection for Sigmund instead. "As soon as the meds take effect, Mr. Lange, we'll release you."

"Fuck you, bitch!" Sigmund began struggling against the restraints. "Ashlyn! Ashlyn, please! Show yourself to these idiots!"

Troy looked at Sigmund, and then scanned the room for the possibility that she might really be there.

Rachel came back to the side of the bed with the syringe, lifted the blanket and Sigmund's gown, then injected him in the buttock.

"Nooooo! You don't understand!" His chest convulsed, the words rattling like broken glass.

"There, there now, Mr. Lange," Rachel said as she rubbed the spot on his hip. "That should make it all better. Troy, can you watch him for a bit while I finish my rounds? I'll document this, then come back and remove the restraints."

"Absolutely, Rachel." Troy gave her a reassuring smile. "And if you see Aislen before I do, could you tell her I'm looking for her?"

"Of course," Rachel wrinkled her nose at him and pushed the cart out of the room.

Troy watched her leave, then moved to the door, shutting it quietly behind her. He slowly walked back to Sigmund's bedside.

The syringe's warmth was still there; Sigmund's eyelids fluttered, and his world smeared. Even if he could have, Sigmund didn't have enough strength to fight them. Troy took his time walking back, the hard tap of his shoes clicking like a doomsday clock.

As the meds worked on his brain, Sigmund's vision began to fog, and suddenly, she was there—Ashlyn—at the end of his bed.

She appeared like a spark through fog, and hope flared. She looked mortified, like she hadn't come by choice. No, of course she hadn't. This was his doing. His pull was too strong, the bond undeniable. This was the proof he had always needed— she could still be his.

"Ashlyn!" His lips trembled as the word scraped free. "I knew you were here! I always knew when you were around. Please, help me!"

Troy walked to the end of the bed, searching for what Sigmund saw, surveying the area for any sign or feeling of her.

Finding nothing, he turned and walked back to Sigmund, leaned down into his face and looked him in the eye.

"Any final confessions, old man?"

Sigmund couldn't speak. The meds had overpowered his muscle control, and his mind was starting to fade.

Please, Poppet, come closer. Make him stop, Sigmund pleaded.

Aislen looked from Sigmund to Troy. "Troy?"

Troy, of course, was oblivious. Only Sigmund could hear her.

"You are no longer needed here," Troy whispered to Sigmund.

Troy clamped a hand over Sigmund's mouth.

Aislen freaked out. "Troy! What are you doing? Please stop!"

Sigmund couldn't breathe. He didn't have the strength to pull any oxygen through Troy's fingertips.

Sigmund watched as Aislen grew even more horrified by what Troy was doing.

"Troy! What are you doing! This isn't okay!"

From the wall behind Aislen, Astrid appeared, the daughter Sigmund had broken. Thomas stepped out of the shadow behind her, eyes full of quiet accusation. And then, at the edge of the room, *Vater*—the source of cruelty and power in his blood.

The room had filled up with ghosts. They weren't here to guide him into the light. They were here to judge him.

A final jolt of survival adrenaline coursed through Sigmund's body, giving him enough strength to fight against Troy's death grip. Troy clamped his face tighter.

Aislen looked around the room and turned back to face him, realizing he was dying. She looked horrified and helpless, yet also something akin to relief.

Troy leaned even closer and whispered, "Just let go, old man. There is no need to worry about Aislen. I'll be handling that. Your legacy will be erased from this planet for good very soon."

Sigmund's body involuntarily sucked at Troy's palm, begging for oxygen and being denied. In a last ditch surge of defiance, Sigmund closed his eyes and began tapping his gnarled fingers against his thumb.

Tap.

Mudra one.

Tap.

Mudra two.

Tap tap.

Mudra three, then four.

Tap tap tap.

Both hands now.

Tap tap tap tap tap.

One, one, two, three, five.

Tap tap tap tap tap tap tap tap.

One, one, two, three, five, eight, thirteen, twenty-one, thirty-four.

Tap tap tap tap tap tap tap tap tap tap tap tap—*POP!*

For an instant, he felt weightless, unmoored, as though he'd slipped past Troy's grip, past the bed, past the room itself. Rupture. Release. *Rebirth.*

EIGHTEEN

RAZE STEPPED out of the house into the late afternoon bustle of the city. Unlike most dreary winter days, it was bright and brisk. The sunlight had burned off any fog that could have provided a cloak of anonymity. He swapped the black suit for jeans and a hoodie, a deliberate downgrade to blend in.

He didn't know where to begin. He was a fish out of water, trying to pass for normal. He hadn't shopped for food in years. His basic needs had always been provided, delivered by Infinium's wage-slaves, which left him to focus on his work. But they had moved into uncharted territory now, and he needed to adapt quickly to this new reality if he was going to survive. He started toward the Embarcadero, remembering that he'd passed a farmer's market there during some of his runs.

The stunt he'd pulled with Grant, Troy, and The 8 would only buy them a day, two if they were lucky. Troy would be scouring Modesto, hunting for Aislen right about now. But after he checked the three or four places Aislen could be, he'd hit a dead end. Troy wasn't dumb. He would be the first to figure out that Raze had sent them on a wild goose chase. But he was so low in the ranks right now that it would take a lot for him to convince the others. They wouldn't gather an emergency session because Troy had a hunch, but two days from now, they would definitely give him a listen and be calling for Raze.

He had to get Aislen up to speed that fast. But what speed? What did she need to know? How was Raze supposed to teach all that to her?

She'd been Traveling since he grabbed her—in the car and again while he met with The 8. And if she was really moving through time, that changed everything.

Most operatives were only trained as Viewers. They either used physical coordinates to enter an aperture of Place and survey what was going on there or acquired people's signatures to Travel and witness their activities.

Time travel, though, was a sealed box. Operatives who slipped into the past were to be strictly observers. Move something and you can unmake people. Raze had been taught the cost: never, ever push history.

Raze preferred to work in the Present Time Zone. As a Control Operative, he manipulated and influenced people to change the course of *future* events. If you did this to targets in a Past Time Zone, it created disruptions that expanded through time, black holes that sucked in future events and even people. One false move and you could suck the wrong people, even yourself, out of existence.

If Aislen truly could cross Time Zones, she had to learn the rules before she accidentally rewired existence.

When he got back, he'd get her nourished and then see what she'd been up to. He could assess where they needed to go from there.

And where did they go from there? There were too few choices. They could disappear off the grid, like her father

Preston had. Raze sure as hell didn't want to do that, and he didn't have to guess Aislen wouldn't be down either.

If she was already that adept, Raze could sell The 8 on using her as an operative. It would solve his problem and save her, both at the same time. Maybe he could convince her of the lifestyle, and she'd go willingly. It was the easiest fix.

Raze felt a sick turning in his stomach as if the idea repulsed him. But it was the best idea! Just turn her in. Use her. Disappear. The options lined up, yet none felt clean. He had always been an operator of hard lines; this was a knot.

The knot untied itself with a jolt—a sting at his thigh. The amulet had woken in his pocket.

He'd been carrying it all day, and while there was a constant low-grade frequency emitting from it that he'd gotten used to, it hadn't done this before.

He dug the pendant free. Platinum rings hunched around colored gemstones—each a tiny node of song. All gleamed—except one. The olive tourmaline had gone black, an onyx scar. When his thumb slid over a bright jewel, it chimed; over the black stone, nothing. A portal had closed.

What had happened? What made the stone change? And what was the significance of the labyrinth anyway? Was it a puzzle? A game? A maze?

Raze moved his thumb along the arcing path. There were no straight lines to the next destination, but what seemed like a dead end was really just a turn. What seemed like going backward was actually moving him deeper into the layers. The amulet was definitely a guidance system.

It sang in his hand in response, a pleasant sensation—*ding, ding, ding!* A yes.

Raze tested his theory that the amulet could guide him. He thought again about making Aislen an operative as a way to solve their problems. The amulet immediately transmitted discord, and his stomach lurched—a definite no.

Raze was holding a powerful tool in the palm of his hand. Even if he didn't know where to begin, the pendant could provide direction. He needed to give it back to Aislen.

The amulet fell back into harmony, communicating its intentions clearly. Raze slipped it back in his pocket and continued toward the market.

TONAL
Adolescents ~ Incubus

EVEN WITH NEW CLARITY, Raze felt uneasy. He was used to relying on himself to make choices, head in directions, and reach goals... but his life hit a turning point the day Aislen showed up in Demesne. And each step along the way, each decision he'd made, a new direction. He was now in a mystery—following the unknown.

He let that sink in as he wandered into the crowded market. He tried to blend himself into the diversity of energy, sound, and color.

A stream of shoppers swept in around him. Raze spotted a woman walking toward him, eyeing him intently. He was used to that. He eyed her back, waiting for her to get uncomfortable, avert her eyes, and shut down. But she didn't. She smiled as she passed, a friendly smile, nothing beguiling or flirtatious, just neighborly, and continued on her way.

This was not a typical reaction. It was either fear or sex, not just...*normal.*

He meandered through the maze of canopies. The aroma of fresh bread embraced him. Fully feeling his hunger, he followed the tempting tendrils to the bread vendor.

"Good afternoon! Can I help you with something?" A man in tie-dye, with long hair gathered in a topknot on his head.

"Yeah. Bread."

"Ha! Yeah, well, this is the right place! We have an amazing roasted garlic & olive oil sourdough today and a sprouted wheat that's a favorite."

"I guess the wheat?" Raze didn't think roasted garlic was a good idea.

"Good choice!" Mr. Man-bun selected a loaf and bagged it for Raze. They exchanged money, and just like that, Raze had acted like a regular person.

He moved on to a stand of fresh eggs and did the same thing. Then into a produce tent where he picked out some spinach, onions, and other vegetables.

As he waited in line to pay for his remaining items, Raze felt something brush against his leg. He looked down to find a small boy looking up at him, a toddler on a leash trying to hold on to his mother's tight yoga pants with one hand and manage a blue sippy cup with his other.

He looked up at Raze, gave him a slobbery grin, and raised his sippy cup up to him. He babbled something incoherent. Was he offering Raze a drink from his sippy cup?

Raze was taken aback. Children usually knew even better than adults to steer clear of Raze. They *never* engaged.

The boy confidently babbled some more gibberish and tapped the cup into Raze's thigh.

"No, thank you. I'm good," he said to the boy.

Yesterday's Raze would have had to resist drop-kicking the toddler into the bay. But today's Raze felt remarkably tolerant and equally confused.

The boy giggled and did it again, a salut to the knee with a juice. Some of the juice spouted out the top and splashed on Raze's pant leg.

Instinctively, LululeMom turned to see what her rugrat was up to, saw the damage, and began apologizing profusely. "Jeffrey! No! Oh my God, I am *so* sorry! Here, let me find a wipe."

Raze stopped her. "It's all right."

And *really* it *was*. He felt officially part of the world now, christened into humanity by an innocent. Another pivot in the path.

Raze paid for the produce and made his way back toward the warehouse in a daze. The air felt different, charged. Raze felt different. He felt energized, like he'd shrugged off the chain he'd misinterpreted as freedom and reconnected in some small way to the real world. He felt capable. Even if he didn't have all the answers, he was certain that he could maneuver whatever was coming as long as he stayed present and in the moment.

He shifted the bags, raised his palm to the Qi.

Nothing. No beep. No click. The door stayed shut.

He grounded himself, pushed his signature into the Qi again. The panel blinked once, then flashed red.

"Unknown guest. Access denied."

A cold burn climbed his spine. Someone, somewhere, had closed a door on him.

NINETEEN

AISLEN STOOD HELPLESSLY at the end of Mr. Lange's bed, watching Troy—*of all people*—murdering her great-grandfather. The look of pleasure, no, outright delight on his face was grotesque. She'd watched his whole persona transform from the charming, charismatic Troy that she thought she knew—and might have loved—into this monstrosity; flirting with Rachel one minute, murderous psychopath the next.

Who was he? The realization that this was the real Troy made itself clear. She'd been played.

Aislen realized she was surrounded by others now: Astrid, Thomas, and Sigmund's Nazi father. They didn't acknowledge Aislen, or each other, for that matter. They just stood impassively at the end of the bed, watching as the murder unfolded, waiting for Sigmund to cross over.

"Unknown Guest. Access Denied."

Aislen looked around to see who had spoken. But besides the faint suckling noise of Sigmund fighting for breath, the room was silent.

Please, Poppet, make him stop! Sigmund found his way into

her head. He glared at her over Troy's clenched grip, eyes wild and desperate.

As much as she was growing to hate him, even though he was more of a monster than Troy was proving himself to be, this frail, broken version of her great-grandfather pulled sympathy from her.

But there was nothing she could do. He couldn't hear her. He was oblivious to all the others standing in the room with her.

Raziel was right. If it were a dream, she could change it. But this was reality. She was witnessing a current event a hundred miles away and was helpless to stop it.

"Unknown Guest. Access Denied."

Aislen couldn't pull her eyes away from Sigmund's pleading stare.

Troy leaned down even closer to Sigmund and growled in his ear, "Just let go, old man. There is no need to worry about Aislen. I'll be handling that. Your legacy will be erased from this planet for good very soon."

Aislen went cold. Troy had *never* been on her side. It was all a sham, a deadly farce that she had fallen head over heels for.

As Sigmund realized his imminent doom, he closed his eyes. Aislen watched the fingers of his restrained hands begin to twitch as the life was squeezed out of him.

Mudra one. Mudra two.

"Unauthorized Subject. Warehouse Door 1."

Aislen recognized the woman's voice now.

Mudra three, mudra four. Sigmund was reciting in her head. She watched his fingers tapping a sequence, a stemming fidget she'd witnessed him do many times before.

One, one, two, three, five... Tap tap tap tap tap.

"Warning! "Unauthorized Subject. Warehouse Door 1."

Aislen could feel the chaise beneath her and the warm blanket around her legs.

One, one, two, three, five, eight, thirteen... Tap tap tap tap tap tap tap tap.

The violent scene playing out before her started fading away as Aislen was pulled backward through the signal line.

One, one, two, three, five, eight, thirteen, twenty-one, thirty-four—

POP!

Aislen felt the energy shift, the void created as Sigmund's life left his body.

The aperture slammed shut, locking her out of the hospital room. She ripped the blanket from over her head. Her throat tightened. A strange, guilty lightness flooded her chest—not joy, not exactly relief, but the longed-for end of something poisonous.

Her great-grandfather was dead! He was an evil, evil man. But *Troy!* How could she have been so wrong about *him?* All the flirting! The feigned care and compassion! He had been working her the whole time. Aislen felt as though someone else, someone more precious, had died in that room. But that person was just a fantasy; the Troy that she had believed in didn't really exist.

"SECURITY OVERRIDE." The woman's voice was more insistent. The chaise lifted Aislen upright, the music stopped, and the room became brighter.

The screen on the wall came to life. On it, Raziel was standing at the door, arms full of groceries, looking frustrated.

Aislen was surrounded by evil. The man on-screen was a murderer, too! He'd used a helpless child to assassinate his own father. He had stalked her ethereally and then had kidnapped her.

She watched him on the screen as he closed his eyes, took a

deep breath, and placed his hand up to the reader. Raziel's signature bloomed on the screen—not the black-blue wash she'd matched to get into the house, but the inverse: silver threaded with midnight, like moonlight trapped in oil.

Had he *changed?*

Aislen thought of Troy, the man she had thought was her safety net. She'd been running toward Troy at the hospital, trying to get to him. And Raziel had stopped her.

Raziel had actually *saved* her.

Did he know that? Did he know what Troy was? Or did he have his own agenda?

Raziel tried the Qi yet again.

"ACCESS DENIED. Calling Authorities. 10...9...8—"

Raziel's face looked muddled; rage, confusion, and panic fought for dominance across his face. This could be her chance; an opportunity to escape. But he had taken care of her earlier. He was bringing her food now. He'd validated her dreams as real and her time traveling as possible.

"7...6...5—"

A gut instinct took over, and Aislen put her hand up to the screen. She projected Raziel's signature, the signature she remembered, toward the panel.

"4...3...2—" The countdown stopped.

"Hello, Raze. Authorize entry?"

Yes and **No** buttons appeared on the screen.

Her thumb hovered over the screen.

Her pulse thudded in her wrist.

She swallowed and tapped **Yes**.

TWENTY

AISLEN WATCHED on the monitor as the back door clicked open and Raziel tentatively walked through.

The door to the lab slid open, beckoning freedom.

Aislen didn't know what she should do. What had just happened? If Raziel couldn't even get into his own house, then he wouldn't be able to get to her in the lab, would he? The thought of making a run for it tempted her. *Find an emergency exit. Go to the police. Then go home.*

She could almost feel the city air on her face, the taste of it. But no, Raziel hadn't left the door open because he was feeling generous. He'd left it because it didn't matter; there was nowhere to go.

And anyway—even though he'd kidnapped her, held her here, made her a hostage for reasons she didn't pretend to grasp —the guy was bringing her food, water. Not the usual psycho move. He was... taking care of her. Whatever that meant.

Aislen decided to find out. She locked in on Raziel's signature, amped it up in her space, and flooded it through the system. Confidence surged—all his. She stepped out of the lab and climbed the staircase, through the mirror that served as a doorway, and into his bedroom.

The house had shrugged off its high alert, back to the lazy jazz and mellow lighting. Aislen drifted through the room, feeling equal parts trespasser and invisible guest. Underneath it all, she could sense Raziel's pride, the ironclad precision in every detail. He'd built this place, made it a kingdom.

She would have expected someone like him, someone who created chaos and wreaked havoc in the world, to live in chaos himself. A man like him would be too busy for laundry or to care about things being neat. But it was exactly that: immaculate, sophisticated in its minimalism. Everything was in its place because everything had a purpose.

She ran a hand across the gray silk bedspread, followed the line of it to the wall, and froze. The mural was impossible to ignore: an angel, massive, spanning floor to ceiling, high above the bed. Blindfolded. Wings fanned wide. Not flying, not moving at all. Guarding. Protecting.

It was breathtaking.

The person who commissioned this could not have been the man she was cloaked in—the man she was about to face.

Aislen stepped onto the landing where the spiral staircase began its descent. Three stories below stood Raziel, clutching grocery bags, his face tilted up toward her. From up here, he seemed harmless—a trick of perspective. He set the bags down, raised a finger to his lips, and motioned her to stay. Then he launched himself upward, conquering the steps in pairs. Before she could retreat, he materialized before her, his presence expanding to fill the narrow landing, any illusion of harmlessness shattered.

He grabbed her hand, sending a jolt of energy through her that made her knees weak. He didn't slow down, just pulled her with him, across a catwalk, past a series of 20-foot arched windows, and through a glass doorway onto a rooftop patio.

The silhouette of the city rose around them, darkening in the fading light of day. She recognized its unique outline: the Transamerica pyramid spiking the sky, the Bay Bridge with its trails of light, the distant gulls threading their cries through the air. Salt, brine, diesel, the rumble of traffic.

Raziel didn't pause; he wasn't in the mood for sightseeing. He took her straight to the wall where water spilled down mossy brick, feeding an urban oasis below. He spun, fixing her with hands locked on her shoulders.

"Did you let me in?" He was his old self, cold, hard, and angry. *This* self could have made it through that door.

Aislen shrank into herself. "You weren't projecting the right signature frequency. Well, not the one you had me match before..."

His eyes slitted. Not surprised, but definitely not pleased. "You could tell?"

"I saw it—on the monitor—" she stuttered. "And the voice said it was calling the authorities. So I used the frequency to open the door."

He looked at her like she'd just announced she could fly. "Why would you do that?"

Great question. She shook her head. "I don't know."

Raziel released her, studying her like she was a cipher. "You did the right thing. They wouldn't have been saving you." That landed hard, and for a few seconds, he just stared back at the house. "This complicates things. We need to see what you're capable of. Get you and get you prepared. You need to be able to start taking care of yourself because I don't know how much longer I can protect you."

"Protect me?" Aislen snapped, incredulous. "You kidnapped me!"

Raziel's face went still; a tiny muscle jumped at his jaw. "I didn't bring you here to hurt you," he said, voice low.

Her shoulders slumped; the protest left her. While kidnapping her was technically true, it was not the whole story. He'd also saved her. From Troy.

All the fight went out of her. "Troy..." She barely whispered his name.

"What about Troy?" Raziel's tone was vicious again.

Aislen shook her head. "It's nothing. Forget it."

"Like hell. You don't know dick about Kellen. Or about anything else. You have no fucking idea."

"Well, actually, I do!" Aislen shot back.

He sneered. "Oh, you do? Enlighten me."

That force between them sparked; she could feel it, an electric tension, friction, and magnetic pull all at once, burning through her skin even though he wasn't touching her. Her heart was a caged bird.

He waited, eyes boring through her, daring her to speak. She didn't want to. Didn't want to confess how stupid she'd been, but she needed him, whether she liked it or not.

"I was wrong about Troy." The confession tasted bitter in her mouth. "I thought he was my friend. But he's not. He never was."

Raze was taken aback. "When did you figure that out?"

"Just now. While you were gone. I fell asleep again."

"I told you not to do that."

"I know, but I couldn't help it. And now I wish I hadn't." The vision replayed: Troy suffocating Lange with his own hands. She trembled.

Raze's anger cooled. "What did you see?"

"That he's a fraud," Aislen spat. "Pretending to care. About people, about Blake and Rachel, about *me*. But it was all a lie.

Everything he says and does is just a manipulation." She met Raziel's eyes, no flinching. "He's just like you."

That set him off. "Like me?" he snarled, closing the gap between them. "Kellen isn't anywhere close to me. First, I don't fake caring. I actually don't give a shit. Second, Kellen only wishes he were capable of what I am. But he is far from it."

"Well, he's got murder covered," Aislen snapped. "So you're exactly alike. Killers."

"Murder?" Raziel's confusion seemed genuine. "What murder?"

"You murdered Blake's dad, and who knows how many more. And he just murdered my great-grandfather! Suffocated him—with his bare hands!"

"He what?!" For the first time, Raziel actually looked shocked. "He killed Sigmund Lange!?"

A dam burst. "I saw everything... just now. Troy went into Sigmund's room. They had him in restraints, and Lange couldn't do anything to stop it. Troy waited until Rachel left, and he suffocated him!"

"That motherfucker! That was not what I told him to do!" Raziel began pacing the rooftop.

Aislen followed him, almost hysterical. "Not what you told him to do!? What does that mean? Are you working *together*?"

He spun, shoving her back to the waterfall. Still pissed, but trying to keep it quiet. "Listen. We don't work together. We work for the same corporation."

Aislen shook her head in disbelief. "He works at the hospital."

"A cover. He was assigned to keep an eye on your great-grandfather—the founder of our company."

"Infinium Incorporated," she whispered, understanding.

Raze was shocked. "How do you know that?"

"The drea—I mean the Traveling."

"Where exactly are you going?"

"Back in time, I guess... 1968? To Sigmund's house... to the experiments he did in the brothel with my grandfather. Then, to when my grandfather met my grandmother and got her pregnant... and to when he started the company."

"All of that? Damn, you've been busy!" Raziel seemed impressed but then grew concerned. "Has Lange been in all of your Travels?"

Aislen thought about that. "He comes and goes. The young version of him talks to me directly, like he knows I am there but can't see me. But Old Lange, he talks in my head. Like telepathy, but different—closer. He says he is showing me the history. Says it's important."

The color drained from Raziel's face. "Holy shit! He's been prepping you! Well, he *was*. Maybe Kellen did us a favor by killing him. That's one less thing we have to worry about."

"I don't understand."

Raziel leaned in, serious. "Your great-grandfather has been looking for a new body. He was getting too old and feeble, and he knew he didn't have much time left. He used Blake at first, as a conduit, to get into *Demesne*. But what he wanted was a real match. He wanted *you*."

Everything inside her recoiled. She knew what Raziel said was true. She remembered feeling Sigmund, his cold clawing at the inside of her skull—trying to pry in. Now she knew why.

"Why me?"

"Genetics. You're related, so you're compatible. You are also capable, a genetic skill set he needs."

"For what?"

"To take over your body. Use you to reclaim Infinium and settle the score with The 8."

Aislen felt lightheaded and sick to her stomach. She staggered, Raziel caught her, steady hands, eyes locked.

"Hey. You're safe from him now. He's gone. Now we only have to worry about Kellen. And The 8."

She yanked out of his grip, stepping away. "But you work with them! You gave him orders! What are you having him do!?"

"I sent him to Modesto. To hunt you down. Kidnap you."

She couldn't believe it. "But *you* already did that! Why would you send Troy to find me when you already have me?"

"To buy us time."

For a second, everything spun. "You didn't kidnap me to kill me?"

Raziel shook his head. "I wish it was that simple, trust me."

She searched his face. No deception... just regret. Like the price of what he'd done was still collecting interest. She realized: he'd saved her. Whether he liked it or not.

He broke the silence.

"Look, we don't have long. A day, maybe two. We need to get you inside, get some food, some real rest, so we can figure out our next steps."

Aislen nodded, numb with shock. Raziel, the villain, the savior. A guardian angel, masquerading as the devil.

He locked eyes with her, all business. "Listen up. Here's what we need to do."

TWENTY-ONE

ANOTHER TURN IN THE MAZE. The game had changed yet again. And again. And again.

When Aislen appeared in the aftermath of what she had done, Raze was caught in a crosscurrent of awe and total unease. She'd not only solved a lethal problem in real time, but in the process, she'd gained control of his house, and in essence, of him.

She knew that he wasn't resonating as himself, and that alone tipped the balance to her favor. Still, she hadn't let The Womb call the authorities. She could have set herself free, at least temporarily, but instead she'd let Raziel in. A walking contradiction, she confounded him.

She'd been moving at full tilt since he'd grabbed her in Modesto. Sigmund had locked her into a deep-dive history lesson: MKUltra, Infinium Incorporated, her family line. Raze had to admit—it would help. At least she'd go into this next phase knowing exactly what they were up against.

Sigmund, of course, had been trying to connect with her in a way that would have blown everything up if it had gone unchecked. Thankfully, that disaster was cut off at the root. Raze wanted to kill Kellen for dispatching Lange without permission, but there was no denying the reality: Kellen had done them a massive favor. Lange was gone, meaning Aislen was safe from any shot at possession. No more risk that Lange would hijack her body, use her to take down Infinium—and Raze right along with it.

And now Aislen knew the truth about Kellen—he *wasn't* her white knight. That made the next discussion easier. Because this wasn't over, not by a long shot. Sigmund might be out of commission, but that meant Troy would zero in on Aislen next. And it wouldn't take him long to realize she wasn't in Modesto. The 8 would be breathing down Raze's neck any time now.

If they were going to survive, they needed Aislen in fighting shape. Fast.

"Listen to me very carefully; here's what we need to do. You have to be me, energetically, in the house... the me I was this morning. You must maintain that frequency cloak. It's the signature the security system recognizes, that will allow us to stay here undetected by Infinium and The 8."

"You can't just go back to that?" Aislen asked, zeroing in as if she sensed a crack in his armor.

Agitation crackled through Raze like static. It exposed his weakness. But if he snapped at her, he'd lose her, and he needed her cooperation. He forced it down.

"I don't think so," he admitted. "It's something natural, not something I had to acquire or commit to memory."

Aislen weighed this. "Could you read me if I am channeling yours and learn it again?"

It was a good idea. He gave a nod. "We can try. Go ahead."

Aislen shut her eyes. Immediately, Raze could feel her shifting, calibrating to the shadowy charge that had once belonged to him. She was good. He let his own eyes fall shut, brushed his open hand through the swathe of space just above her shoulder, feeling for the obsidian current that was his signature. There it was, cold and magnetic, haunting the air.

He reached for it, trying to slip his own skin back on—but the energy was flat, husk-alike. Lifeless. A discarded molt that he couldn't inhabit.

He reached in deeper, trying to crawl into the empty skein. Beneath his old resonance, he could feel the strong pull of Aislen's natural frequency—the irresistible temptation to sink into that was almost overpowering.

He yanked his hand away, shoving her energy back. "That won't work," he said, gruffly. She staggered back as though he'd actually touched her.

She blinked at him, confusion and something raw flashing across her face. "I don't understand. Why is your signature different now? What happened?"

You *happened!* Raze raged internally. The truth he wouldn't admit aloud.

Aislen recoiled, understanding flashing in her eyes, shock flickering through her body.

She'd heard him. Raze had forgotten she was telepathic, too.

"It's not important why," he said, voice brittle, forcing the storm beneath the surface. "But we have to work around it if we are going to stay alive. So, back to my original plan. You need to keep broadcasting my original frequency, as a primary over your own."

And I'll be the "guest" in my own house, he grumbled to himself. *Which is just really fucking fantastic!*

Aislen winced in reaction.

And we are going to utilize those telepathic skills of yours, too. Raze threw at her, wordless and precise. "You can only speak your real thoughts out here. There are no Qi Readers, and the waterfall creates enough negative ion interference to scramble signals.

"But inside, when you speak as my... let's just call it my 'romantic' guest. Which means you don't talk much at all. Do you understand?"

Yes.

Smartass.

Now Raze got ice-cold serious. "Let me be very, very clear. The 8 will be looking for discrepancies. Whether you believe me or not, care or not, I am balanced on a fucking knife-edge trying to hold this together until another option presents itself."

Aislen nodded tightly: she got it.

"Are you ready?" Raze asked.

Aislen amplified his energy in her space, full blast. "Ready."

Raze stepped aside and let her lead, back into the jaws of the shark tank.

TWENTY-TWO

"TWO STICKS AND A BUCKET."

"Two sticks and a bucket."

"Two sticks and a bucket."

Over and over, Blake spun the phrase through his head, a worn-out spell meant to hold the ghosts at bay, to block the flickering phantoms that came for him in the dark.

It didn't work. They wouldn't leave him alone. The cops. The doctors. The memories.

The only one who never came... his dad. Not once.

Blake missed him, bad. Missed him more than his mom, more than his sister, missed him more than anything. Even more than he missed his video games.

And he really missed his video games.

He heard the click-clack of heels out in the hallway, sharp as a countdown. Another one on the way.

"Two sticks and a bucket."

Muttering now, low voices. The cop guarding his door; another voice, one he half-recognized. Keys rattling, metal slicing the lock, bolt scraping back.

"Two sticks and a bucket."

Mr. Troy came in, dragging a battered chair behind him. He parked it right up next to the bed and then sat, arms on knees, leaning in way too close. Group-therapy close, except now it wasn't camaraderie, it was a threat, heavy and sour.

"Two sticks and a bucket."

"Two stic—"

"Shut the fuck up." Not Mr. Troy's therapy voice.

Blake did as he was told. He didn't remember how not to anymore.

"Okay, you little shit. You're on assignment. I need your help with a new adventure. Remember that woman who showed up in your little video game? The hot redhead? The one in here with me a couple of days ago?"

"Yeah, uh, I mean yes, Mr. Troy."

"I'm sure you do. Well, I need to know where she is. I know some of those skills you've been practicing have probably rubbed off on you, and I need you to tap into them and tell me where I can find her."

Blake began rocking back and forth. Reciting his prayer, but in his head.

"Knock it off!" Troy's hand smacked into Blake's skull. "I said, tap in and figure out where she is!"

The slap spun stars through Blake's eyes. Troy leaned close, nose almost touching. "That sound," he murmured, "is like a dinner bell. Find her for me, or I'll see what other noises you make when bones break."

"Ichiban," Blake whispered.

"Fuck Ichiban! He's no use to us now. But Aislen—*she matters*. So use that voodoo shit and find her."

"But I don't know how to do that," Blake said. "Ichiban does."

Troy's hand curled into a fist. "Goddammit, Blake! Try to remember how he did it and do it yourself."

Blake's eyes went out of focus. "Bet you wish you didn't kill him now, huh?"

Troy blinked. "Excuse me?"

"Ichiban," Blake said again, voice gravel.

"I don't know what game you're playing, but I'm not in the mood. Ichiban's gone. He's in hell having coffee with your dead dad."

Blake's rocking stopped. His head lolled sideways, almost breaking his neck, then snapped up sharp.

"Well, that was really uncalled for," Sigmund said, using his own voice now.

Troy sank back in the chair, eyes going huge.

"Don't look so rattled, Kellen. It's me." His voice dripped with mockery, too old and knowing for a twelve-year-old throat. "Sigmund Lange. Your murder victim."

"Jesus Christ..." Troy's jaw unhinged, color draining. "What the fuck are you?"

"Everything all right in there?" the cop outside called.

"It's fine! My fault!" Sigmund answered, mimicking Troy's voice, pitch-perfect casual.

Troy stared, not even breathing.

Sigmund tilted Blake's head, a wicked grin spreading across the boy's face. "Pretty impressive, right? Bet you didn't know I had an 'in' with Blake here. I've been running things behind the curtain for months. So this? Cakewalk."

Troy shook his head, his brain trying to process this turn of events. "I've seen some fucked-up split personality cases. But never an outright possession."

Sigmund's smile sharpened. "You left me no choice when you murdered me. I needed a place to go. I'm not done here, yet."

"Murdered you?" Troy barked out a laugh, thin and sharp. "Looked natural enough. Nobody's crying for you, old man. The 8 would thank me if they had half a clue."

"Wrong." Sigmund's voice went low, conspiratorial. "They need me for the rest of their plan first. I'm the key to finding Preston. I am the key to *owning* Aislen. When The 8 finds out you killed me off-script, rest assured, they won't reward you. They're gonna gut you and feed you to the dogs."

Troy closed the distance, fingers like clamps around the boy's throat. "That's an easy fix. I snap this boy's neck, and there are no more witnesses."

"Ahhhh, wrong again," Sigmund said, with buttery calm. "There *was* another witness."

Troy's face hardened into a question. "What—who?"

"She was Traveling. Standing at the end of my bed like a guardian angel. And she saw *everything. Ashlyn was there.*"

Troy's hand dropped, the color draining from his face. "No," he said, too quickly. "Aislen Walker? Was there?"

Sigmund's smile spread, slow and venomous. "Ashlyn," he said, the name a caress. "She can slip between places. Rooms, cities, time itself. She's the culmination of everything I've been building. That's why she's valuable. And that is why I *need* her."

"Where is she now?" Troy demanded, voice clipped.

"Protected. Hidden in the eye of the storm."

"Protected by who? Preston Reed?"

Sigmund shook his head, his grin thinning into a blade. "*Raziel.*"

Troy laughed, a chopped sound. "Raziel? You're outta your fucking mind! No way Raziel would help her! It would end his career!"

"That may be," Sigmund said with a shrug. "But I can feel him there. His energy's all over her, every time I try to tap in."

Troy was on his feet, agitated. "But that asshole told *me* to find her! Gave me the plan! In front of Infinium and everyone! Are you telling me that he's had her all along?!"

Sigmund gave a lazy shrug. "I am only saying that there is a very strong energy around Ashlyn. And it reeks of Raziel. He is hiding her and setting you up to fail. Make you look like an idiot with The 8."

"I'll kill him!" Troy spat, pacing, fists balled.

Sigmund's grin was slow and mean. "Fantastic. Because I need you for this."

Troy came to a sudden halt, pinning Sigmund with a glare. "Why the hell would I help you? With proof Raziel stabbed Infinium in the back, I could go straight to them and snag Aislen myself."

Sigmund's tone dropped. "Because, alone, you don't stand a chance. But me?" He let the words slither, burrow. "I've already been inside her mind. I can reach her. I can *become* her. If you want to be the hero who brings her in—even get so much as a whisper of glory—you need me."

Troy's jaw worked, the muscles clenching, unclenching as he weighed his options: call Sigmund's bluff, snap the boy's neck, and be done with it. Or the promise of power, Aislen, and the chance to humiliate Raziel.

"You really think you can get Aislen?" Troy asked.

Sigmund's eyes glinted. "I know I can."

"And you'll leave Raziel to me?"

"Raziel is all yours."

Troy let out a dry laugh that wasn't happy. "I'll do it—for now. But I don't forget. You fuck me over and I'll end this brat's body and you with it."

Sigmund's grin was ice. "Good. Now pick up that chair and sit the fuck down. We've got a full night ahead."

BEAT
Psycho ~ Muse

TWENTY-THREE

AISLEN REACTIVATED Raziel's old frequency cloak and followed him inside, both of them sharp with the need to avoid another alarm. Once they knew the system wasn't going to sound, they descended the spiral staircase into the living room.

Once again, Aislen was struck by the sheer power of the converted warehouse. Three-story ceilings, brickwork left raw, and the wound-gray of unfinished concrete, steel beams, and ribbed pipes like exposed sinew. The place should have felt cold, industrial. But it didn't. The furniture was all clean lines and geometry, masculine but not severe, accented with the wild risk of color: a bruised cobalt rug, a flash of orange in the throw pillows, the deep wine of leather. Four arched windows—each one huge enough for a cathedral—punched through the far wall and at this hour framed the city in glitter and blackness.

The kind of room that belonged to someone who had never belonged anywhere. Aislen stared at it, wondering about the man who'd shaped this strange oasis.

She watched Raziel surreptitiously. He plucked the bag of groceries off the floor, moving with easy, predatory confidence into the kitchen, and began unpacking supplies. This was not the Raziel of the black suit, which amplified his power and presence. This version was stripped down and unofficial. Black v-neck sweater that clung to the definition of his torso, graphite slacks loose at the hip. Even in the absence of formality, the carved lines of his physique refused to hide. If anything, the new look, coupled with the altered frequency, made him more arresting, stirring something other than fear but equally unsettling.

And then there was his hair: obsidian, tousled, almost untamed, the curtain of it framing cheekbones that could have been hewn out of the foundation stones of the building itself. Now that terror had receded, Aislen could see how extraordinary his features were--how his beauty was as inescapable as his presence.

Sensing her attention, Raziel glanced up, and a flash of glacial blue burned through the black strands, fixing her in place. Air vanished from her lungs; her pulse detonated.

"Before we continue with our extracurricular activities this evening, I need nourishment." Raziel's tone was dry, matter-of-fact, but the amusement in his eyes was diabolical.

The phrase "extracurricular activities" lashed at her, summoning a reel of images: not her own memories, but raw sense-data from his energy field. Skin and tangled limbs and breathless, liquid sounds—the couch, the rug, silk sheets twisted, the tile of the shower wall. They weren't hers, but the effect was. Heat stung her cheeks. She pivoted away from him so that he couldn't see the flush on her face.

"I like breakfast for dinner, so I'm making eggs." Raziel's voice had its familiar edge for the listening Qis. "I don't usually feed my playthings, but I am feeling generous tonight. Do you want some?"

The word plaything shocked her system, igniting a charge

of anger. That was his reality, wasn't it? Everyone was his toy. And she was caught in the game, ready to be tossed and spun for his amusement or advantage.

Aislen's emotions stuttered. The idea of being his plaything rekindled the electric awareness in her body that she'd tamped down on the rooftop. It also lit a spark of anger. She really was just a plaything in all of this, wasn't she? A toy caught in a game with all the players batting her this way and that.

Aislen! Raziel snapped subliminally, the sharpness cutting through her, snapping her to attention. She met his narrowed eyes.

Say yes.

He held her in his gaze until she found her voice.

"Um, yes, please."

Good girl. His mouth quirked as he reached into the knife block without looking and drew a cleaver that might have cut through bone. "I can make omelettes or a scramble."

Your playthings?

I usually call them worse. How do you want your eggs?

Scrambled is fine.

Raze tilted his head and waited.

"Scrambled, please," said Aislen, and tried not to flinch watching the knife go to work on vegetables.

Don't take what I say personally. It isn't about you. His voice came again, private, softer. "Part one of our evening was exceptional, by the way. I'm really looking forward to seeing what else you have in your repertoire later."

Her body went still at the words. Whether he was just performing for the Qis or not, it felt real enough to scorch her. Every nerve raw and open.

I don't know what to say.

Do your best. He responded, still chopping.

Aislen closed her eyes and tried tapping into the memory of

Sigmund's brothel girls, their voices dripping suggestion and invitation. If she didn't look at him, she could imitate them, could let the words flow without shame.

"I'm glad you enjoyed that." She copied the purr of Candy welcoming Sigmund at the door. "If you thought that was good, wait until you let me put my mouth on you."

The sound of the blade stopped cold.

Aislen opened her eyes and found Raziel staring at her, wide-eyed, the beginnings of a genuine smile threatening his composure. He looked both startled and deeply amused.

That bad?

Raze shook his head. *No. That was... impressive. Just... unexpected.* A pause. The knife resumed its rhythm.

"We'll have to see about that," he said for their audience. "If you're up to the challenge." He flicked a glance at her, eyebrow cocked, unmistakably taunting, but the spark between them arced higher with every word. He wiped his hands clean, leaned on the counter, and locked her in his gaze. *You don't have to respond. They're used to there not being a lot of conversation in here.*

Aislen caught herself, relief and something hotter twisting together. Her mind flooded with what happened here that was wordless.

"Have a seat," he ordered.

Aislen was reluctant to move any closer to him, not for fear of violence anymore. But obedience was easier than resisting.

Raze cracked eggs into a bowl, eyes never leaving her. *Where'd you learn that line? It didn't sound like you. I mean, I don't know you, but... it was definitely an imitation.*

From the girls at Sigmund's brothel, she responded. *Where he experimented on Thomas.*

Ah, of course. The CIA really liked the brothel theme. And

Sigmund Lange did a lot of groundbreaking work there. Not just with Thomas Reed, either.

Aislen shuddered. *I think Thomas was his favorite, up until...*

Until he impregnated your grandmother? Don't kid yourself. Lange did that intentionally.

Aislen was shocked. *What do you mean?*

He needed more than one Thomas for his legacy. He used his daughter as an incubator. Breeding another Thomas was the only way to scale what he'd built. He learned that in the Reich: if you want a superior world, you breed superior stock.

How do you know all this?

Raziel's focus never broke, whisking the eggs now, coldly efficient. *Lange is the architect of Infinium Incorporated. If you were in, you learned the history. But what I didn't know was how The 8 ousted Sigmund, option-locked him, and put him in a nursing home to rot away in his final days. It's no wonder he was searching for a way out.*

He poured the eggs into a pan, heat hissing, and spoke aloud for the Qis. "Making breakfast is a distraction. I'd rather have my hands on you." Nothing about his demeanor changed, same posture, same placid gaze, but the words were silk and smoke, and the effect was physical. Her skin prickled, senses shaken.

Aislen compared it, unbidden, to Troy: all the effort he'd put into seduction, trying to make her feel wanted or enchanted for his own ends. Raziel barely had to move, barely had to try, and the undertow was relentless.

Do they train you guys to do that or something? She asked, then tapped into Candy and Misty for inspiration. "Well, hurry up then, baby. I'm wet with anticipation."

Raziel only arched an eyebrow, and again his lip curved upward slightly in amusement.

They train us to manipulate energy, yes. Seduction is just one expression of that. But you seem to be a pretty quick learner there yourself. Channeling overt sexuality like that--convincing. But don't worry, Aislen, I'm not trying to seduce you. It's all for show.

He turned away, serving food with mechanized precision. The words should have been reassuring, but instead, she felt the sharp sting of rejection. What she felt between them was not a performance. It crackled in the air, thickening by the hour. Did he not sense it? Or was he just immune, so used to having this effect on women that he was impervious?

He changed the subject. *What else have you learned while I had you in The Womb?*

The Womb? Is that what you call your lab?

It's my nickname for her. It's an isolation chamber, designed to mimic the embryonic environment, for channeling conscious-ness in and out of the body.

Aislen was taken aback. She hadn't thought about what she was doing in that light and was surprised that Raziel would describe it in such a way.

You sound more like a yogi than a top-secret manipulation spy.

Control Operative, he corrected. *That's the correct term. At Infinium, we strip out the dogma and superstition, but retain the practical, scientific application of the technology. Then we monetize the hell out of it. The Church had its own business model, but Infinium scaled that up.*

He brought out two plates and set one in front of her, taking the seat beside her. Energy clouded the air between them. Aislen's stomach knotted so tight she doubted she could eat.

He read it instantly, picked up her fork, and handed it to

her. "Eat," he said flatly. "You're going to need the energy for what's next."

She stared, speechless.

Take the fork, Aislen. And put that food in your body. We need you at 100%.

She reached slowly, wary of touching him, panic rising.

He watched, unblinking. "Take off your clothes. I want to watch you eat naked."

She nearly dropped the fork. *You have to be kidding.*

"Then I'll have you for dessert." For a second, he let himself have a real smile; then he turned from her and started eating.

Aislen just stared at him. *Is this how you always are with women?*

He shrugged. *Most don't get this much conversation. Eat.*

And that works for you?

I get what I want.

And that works for them?

He cut her a glance, flat and cold. *They get paid in money, not congeniality. So yes. It works. Eat, Aislen.*

She forced herself toward her food, appetite gone dead. She picked at it with her fork.

Raze leaned over to her ear, "Eat."

Though it was the barest whisper, the command was absolute, vibrating down her spine. Every part of her body became completely aware, and she felt like she would fall out of her chair. She forked a piece of food and placed it in her mouth, desperate for focus. Anything to distract her from the touch of his voice.

He went back to eating in blessed silence. Once Aislen started eating, she found she was ravenous and devoured her entire plate before he even finished. She looked up and found him watching her.

More? He had that amused glint in his eye again. It threw her. This from a man who never looked like he'd laughed a day in his life. And although she was embarrassed by her unladylike gluttony, she was still undeniably famished.

She slid her plate his direction. *Yes, please.*

Told you, he said as he took her plate and refilled it. He waited, patient, until she finished, then shifted back to purpose.

We have to decide what to do next, Aislen.

She was startled by the "we." Was he giving her choices? Including her in the decision-making? An alliance where she'd expected only orders?

The way I see it, we have two options. He stopped and looked at her like he knew she wasn't going to like what he had to say. *Do you want the bad option or the worse-than-bad option?*

Dread settled in her gut like wet cement. *Worse first.*

He inhaled slowly, measuring her. *Worse is, we do what your father did: go into hiding. We switch frequencies every five minutes for weeks, bounce across the globe until we find a dead zone, then slow it to once daily. Then we reach out to your dad, see if he can guide us to his location. I can hand you off to him and then go my own way.*

He let her sit with that, then, for the Qis, "I needed that. But I think I need a shower before we resume our activities."

Aislen was unfazed by the innuendo this time. *You know about my dad?*

I do. I've hunted him.

Hunted?

Yes.

Aislen got a chill at the thought of her father as prey. It reminded her that she was, too. *And the other option?*

I call a meeting with The 8, take you to Infinium, and convince them to train you as a Control Operative.

Aislen could feel the blood draining from her face. *How is that better? I mean, both ideas suck! But at least if I could find my dad, he could help, and I could be safe.*

Raze kept his gaze steady on her. *Running isn't easy, Aislen. Your dad had decades of training. Even then, he had to give up something very important.* Raziel's gaze felt like it would cut through her.

The weight of his words sank in as Aislen realized he was talking about her.

You are new to this. And you aren't ready for that kind of sacrifice, Aislen.

Aislen thought of her mom, of leaving her forever, and her heart broke.

Reading her mind, Raze continued. *He gave her up... and he gave you up. It destroyed him.*

Aislen searched Raziel's face. *How do you know all this? How could you possibly know?*

He told me.

Her head spun. *He told you?! When?*

He came into Demesne while I was destroying it. He asked me to help you.

Aislen shook her head in disbelief. *No! He would never! He wanted to protect me! You were trying to kill me!*

Raze didn't argue or try to defend himself. Then, without a response, he gathered their plates and took them into the kitchen. He cleaned the kitchen in silence. Aislen tried to read what he was thinking or feeling, but there was a block up, and though she was sitting in his old energy field, it wasn't a key.

"Would you like a cocktail before I shower?" Raze broke the awkward lull. *Say yes, it buys us more time.*

"That would be lovely," Aislen murmured.

Raziel pulled a glass and a bottle of amber liquor from the cupboard, poured, then emptied it in one fluid motion.

Raze set the glass on the counter and finally looked at her again.

Look, I know it's not ideal. It might not even work. But making you a Control Operative takes the pressure off. We work with Infinium instead of against them. It still leaves option two open. And even though you wouldn't be able to see or contact her, you'll still be close enough to your mother. You'd be paid exceptionally well, enough to take care of her secretly. And there may be a way to connect with her, through Sgt. Mathis and the game.

Aislen weighed it. It wasn't good enough.

I want to go home.

He shook his head, mouth set hard. *That's impossible.*

Aislen glared at him. *I go home. You run.*

His jaw knotted, voice ice. *That's a death sentence. You don't understand these people. If you're not with them, you're against them. You wouldn't survive the night. Neither would your mother.*

She flared with sudden fury. *If you hadn't told them about me, I'd have had a chance.* She threw a harsh, stinging energy at him with her words, hoping he would feel it. He winced.

I wouldn't have told them unless I had no choice.

That sucked the fire right out of her. Raze poured himself another drink, a double this time. He contemplated the golden liquid as if reading his fortune in its reflection.

When you came into Demesne, it set off a chain reaction of failures. Mine. You became my problem. I tried to keep you a secret because I was going to handle you myself. But Troy found out you'd been in Demesne. Because you told him.

Aislen felt ill, remembering all her confessions to Troy about her dreams.

Troy was going to out you... to ruin me. So I preempted him:

told them who you were, before he could, so that I... his thoughts trailed off.

So you could kill me. Aislen finished his thought for him. A chill went down her spine.

Raze eyed the drink in front of him. *I told myself that, yes. It's how I justified rushing halfway across the state to get to you before Troy could. So I could permanently handle you—and save my own ass.*

He looked up at her. Cerulean scorched through the air between them, burning her where she sat.

But it was a lie. And the real reason doesn't make sense.

He emptied the glass.

"I'm taking that shower now." He rounded the counter, brushing past her, refusing to meet her gaze, and headed toward the spiral staircase.

"Follow me," he called back, a command with no room for argument. And Aislen rose, feeling the invisible tether that drew her after.

TWENTY-FOUR

RAZE MOVED THROUGH THE BEDROOM, Aislen following close behind. He entered the bathroom first, a sweep of his hand summoning the water and the music: "Shower on. Relax."

The sound of streaming water filled the space. An ambient spa mix, not something he'd ever choose, but this wasn't for him. He glanced back at her. Uncertainty and trepidation flashed across her face. Strangely, he understood how she felt.

You are the one who has to take a shower, so your energy reads like mine in there. I'll wait in the bedroom.

Relief visibly loosened her posture. She nodded, still watching him as if a predator might spring at any moment.

Wait here. I'll find you a change of clothes.

He rummaged through his closet in search of something, anything, suitable. Why hadn't he kept the leftovers from past visitors? Instead, he'd tossed them out, as though erasing every trace mattered. All he found were a pair of fleece joggers and a muscle tee, both too small for him but good enough for her. He set them on the bathroom counter, fetched a clean towel, and hung it within arm's reach of the shower.

Aislen watched him with dubious suspicion, like he'd pounce on her any second. He couldn't blame her. That's how these exchanges usually unfold.

Take your time, he said to her as he left. *It's what I would do, and it will keep the watchers fooled.*

He could still feel her eyes on his back as he retreated into the bedroom, the moment stretching, taut with invisible threads. He settled onto the edge of the bed and let the veil of calm and control he'd been maintaining fall away. Below the surface, chaos howled—a twisting knot of energies and emotions, barely contained. His self-control had thinned to a brittle veneer.

They were on the edge, their safety insanely precarious. This little charade they were playing wouldn't fool a real watcher for long. Nothing in this scenario resembled his usual routine. Women came; sex followed, then an exit.

Either The 8 weren't watching, or they were dumber than he thought.

But that was the least of his problems.

He rested his head in his hands and applied hard pressure into the corners of his eyes. He was like a hot can of beer, and someone was shaking it. Aislen Walker.

She was undoing him, strand by strand, every line of self-control fraying in her presence. Raze was used to women reacting to him, and Aislen was definitely caught in the current. Every tell was visible: the rush of color over her cheekbones; the fluttering, quickened breath; the pulse hammering at her neck, visible and vulnerable.

Tonight, though, it was worse. Tonight, he felt it too.

There was something unnatural about the force barreling between them, a magnetism that defied analysis. It was growing, feeding on itself, short-circuiting his discipline, disrupting rational and emotional control. It scattered the electric impulses in his limbic system, sucking it into raw animal longing. The urge to reach for her, to obliterate distance and restraint, curled through him with barbed hooks. That kind of energy was distracting, hypnotic, and for them, deadly.

He needed to hit something. Or to run. Or to lose himself in one of his regulars for hours until the heat had nowhere left to go. But all those outlets were out of reach now, and the pressure kept building.

Even more dangerous were the other emotions taking root inside him. Watching her play the part, adapt, spar with him, keep the illusion intact—it was unexpected. Her acceleration in the last day was staggering. Other women would be in pieces by now. Aislen, so new to all this, was not only controlling herself but also maintaining his old frequency at the same time, keeping them both hovering at the edge of disaster, but not tumbling over.

It was effortless for her. She was exponentially more adept than either Thomas or Preston Reed. Sigmund Lange's legacy, whether by design or accident. She was probably Sigmund Lange's greatest achievement—may he rest in Hell.

He was in awe of her. That feeling itself was foreign, unwelcome. He respected her; a word he'd never uttered in his life. And he felt a need to protect her, almost compulsively, even from his own grasp. Every new emotion was a crack in his armor. They couldn't afford the weakness.

Every second they wasted pushed them closer to disaster. They needed to make a move: run or go to Infinium. All their paths narrowed to that fork in the road.

The amulet pulsed in his pocket. In all the chaos of the evening, he'd forgotten about it again. He pulled it out, hoping it would somehow give him another option, a direction they desperately needed. He was stunned to find that it had changed again. Instead of nine colored gemstones, only six held their vivid sparkle. Two more, the tourmaline and citrine, had turned to onyx.

He frowned. The pace was accelerating. Whatever was happening, it wasn't random. Was it something they'd done?

The pendant sparked with static in his palm.

No.

That was a relief, but he needed to pay more attention to the amulet. He needed to figure out why it was mutating.

Another sting of static.

No, again.

He paused, trying to decipher what it was saying, and he realized—*he* wasn't the one meant to decipher the amulet. It belonged to Aislen. The answers were for her.

The amulet dropped into a mellow hum. That was the "yes."

As if on cue, Aislen emerged from the bathroom, wreathed in steam and the scent of citrus. Her hair fell in wet curls over her shoulders; the soft cotton clung to the lines of her body. Every detail about her seemed magnified, electrified.

A palpable charge ignited the room, and the air between them snapped with white heat. A disruptive sizzle glitched his synapses, and the familiar need to have, to possess, to claim —*right now*—surged through him. It moved him across the room, within mere inches of her body, before he could check it.

Aislen didn't flinch. She didn't move away. She met him open, unguarded, the naked edge of her want visible and unapologetic.

They hovered in the space, breath held, the world around them blurring into white static. Raze felt the shift in her frequency, an opening resonance, a bass note beckoning him closer. It undid him. He clenched his hand, fingernails carving half-moons into his palm, pain a desperate ballast.

The amulet agreed and stung his other hand with a violent bite, strong enough to wrench him back a step.

They hung there, wading in the excruciating undertow of desire, a war fought in inches. Again, the pendant intervened, sending a cooling surge through him, dousing the worst of the fire. He stepped further away from her, raising his hand up into the space between them, a fragile line in the sand.

Her face stilled, the heat ebbing from her eyes. Good. He needed boundaries, and so did she.

The amulet rumbled, not to be denied, reminding him of what he was supposed to do. He extended it to her, palm open.

This is yours.

Aislen looked down at the amulet, then at him, unbelieving.

You need to wear this. It transmits messages, and I think it's trying to give direction. But it's meant for you.

She reached out, hesitant, and the moment her finger brushed the silver, the amulet sang for her, harmonies Raze could feel in his bones. She traced the spiral with one fingertip, evoking a chorus of resonant overtones. When she touched one of the onyx stones, the pendant went silent. Her frown was immediate.

Did you break it?

Raze shook his head, feeling strangely gentle. *No. It's mutating. This morning, they were all gemstones. By afternoon, one was dark. Now three.*

He trailed off, unsettled.

Maybe it's connected to your Traveling—because you're changing just as quickly.

She cocked her head to the side, considering him. *I could say the same for you.*

He grunted. It was no use arguing.

She gently picked up the amulet, holding it as if it were a precious gift. When she looked up again, her eyes shimmered.

Without thinking, Raze reached up to unclasp the silver chain from around her neck. As his hand moved under her wet hair to the back of her neck, he could feel her skin rise up to meet his fingertips, blooming into a field of goosebumps. A voltaic charge zapped through his fingers like quicksilver through his veins.

A whisper of sound escaped her lips. She met his eyes, an invitation in the space between them.

He felt it—a fracture. Something snapped within him, cracked open so profoundly that if he went there, he wouldn't be able to put it back in the box. If he kissed her, it would unravel him completely, a temptation that tasted like surrender.

Fighting the pull, he slid the chain away from her neck, the silver thread snapping with latent current between them. Then, using the last shreds of will, he pushed her gently but firmly away, stepping back.

No! He telepathed, charging his space with any kind of emotion that could push out the spellbinding temptation of her. If they fell into that vortex, they would be lost—exposed, defenseless, and utterly incapable of regaining control.

She staggered back as if hit, clutching at air, the agony writ large on her face. He tore his gaze away, unable to stomach the destruction.

"Why don't you take a shower now," he said, voice rough, uncaring if it cut her. "I don't want to contaminate myself with you."

He stalked out, already reaching for cold water. The words still burned on his tongue. *Contaminate myself with you.* A lie, every syllable of it. The truth was worse: if he didn't keep his hands off her, he couldn't stop himself from unraveling.

Cruelty was safer than surrender.

∞

AISLEN DOUBLED OVER WITH REAL, wracking pain, arms wrapped tight, as if that might hold together what Raziel's rejection had torn inside her. This wasn't some bruised ego; it was as though he'd reached inside and yanked something essential free, leaving behind only hunger and humiliation—a raw ache of want that throbbed, unfulfilled.

She was mortified by her own irrepressible, wanton reaction to him. She wanted to be sick with revulsion, to conjure up the old fear, the loathing, but those feelings had evaporated. Dissolved sometime in the last hours, burnt away by their strange, impossible intimacy. She'd do anything to get those feelings back, to shield herself again, but now she was only exposed and trembling and more vulnerable than she'd been when she thought he would kill her.

She staggered to the bed and pressed her face into the cool sheets, eyes burning. The long shower had offered some relief. She hadn't realized how tightly she'd been wound until the water beat down, loosening muscles gone brittle from the car and The Womb. Eighteen jets worked every knot until she finally surrendered—and even that embarrassed her, how easily the shower coaxed her body into letting go.

But when the steam dissipated, and she wrapped herself in the thick towel Raziel had left for her, she caught the essence of him buried within the plush cloth. Her senses woke up, the tightness returned, coiling inside her like a live wire.

What was happening with her? Better yet, what was happening with him?

Raziel had left out the towel, the clothes, had made her a meal. He'd made her safe, despite everything. She looked at herself in the mirror and didn't recognize the girl who looked back; this one was stripped down, her innocence in tatters, face sharper, gaze more certain. She wasn't who she'd been, either

They both were becoming different people.

Staring at her own bare skin, Aislen realized what had to come next. It was inevitable: they'd walked themselves into this corner, and if they were going to keep up the charade, if they were going to keep the enemy from seeing through the Qis, they had to deliver. All that talk in the kitchen—they had to make good on it, or the watchers would know something was off. The certainty of it made her heart skip a beat.

She was no ingenue, but nothing in her past prepared her for this. Every attempt at romance had been shy, pale, with boys fumbling in the dark; Troy in the dream temple had come closest to something real, and she was so grateful that disaster had been sidestepped. She would have felt ruined.

But Raziel? Would she feel used? Would she care? The heat that crawled over her skin told her the answer before she could avoid it. She blushed with the realization that she didn't care. She wanted him. Maybe more than he wanted her.

She studied her reflection, trying to see herself through his eyes. Pretty, maybe, but hardly the image of someone who might attract him, the way his world must offer him every possible temptation. Wondering if she was good enough for him was its own embarrassment.

She slipped on his fleece joggers, shivering at the friction of his clothes against her skin, and then the T-shirt, thin and soft, shot through with his scent. She left her bra behind, a small attempt at boldness, and raked her fingers through her hair. It was the best she could do: barely presentable, but real, and honest, and her.

She inhaled, steadying herself, willing herself to trust the chain of events that were sure to follow.

Oh, how wrong she had been!

She flopped onto the bed again, desperate to erase the last few minutes, to sweep away the memory. When he'd looked up at her from the mattress, time slowed to a crawl. His gaze tracked her, mapped every line, and each place his eyes lingered burned. Her body responded, helpless, as though he'd touched her outright, every nerve exposed. In that endless second, she wanted him, and she believed he wanted her back.

Then, he was there. Before she'd even seen him move. His presence filled all the space between them, obliterating any last defense. She would have given in, no resistance.

But he rejected her—not once, but *twice*. The second time was a slap: disgust, contempt, as if she'd made herself filthy by wanting him. Then he was gone, tearing himself out of the room, leaving her hollow, humiliated.

Of course, it was her fault. She'd misread everything. But another thought rose, sharp and unwelcome: or maybe it was his fault. Maybe he wanted her to misread it. Maybe he'd been playing her the whole time, the way he played everyone else—a job that he was trained to do. The thought burned, then guttered, leaving only shame.

Aislen sat up, numb, and stared at the pendant in her palm. The fact that he'd given it back to her had been a gift, more intimate than any touch, and that made the rejection bite deeper. She glanced to where they'd stood together, where he'd clasped the chain around her neck, where she'd let her control slip, and flushed with shame all over again.

The chain was still on the floor, abandoned; he'd dropped it in his rush to escape her. She got up and gathered it, threading the pendant back onto it, fumbling it behind her neck. His touch lingered there, ghostly, and she nearly shuddered. But when the pendant settled onto her skin, it erupted with warm, thrumming harmony, soothing her wounded heart.

She looked down at its spiraling shape, turning this way and that, pondering how it represented everything she was feeling. Twisted. She wondered why it was changing, why color had desaturated from three of the stones, transforming them into something completely different. Was it because she was changing into something completely different?

The pendant zapped; a charge of static she could feel through the thin t-shirt.

Was it because Raziel had changed?

Another slight sting.

Would it tell her when she finally understood?

Harmony reverberated through her chest.

Raziel had done the right thing. He had given her back this precious gift. The harmonies grew stronger, and all at once, Aislen understood.

She felt his presence before he said a word; the room shifted, energy cooling, all the searing heat banked down—but it was still him. She kept her eyes locked on the pendant. She dared not look up at him.

I'm sorry. He said. *I didn't mean to be so aggressive. And it wasn't my intention to hurt your feelings.*

She nearly choked. An apology? Aislen pressed her lips together, refusing to look up, fingering the pendant for protection.

I... I thought we were supposed to... the words jammed in her throat; she couldn't bring herself to say them. *...because the readers—they'd expect—*

You're right. Raziel cut in. *Normally, that would be the correct choice.*

Her head spun. Now he thought she was right? She couldn't help but look up at him now. He was dressed similarly to her: joggers, t-shirt, his hair blacker than black in its wet state, making his eyes bluer than blue if that was even possible.

Don't go there, Aislen, she warned herself, trying to shield the thought from him.

Raziel went on. *I'm pretty sure whatever just happened between us registered stronger than anything these walls have ever recorded. The Qis won't question it—they'll think we over-delivered.*

Relief and shock collided; it wasn't just her. He'd felt it too. The sharp edge of rejection dulled, replaced by something stranger.

I am sure you would agree that, regardless of whatever this thing is, he gestured to the air between them, *it is for the best if* that *doesn't happen. You can see it's disorienting. And if we're not vigilant, we're vulnerable.*

Aislen nodded, stunned by his command of the situation.

That being said, he straightened, more formal now. *I am sure you realize that we do have to sleep here together.* He angled his chin toward the bed behind her.

She felt the "whatever it was between them" flare up again and caught herself, trying to mirror how he was handling himself instead.

I would never go into The Womb when I had a guest staying, he explained. *It is a violation of protocol. And obviously, you can't leave like my other visitors do. The Womb isn't a good place for you right now anyway. You need a few hours of real sleep. Not Traveling sleep. And you shouldn't be time-traveling until you know the rules better. We can't have you going into the past and altering the future accidentally. You could alter us out of existence.*

He watched her intently, making sure she wasn't going to lose her composure.

She looked at the bed, then back at him.

It's an enormous bed, he offered, attempting to reassure her. *And we can put pillows between us if that will make you more comfortable.*

There he was again, thinking of her comfort when her own resolve was in pieces. As if that wasn't its own type of seduction, nothing was.

Sound like a plan? Raziel asked, blowing her mind again by asking her consent. If she was feeling like she was a completely different person, she couldn't imagine how he was feeling.

Aislen nodded. *Sounds like a plan.*

But as she glanced at the bed, its vast expanse suddenly felt too small. And she wasn't sure pillows would be enough.

TWENTY-FIVE

THE DAYS ARE A BLUR.

Or are they weeks?

Months maybe?

Mathis can't tell.

Nurses sweep in, then out. Doctors, too. Mathis himself drifts in and out, rising and falling through layers of oblivion and broken lucidity.

But mostly he dreams.

He dreams of dispatchers and cops in a standoff over the last donut in the Mr. T's pink box. Not just any donut—the maple twist, obscene with chocolate chips and bacon. Mathis lunges, but Alpha Dispatcher zaps him with a laser gun, blue-hot light ripping through his chest. His heart sears.

It could be real.

His chest hurts like a motherfucker.

Then he's in his LaZBoy, skivvies, PBR, remote in hand. Every channel is static. Static. Static. Even QVC turns to snow. He can't find the Giada porn, so he gives up and watches the fuzz dance.

He's somewhere else now, standing alone in a room. Before him is a black box. Not just black, but blackness distilled, pulling at him with an impossible gravity. This thing wants him whole, and Mathis knows—if he crosses its event horizon, oblivion wins.

In the lucidity between dreams, Mathis surfaces. A new nurse. More meds. A grim-faced doctor with an update about his laser beam wounds. It all sounds like static.

There is one constant that shines steadily just outside the boundaries of this in-between.

Sabine.

She is always by his bed, holding his hand. She speaks to him: maybe coaxing him back to the world, maybe promising that everything will turn out okay. Maybe she whispers sweet nothings and confessions of love.

Mathis cannot tell. It sounds like static.

He clings to Sabine's presence as long as his battered mind and body allow, but the pain and exhaustion always win. He slips under once more.

Sometimes he falls into a gap: not a dream, not awake, and not the oblivion that stalks him, but a neutral interlude where he floats on a blanket of ease and perfection. The clarity here is scintillating; the respite, profound and nurturing. Nothing is important here, and yet everything is. It's like nothing he's felt before, and exactly what he's been missing all his life.

In this place, Mathis notices he's always seen the world in black and white: 1's and 0's, this or that, yes or no. Here, he realizes there's so much more—not complicated, but suddenly, beautifully simple.

He loves the space, though he doesn't know it until something starts to drag him out of it. It never lasts. There's always another shift.

Like now. There's a tapping. Gentle, insistent. Mathis

resists; he wants to stay sheltered in this sanctuary of grace. But this tapping unsettles him. It triggers a fight response in him. He wills himself to float up into a haze, not knowing if a dream or lucidity waits for him on the other side.

He opens his eyes and realizes he is floating near the ceiling —looking *down* at his body.

It's me! He thinks before the horror sets in. He's wrapped in tubes! Wires snake around him like a net. Dead! He looks dead!

He must be! Otherwise, how could he be up here, looking down at himself? He feels like he's about to pass out, but dead men don't pass out. And the machine is still bweeping. So there's still a pulse.

The tapping grows louder. A man enters.

"Hey there, Ms. Walker."

Words! Not static. Real words, ringing sharp and bright.

Troy Kellen. No mistaking that haircut, that glossy arrogance.

Rage ignites, raw and fierce—a bonfire in his chest more intense than any wound. The heat of it slams him out of the rafters, back into his body. Sabine's form blurs, swallowed by darkness.

"Oh! Hello, Troy."

Speech, again. This time, Sabine's voice is musical, gentle, a balm after eternities of static. Her hand encloses his, real and warm.

Mathis pushes against the torpor, desperate to move. Just one thing. A pinkie, maybe. He wills it to flick, a warning to Sabine. But his brain is too far from his muscles. The command can't travel all the way down his arm.

He redirects. Eyes, then. He concentrates all his power forward to lift the thin skin flaps from his eyeballs so he can glare death beams at Troy and get him to back away. But damn, if they aren't the heaviest! They must weigh 100 pounds each!

Mathis persists and finally gets one eyelid to partly unstick. It is just enough that he can see the shape of Troy sidle up beside the bed, drifting close to Sabine. From here, even if he strains his eyeballs hard left, he can't see Troy's face. He can't see Sabine at all.

"How's this going?" Troy asks, waving a half-assed hand over Mathis' body.

"If you mean how is he doing, he is going to be fine." The frost in Sabine's voice is unmistakable. "Robert is a very strong man," she adds, giving his hand a squeeze.

"Hm. I see." Kellen's voice is flat, uninterested, devoid of charm. He's not even faking it. He's just Dookie, the game avatar, all the smarm peeled away.

"Well, I hate to bother you again during this difficult time," Troy continues, saying the right words, entirely void of sincerity. "But has Aislen come back by here tonight?"

"Why do you ask?" Sabine is all business. No answer, just the question.

She doesn't trust him. Mathis thinks. *That's my girl.*

"She never showed back up at work last night, and she's not answering her phone. I went by to check your house, but there was no answer at the door. We're all very concerned."

Mathis feels the warmth drain from Sabine's hand. Troy has her now; the hook set deep.

Once more, Mathis fights to open his eyes, pouring all his will to the front of his skull. The best he manages is a flutter, a shudder of lids.

"Oh. That's not right," Sabine says, distracted. Mathis can tell just from the timbre: Aislen hasn't returned, and already Sabine's mind is racing through every part of the city, search-ing. He tries to roll his eyes beneath his lids. Maybe Sabine will notice, think he's having a seizure, and stop this before it spins out of control.

"I was afraid of that," Troy says. "To be honest, I've been worried all day."

The lie is so bold it makes Mathis' skin crawl.

"I didn't want to pry or seem like a stalker, but it didn't feel right to me either. So I had her phone pinged."

"And?" Now Sabine is brimming with worry, teetering on the edge. Mathis can feel it—a familiar anxiety from a thousand mothers before her.

Through the slits of his barely-cracked eyelids, Mathis watches Troy fish a phone from his pocket. There's a sharp, shocked inhale.

"That's Aislen's phone!" Sabine's voice spikes, panic blooming. And panic is exactly where Troy wants her. "But how—"

"I found it in the bushes at the hospital. And her car is still in the parking lot." Troy's face pinches into a mask of concern. "I didn't want to sound alarms until I was sure. But when I found this, I knew something was wrong. I came straight to you."

Sabine reels, caught in disbelief. "Oh my god!"

Mathis sees Troy reach out, hand extended toward Sabine, pulling her hand away from Mathis' grasp.

"I know how alarming this all is, Ms. Walker. But I think I have a lead on where Aislen might be. If you could come with me, I could use your help."

No. No! The scream rips through Mathis's mind but never escapes his mouth, ricocheting in his skull. There's another way. Mathis has resources. They could have the whole state looking for Aislen within minutes. If he could only get Sabine to hear him. He tries with his eyes again, striving to send an SOS through the flickering of his lids. But he has spent all his energy, and lethargy is creeping back up to pull him back down.

"Absolutely!" Sabine says, already gone in spirit, her mind halfway out the door.

Dread sweeps through Mathis, heavy and cold, giving lethargy the upper hand.

Mathis feels Sabine press her lips to his forehead—hears her say something to him. But it's nothing but static.

Through the narrowing slit of heavy lids, Mathis watches Sabine walk away. The sinking feeling in his gut gives way, and Mathis slips back into the darkness. He knows one thing: he will never see Sabine again.

TWENTY-SIX

A THICK, white fog encircled her, billowing and wafting. The hush was thick and heavy, easy to sleep in. But is it really sleep if you are aware?

Her awareness increased as the thick billows pulled away, revealing a green sea of hills. Cypress spires and eucalyptus crowns broke through the pale brume like islands. In the distance, the twin vermilion towers of the Golden Gate Bridge rose against a periwinkle sky. San Francisco, rendered with the stillness of a painting, too quiet to be real.

She was dreaming. She could tell by the quality of the experience now.

Raziel would be pissed. She was supposed to be resting, not Traveling. But the View and the surreal quiet were so tranquil, she didn't make any attempt to wake.

What he doesn't know won't hurt him, she reasoned.

She let the sidewalk guide her, winding downward into a row of perfect, white Victorians, gabled roofs painted a red that rhymed with the bridge in the haze below. One house stopped her cold, nostalgia rising like a tide, unplaceable and urgent. Numbers glinted on the siding—59.

By the time she climbed the steps, dread was already curdling in her stomach.

She would have turned back, but the dream had her now.

She put her hand to the doorknob, hesitated; unnecessary. It didn't need to be opened, not in a dream. All she needed was focus. She drew herself tight, packed her energy small as a needlepoint, and forced herself through the door. A thunderclap in her ears, like a cork popping.

Inside, she expanded again, awareness unfolding, and was immediately hit with a rush of recognition. Sigmund's house!

Aislen didn't want to be here. She didn't want to see the aftermath of Sigmund's showdown with Astrid and Thomas. She turned to fly back out the door, or out of the dream back to pure sleep instead, but a small voice stopped her cold.

"Mommy?" The word came trembling, afraid, and *familiar*.

Its timbre carried a frequency that collided with Aislen's, triggering a matching response, like a tuning fork hitting just the right note.

"Mommy? Open the door." Soft knocks rattled against wood from the top of the stairs.

Aislen turned, drawn inexorably to the top of the stairs, hunting the source of the frightened voice. There—a child, half-wrapped in shadow, half hidden by a banister. She couldn't tell if it was a boy or a girl by the silhouette, but her mind scrolled backward, and she knew. Of course, she knew. She climbed, pulled by the gravity of the small boy who would become her father.

He stood poised before the door, pleading with it, willing it to open. Hair a shock of pale gold, untainted by years. A shirt with navy blue stripes, collar sharp, tucked into pressed navy slacks; a shiny belt buckle and black shoes, so neat they looked drawn from a catalog. Five years old, maybe.

Little Preston turned and looked up at Aislen. *Directly.* The quick focus of dark blue irises chasing her features. Not just a feeling—actually *seeing.*

"Mommy's in there," he whispered, softer now, pointing a pudgy finger at the door. He looked from the door to Aislen, helpless. "And someone else," he said. "A bad man."

Aislen eyed the door, then the boy. "Do you want me to go in there?"

He nodded, solemn. "Yes, please."

Aislen didn't want to. No telling what waited on the other side. Dread that Sigmund would be there, and she didn't want to witness any of the disgusting things he was capable of. But Preston stood so alone and helpless, needing his mother, that Aislen felt compelled to get Astrid to come out of the bathroom and comfort her son.

Aislen contracted herself again and oozed through the keyhole, careful, silent—a shadow passing. No sudden noise to betray her.

Inside, she fanned herself out, observing: The bathroom. The tub. Astrid in the water, clothes still on, limp and sodden. Water bled over the rim, the faucet keeping up a slow, relentless trickle.

A man hovered over her, more wraith than flesh, and it *wasn't* Sigmund. The ghostly outline leaned close to Astrid in the tub, mouth slanted to her ear, voice a steady drip Aislen couldn't quite decode.

He didn't pause when she entered. Didn't react. She crept closer, trying to catch the shape of his whispers.

A tan suit, sideburns, a damp sheen of sweat on his forehead. Not solid—a Viewer, a Watcher from somewhere else, projecting.

Astrid's head bobbed just above the water, eyes flat and distant, nose and lips barely clear. Her hair was soaking wet, like she had already been under several times. Aislen couldn't tell if it was tears or water from her wet locks streaming down her face.

As Aislen edged nearer, scraps of the man's muttering took shape.

You can do it. C'mon, Astrid, you know you want to.

Wants to what? Aislen froze. The man had a dew of perspiration across his forehead. He was working hard at whatever he was doing.

Just sink, Astrid. But stay there this time. Join Thomas. He's waiting for you.

Aislen went cold. Was this man trying to convince Astrid to kill herself? Why? What purpose did that serve? Was Thomas dead?

The sick feeling in her stomach cranked up a notch. Whatever happened with Thomas would not have been an accident. And Aislen realized this man was a *Control Operative*, an earlier version of Raziel.

Go on, Astrid. He's just on the other side. You know you want to see him again.

Astrid slid under the water, deliberate, surrendering. Aislen wanted to shriek, to explode in the room and blast this Grant out, destroy his influence. If she could scatter him, maybe Astrid could surface, break the spell.

But Raziel's warning echoed: change the past, risk obliterating the future. If she changed the course of events as they happened on this day, she could alter her father's life. Not necessarily a bad thing. Unless she altered herself out of existence in the process.

Astrid drifted at the bottom of the tub now, limp as a

drowned leaf, gazing up through the water's meniscus, utterly still.

"Mommy?" Preston whispered from the hall, knuckles pattering on the panel. His voice was a life raft, tugging Astrid back to the surface. She broke through, gasping, water streaming from her mouth.

God damn it, Astrid! The Viewer swore, wiping the sweat from his forehead with the back of his hand.

How long had this been going on? Astrid looked drained; tired lines etched her face, dark circles weighted her eyes. The past few years had aged her, and this final hour had left her wasted.

Yet beneath the exhaustion, something stirred. At first, Aislen thought she'd imagined it—the faintest flutter, so slight it might have been the ripple of bathwater. But no. Astrid's fingers twitched once against the porcelain rim, a tremor so fragile it nearly slipped past notice. It was the smallest act of defiance, like a candle flame shivering in the draft, perilously close to snuffing out—yet alive.

Aislen's heart crumpled—for Astrid, for the boy in the hall-way, waiting for a mother who couldn't reach him. She couldn't freeze, not now. Preston deserved better. She took a deep breath, preparing to unleash a storm of energy in the room, but a key rattled in the lock downstairs and stopped her cold. Footsteps, measured and menacing, pounded up the steps. She recognized the rhythm. She knew who it would be.

As another key slipped into the lock of the bathroom door, Aislen flung herself across the room to hide her presence.

Another key rotated in the bathroom lock. Aislen flung herself to the wall, blending with the margins, hiding.

The door crashed open. Sigmund Lange, in full stride, holding Preston's hand in a vise. The Viewer jolted back, his composure shattered. Pure, undiluted terror in his face.

"C'mon, Preston. Let's have a looky now, shall we?" Sigmund's voice oozed saccharine.

Preston followed, looking up at his grandfather with distrust.

"Yep. Just like I figured," he said, looking down at Astrid in the tub. She continued staring blankly straight ahead. "Look at her, Preston. This weak bitch is your mother."

Aislen nearly buckled. What kind of man said that in front of a child?

This kind.

Aislen's scalp prickled, a phantom memory of Sigmund's clawed hand scrabbling at her skull. She shuddered, desperate to shed the touch. Thank god he was dead. She couldn't believe she'd actually felt pity when Troy squeezed the life from him. Good riddance.

"She is a feeble, witless slut," Sigmund spat down on Astrid. Each insult made Aislen flinch, but Astrid didn't react. After suffering for so many years, she had become immune.

He paused, gaze flicking to Preston, then back to Astrid. His breathing slowed. He looked like a man lecturing in a classroom.

"You see, Preston, she was never going to be more than this. I knew it the moment I cut her out of her mother. She was weak in the bone, in the blood. And weak things... weak things are meant to be broken."

"Grant!" Sigmund barked, and the Viewer jumped as if on a string. "Where are you?!"

Grant sidled to the window, reluctantly laying his palm on the glass, frosting it over from the inside. Sigmund stalked across the room to loom over the specter.

"You're almost as worthless as she is! What the fuck is taking so long? I've promised the board that something like this would work—I need that funding!"

Sigmund's rage was unbridled, Astrid still lay unresponsive, and Preston focused only on his mother. Preston quietly inched closer to the tub's edge, brushing trembling fingers against the water.

"We can't wait for Preston to grow up to do this! We need results! NOW!" Sigmund's voice whipped Grant.

Astrid stirred, her head drifting toward Preston. Tears slid down her cheeks, rolling down her face into the bath water. She summoned every drop of strength, lifting her fingers to touch Preston's. He latched onto her index finger, a lifeline.

"I am *not* going to be a government shill the rest of my life!" Sigmund thundered, Grant crumpling in on himself.

Preston's eyes became magnets, dragging Astrid back to the here and now. And it worked. She began hauling herself upright, surfacing from the murk of surrender. Water rippled. The rhythm of her soaked clothes and hair splattered onto the tile. Sigmund's head snapped to her, animal-fast.

"Don't you dare!" Sigmund roared—not at Astrid but at Preston.

It almost shocked Aislen out of the View, but Preston, the boy who would someday be her father, locked in, concentrating on his mother, she on him.

"God damn it! If you want something done right..."

Sigmund stripped off his jacket, laying it over the chair with surgical care. He rolled his sleeves up, eyes locked on Preston and Astrid. He paused to savor it, a smile blooming on his lips, as if he were anticipating the pleasure of a good meal. He loosened his tie and marched to the tub, ripping Preston's hand away from his mother's and shoving him aside.

"Don't think I don't know what you are up to, you little brat!" Sigmund growled. He turned back to Astrid in the tub. She shrank back, trying to protect herself in the water.

"You've outlasted your use, Astrid. Time to join Thomas."

He smoothed his tie, tugged the knot until it sat neat against his throat. His voice dropped to something quieter, measured, almost reasonable. "You were never meant to last, you know. Weak stock produces weak stock. Nature culls the feeble—it's simple mathematics."

Then, with sudden violence, he grabbed Astrid's hair, twisting a fistful, wrenching her head. She cried out.

"Pappy?" Preston whimpered, voice breaking.

Sigmund shot a glare at him over his shoulder. "Watch and learn, boy."

He shoved Astrid under the water. Astrid tried to resist, kicking and clawing at his arm, but she was no match for the fury of Sigmund Lange. He shoved her deeper into the water, flattening her to the tub's bottom.

"Pappy?" Preston pleaded again, but Sigmund was gone, lost in the brutality, focused on the struggle, eyes crazed with satisfaction.

Astrid's body convulsed, water slapping the porcelain. Sigmund bent close, almost tender, brushing a strand of wet hair from her face. "Don't worry, Astrid. I'll make sure your boy grows up strong. Not like you."

Then his grip tightened, and he shoved her head down harder, savoring the last of her fight.

"Mmmm, that's right," Sigmund exhaled, pleasure rippling through him.

"Mommy." Preston, barely audible, watching through a curtain of tears.

Sigmund finally let go, standing up, surveying Astrid's limp form at the bottom.

Aislen's insides twisted, nausea and grief spiraling together, her energy spinning wildly.

Sigmund casually walked to the mirror, unbothered by his now soaking clothes. He washed his hands and smoothed his hair, savoring his own reflection in the mirror. Then he carefully scooped up his jacket and draped it neatly over his arm.

He shot a look at Grant, still standing in the corner, pale as moonlight, horror frozen on his face.

"That, Mr. Parker, is how it's done. Figure it out, or you're next." Sigmund turned his back on him and headed for the door.

Grant bolted, compressing himself into a bead of light and streaking out the window.

As Sigmund approached, Aislen couldn't hold back anymore.

You are EVIL!!! Aislen screamed, with a raw surge of hot energy. The walls shuddered with the force of it, floorboards rattling, the lightbulb above flickering in spasms. For a heartbeat, the whole house seemed to groan under the weight of her fury.

Sigmund only paused, cocking his head, a slow smile curling at the edges of his mouth. The tremor didn't scare him; it delighted him.

He advanced on her, savoring the moment. Standing in front of her, he inhaled, then locked eyes with her.

"Preston!" he barked. "Is there someone else here?"

Preston looked her straight in the face. "No, Pappy. I don't see anyone."

Sigmund glared, drilling into her, then grinned, wicked and knowing.

I always knew you were there, Poppet. A gnarly unseen hand ran its fingers through her hair and began scratching its claws at her skull. *I could smell you,* it whispered huskily in her head. *It's how I found you again.*

No! Aislen pushed herself away from Sigmund, charging her space with a fiery energy, scorching the hungry ghost of her great-grandfather out of her head. But the Sigmund that stood before her was unfazed, gloating with validation. He jerked away from her toward Preston, bending over and getting into his face.

"Don't think I don't know when you are lying, you wretched brat. And don't think that because you're a child, I won't do to you what I did to your mother and father. You will be doing exactly what I say from now on."

Sigmund stood upright and marched out, not looking back. "Follow me," he tossed over his shoulder. Preston lingered, staring at Aislen, with a sadness that broke her heart.

He glanced towards the bath one last time, then slowly bent to his fate and followed his grandfather.

No! Aislen reached for him, desperate to grab hold of him and steal him from this time and place... bring him into the future with her, where none of this could touch him.

Preston stopped at the top of the stairs, pausing for a moment, then shifted his weight on a loose board, making it creak loudly. He looked back at Aislen, eyes impossibly solemn for a child, and pressed his finger to his lips.

Shhhhh, he sent, the telepathic note wrapped in the innocent cadence of a child's game—yet threaded with a resonance far older. For an instant, Aislen felt the gravity of it—the boy, not just a child but a soul already aged by what he'd endured, reaching for her across time.

"Preston, stop that right now! This is no time for games!" Sigmund's voice roared up the stairs. "Get down here!"

Aislen watched, powerless, as he turned away and headed for the open door, the shadow of Sigmund Lange swallowing him. She hung there, at the top of the stairs, a ghost left in the shell of this house.

Pain, grief, loss—they shattered her, splintered her open. Her head fell back and she opened up, letting it all out in a wail, a keening of lament and agony that soon morphed into a primal scream of rage.

Something grabbed her and yanked her up... up, up, up, out of the house and out of the View. She surfaced, gasped, her eyes meeting Raziel's as he held her by the shoulders, searching her face, waiting for her to recognize him and where she was.

She collapsed into him, face drenched, tears everywhere. Raziel's arms came around her, holding her together.

"I got you," he whispered into her hair. "I got you." He rocked her, gently, letting her grief spool out against his chest.

Her poor dad! All of that misery, that was his childhood? No wonder he ran. His mother, his father—all of them—victims of that monster, Sigmund. If any spirit deserved oblivion, it was him. Aislen shivered through the aftershocks.

Raziel crushed her closer. "It's a dream, Aislen."

"But..."

"Shhhhh, I know it's real," he whispered, "but it's not real *right now*."

She didn't know how long he held her. She rested her head against the curve of his shoulder, which felt made especially for her head, and slowly, slowly, the pain abated, terror trickling away.

"I need to go to a house tomorrow," she finally said, careful, measured. "I think I need to find something there. Will you take me?"

Raze was quiet for a long moment. "Yes."

He paused, weighed it. "Yes."

Aislen exhaled, relief washing her clean. Raziel stroked her hair, smoothing her down, easing her back into the peace she craved. The amulet at her throat hummed its assent, a lullaby that swept her off into dreamless sleep.

∞

WHEN THE SHRIEK first punctured Raziel's semi-conscious alpha state, he had filtered it out—filed it as just another city siren, one among thousands, mewling in the night. It was distant, ignorable. But it sharpened, deepened, slipped past his mental filters and forced its way in: Aislen's cry, escalating into a keen of such agony that the hair along Raziel's arms stood straight. There was nothing ordinary about it; this was pain, raw and scraping, and the city's noise had never sounded like that.

He reacted—no thought, just action. He tossed the bedding aside; pillows tumbled, sheets tangled, his hands reaching for her. He caught her by the shoulders, lifted her clear from the mattress, a rough jerk meant to jar her out of the View.

It worked. She came to with a gasp—saw his face—and instead of flinching, she folded into him.

He wasn't ready for that. He went rigid, arms hovering, caught in habit. But instinct slashed through: he wrapped her in tight, pulled her close, felt her warmth radiate into his skin and the wet heat of her tears bleeding through the fabric of his shirt. The grief coming off her wasn't hers alone; it tore through him, stripping the last defenses he thought he had left. Every layer of defense he thought he'd constructed—every barrier— she breached them all. He was exposed to something he hadn't even known was possible.

"I got you." His own words startled him—the rawness of them, the way he rocked her, steady and slow. Maybe this was for her; maybe it was for him. He'd always lived sealed off and untouchable, immune, but here she was, undoing him, unwinding every barricade he'd ever built to keep himself alone.

Aislen shivered; he tightened his grip, as if he could draw out the last vestiges of the nightmare through sheer force.

"It's a dream," he said, because that's what people say when they need to plant themselves back in the present, anchor themselves to the third dimension.

"But—"

"Shhhhh, I know it's real," he whispered, "but it's not real right now."

She accepted that without argument, turning her head in and resting her cheek against the hollow of his shoulder. She didn't turn away. He could feel her breath against the line of his throat; her scent filled his lungs, sharp and close, almost a taste. Another layer, melted away.

He considered the old reflex: put space between them, raise a wall, push her out, protect himself. But the urge died the second he acknowledged it. He didn't want to. This—this closeness, this warmth, this woman—it was the only thing in his life that felt unequivocally right.

"I need to go to a house tomorrow," she said at last. "I think I need to find something there. Will you take me?"

He weighed it. Risky. Too risky. Two targets, exposed. But it was no less dangerous than sitting here. Moving was harder to track, and maybe it was the next step they needed.

"Yes." He said it with no hesitation.

Aislen loosened her hold—not all the way, but enough for the tension to drain out of her. Between them, the amulet vibrated, a low purr of contentment. The right choice.

Raze found himself running his fingers through her hair, soothing, unconsciously steadying her until her breathing evened, her body relaxed, her consciousness sliding back toward sleep. He thought about holding her there, keeping her tethered to the present, making certain she didn't start Traveling again. He lowered himself and Aislen gently to the mattress, arranging her so her head came to rest on his shoulder, his arm still bracing around her.

He didn't know how this became his axis, but it had: the anchor point, this closeness, the heat in his chest, the drive to protect her from everything that could get through. He had always been defined by his barriers, by the distance he kept— but now, he was cracking open from the inside. A voice in him screamed: it was a mistake, it was weakness, it was reckless. And all of that might be true. But it was too late; he was out of bounds, and there was no going back.

He wouldn't be going back to Infinium. And he wasn't going to turn her over to them, either. The only path left was to run, and soon. His contingency plan was primed: backpack in the safe, currency in five denominations, five passports, a cache of debit cards, two burner phones. He had prepared for this, even if he hadn't known it until now.

First, they would go to the house Aislen mentioned. Whatever she needed to retrieve, they would get it. After that, they'd disappear. Total blackout. And he was certain Aislen would resist—but it's all they had left.

Against his chest, her breath hitched as she hovered on the edge of sleep, words slipping out, soft as vapor:

"Don't let go."

TWENTY-SEVEN

BLAKE LAY COILED on the bed, bundled tight in his blankets—a literal burrito, if anyone asked. Orders, straight from Ichiban: stay still, rest up, don't get any ideas.

Ichiban had said, "This is my body now, and don't you forget it."

Still, even Ichiban admitted sometimes he'd have to submerge himself, let Blake come up for air, and give the cells in his muscles and brain some of his own juice.

"You are the gas, but I am the driver," Ichiban said.

Blake wasn't even supposed to think "Two sticks in a bu—" though that phrase looped in his head like an old loading screen, keeping everything level. But Ichiban was "fucking sick of hearing it."

That was fine, though. Having Ichiban back made every-thing smoother, like the world had settled into a track and was just rolling forward. Ichiban said, "Everything is going to be fine." Blake believed him. Because Ichiban wasn't just a voice or a presence; Ichiban was a badass.

All night, Blake lay there, juicing his cells, watching the

ceiling tiles, and making up brand new Minecraft mobs in the negative space. He was halfway through inventing some kind of alien beast (tentacles, probably, for bonus points) when Mr. Troy's footsteps sounded down the hall. Mr. Troy stood outside, having a whole conversation with the police officer in his customer-service voice, stretching it out until finally, he stepped inside.

"Let me talk to Ichiban," he snapped, door barely closed, zero nice left in the voice for Blake anymore. Mr. Troy had gone full jerk, and Blake was getting tired of it—but there was no point arguing. Ichiban was expecting him. With luck, "I'll take care of everything" included taking care of Mr. Troy, too.

Blake shut off, closed his eyes. A cold pressure uncoiled inside him, iron jaws closing, and the boy's thoughts snapped dark.

The body sat up stiff as a lever. Sigmund was awake. "What took you so damn long?"

"I got here as soon as I could," Troy said defensively. "There was a lot to do, and I still had to wait for visiting—"

"Enough! Give me an update!"

Troy dropped a duffel on the floor. "Got into Blake's house. Still taped off, but no cops inside. Place smelled like bleach and stale takeout. Found some clothes and found Blake's passport. Well, *your* passport now, I guess."

Sigmund was already up, stretching, reacquainting himself with the Blake-body. "Go on."

"I moved the money like you said. Pulled cash, too—for Ms. Walker."

At that name, Sigmund perked up. "And?"

"She was desperate. The second I said Aislen, her eyes went wide. Hook, line, sinker. Told her Preston had her—that he'd only give her back if she came alone. No cops. No boyfriend. No witnesses. I made it clear—one word to anyone and they're all dead."

"And she swallowed that drivel?" Sigmund asked, dropping to the floor. His arms churned the boy's muscles like a rusted engine long starved of oil. The strain was exquisite.

"Didn't even blink. Must've known enough of Reed's life to make it feel real. She didn't circle back, didn't say goodbye. Just bolted. She's probably booking a flight already."

"Good. Very good." Sigmund switched to one-handed push-ups, savoring the new balance. "What else?"

Troy pulled papers from his pocket. "I forged new dates on the transfers I lifted from Parker. We can leave as soon as you're dressed."

Sigmund yanked a polo from the bag, teeth bared when it squeezed his chest. "Pathetic. Too small."

Troy only shrugged. "You look harmless. That could help."

Sigmund snorted but didn't argue. "And my carcass? Threads of my frequency are still snagged there, dragging like anchors. I want every atom reduced to ash. I need to keep hold of Blake until I switch to a better body."

Troy looked confused. "A better body?"

"Yes! I can't stay in here! Blake's code isn't good enough. I need a genetic match."

"Aislen," Troy said, as if he'd just figured it out..

"Yes, *ASHHLYN!* How hard is it to shape your tongue correctly? Idiots, all of you."

"Well, the doctor didn't see anything wrong. You were fucking ancient. So no autopsy. It'll be cremated by this afternoon."

"Perfect. We're good to go." Sigmund sauntered for the door, hungry for that first taste of freedom after two whole decades.

Troy grimaced. "Uhhhhh, the officer needs to... put hand-cuffs on you."

"What!? You gotta be kidding me!? I'm only twelve!"

"Murderer's a murderer. They won't risk it, not for age. Also..." Troy looked uncomfortable. "You should let Blake come back for a bit. You can't go around talking in the old-man voice. Even with puberty, it's weird."

"I just won't talk."

"You think you're gonna keep quiet if someone bugs you? I don't wanna gamble on that."

Sigmund wanted to scream, or maybe punch something. He'd waited forever for this. And now? Stuck again. He stomped to the bed and flopped down. "Fine. But once we're in the clear, I want out. You got it?"

Troy nodded, but Sigmund detected a slight smirk on his face. Something to file away. With the fact that Troy was a murderer, too. Of him. There'd be payback at some point, no question.

Sigmund let go, pulling his energy back, allowing Blake control of the body.

But one day... one day soon, he would be out of his prison for good. And when he was, everyone who had dared to bind him was going to pay.

TWENTY-EIGHT

THE GRAY of dawn pressed at his eyelids, burning through sleep, dredging him up from a depth he hadn't meant to reach, maybe deeper than any rest he'd known in years. Then he remembered the whiskey, his general lack of discipline the past week... and Aislen. No wonder he'd lost control of his sleep cycle.

He rolled onto his side and opened his eyes to the angel, poised forever in her silent vigil above him. He'd commissioned the mural on impulse—after seeing raw, photorealistic truths distilled on alley walls, strangers immortalized for other strangers to find.

Raze hadn't given the artist instructions, just the expanse of wall. And the artist had given him her: serene, unblinking, blindfolded to the faults of those she guarded. Raze wished she could take her blindfold off now. He wasn't the person who needed to hide from her anymore. That person had been burned away by the alchemy of another supernatural creature.

He turned and looked across the vast expanse of the bed to

where Aislen would be sleeping. But all that was there was rumpled linen, a void. She was gone.

His chest tightened, every instinct screaming she'd slipped away. If she'd left for the house alone, he couldn't protect her. If she'd escaped... or God forbid, went back home... his stomach turned at the thought.

Raze shot out of bed, fully awake and alert. He crossed the floor in two steps and checked the bathroom. Nothing.

Then, a sound below. Movement. The muffled hush of bare feet, the percussion of dishes. He found her—in the kitchen, trying to be quiet as she made breakfast.

He watched her from the stairs, unseen. She moved like a rumor along the tile, hair bound up with stray strands in her face, a borrowed sweatshirt hanging from her frame. She looked almost like she belonged.

He marveled at the fact that none of the alarms in the house had been triggered. She'd maintained his old frequency all night and kept the system on standby. And she had moved through the house without stirring *him*, which was almost as impossible. She was like a ghost in 3D, too, if that was even possible. But Raze was starting to believe that with Aislen Walker, anything was.

It was a view he could have gotten used to, in another world—an alternate reality where he could walk into the kitchen, pour coffee, brush her hair away, maybe even plan a life. But that world didn't exist for men like him. Ordinary was for other people. Maybe it could have belonged to her if none of this had wrecked her path. If not for Sigmund, and Infinium, and for Raze himself. He was the reason she was in danger. And if anything happened to her, he'd never forgive himself.

She sensed his presence finally and looked up at him. Her smile came slow and bright, unafraid.

Good morning. I thought it was my turn to cook.

The flood of feeling hit him again: protectiveness and possessiveness, desire and... *no*. Raze pushed it away. You didn't hurt the things you cared about. You didn't destroy the lives of the people you loved. And he was about to do both. He was about to shatter whatever hope she'd built up overnight because there was no scenario where they found that house, no scenario where she could see her mother again, and survive. If he wanted her alive, they had to disappear.

Come on down. It's almost ready.

Raze wanted to go back to the bedroom, grab the contingency bag, take her by the hand, and vanish. But he couldn't do it. Not with her standing at the counter in his sweatshirt, smiling at him like that. He hesitated on the stairs, heart in his throat. He'd try to soften the blow.

He reluctantly descended the staircase, sat down on the stool in front of his plate, and though it looked delicious, his stomach was already full of dread. He didn't know where to begin.

Aislen hopped onto the stool next to him and started eating with enthusiasm.

Can we leave as soon as we eat? I have a general idea of where we need to go.

Raze winced. She still believed there was something to find in that house. That an answer was waiting for her, if only she could get there. But he knew better. Even if they found it, it wouldn't fix what was broken. The only move was to run.

Raze groaned internally. She had such high hopes about that house and what she thought she would find there. But it wouldn't matter what they found there; it wouldn't solve their problem. They still had to leave.

He turned to face her, caught her by the thighs, and pivoted her on the stool so she faced him.

Aislen... I'm sorry to have to tell you this... but we've over-

stayed our safety net here. And in my new state, I can't fake it with The 8 or Grant. And I can't take you to Infinium and subject you to that life, even if it buys you time. And we can't waste time looking for that house, or looking for what you think you will find there. We have to go.

Her eyes darkened instantly. *But you promised! Last night you said yes!*

He pushed out a breath. *I know. I wasn't thinking clearly. I wanted you to calm. I wanted you to rest. But it isn't a good idea. It's dangerous.*

You don't even know what I saw! How can you say that?

He shook his head, voice flat. *I know from my experience with Infinium. If we stay, we die. But I planned for this. I have money. Passports. Burners. We cut loose, throw Infinium off our scent, and buy the time we need. We can't waste another second here.*

For a heartbeat, she just stared at him, then the storm broke. *You go! No one is stopping you! But I am going to find that house! Sigmund murdered my grandmother there! Right in front of my father! He was only a child—and then Sigmund took him, and God knows what he did to him!*

Whatever it was, it made him run. He's still running! I am not running, Raziel! I am not leaving my mother and running for the rest of my life!

Aislen, look—

No! You look! She held the amulet from her neck and thrust the labyrinth toward him. It had grown darker by another two stones. The emerald and topaz had turned to onyx. Her eyes were rimmed with tears. *Astrid and my father. I lost them last night in that dream, and when I woke up, the stones had died.*

He stared at the darkened gems, uncertain. *What makes you think that's it? Who else have you lost? Why the other stones?*

She didn't falter. *I think the first one was Thomas. The second, my great-grandfather. And I think the third... is Troy.*

Sigmund? Troy? He tried not to show his annoyance, but it bled through. *Troy killed Sigmund... was using you. Why count Troy as a loss?*

When Troy killed Sigmund, a piece of my bloodline ended. I'm glad it happened, but I'll never know what else might have come from it. She gazed down at the pendant. *And before that, I believed in him. He was my ally, my friend... maybe even more. I lost who I thought he was. What I thought we could be.*

There it was. What he'd feared most. The familiar edge of jealousy cut through him.

You can't change what Troy did to your great-grandfather. Raze said, trying to keep his energetic tone even. *And you can't change what Sigmund did. The past is done.*

No! I could have! I could have changed everything! I could have distracted him, helped Astrid fight, helped my father. But I didn't. I just stood there and let Sigmund drown her. My father saw me. He was so small, and he recognized me, but I didn't save him.

Raze didn't know all the details of what had happened. He knew that Astrid and Thomas had been eliminated. But not the how of it.

It was good you didn't interfere. If you'd changed the course—

I know! I could have erased myself. But seriously? Who cares? I am alive for this?! So I could run? So I could leave my mother behind? Maybe it would have been better to risk it and give my father a chance instead.

"No!" The word burst out before he could check it. He was angry now, and surprised by it. *Don't ever say that. If you didn't exist—*he stopped.

What would he be, without her? He'd be the same Raze

that he was before. A blunt instrument. Or maybe Preston wouldn't have unwillingly built a mind control empire for Sigmund. Then Raze would be nothing, just a burnout wasting away on video games in his parents' basement. And he never would have met Aislen, or had his world blown apart, or his soul scraped clean.

Aislen was watching him. *What? If I didn't exist... what?*

Raze shook his head. *Never mind.*

She gave a short, sharp laugh. *See? The world would have been better off.*

But he didn't see, not the way she meant. He let it lie.

She reached for his hand, and when her skin met his, sparks traveled up his arm. *Listen to me. My father showed me something in the View... before he left. He showed me where to find something. And he wants me to find it. You felt the amulet last night.*

She gripped the amulet in her other hand, holding onto both as if she could fuse him to her will. *If this amulet is a guide, and you know it is, this is the right path. It's the next step. Please, Raziel. Let's take this one step. After that, we do whatever you want. If we run, I'll run. But I owe it to him to see what is there first.*

Her eyes were wild with certainty. *I have to go there, Raziel. If I don't, I may lose everything else. People I can't bear to lose.*

She glanced down at the stones, then back up at him, and he wondered if his own name was written in the color of one of those stones.

A part of him wanted to ignore her, to drag her away. But the amulet's resonance was undeniable, as real as her pulse in his palm.

He let out a slow breath. *Okay. We'll go. But after that, you have to be ready. No arguments. If we need to run, we run.*

Her smile was sunlight punching through the storm cloud. *Deal.*

He wanted to believe it would be that easy; that the amulet's guidance would bring them answers, not more danger. But he'd learned to be suspicious.

He let go of her hand. *Eat now. It might be a while before you get another meal.* He wanted to make it sound as grim as possible, because it was. They were trusting a piece of stone more than instinct.

Raze just hoped it wouldn't cost both of them everything.

TWENTY-NINE

MATHIS INCHED his way down an endless hallway, lugging a tall pole laden with IV bags and monitors. A purple haze beamed through a portal at the end of the hall—not the gentle kind of "light at the end of the tunnel" crap people talked about. This glow felt wrong. Too bright. Too fake. Like some lunatic had spray-painted the afterlife.

It should have made him turn around and go back to his room, but there was also laughter and voices coming from the other side.

And Mathis could use some company. Maybe Sabine was down there.

Mathis plodded forward, schlepping the bweeping machine beside him, not even registering anymore. But the wheels refused to roll, bogged down in thick, tan carpet.

Carpet? In a hospital?! That was nuts. But then the smell of old beer and Doritos registered. He knew this kind of carpet —cheap, stained, too familiar. His gut clenched. This wasn't a hospital floor at all.

He grabbed the IV pole and hefted it off the floor, surprised when it weighed next to nothing, even fully loaded. *Weird.* He half-lifted, half-marched the machine toward the glow, following the noise.

As he stepped through into the purple room, he braced himself for hospital misery, but... it wasn't a waiting room at all. It was someone's living room. A true bachelor pad. A battered couch, a gnawed-up LaZBoy, the coffee table buried under Funyuns and Big Gulps, and pizza boxes sagging with half-eaten slices. The carpet here looked like it hadn't been vacuumed since the Clinton administration.

And no Sabine. Just a bunch of dudes, a messy wolfpack: two on the couch, one on the floor, one in the LaZBoy, another in a fold-up metal chair they probably dragged in from the garage. All of them were wearing visors and a single black glove, all clutching simulated weapons, all locked on the wall-sized screen across the room. *Huge.* Seventy-five inches, at least.

Mathis recognized the image on the screen instantly. In Ultra 8K, they were playing *Demesne.* Octave 6. Primeval Forest. The violence was unreal, or *too real.* Limbs flying, blood spraying, the carnage so close you could smell it. And these guys weren't dying—they were the ones doing the killing.

"Hey, guys! When this round's over, you wanna take a break and hit the 9th? I gotta try these Beta tactile gloves G just got. Word is, when you grab some chick's titties, you can actually feel them."

"No shit?" Couch Potato 1 said, barely looking up from the slaughter.

"For real! Been dying to test drive them ever since G got new gear from QGS. God knows Amanda doesn't let me near *her* rack anymore."

Laughter, a burst of digital gore, and a round of comments:

"Ha! What I tell ya, Merch? Get married and the tits are history. Just wait til you pop a kid out."

"Whoa whoa whoa," Merch barked. "No one told me when we tied the knot, it meant my balls were getting tied!"

"Dude, we *all* told you that," said a guy in the man-chair. Mathis immediately noticed his visors. They were different than the others—a pair just like the ones Mathis had swiped from the Parrish house.

"Fuck that!" Merch roared and went ballistic, his avatar turning into a one-man meat grinder. The others just watched, hyped him up, and when the last three enemies ran for the trees instead of dying and losing their grind, Merch howled like he'd won the Super Bowl.

"All right, guys, c'mon. After that, I deserve a little sugar." He honked his gloved hand at them.

"Okay, I'm down," said Couch Potato 1.

"Me, too," said number 2.

"Yeah, you guys go on ahead," LaZBoy said, peeling off his glowing glove. "I need to take a leak and grab another beer. I don't need to circle jerk with all you."

"Yeah, right, G! We know you like to bang octagons when we're not around," Merch shouted.

"Ha! He's a secret shaper in his private time," a voice from the floor added.

"Ha. Ha. Fuck you. Y'all are just jealous I'm gettin' laid." G said.

"Badge will get you pussy..." Mr. Metal Chair added, to which the rest of the group chimed in, "But pussy will get your badge!"

Mathis froze. That's an old cop adage. Were these guys cops?

"I'll remember that," G said as he pulled his visor off.

Mathis froze. It wasn't just "G," it was *F'in G!* The rookie on his watch!

Mathis scanned the room, wondering how many other familiar faces hid under those visors. Was this what the squad did on their RDOs? Kids these days... But then again, he'd blown his whole last day off inside that damn game and wound up hooked to a beeping machine.

F'in G laughed as he made his way toward the bathroom. As he passed by Mathis, he paused, cocking his head quizzically toward him as if he was aware of something, before shrugging and continuing down the hall.

The rest of the pack was already whooping and whistling, which told Mathis they'd made their way into the debauchery of the 9th Circuit. Merch was already pawing at the air with his glove, slack-jawed and wowed, grabbing something massive and invisible.

Mathis realized "Merch" was Officer Merchant. Mathis had seen that same look on his face every time he caught him sleeping behind the old Kmart at 3 a.m.

The toilet flushed down the hall. F'in G came back, grabbed a beer in the kitchen, then, standing in front of the TV, called out, "Hey! Y'all hear about Sarg?

"Yeah, it's pretty bad," Metal Chair said. "But they think he's going to be all right without open-heart surgery."

Open-heart surgery!? Mathis's heart stuttered. *Is it that bad?* And how did this guy know so much about his medical condition?

"Open-heart surgery at his age! Brutal," Couch Potato 1 said.

"Maybe he *oughta* cut the beer and lose some pounds," the voice from the floor added.

Maybe you oughta go fuck yourself, Mathis snapped silently.

"Maybe it's a sign to finally hang it up. Jezzus, do we really need senior citizens on the force?" added the other Couch Potato.

What the fuck? Who did these asshats think they were?!

"Aww, guys, stop. He's a good dude. He gotta a good heart, even if it's a bit busted right now. And he's a helluva boss. I've learned a lot from him this year." It was F'in G.

Mathis stared at him, throat tight. Of all people to say that.

"You're right, G. Sorry. I'm just selfish—I'd like to make Sergeant before my kids are in college. But I'd rather he retire, not die, to open a spot," the floor-man said. "We should go visit him tomorrow if he's up for it."

"You don't have to worry about Mathis," Mr. Metal Chair said. "He's keeping some pretty fine company right now... that smokin' hot waitress from the Old Mill..."

For fuck's sake, how did this fool know about Sabine?

Mathis took a closer look at Mr. Metal Chair: arms, thick with golden brown hair. Hairy as a damn bear! And was that a pornstache peeking out from under the visor?

Fucking Jackson! What was he doing gaming with a bunch of Millennials?!

"Say what!?" Couch Potato 1 squawked. "Mathis is knockin' boots with someone and we didn't know about it?"

"Yep. And she is fine as fuck, let me tell you."

Whoa! Watch your mouth, that's my lady, Mathis bristled.

"Good for him!" said the floor boy. "Maybe it will give him something to retire for."

Brutal. They were fucking brutal.

"Damn, you guys are brutal," F'in G said, giving voice to Mathis's own thought. *Had he heard him?*

F'in G headed for his chair, but as he passed Mathis, he paused.

"Hey! Anyone hear that beeping?" F'in G asked, eyes locked on Mathis.

"Hey! Did anyone hear someone say I don't give a fuck?" Merch yelled. "Just get over here and get back in the game! You're missing out!"

F'in G frowned but sat down, put the visors on, and disappeared into the game.

Mathis just watched, a tired ghost in the room. He wanted to go back, crawl under a blanket, and shut down. He turned, shuffling toward the door, passing the black cube glowing purple on the carpet.

This was what got me here in the first place, he thought, and he gave it a swift kick. The image on the massive screen went straight to static. The whole crew behind him exploded in cursing. But the static wasn't normal, and it sucked Mathis into the screen like a drain.

THE INTERLUDE BETWEEN
Oh What A World ~ Erasure

THIRTY

THEY STARTED their journey by heading for the Golden Gate Bridge. Aislen knew Sigmund's house had a view of it, and when she described her vision to Raziel, he knew immediately: The Presidio.

It would make sense, he said, while they prepared at the warehouse. *The CIA brought over a slew of Nazis after the war, specifically for MKUltra. They probably provided Sigmund a house on base so he'd be close to the Army hospital and would have an abundant supply of test subjects.*

He grabbed one of his burner phones and a prepaid Visa from a safe in a hidden panel of his closet. As soon as they stepped outside, he told her to drop his signature and find a fresh one.

"We should get used to this now, just to be safe." He set the alarm on his watch to buzz every five minutes, a reminder to shift frequencies. Really, it was for her benefit; Raze was already an expert at staying off the radar.

Walking toward Market Street, she dropped his signature and acquired another. The new frequency, the sunlight on her face, the sheer pulse of the city, infused Aislen with a sudden, leaping vitality. Her steps were lighter, almost buoyed. Hope kept bubbling up from her core, impossible to tamp down.

And the amulet throbbed in tune with her chest, pitch-perfect, assuring her she'd made the right choice. And she was with Raziel. After what he'd done for her over the last day, she had no doubts about his intent or his integrity. He was on her side, even when it meant going against his own instincts and taking her to Sigmund's house. Aislen trusted him completely now.

She could feel the tension radiating off of him as they walked side by side. Every time they crossed the street, every turn, he moved to the outside, always placing himself between her and the traffic. His eyes were in constant motion, sweeping the vicinity for any possible threats.

Aislen risked a sidelong glance. He looked like the man who'd confronted her in *Demesne*: same impossible magnetism, same confidence forged in steel. But there was something else now—a difference she couldn't name. Not softened. Tempered.

Walking next to him, his presence pressed in close: solid and unwavering, a shield at her back that left her feeling both protected and dangerously small.

Raziel touched the small of her back, steering her around a corner; a gentle nudge that also meant, *Shift now*. She still wasn't used to the flicker of shock that came whenever he touched her.

Aislen reached out, snagging a signature from a business-woman striding purposefully down the far side of the street. She seemed determined, all drive and resolve. Maybe Aislen could borrow a sliver of that, too.

Raze flicked his hand out toward the street and—on cue—a taxi pulled up to the curb. He could summon anything he wanted energetically, and Aislen was more than a little awed by it. He opened the door for her, guiding her inside with his burning touch.

Shift again, just to be safe, he told her telepathically as he slipped in beside her.

Aislen latched onto the signature of a man sitting on the corner, brown paper bag in one hand, cardboard sign in the other: "The Father Knows The Way," scrawled in Sharpie. A strange electricity tangled down her spine. In one of her first dreams, her father had carried such a sign. Her stomach lurched. This wasn't déjà vu. This was the same sign from her dream. It was almost as if the universe was tapping her shoulder to say: yes, you are on the right path.

"Palace of Fine Arts," Raziel told the driver. *We'll walk from there,* he sent her privately. *Shift the second you're on the sidewalk.*

She nodded.

It didn't take long, partly because San Francisco really wasn't that big for a metropolitan city and also because the driver drove like he was chasing a deadline. As soon as they stepped out, Aislen switched her cloak again, taking the taxi driver's signature with her.

Raziel led them west from the Palace, ducking into another park across the street.

"This used to be the site of the old hospital," he pointed out. "There was a psych ward here that funneled patients into MKUltra programs like your great-grandfather's. They ran their own experiments here, too.

"They used it for only twenty years before shutting it down. People thought it was haunted by soldiers who died from war injuries—but in the early days of MKUltra and Remote Viewing, the Viewers didn't always make it back into their bodies. Too many drugs, too much strain. Their disembodied selves wandered the grounds, searching for their lost bodies.

"The Army finally blew up the building to stop prying eyes and erase the evidence. I'm sure there are still Wanderers here, though."

A few days ago, Aislen would have dismissed the story as a conspiracy theory outright. But now she didn't even question it. Five days ago, she'd been a student nurse in a dull town, content with her quiet life. Every day since, she'd woken up in a different reality.

They headed up a hill, passing the stands of cypress and eucalyptus Aislen had seen in her Viewing.

"I want to try something when we get to the house," Raziel said. "I'm not sure if people live there now, or if it's offices. Either way, I want us to try to hide in plain sight."

"Like, make ourselves invisible?" Aislen asked.

"Kind of. We obviously can't dematerialize, but we can try to blend in energetically, enough that the average passerby might not notice us—in case we need to break into the house."

Her heart skipped. She hadn't thought about that. In her mind, it would still be Sigmund's house, and she could just walk into it because he was dead. But that was 30 years ago! Of course, it would be something else now.

"It'll be fine," Raziel said, sensing her tension. "I can disable alarm systems telekinetically. But if anyone comes by, I want them to just... skip over us. You know how when you look at a brick wall, if there's a brick missing, your mind fills it in automatically?"

Aislen nodded.

"That's what I want us to be, the missing bricks. So instead of matching the frequency of a person, try to match the frequency of the environment." He checked to see if she was understanding. "It's all frequency, right?"

Aislen thought about it. It sounded like something her father would have said. "Makes sense. Will it work?"

"I have no idea," Raziel admitted. "I've never tried. You gave me the idea this morning." He gestured up the incline. "But we're about to find out."

The houses from her dream shimmered ahead, picturesque against the dewy sunlight.

As they drew nearer, Aislen felt Raziel's energy downshift, her cue to do the same. She tuned into the frequency of the cypress trees on the hill. For all their size and solemnity, their frequency was astonishingly subtle—a placid, contained hum, nothing like the loud neural blare of human signatures. She slowed her own vibrations to match. Once she made the connection, a profound calm seeped through her.

Raziel felt her lock on and gave a small, impressed smile. In silence, they moved up the path to the row of houses.

At #59, Raziel pointed to the shrubbery bordering the lawn. Aislen sank into their vibrations, which were higher-pitched than the cypress: a bright, collective trill, all the plants in chorus, more hive than individual.

Raze motioned for her to stay by the shrubs while he ascended the porch steps. He held his left hand up, feeling for something. Aislen realized he was scanning for signature frequencies inside the house. He tried the front door—locked. He drifted to the windows, peering in, testing each one.

Across the street, a couple strolled past; the woman pointed toward the house, and Aislen's chest squeezed in panic. She and Raziel were definitely suspicious, and he wasn't hiding the fact that he was looking for a way in. But the woman's gesture kept rising, and she pointed out the gingerbread trim on the gables, not the two of them.

Raziel returned to Aislen at the side of the house, watching as the couple continued.

Not bad, he said. *That's exactly how most people see the world. Let's check around the back.*

They crept along the side of the house, checking every window. No luck. At the back, up the steps, he tried the door—it was locked. He motioned her onward, and they circled to the final wall. This side was more exposed: trimmed shrubs, facing a slightly busier street.

He pointed to a line of basement windows. He crouched along the wall, testing the panes. Just then, a white patrol car rolled up, the officer scanning the houses. Aislen froze. Raziel was pushing against a loose window, trying to force it open. She dropped into the frequency of the lawn, barely breathing, while the officer's gaze scanned past her, right toward Raziel, who slipped the window open and ducked inside.

The officer turned, waved at the couple across the street, and drove on.

Aislen let out a shuddering sigh, her knees threatening to fold.

Aislen! We're in! Raziel called to her from inside the basement. She scurried to the window, her heart pounding. She was about to enter the basement where her grandfather was imprisoned, where her grandmother had been brutalized. Raziel looked up at her, reassuringly. *It's okay, there's no one here.* He reached up to her.

Aislen steadied herself and dropped through the window. Raziel caught her, easing her to the floor. Instantly, her head spun—not from his hands, but from the tide of memories that crashed into her.

The room didn't just hold memories—it was the room she'd entered in her Viewings. The Army bed was gone, and the filthy mattress Astrid slept on. But Astrid's energy was still embedded here, layered into the bricks. Thomas was here, too; his signature was a deep well of regret, loss, and the shame of having failed Astrid.

Raziel watched her face. "You saw things here?"

Aislen nodded, a tear unwillingly escaping from the corner of her eye. She quickly swiped at it with her sleeve.

"What happened to Thomas?" she whispered, hoping Raziel would know.

He hesitated. "Are you sure you want to know that?"

"Yes."

Raziel's voice lowered. "Thomas fought Lange and Infinium all the way. Refused to Travel on command. If they suspected he'd seen something, they tried to torture it out of him. He used his energy to counter the psychotropics, so Lange kept increasing the doses. His body finally gave out. Officially, it was an overdose. There are rumors that they're both buried at Headquarters. I used to think that was a lie, but now..." He didn't finish.

More tears slid from her eyes. This time, she let them. Raziel waited quietly, allowing her a moment to grieve the loss of family she'd never met but knew better than anyone.

After a while, he gently rested his hand on her shoulder, bringing her back. "Let's go find what you're looking for."

She led the way, climbing the wooden staircase, pushing through the echo of Astrid on these steps. She pushed open the door, checking no one was home. The house felt staged, hollow. No signs of life, only the past flowing through its walls.

She stepped into the kitchen, a hurricane of anxiety and fear paralyzing her. Raze stepped in behind, catching the ripple, sensing it, too.

"Is it her ghost?" Aislen asked.

Raziel shook his head. "No. It's a signature remnant. When something traumatic happens, it leaves an imprint—a shadow of energy. Astrid's routine here was so intense it left a vortex. Anyone living here would definitely think it's haunted."

He pointed back to the task. "Let's see if we can find what Preston was showing you."

Aislen looked up at him. She wanted desperately to search, but didn't want to go upstairs. If it was this overwhelming here, what would it be like above?

"You can do it," Raziel said. "I'm here with you."

She nodded, turned, and walked up the stairs. The bathroom door at the top of the stairs was open. In her mind's eye, she could see her father as a child, standing in the doorway. Aislen, afraid of what she might find, moved anyway, compelled to face the memory. She stepped into the bathroom.

The tub was gone. The whole room was redone, bright and clean. From the window, she could see the top of the Golden Gate Bridge. There was nothing left of the old energy. The memory of Sigmund, Astrid, what took place in this room—was wiped out. The house should be gutted or demolished, she thought.

A loud creak sounded behind her as Raziel reached the top of the stairs, snapping her out of the ghostly overlay. She turned and looked to where he stood, exactly where Preston had pointed, all those years ago, and just last night.

"It would be here," she said, pointing to the squeaky board.

Raziel knelt, examining the oak floorboard at the landing. Secure; one end under the banister, the other under the baseboard. He stood and shifted his weight side to side, making it squeak, just like Sigmund and Preston once did.

He bent again, this time to the panel at the front of the top stair. He made a fist and knocked hard. The panel dropped, revealing a cavity. Raziel peered inside, then up at Aislen, eyebrows arched.

"You were right." He reached in and pulled out a doll, studying it before handing it off to Aislen.

"Is this what we came here for? An old toy?"

Aislen stared at the doll. He looked like a Ken, but dressed like GI Joe. Jet-black hair, obviously trimmed and painted, piercing blue eyes. On the shoulder, a bit of white tape, neatly inked with a hand-drawn infinity symbol, different colors overlapping.

She looked back at Raziel and held it up to him. "Don't you see? It's *you*... in *Demesne*."

Raze took it back, turning it in his hand. "No shit," he breathed, the awe in his voice betraying how deeply it struck him.

He handed the doll back, then reached into the hole again, groping with his fingers until he surfaced with two more dolls: another Ken, tuxedoed in black, and a red-haired Barbie, green eyes glittered with gold flecks and freckles.

For a second, Aislen just stared down at the doll, the shape of her own face rendered in miniature; her father hadn't invented her, not out of thin air. He had *seen* her. Across time.

"He saw the future," Raziel said.

Aislen marveled at the extra details her young father had painted on her face. "But why am I wearing this?" she wondered aloud, pointing at the clothing, a sharp black suit, identical to Ken's.

"Maybe it was the best he could do," Raze said quietly.

But that wasn't it. A chill trailed up her arms. She wasn't wearing a black suit now. Not yet.

Raziel slid his hand around the compartment one last time, "Wait. There is something else." He peeled something off the bottom of the compartment and pulled out a folded piece of paper.

"AZLYN," written in crayon, a child's scrawl.

"It's for you," Raze said, standing up and handing it over.

Aislen unfolded the fragile paper, revealing a hand-drawn labyrinth—the same design as the pendant she wore around her neck. But in this drawing, there were only two dots—a white one, and one in glitter glue, like the diamond and the rainbow stone. The labyrinth was ringed by a whole field of colored dots and strokes.

"It's my necklace," she said, looking at Raziel as he examined the drawing.

"No," Raziel said. "It's a map."

Aislen looked back down at the drawing.

"We need to go here," he said, pointing to the white dot on the page. "That is the last place your father was tracked to on the planet.

"Then," he said, as he slid his finger to the glittered dot in the center of the page. "We go here."

He looked at Aislen, a fresh certainty and what looked like hope in his eyes.

"And that is where we will find your father."

THIRTY-ONE

AS THEY MADE their way back to the warehouse, Raze thought about all that had transpired at The Presidio and with Aislen. It was wild, nearly absurd, to think she had stumbled into The Stratum and his *Demesne* a mere 84 hours ago, an innocent lamb in a lion's world.

She had been with him for 36 hours. Barely twelve in The Womb itself, and already she had Signature Acquisition locked down, Remote Viewing like she'd been born to it. She had also In-Stepped—channeled into another person's perspective, being Thomas during some of his journeys. She had traveled backward on the continuum and witnessed the history that created her and, in essence, created Raze as well. Not even the most seasoned operative could do that with her speed or clarity.

She could match signatures of non-human life forms. Raze was pretty sure she could mimic the signature of a stone or a river, or the shadow of a current in the air if she wanted. Blend into the world, vanish in plain sight. That was the level she'd reached.

Raze wanted to say he was impressed, but "impressed" was a word for lesser things.

Whatever Sigmund had discovered and developed in Thomas Reed was passed down and refined in Preston and then poured undiluted into Aislen. It was compounding, exponential, the power gathering force every generation. Raze couldn't imagine what Aislen had the potential to become. It would put his own abilities to shame, if it didn't already, and he shuddered to think of what could be done if she were in the wrong hands.

And then there was Preston. Five years old and already able to see the future. He had created little effigies of Aislen and Raze, knowing they would be drawn together. He drew a map, his future escape route, but it was also a bread-crumb trail for Aislen to follow when her own moment to run came.

Now: they had a place to go. And Aislen *would* go, because her father had set it in motion. Yes, she'd be leaving everything, her mother included, but maybe—with her and Preston together—they could find a way to bring her mother in, fold her into the plan. Raze didn't know how... but stranger things had happened.

Raze could see the map in his head even now, the way Preston had drawn it. Even at five, the kid worked in that dotted, cross-hatched motif, Aboriginal Dreamtime style, a top-down vision of the sacred grounds in the Outback. Raze had astrally scouted that terrain again and again during his training, a bloodhound trying to pick up Preston Reed's scent through the ether. It was the Prime Directive for Infinium: track and destroy Reed. It had been Sigmund's personal gospel, predating Raziel's first breath as an operative.

It was a map to the last known place that Preston's signature was ever tracked to: Australia.

But how? How does a five-year-old chart out his own

twenty-year-old future? Did he simply "see it?" Or was Preston doing something nobody else could: stepping *forward* through the continuum, picking the lock on time itself, and walking right through?

Raze had thought he'd learned every trick this world offered. And he'd been dead wrong, as blind as the rest, maybe more so, because he should've known better.

When they got back to the warehouse, Aislen cloaked herself in his old frequency shell and unlocked the Qi to the house.

They were greeted by a loud alert tone that echoed through the vast space.

"Urgent! Incoming communication from *Demesne*," The Womb blared.

Raze felt a sick twist in his gut.

He caught Aislen before she got three steps, hand clamping around her arm, pulling her flush against him. *Game's up, Aislen. Be ready to run. Understand?*

She nodded, eyes wide.

Wrap me up in your frequency grid and stay as close. We can't play the "playmate" card anymore.

She nodded again and pressed herself backward, spine to his chest. Her energy flared, enfolded him, a nest of static. He tried to weave himself into her field, merge the signatures, but he hit a wall: his meridians snapped shut, repelled the attempt as if it was toxin. They'd have to make do with the superficial veil Aislen provided.

Raze quickly assessed their options: bolt now or see who was trying the line. No hounds waiting. A good sign. If The 8 or Grant were trying to communicate with him, they wouldn't use *Demesne*. It had to be Troy. He was probably reeling because he'd failed to find Aislen. And he couldn't just call Grant and The 8, not after he killed Sigmund.

If Raze ignored the call, they'd have a thirty-minute head start before the Infinium RRT landed on them. Answer, play along, and he might get three hours. He could tell Troy not to call Grant, bring him to the warehouse to "hunt" Aislen together. It was a classic shell game.

He made the call. *I'm answering it,* he said. *It's Troy. Stay close until we're in the game.*

She was up the stairs like a shot, Raze on her heels, hand at her back to keep the connection. At the top, he veered her to the panel opposite the bed.

"Access Game," he commanded.

The wall began to open, and the angel's painted wings folded in, exposing the black gaming cube pulsing in its cradle.

Project my signature into the box, then move to the side wall. Stay invisible, but keep that net around me.

Aislen didn't even hesitate. Her hand extended, the Q came to life, then she slipped aside, out of sight. Raze slouched back onto the bed, composure set to nonchalance, waiting for the show.

Troy Kellen blinked onto the screen, face pinched and sour.

"Fuck, dude. What took you so long? We're making progress here, and you're out fucking around?"

Raze didn't blink. Held the mask. "Progress? You should be here, then. Did you get the target?"

Kellen was gloating, a greasy, self-satisfied grin spreading across his face. Raze wanted to crack it open with his fist.

"The next best thing? Enlighten me."

Kellen's smile split wider. "Her mother."

Raze registered the sudden tremor in Aislen's field, but kept his gaze steady, unwavering. "What do you mean, her mother? That wasn't your directive, Kellen."

Troy shrugged. "Aislen's vanished. Even her mother

doesn't know where she is. So, instead of using Aislen to get Reed, we're going to use Mommy to get Aislen, to get Preston. And then we will eliminate all of them at once."

Raze could see Aislen go white from the corner of his eye and felt her amplitude shift. Shock, panic, whiteout. He hammered a downshift at her, pinning her energetically against the wall. *Hold the frequency!*

Jaw clenched, seething, "Where is Sabine?"

Troy basked in the moment, eyes bright with malice. "Already in motion. We told her Aislen tracked her father to Australia, and that she was in danger. Mom bought it, and she's doing exactly as she's told, all to 'save her precious daughter.'"

The amperage from Aislen pulsed powerfully, pushing at Raze's control hold. Raze doubled down, anchoring her, trying to force stability.

"And who the fuck is 'we,' Kellen? Last I checked, you reported to me. Is Grant in play? The 8? Did this even make it up the chain?"

A smirk. "Not exactly. There's been a hitch."

"A hitch? You mean *another* one?"

"Maybe I should let him explain." Troy flipped the webcam, camera drifting to a new face.

Blake Parrish. Grinning at the lens.

"Jesus Christ, Kellen. How's he gonna help us?"

"Hello, Raziel. We meet again." There it was. Not Blake's voice. Sigmund's. Not dead at all. Piggybacking through the flesh of Blake Parrish.

Aislen turned chalk, shaking her head, a silent, frantic denial. Raze held her, ramping the current until her resistance flickered. The drawings and dolls she'd been holding tumbled from her numb hands. *Steady, woman. Any more energy from me will kill you.*

"You are probably figuring out," Sigmund's voice crawled

through the speakers, "you aren't in control of this little opera-tion anymore. In fact, this world is no longer yours. It's mine.

"I know you have her, Raziel. I don't know what you were planning on doing with her, but those plans have now changed. You'll bring my Ashlyn to our little rendezvous in the Outback, or her mother is going to suffer an untimely and immeasurably painful death. You have a week."

The camera snapped back to Troy's gloating face and a finger gun

"See you soon." He mimed the shot. The screen went black.

∞

THE AFTERSHOCK of Troy's voice sent a shudder of revulsion through Aislen. How could she have been so stupid? Let him touch her, hold her, taste the lies on his tongue? The thought of it made her skin crawl, made her want to be sick.

When he said that they had her mother, she nearly broke cover, instincts screaming to launch herself through the screen.

But Raze's energy slammed her back, unyielding, pinning her hard. *Hold the frequency!*

His thoughts were harsh. He was barely containing his rage. Aislen hadn't ever felt this ferocious an energy from him. She had forgotten who he had been before.

She couldn't move—could only stare, and watch him play it cool for the enemy as if nothing at all was cracking inside him.

Troy's words gutted her. He was right: her mother would walk into any trap, abandon reason, if it meant protecting Aislen. Her father had tried to warn her; they had all been in so much danger, but she'd been oblivious. She'd missed the signs until it was nearly too late.

Raziel tried to ballast her, press calm through her panic, but she was shaking with terror, and it only got worse.

Then, in stereo, her great-grandfather's voice: "Hello, Raziel. We meet again."

It hit like ice. Sigmund was alive. Troy hadn't killed him after all! She couldn't believe it.

But the real shock came when he slithered into her thoughts.

Well, hello there, Poppet. Fancy meeting you here.

A frigid caress brushed across her scalp. She shook her head violently, trying to get him off and out.

A harder blast of energy slammed into her as Raziel held her down even tighter. *Steady woman! Any more energy from me will kill you!*

Aislen froze. She was trapped. Caught between Raziel's grip, iron and unyielding, on her body and Sigmund's spectral invasion, worming through the cracks in her mind. She heard the voice over speakers *and* inside her head, felt the probe of Sigmund's energy sliding along her temple, worming for weakness, and then—the breach. He found a weak spot and embedded into the soft tissue of her brain. Her neurons caught fire, trying to ward him off.

Do not be afraid, dear Ashlyn. I'm not going to hurt you. That is the last thing I want to do. I want to take care of you. You are my greatest pride and joy. Apple of my eye.

He stroked her mind, twisted her senses, made her retch with disgust. Raziel's grip was relentless. He was trying to protect her, not realizing he was hand-delivering her to the thing he was trying to protect her from.

Just let me in, Poppet. Give me a place here. You won't believe what we can do together. I will be so good to you.

Pressure, relentless. Sigmund's energy stabbed deeper, and Aislen felt herself slipping, dissolving into the current. Instinct kicked in: she grabbed a handful of Raziel's freezing voltage, yanked it into her mind, and slugged Sigmund with it. It worked. His energy recoiled, shriveled away, like acid splashed on a parasite.

But he was still at her ear, seething. *Have it your way this time. But listen to me very carefully. You will get your ass on a plane as soon as fucking possible, or so help me God, your mother dies.*

Your new friend here knows the way. And I am sure if you bat your lashes and shake that ass just right, he'll bring you right to me. You have a week.

And let me tell you: if you don't show, her death will make Thomas' and Astrid's deaths look like a cake walk. Do not doubt me on this. It has been such a long time since I've had the plea-sure of extinguishing the life force out of someone, and you are the only thing that can stop me. You understand?

Nod your head for me now, like a good girl.

Aislen nodded her head. Raziel's grip tightened. Then the pressure collapsed—a vacuum. Sigmund's presence vanished from her brain as the glow from the television went black.

She dropped, boneless, all the energy shields gone. Hit the floor, emotions detonating inside her.

"Unauthorized entry. Unauthorized entry." The Womb, monotone, uncaring.

Raziel was already moving, off the bed and across the space in a blink. He hauled her up, hands like clamps. "We have to leave, NOW!"

She stumbled after him, barely registering the movement, dimly aware as he swung for the hidden compartment and yanked free the large backpack.

"Notifying the authorities. Notifying the authorities." The

Womb's voice synced with a blaring klaxon, alarms ricocheting off the warehouse walls.

Down the stairs, every step a blur. Back door in sight.

"Wait!" Aislen, suddenly finding her voice, her legs. She tore free, sprinted back up the stairs as the Womb counted down:

"Engaging locks in 10, 9, 8..."

She dashed across the bedroom, grabbed her father's drawing from the floor, left the dolls, and pivoted for the stairs.

"...7, 6, 5..."

Aislen barreled down, Raziel already at the door.

"...4, 3, 2..."

She grabbed his hand and they both raced toward the street. The bolts locked behind them, sealing off the life they'd just abandoned.

THIRTY-TWO

TROY DISENGAGED FROM THE GAME, grabbed the sledgehammer, and pulverized the box until it splintered into dust and chips.

"Grab the bags," Sigmund ordered. "We have a flight to catch."

Troy let the sledgehammer clatter to the ground. "Whoa! Slow your roll! We got plenty of time."

Sigmund ignored him, already yanking his bags toward the door. "Like hell we do! Every minute my carcass rots in a morgue, more of me rots with it. I need Ashlyn, and I need her now. She could be on a plane within a day. She isn't as helpless as you think."

Troy snorted, letting his gaze drift to the fat duffel of cash by the door. "Aislen? Please. She may have 'gifts,' or whatever, but she has zero emotional fortitude. She's gonna panic."

"She has Raziel," Sigmund bit out, "and *he* isn't going to panic."

Troy barked a laugh. "Raziel!? She doesn't have Raziel. Didn't you see his face just now? He didn't even flinch. He'll either drop her like a bad habit to save his own ass, or he'll bring her in to Infinium. That's what you should be worried about, Sigmund. Him hauling her to The 8. We should probably beat him there to get Aislen."

Sigmund just glared at him, unblinking, cold. "Are you done? Do you really think you know more than I do?" His voice was ice. "Ashlyn was right there in the room *with* him. She was covering her natural frequency with his, but she was there all right. I felt her flutter like a moth trapped under his shadow."

"And I was so close, so very close to attaching to her, but she was able to use his frequency to throw me out. No, he didn't kidnap her to be the hero for Infinium. He took her because he has *feelings* for her. They are working *together*."

Troy's fists clenched. "What?! "You gotta be fucking kidding me!" He started pacing, seething. "How did she win that maniacal asshole over?"

Sigmund's voice was heavy, final. "I've learned not to underestimate people, especially where women are concerned. I learned that the hard way years ago. Raziel has resources. He has dangerous capabilities. It isn't going to be easy to persuade her to let me in with him around. That's where *you* come in. Now get the fucking bags and let's go."

PRELUDE TO A NIGHTMARE

Dream Within A Dream ~ The Glitch Mob

THEY RAN, zig-zagging through the city, down alleys, between buildings, turning this way and that so as not to leave a clean trail. Mirrored, bullet-gray towers glimmered down on them ominously, watchers they couldn't hide from. Raze kept scanning, all directions, on the lookout for Infinium's vans—the kind with no redeeming markings, just the matte black death of corporate muscle on the hunt.

"Drop your signature," he snapped at Aislen, not slowing. "And any remnants of mine, if there's anything left."

Raze felt Aislen's own energy blaze like a wildfire backdraft when she dropped his tattered, energetic skein. Panic radiated off her. If she couldn't shed her own signature—the frequency of her fear would make her more visible, more obvious, a beacon. They were exposed.

Three sharp barks of a siren sliced through the next block. Police. The sirens weren't coming to help—they were here to trap. Cops couldn't be trusted. Infinium had moles on police forces everywhere and used them for cover in situations like this, to contain the situation until Infinium's Rapid Response Team arrived.

Yanking Aislen into the alcove of an apartment building, he shoved her up against the wall. "Think of your friend," he growled. "The little blonde—Genesis! Use her signature." Aislen closed her eyes, trying to conjure up her friend's frequency, but couldn't tamp down her own enough to hone in. The siren fired up full blast as it turned the corner. There wasn't time.

Raziel pulled Aislen off the wall, crushed her body against his, and wrapped her, field and arms both, in a shield he built from adrenaline and need. His fingers tangled in her hair, jerking her face up, and he kissed her—not for pleasure, not even comfort, but to overload her with his own frequency, armor her with all of himself.

The cop car blew past, followed by another, then a third. Raze held the contact, buried her in his energy, not trusting the thin walls or the seconds between danger. Only when the sirens faded into a distant wail did he ease back, releasing her.

She sagged against the wall, unsteady, high on the rush of his field. He didn't apologize. No time, no space for that.

"Get her signature now, Aislen!" he said as he grabbed her hand and pulled her back into motion. They sprinted north, then west, then south, doubling back several times to muddy their energetic footprint. It took Aislen time to wade through her emotional turmoil, but the running helped. After a mile, her frequency cooled and blurred, taffy-pink and strange enough to pass.

Union Square opened ahead, a crush of shoppers and noise. *Every five seconds, grab a signature, and then swap it for another,* he telepathed, rather than shouting over the din of the crowd and traffic.

Aislen got it, finally. She started to cycle signatures, jump from one energy to another, and together they hopscotched their trail down the street, leaving confusion in their wake.

Then a low, bone-deep thrum rippled through his field, a subsonic drone only Infinium rigs carried to sweep city streets for target frequencies. He spotted it in the gridlock—the van with matte finish that drank light instead of reflecting it. Infinium camouflage paint. Predatory.

Raze didn't wait to confirm. He yanked Aislen into a department store, straight into an elevator, and jammed the doors closed before anyone else could come in.

She started to speak, but he cut her off: *Not now.*

At the 8th floor, they slipped out, crossed the lobby to another car, and jabbed the down button. The thick metal box, sliding on its column of electricity, would cloak their presence long enough to breathe. Up, down, switching cars four more times, until at last Aislen looked steady enough to take a few more miles at speed.

Keep hopscotching signatures for a little while longer, he said, as they slid out the rear of the store and took to the alleys again.

Through Chinatown, ducking and weaving, signatures layered and abandoned every block, they moved. Only when the city thickened, when the press of humanity closed in around them, did Raze dare to slow. There, lost in the tangle, he felt sure Infinium's sweep wouldn't catch their trail.

Because that's what chased them now: Infinium. The 8. Not just the law, not just some syndicate. Fuck Sigmund Lange and Troy Kellen. Lange thought that this was his world now? Well, Lange was wrong. Without Aislen, Lange had nothing. Raze had Aislen... and would do anything to keep it that way.

And fuck Infinium Incorporated, too, for that matter. Plenty of organizations would pay for them, protect them. But first they had to vanish.

Raze guided them toward the bay, across the Embarcadero, walking them alongside the water. *Bounce your discarded signatures across the water,* he said as he pulled her alongside him. *It will diffuse and scatter them—they'll never get a lock.*

They kept to the waterfront, following the fractured lines of light and shadow, until they reached the dark underbelly of the Bay Bridge. The static of the traffic and angry buzz of the commuters overhead was like a clogged energetic artery to and from the heart of the city, which provided enough of a cloak for them to stop and catch their breath again.

Raze turned to Aislen. She was a mess—hair wild and curly from the wind and running, damp curls plastered to her cheeks, sweat streaking down like tears. She was shell-shocked, staring blankly across the water in a daze. The energetic residue of a thousand people clung to her, and her own turmoil had been so great that she had emotionally flatlined in order to function.

Raze stepped in, lifted her chin so she was forced to meet his eyes. Gently, he brushed the dripping curls from her face. "We're good, Aislen. You did what you had to. The worst is behind. But we have to keep moving, all right?"

She breathed in, hard, then let it out in a shudder. Tilted her head back, searching for the sun, but got only the steel grid and concrete of the bridge. She studied it, the darkness above, then followed it back across the water. Maybe she was picturing home. Maybe she knew she'd never see it again. Her jaw tightened, the faintest shadow of determination cutting through the daze. Whatever thought had surfaced, she wasn't sharing it.

When she finally made eye contact with him, there was nothing broken in her eyes. Just green, vivid, crackling with force. Raze felt something catch in his chest. This was not the terrified girl he had been face-to-face with in *Demesne* less than four days ago. She was changed, equal parts danger and iron. She was his equal.

Remorse hammered in his chest—for being the one responsible for putting her into this terrible situation. But stronger was the overwhelming need to protect her from Infinium and Sigmund Lange. And another emotion gripped him as well, one that he dared not name in case he became lost to it, and to her, forever.

"We have to go dark," he said carefully, concerned about how she was going to take it. He reached into his backpack, pulled out a watch, set the timer on it, then put it on Aislen's wrist.

"Every five minutes, we shift our frequency. Once we're out of range, every fifteen."

Aislen nodded, looking down at the watch.

"And we need to decide where we should go first."

Aislen stopped breathing and slowly looked back up at him, brows pressed together. "What do you mean, where we need to go first?"

Raze blinked at her, thrown. "You want to split up? You think you can handle this solo?" Twenty-four hours ago, Raze would have been fine with this idea. But now, not so much.

Aislen shook her head, looking at him in disbelief. "No. I mean, it's obvious where we are going."

Raze didn't follow.

"We're going to save my mom!"

Raze stared at her, sure he'd misheard. For half a second, the words didn't compute—then the meaning hit, hot and sharp.

"Are you fucking nuts! We are absolutely not going to save your mom!"

"We absolutely are!" Aislen snapped back, jerking her arm free. "Are you kidding me? She's my mother, Raziel. I am not a monster like the rest of you! I am not leaving her to Troy and my great-grandfather! They'll kill her!"

"First, you don't know if they really have her. They could be bluffing. Second, once they have you, they will kill her anyway. And me. And, in the end, *YOU*!"

"You're right, they don't have her now," she said, exhaling sharply. "But they will. And Sigmund will kill her... if I don't stop him." Her voice didn't waver. Her eyes were deadly clear.

"How the fuck do you know this?" Raze demanded.

"Sigmund told me. Telepathically." A tormented shadow passed across Aislen's face. She reached her arms around herself, unconsciously rubbing her hands down her arms, like she was trying to protect herself or brush something away. Whatever had happened, it was more than a simple telepathic conversation.

Raze closed the gap and caught her arms, searching her eyes. "Explain, Aislen. Tell me."

Her gaze slid away to the water. "He said if I'm not there in a week, he'll kill her. And it'll be worse than what he did to Thomas and Astrid." She looked back at him, tears slipping down her cheeks. "He'll do it, Raziel. It's not just what he says... it's how he feels when he says it."

"What do you mean, *how he feels*?" Dread coiled inside Raze.

"He gets inside my head, Raziel." She pressed her fingertips tight into her temples. "It's not like when you speak to me telepathically. He forces himself in. I can push him out sometimes, but just now, in your room, when you were holding my energy down, he got through. I could feel him everywhere, like a virus." She shuddered, disgust and shame in equal measure.

"He in there now?" Raze asked, bracing for the worst.

Aislen shook her head. "No. I used your energy to kick him out."

Relief and regret warred in his chest. He tried for calm. "Good." But the truth punched through: in trying to protect her, Raze had effectively fed her to the wolf. Sigmund had found his way in. Fury slammed through him so hard he almost welcomed it—rage was easier than the sick twist of failure in his gut. His aura flared, sharp and jagged, before he forced it down, shards of heat flickering across his field.

She'd managed to fight Lange off, for now—but Lange had already established a line in. Raze knew all too well that was the hardest part, and once you were in, you always had an unlocked door.

And there was only one way to shut that door for good.

"Did he say where they're going?" Raziel asked.

"No." She held up the map. "But he said you would know."

Of course.

He looked at the map, then at her; eyes fire in a sea of green.

He couldn't believe what he was willing to do for her. If he thought it was incredible that he was willing to run away with her, he was astonished that he was willing to die for her.

"You'll need a passport," he said.

"I have one."

THIRTY-FOUR

MATHIS WAS BORED. Bored to near-death. He understood that now: he was dying.

He floated in a sea of static for what seemed like an eternity with only the never-ending bweeping for company. No Sabine at his side. No voice reaching through the ethers. No hand-holding as a tangible reminder of reality. There was nothing tethering him now. He was lost to the world he once knew and was pretty certain that he wasn't going to be able to find his way back.

But what was there to come back to, anyway? A world without Sabine? A world without the job? Next stop for him: LaZBoys and barflies. How many years could he take of that?

"Fine, you win!" he hollered out to any gods that may be listening, though he was convinced now there were no gods of any kind, by any name. There were no angels. There were no harps. And Denise? She wasn't even here to greet him or help him cross over. If she was coming, she would be here already. There was only the static and the fucking bweeping.

"You want me? Come get me!" he screamed into the static.

And the static responded, moving and twisting. Infinite bits of dark matter churned together and pulled apart, shapes shifting and swirling around him like a starling murmur against a slate sky.

The whole swarm collapsed inward, folding itself into a deep black hole, and then exploded open into a flash of light—a portal burning and beckoning in the dark.

Finally, the tunnel of light Mathis had been waiting for!

He was so ready.

Mathis moved into the mesmerizing vortex, a psychedelic display of color and images. A movie played out to the left: his grandfather tilling soil, his face beaming down at young Mathis, ruffling his hair, telling him he'd done good.

Another reel spun up on the right. Teenaged Mathis, tearing down a dirt road in his white '57 Chevy pickup, O'Susanna. His buddies are yelling in the cab, a cooler of stolen beer from the Bait and Tackle rattling around in the bed. They'd cut class, fish the reservoir levee, pretending at manhood. God, he loved that truck!

Memories appeared and slipped away. Mathis getting his badge and being sworn in. Mathis in his first pursuit. Mathis barking *his* watch expectations to his first team of officers.

Damn, he was going to miss that job.

A brilliant explosion of stars spun around him, and he was standing on a stage. He was singing his favorite song, and he sounded *fantastic!* So much better than he ever had at Sammy's Sushi Boat. The disco light sent a thousand tiny stars in every direction on the horizon as the mosaic of his life ended, fading into the gauzy clouds he had also been expecting.

A doorway appeared. It was your run-of-the-mill doorway, not the gilded gate Mathis had hoped for. Just a shitty, brown door. And no Archangel Peter was waiting to greet him.

"Ah, hell," he thought to himself, pun totally intended. He

didn't think he'd been that bad a person. He'd given his whole life to loving a woman and serving his community. *Really?* This is what he got?

It was too late to turn back now, so Mathis reached down and opened the door. When the light cleared away, Mathis was back in the recurring nightmare of the empty room: just him and the black box. Indeed Hell, and there was no escape. The door had disappeared.

The box came to life, igniting into a rich purple glow. It throbbed and pulsed, singing a siren song that Mathis could feel in his chest but not hear.

There was no pain. In fact, the box caressed him with soothing undulations, like a cat purring on his chest.

He moved closer to the cube. With each step, the heartbeat of the box grew stronger and larger. There was no need to resist, no need to fight. By the time he reached its threshold, it was as large as Mathis, a black coffin, and a perfect fit.

Mathis took one last deep breath. Stepped into the box. The lid of night sealed shut.

"Game over," the box said. Final. Absolute.

REQUIEM

Into The Black ~ Chromatics

THIRTY-FIVE

THE MOTHERBWEEPING BWEEP was still bweeping—
and louder than ever.

And the blackness he had been looking forward to was now
light gray and blinding. His skin crawled. Every inch of him felt
wrong and restless. He wanted to get up, move, stretch, take a
run—a first for him—and definitely unusual for a dead man. He
opened his eyes.

A woman loomed over him, fiddling with the machine, then
shut it off. Thank God. An angel! Odd, though, her halo
seemed to be blue scrubs. And beside her, a guy in a white lab
coat, scribbling away on an iPad. Gatekeeper of heaven? They
used computers?

"Well, hello, Mr. Mathis!" Angel in blue gave him a perky
smile. The man glanced up from his tablet. "Yes, indeed!
Perfect timing!"

"Am I dead? Is this heaven?" Mathis's brain spun, utterly
lost.

The man just cackled. "Nope, you're alive. But you probably slept for a good twenty-four hours."

"I'm alive?" Mathis blinked down at himself; tubes stuck in his arms, wires running every which way, sticky patches all over his chest. "Do I have to have open heart surgery?"

"What? No, not at all. It's not that bad."

Mathis remembered the pain in his chest, how it felt like some wild animal ripping him open from the inside. Now? His heart felt fine. Weirdly fine. "Was it a heart attack?"

"That's what we thought at first. There were some pretty strange readings on the EKG when you came in. But all your other tests are normal, no blockages. You had what we call stress-induced cardiomyopathy. Usually comes from trauma or a stressful life event. Anything like that going on?"

Mathis thought of the murder, mayhem, his nosedive into crime, and a video game experience that wasn't really a game at all. "You could say that," he admitted.

"Well, it got the best of you. Your body's way of saying enough's enough. What you need is serious rest. And you could probably stand to eat better and lose a few pounds."

"So I've heard," Mathis muttered, remembering his coworkers' assessment.

"We'd like you to keep you through the night just to be on the safe side. We'll get you more meds to help you sleep, and I'll sign your release papers in the morning." Before Mathis could get a word in, the doc and nurse beat a hasty retreat.

He didn't want to stay! He wanted the fuck out of here! And he definitely didn't want any more meds! He'd never had such crazy dreams in his whole life!

He hadn't realized until now how empty the room sounded without Sabine's voice. The silence pressed in like static, louder than the bweeping had ever been.

Had she even been here? And what about Troy Kellen? Did that bastard really get Sabine to leave with him?

Mathis's whole sense of reality was shot to hell. For all he knew, nothing about the past day was real. Or...*all of it was.*

What if it *was* real?

Mathis didn't completely understand what had happened in the game. Didn't understand exactly where he'd gone or everything that had happened during his coma-dream trip. But if any of it *was* real, the world as Mathis knew it... well, he didn't really know it now, did he?

And if it was all true... that game was up to nothing good. And Sabine and Aislen were in the crosshairs.

Mathis was betting on real. He grabbed his phone and punched in Jackson's number. He didn't care if he interrupted his video game sesh with the guys. Mathis needed a patrol car sent to Sabine's house, check on her and Aislen, and set up extra patrols through the night to keep them safe. And if he couldn't find them? Mathis's heart sank. Then he'd have to file a missing persons report.

The phone began to ring. Jackson was notorious for never picking up on the first try. Tonight was no exception. With each ring, Mathis felt a queasy lurching in his gut. Possibly because he was starving.

"Hello!" Jackson finally answered. From the background came the tinny explosions of a video game—except the sound looped, the same pop-pop-pop repeating, like the controller was stuck.

A gut punch doubled Mathis over. He grunted.

"Mathis? Is that you, buddy?"

"Yeah, uh, hey there, Jackson." The ache in his guts didn't let up. It crawled upward, tightening under his ribs, an echo of the pain from before. Not hunger. Not normal. Definitely not just stress.

"Man! It's so good to hear your voice! We were all really worried about you."

Mathis took a deep breath, tried to wrestle his body under control. "Yeah, I'm gonna be fine. Just stress, they say. So, um, I have a question... were you here at all when they brought me in?"

There was a long pause. Too long. Static hissed faintly on the line before Jackson's cheerful voice came back, a half-beat late, like a recording catching up.

"Of course! I was the first one they called! Stuck around for a couple hours. Why?"

"Just wondering. It's all really fuzzy." Mathis's stomach rumbled. It felt like an alien trying to find a way out. "So, when you were here," Mathis pushed on, "did you happen to see that waitress from the diner? Sabine? Or her daughter?"

Jackson paused. Then laughed. "Buddy, you must really have been out of it!"

Mathis sighed with relief. She had been there! But if that was true, then she was in trouble.

"Why would I have seen *her*?" Jackson barked another laugh. "Those must be some good drugs you're takin'! I mean, I know you're lonely and all, but Sabine is waaaaaay out of your league."

Jackson's laugh landed like gravel in his stomach. The pain surged again, burning behind his sternum, the sure sign that his gut was calling bullshit. She hadn't been there? Was it all in his head?

"Yeah, you're right," Mathis said, trying to hide the disappointment. "Must've been the drugs making me see things."

"Damn! See if you can score some more from your nurse before you leave."

Mathis's stomach twisted, his chest squeezing tight. He didn't have time for this. Even if none of it was real, he had to know. He needed Jackson to check on Sabine and Aislen.

"Hey, Jackson, would you mind doing me a favor?" His gut screamed as he said it.

"Oops! Sorry to cut you off, buddy. I'm getting another important call. I'll check in later—" Click. The line went dead.

Mathis stared down at the phone in disbelief. Did Jackson just hang up on him? What the hell? The pain in his gut faded, but it didn't erase the warning bells ringing in his head. Something was wrong.

He didn't know what to make of any of it. But he knew this: he needed to check on Sabine. Even if that meant doing it himself.

Old habits died hard; a good cop trusted his gut, even when it hurt like hell. He'd already died once tonight. Staying put felt like doing it again.

He picked the phone back up and ordered an Uber. Gritting his teeth, he yanked the IV from his arm and ripped the pads off his chest. He slid off the bed, testing his legs, made sure he wasn't going to eat shit on the linoleum, then shuffled for the door.

He had no clue where his clothes were and couldn't exactly ask the nurse to help if he was planning an escape. The Uber driver would have to deal with him in a hospital gown. They probably saw worse.

Ignoring the blood dripping down his arm, Mathis scampered barefoot down the hallway toward the elevators, bare ass flapping in the breeze.

REPRISE FOR A DRIVE

Come Undone ~ Duran Duran

THIRTY-SIX

THEY STARTED by syncing their watches, lining up their frequency shifts, the seconds ticking away in perfect tandem. Then he taught her how to steal cars.

They started with a Prius. Although Raziel seemed more than a little put off by it, there were plenty to choose from in the lot. They stopped at the first one they found, just so he could show her what to do.

"Send a feeler down into the electrical system," he instructed, raising his left palm toward the car. "Once you capture its unique combination, project it back into the system." He made it look so simple: left hand to sense, right hand to command. The engine came to life with a quiet readiness. It felt wrong, but right—the only way.

He stepped away from the running car and moved to the next, a same model as the first, parked right next to the other.

A pulse of his energy brushed hers as he passed—a flicker, like connecting wire. Her field hummed for a heartbeat, answering his. "Your turn."

Aislen mirrored what he'd done. The Prius started for her, immediate and compliant.

Raze nodded, impressed. "Good. Now, you drive. I don't want to be seen behind the wheel of a Prius."

"Seriously? At a time like this?"

"Hey, I have standards," he said with a grin. The humor cut through the tension but didn't lift it. She wanted to laugh, but there were deadlines, crimes, and lives at stake. "When we get out of the city, we'll find something a little faster, and I'll drive."

He took the passenger seat. She drove. They slipped away from San Francisco as the sun bled out behind the Golden Gate, painting the windshield with cold fire. A strange calm settled between them, soft as static. Beneath it, their frequencies kept slipping into sync, tuning closer every mile.

After an hour, he directed her to a Walmart parking lot where they dumped the car. He bought some water, protein bars, and two pairs of leather gloves. "Wear these now so no one can trace our prints," he said.

They ate quickly, prowling the lot. Raze found a Tesla that met his standards. She started it; then he slid behind the wheel, and they raced through the back roads that cut through the Central Valley. The curves and straightaways felt familiar to Aislen. This was the route he'd taken when he brought her to his warehouse—the memory of it echoed in the way the car moved, in the line of the road through the dark.

Time and again, she would glance at Raziel in the seat beside her. He looked as concerned as she felt, but moved like he'd done this a hundred times. While she moved like she was trying to remember gravity.

He didn't have to do this. There was nothing in it for him. He could have just run, like he wanted. Go dark, he called it. But as soon as she told him that Sigmund had been in her brain, he'd changed his mind in an instant, bought into her plan entirely. He never said it, but she knew he was worried about her, about that.

Truth: She was worried, too. But she'd been able to fight him off before, and now that she had her own energy back, she felt she was strong enough to fight him off again. And with Raziel beside her, she felt even more confident.

She knew Raziel was putting his life on the line. She was also very clear about the person he had been. She knew he'd had every intention of killing her in the beginning and had done such evil things in his past. Yet, she couldn't deny how fiercely he wanted to protect her now. She felt it, humming under every word, every motion, every shielded look.

And there was that kiss. She'd been nearly out of her mind in that moment, and he had used that kiss to cloak her chaotic energy with his. Yes, he was trying to make them look like they were merely passionate lovers to the responding officers. But there was truth in it as well. Aislen felt everything in her being realign, and she could feel that everything in his already had. It was perfectly right, and so completely wrong.

"We should steal a different car," she said to Raziel when the farms outside her hometown started to flicker past the windows.

Raziel slid her a glance. "What? Have I created a proper felon out of you? You enjoy the rush now?"

She shook her head, "It's not that. This car is too nice for my neighborhood. It'll stand out."

He actually laughed. "Damn. Maybe you don't need me around after all."

She didn't respond. It wasn't just that she needed him around; she wanted him around.

She guided him to a neighborhood where Teslas were a little less suspicious. He parked on a side street and, within minutes, had another Prius going, this time taking the driver's seat himself.

Aislen couldn't help it. "Damn, the things you will do for me," she said, sliding into the passenger seat.

"No shit," he said, dry as dust.

He didn't need directions. He already knew where she lived and how to get there. He'd been there. When they pulled into her neighborhood, Raziel slowed. Up ahead, there were headlights, nothing unusual to her, but he seemed to know better. Aislen shouldn't have been surprised when a patrol car turned onto a street. Her street.

"We need to go in on foot," he said. "Is there a back way?"

She nodded and directed him past her street and into a nearby orchard. "We can take the train tracks to my house from here," she said, pointing through the trees toward the Santa Fe.

"That was smart," Raziel said. "How did your mom know to do that?"

"Do what?"

"Buy a house near the tracks. Railways carry the residual energy of travelers. It is hard to hone in on any particular signature. It helped protect you all these years."

"You found me," she said flatly.

"Technically, you found me," he said. "Or else, no one would have known you existed. I found you at a nightclub, dancing alone in a crowd."

A flash of that memory came into her mind. The energy she'd felt on that dance floor that night, the invisible presence: *it was him.* The resonance had been there all along.

"I snagged your signature there, which is how I found you here." She couldn't be sure, but he looked a bit ashamed now.

"My dad may have told her to buy a house near the tracks. He'd sent a letter and money."

"Well, it was a good idea." He looked back through the orchard toward her house. "We should get in there. Time is short."

They darted through barren peach trees, following the side of the tracks until they reached the back gate of her house. Raziel motioned for her to stay low while he circled the perimeter.

He came back a few minutes later, unsettled. "He just left," he said. "Is this city or county?"

"County. Why?"

"Because it was the police cruiser, not a deputy. And it couldn't be Sergeant Mathis."

"Wait! You know him?" Aislen didn't know why she was surprised.

"I do. But unless a miracle happened, he's probably dead."

She stared at him, thrown. "What? How would you know that?"

"It's a long story, Aislen..."

"Then tell me the short version."

Raziel hesitated, voice flat. "He got himself a Q and a special set of visors he shouldn't have, and he got into The Stratum. And *Demesne*."

She blurted, "So you tried to kill him?"

Raze flinched, looking wounded. "No! It wasn't like that. He was an innocent bystander, like you. He suspected the game had something to do with Blake and Scott Parrish. So he investigated, stole the console and visors, and got into the game. Then he met up with two people who helped him into *Demesne*."

He drew a shaky breath and looked her in the eyes. "Troy. And Sigmund Lange."

"So why kill *him*?! Instead of Troy? Or Sigmund?"

"I didn't kill him, Aislen," Raze snapped. "*Troy did.*"

She gasped, once again disgusted by the maniac that Troy had turned out to be.

"I actually tried to *stop* the damage before I sent him out of *Demesne*—I just don't think it was enough. He took a heart-stopping blow to the chest."

Aislen felt ashamed. First, for assuming that Raziel had been the one to hurt Sergeant Mathis, and second, for being surprised that he'd tried to save him. He had changed—even before she realized.

"Well, he was still alive when we got to the hospital. So maybe he's okay."

"Maybe," Raziel said, but he clearly didn't believe it. "We should get in and get that passport. If Infinium has patrols set up, we need to get in and out as quickly as possible."

She nodded and followed him through the back gate. They moved through the shadowy yard, passing her mom's beloved rose bushes. Aislen felt a stabbing pain in her chest. Her mom... God, she missed her. She would do anything for her calm reassurance right now; anything to hug her again and tell her she loved her.

Raze must have felt her energy shift. He reached back and grabbed her hand. His touch didn't feel like contact—it felt like calibration, two waves finding the same crest.

Do you have an alarm? He asked telepathically, as they approached the back door.

She shook her head.

He tried the handle, and it opened. It was unlocked. He looked back at Aislen, eyes narrowed.

Did you guys make a habit of that?

No. Never.

Stay close to me, he said and slipped inside.

They crept through the kitchen, Raziel's gaze darting ahead, sweeping for any threat. Another wave of grief hit Aislen. This had been home, her sanctuary. Not anymore. Even if they survived, they would never come back.

The downstairs was clear, so they headed upstairs toward her room. It was dark except for the green glow from her clock. She bent to the floor and felt her way toward the end of her bed. She reached under, feeling around for her shoebox. It was gone.

"It's not here," she whispered. "My shoe box with our passports."

"Is this it?" He asked, pointing to the bed.

The shoebox was there, lid off, contents scattered..

Her mom must have known about the passport. She'd found it. That could only mean that she was definitely on her way to Australia to find Aislen.

She rummaged through the travel brochures, searching for her own passport in the mess.

"It isn't here. Why would my mom take my passport?" The panic spiked. She tore through the papers again. Still gone.

Raze caught her by the shoulders. "Stop, Aislen. Take a breath. She may have put it somewhere else."

She wanted to argue, but Raziel cut her off. "Close your eyes, and tap into the energy of the passport. Remember holding it, and try to feel its connection. Then let it go so it can tell you where it is."

Aislen forced herself to breathe, to focus. She remembered sitting on her bed, passport in hand, dreaming of beaches. Then she blanked her mind—and instantly, a teacup flashed in her head.

She opened her eyes in disbelief. "Really?"

He just nodded, "Nice trick, eh?"

She bolted down the stairs and into the kitchen. There, on the teacup shelves, under the nightlight's cold glow, was her passport. Next to it, a teacup she'd never seen before, burnt orange with tiny black and white dots painted in concentric circles.

"That pattern," Raziel whispered behind her. "It's the same as the map your father drew."

He was right. And with it was a handwritten note, along with a sealed envelope.

She picked up the note. Her hands trembled; she already knew this was a goodbye.

MY DEAREST DAUGHTER,

If you are reading this, Troy lied to me.

I have a feeling he is a liar and a snake, but this has to do with you, and I can't take my chances.

If you get this letter, please, I beg you: DO NOT FOLLOW ME TO AUSTRALIA.

Run like your father. There was a good reason he ran. I don't know all of them, but he ran to protect us.

I also lied to you, Aislen. I told you the cups stopped coming two years ago. But they didn't. They stopped one year ago. Last year, your father sent this teacup, a letter for you, and a note to me. He told me only to leave this for you if the day came. And unfortunately, it has.

Dear sweet Aislen. I love you more than words could ever express. You are and have always been my greatest treasure. Please, forget about me and save yourself.

Like your father said,

Love travels a straight line, from my heart to yours.

Distance, time, death cannot disrupt the connection.

Every drop of my love belongs to you.
From across eternity.
Mom

AISLEN'S LEGS BUCKLED. "MOM!" The word cracked through her like lightning.

Raziel didn't even ask what the letter said; he just pulled her into his arms and let her cry into his chest. His field wrapped around hers, steady and quiet, a resonance of compassion that made her cry even more until every last drop of her was spent.

She lay against his chest as the tears subsided, and still, he held her through the aftershocks, staying like that, while the world held its breath around them.

Their watches chimed.

"Are you able to shift frequencies again, Aislen?" he whispered against her hair. She nodded and chose her mother's frequency, channeling her calm, collected vibration, a solid blue like the deepest of seas. Aislen could almost feel her there, and it settled her soul.

She reluctantly pushed herself off of Raziel's chest and looked up at him. "Thank you," she said, truly grateful.

A sudden light fractured their shared field, snapping the harmony. Headlights swept his face and cut across the wall as a car turned onto their street.

"Duck," Raze said, pulling her down toward the floor. "It may be that cop."

Instead of going out the back door, Raziel pulled her forward into the dining room. They ducked behind the table, shadows folding around them as the car's beams went dark in the driveway.

Stay here, he he told her, leaving her huddled beneath the table, half hidden by chair legs.

Raziel low-crawled to the window, peeled back the curtain, and peeked through the slit across the front porch toward the driveway.

He was quiet for a long moment before she heard him whisper, "You gotta be fucking kidding me."

THIRTY-SEVEN

HOSPITAL GOWN, bare legs, blood dripping down his arm. The driver clocked it, offered him a tissue. Bottled water, granola bar. Mathis took both, barely a thank you. He pressed the wad to his arm and told the man to head for Sabine's house.

"That bad in there, huh?" the driver asked.

Mathis grunted, scarfed down the bar in two bites. The guy passed him another one, then another. Mathis didn't refuse.

"I hate hospitals," the driver said. "They're the worst."

"Got that right," Mathis muttered, his focus already outside the window, scanning for tail lights or shadows.

The driver kept talking. Mathis tuned it out, turned it into static—the same static he'd lived in since the hospital.

What would he say, showing up like this? Sabine was going to think he was a lunatic, a stalker. If he ever had a chance, this would torch it. Hell, Jackson was right: she was out of his league. He knew that. But she'd given him her number and had flirted with him... that had to count for something. It didn't mean she'd shown up at the hospital and sat bedside with him through the night.

But Mathis had *felt* her there. Felt her hand in his, heard her voice, saw her in the room. That's right! When he'd been on the ceiling, out of his body. Didn't that shit happen sometimes? He'd skipped past some crazy, woo-woo shit like this on a cable channel before. He'd never believed it, but maybe—

It had felt real. Too real. Jackson was wrong. Sabine had been there. They just missed each other.

The driver eyed him in the rearview. "You sure you're not bleeding out or something, man?"

"Nah," Mathis said. "Just bleeding common sense."

Mathis pointed him into Sabine's neighborhood.

"Go slow," he said. "I want to make sure the streets are clear."

The driver complied, which allowed Mathis to survey the side streets for anything suspicious.

"Turn left at the next street. It will be the house at the end, on the left."

From the end of the block, the house was mostly dark, except for a faint glow from the kitchen window. Mathis saw a shadow moving inside. His heart leaped. Sabine was home!

But then he noticed—there were no cars in the driveway. None on the street.

"Kill the lights," Mathis said.

The driver did. "Uhhhh, I'm down for some excitement, just don't get me into any trouble."

Mathis ignored him, leaning forward, studying the shadows inside, the curtains, the window glow.

"Pull in the driveway and put the car in neutral, in case we need to take off quick."

The driver hesitated. "Yeah, I'm not too sure about this..."

"I'll pay you triple. It'll be fine." Mathis kept his eyes scanning back and forth through the windows. There. The dining room curtain moved. Or had it? He couldn't be sure.

He turned to the driver, eyes wide. "I'm checking it out. Don't freak out and leave. I'm a cop—someone inside could be in danger."

The guy nodded, swallowing.

"You wouldn't... by any chance... have a gun, would you?"

"How much are we talking about?" The driver's eyes narrowed.

"Two hundred. I won't use it unless I have to. And I'll give it right back."

The driver thought for a moment, then nodded, reaching down under his seat and opening a hidden drawer. He pulled out a gun and a magazine and handed them back to Mathis. Mathis wasn't even surprised. This was Modesto.

"I said excitement, no trouble," the driver warned.

Mathis nodded, slotted the magazine, chambered a round, and eased open the car door. He probably should have asked the driver if he had shoes and a pair of pants.

Mathis started toward the side of the porch, moving as tactically as possible, crouching below the sight line of the windows. He ignored the pebbles and thorns stabbing his bare feet, the pain in his arm, and the fact that the driver had a prime view of his ass hanging out of the gown.

With his back against the wall, he crept up the porch steps and peered through the dining room window. Not much to see: nightlight glow from the kitchen, shapes of the table and buffet, tumble of chair legs. Living room blacked out beyond the curtains.

Confident that the room was clear, Mathis slipped to the front door. All or nothing now. Sabine had to be in there.

He rang the doorbell.

Diiinnng Dooong.

In the dead still of the night, the bell might as well have been a foghorn. A dog down the street started barking. Mathis pressed his ear to the door, straining for any sound, any trace of movement.

He'd done this a thousand times. Usually, the house was empty. Or someone immediately started to move. Last time, there had been a corpse and his blood-soaked son.

He pressed the doorbell again.

Diiinnng Dooong.

Even louder in his ear because it was right by the door. He leaned closer, reaching his instincts through the wood panel, and felt for the presence of life beyond the door. Nothing at first. Then every hair on his arms stood on end. His breath caught when he felt something press back. There was definitely a presence there—someone right behind the door.

Mathis adjusted the handgun, flattening himself against the frame for cover. He kept his ear to the wood, tuned in to the presence. It tracked him, moved as he moved. He had never felt anything like this before. Well, not until the game. Not until the hospital. He felt raw now, the world more electric, his nerves broad as antennae.

Mathis pressed his own energy back. Again, there was pressure. Someone was definitely there. *Friend or foe?* Mathis wondered. He scanned the presence, trying to feel the quality of its energy. It didn't feel threatening, but it felt *familiar*.

"Sabine, is that you?" he whispered through the door.

The force shoved back, hard, right into his heart. White light shot through his chest, and for a second, he braced for agony. But the ache dissolved. Gone, erased, like it had taken the pain with it.

That felt familiar, too. He remembered lying on the ground, in the deserted streets of a destroyed city, a dark figure looming above. A man, black hair and eyes of ice. He knelt beside him, placed his hands toward Mathis's chest, sucked all the blue energy of Dookie's bullets out of his heart, and then sent him out of the game.

They had called him Raziel.

"Raziel, is that you?" Mathis whispered through the door.

Quiet, a voice hissed loudly. Not through the door. It was in his head. Mathis almost lost it completely. He really was losing his mind.

What the hell is going on? Mathis thought to himself. The voice answered.

Listen to me, Mathis. You are no good here. In fact, you could be in danger. Just go home. Get well. And forget about all this.

Mathis stumbled away from the door, reeling. If Raziel was there, why not just open up and speak like a man? "Hey, Ra—" he tried.

A sledgehammer of energy hit him in the chest, knocking him back. Another force latched onto his throat, pulling him upright while holding his tongue still.

When I said QUIET, you didn't think I meant it?

Mathis nodded his head. *I get it. You meant it.*

He also got that he had completely lost his fucking mind. In the distance, a train whistle howled, long and cold in the night. Its plaintive cry reminded him of Sabine. It felt like a warning. She had to be in danger.

She is, the voice said, reading his mind. *But you aren't capable of fixing that. Let me handle this, Mathis. Save yourself. Sabine is going to need someone to come home to.*

The train rumbled closer, sending tremors through the floorboards of the porch. The grip loosened around the muscles of his throat, and Mathis was able to catch a breath. The energy evaporated from his chest, leaving him standing on the precipice of the stairs on his own.

The train bellowed, right on top of the house, sound tearing open the night.

GOOOOO!

Mathis scrambled back, winced, barely sure if it was the train screaming at him or Raziel. He sprinted for the car and dove into the back seat.

The driver looked back at him, his face white and eyes wide. "What the fuck was that all about? Is this place haunted?"

Mathis rubbed at his neck where the phantom hand had been. "You saw that?" His voice came out in a rasp.

The driver nodded. "Looked like something had you by the throat."

Relief. He wasn't batshit.

But that meant someone *was* there.

"Wait here," Mathis said, and bolted from the car. He ran around to the backyard. The back door gaped open, the freight train howling by on the other side of the fence. The back gate was swinging wide.

Mathis sent his feelers out that direction, searching for Raziel's presence again. But there was only static and the train screeching its lament against the tracks.

Gone. He watched the engine and cars thunder into the distance, wondering what would happen to Sabine, Aislen, Raziel, himself. The world was off its rails.

And it all had to do with that game.

∞

RAZE STARED, barely believing it. Mathis, upright and alive, in the back seat of an Uber. Not in any hospital, but here, at Sabine's, in a hospital gown, gun in hand.

Raze almost laughed. The old man had guts, but no finesse. His field was like a floodlight—bright, blunt, and impossible to ignore.

As Mathis passed in front of the window, Raze heard Aislen gasp under the table.

Quiet! We don't want him to hear us!

She nodded. Ready.

When I say, we run.

He slipped around the corner and pressed his body up against the door just as the doorbell rang. He checked the lock, but added a shield of energy for good measure. Mathis was the type to kick his way in.

Raziel could feel Mathis move closer to the door. He could also feel him reach *his* energy into the house. A cop's intuition gone mutant; Mathis's spidey sense was off the charts.

Doorbell, and more of Mathis's energy pushing through the door. Raze felt it against his skin and pushed back. That was a mistake. Mathis sensed it, recalibrated, pressed harder.

He has more than just hunches now, Raze thought. Mathis was scanning, not threatening, but insistent.

"Sabine, is that you?" Mathis called, barely audible.

Aislen sucked in a breath, startled at her mother's name. The vibration of her field spiked, brushing his like static— sharp, alive. Raze fired a warning at her, then threw a jolt at Mathis too—a white flare meant to jog his memory, remind him why he'd ended up in a hospital bed. Maybe this time he'd get the message and leave.

"Raziel, is that you?" Mathis whispered through the door.

Raze was flabbergasted. He remembered him? Aislen gasped again.

Quiet! Raze snapped.

Raze felt Mathis snap to attention, sharp and astonished, retreat a step.

What the hell is going on? Raze heard Mathis thinking. Had Mathis heard him? What, was everyone in this town psychic now?

Raze decided to test him. He sent the thought: *Go home. You're no good here.*

It was meant as mercy.

There. Mathis backed further away. He had heard him! Good! Hopefully, he'd give up.

But Mathis started to shout, "Hey Ra—"

Raze didn't give him a chance to finish. He smashed him with another jolt of power, lifted him by the throat, and still his tongue with a lasso of energy. He had saved this guy once. He wasn't killing him now.

Raze! Don't kill him! Aislen shrieked in his mind. He shot her a glare. It was the last thing he wanted to do. And still, it was the first thing she thought he would do.

He focused on Mathis.

When I said shut up, you didn't think I meant it? Raze roared at both Mathis and Aislen.

Aislen shrank behind the chair. Mathis cowered under his hold.

I get it. You meant it, Mathis thought.

Raze heard the horn of an approaching train. Perfect timing. They could use it for cover when they ran.

Sabine. She must be in danger. Mathis's thoughts, clear as a bell.

She is, Raze answered. *But you aren't capable of fixing that. Let me handle this, Mathis. Save yourself. She is going to need someone to come home to.*

Hopefully, the promise of seeing Sabine again would be

enough. The train was nearly on them. Time to move. Raze released Mathis and lunged for Aislen, snatching her hand.

The train's scream rattled the walls, covered everything.

GOOOO! He yelled at Aislen, shoving her toward the back.

They hit the yard running, out the gate, and into the orchard.

The train kept pace, blurring their transition. *Change frequencies!* he ordered Aislen, and phased his own. They sprinted half a mile, orchard blurring, all the way back to the car.

They dropped inside, and Raze floored it, driving hard in the opposite direction, leaving the house and Mathis behind.

After twenty minutes, when the rearview was clear, he finally slowed. "We need a safe place, Aislen," he said. "A place to rest before we go to the airport. Might be our only shot at sleep. Can you think of somewhere?"

Aislen sat quietly for a long time, tracing the two letters in her lap. When she looked up, her eyes were clear.

"Yes. I know a place."

THIRTY-EIGHT

THEY DROVE IN SILENCE, winding through more back roads than necessary to scramble their trail. The silence between them wasn't just tension now—it felt like distance forming, quiet and invisible, the kind that no words could bridge.

Aislen could sense the storm thrashing inside Raziel—a riot of anger, apprehension, and something else she couldn't place. She couldn't tell which emotion was winning. But she knew that it was all because of her.

Was it because she couldn't stay quiet even when he asked her to? Because he was sick of having to help her when she kept messing up? Because Sergeant Mathis was alive when Raze had thought he was dead? The uncomfortable answer pressed at her: it was none of those things.

It was because, when it mattered, she had assumed the worst of him. Because she had assumed he was going to kill Mathis on the porch. She'd screamed at him, and the look on his face—that had said it all.

She realized then what the other emotion was: hurt. Raziel,

ironclad, untouchable Raziel, was hurt by her. She felt it in the field between them—a static crackle, sharp and blue.

His silence hurt worse than shouting would have.

She wished he would let down his guard just enough for her to say she was sorry. She reached out to him, telepathically, but his mind was locked, refusing her entry.

Her hands drifted to the letters in her lap. The envelope from her father remained sealed; she couldn't bring herself to open it yet, not with her mother's words still heavy in her heart. She stroked the paper, searching for warmth, some trace of comfort left behind by her parents. But they felt like pulverized wood pulp, no life in them at all. She tucked them into her pocket as they pulled into the dim parking lot of the lotus garden.

Raze turned off the lights, steering the car into a thicket of bushes. He did his best to mask it with branches, working with deliberate care. "We'll need to steal a new one first thing," he said, voice cold and even. When the car was hidden, Aislen led him down into the gardens.

She had never come into the grounds this late, never felt the solitude so complete, so sacred. They walked the emerald corridor between lotus pools, the choir of frogs hushed, and the statuaries of the Buddha and Quan Yin bore silent witness to their journey toward the temple. Even the lotus blossoms seemed to hold their breath, petals trembling with the effort of staying open just a little longer. Above, the vault of night blazed with a million stars, each another world, another place that she would rather be than here.

They climbed the temple steps, and Aislen pushed open the door. She entered first, holding it for Raziel. Inside, one small candle glimmered on the altar, dancing shadows across the walls. Raziel removed his shoes and slipped off the backpack, placing them by the entrance. He already understood the ritual; he moved with ease. Aislen watched him as he found the box of candles, carried them to the shrine, and kindled each one from the central flame. Light grew and expanded around them, soft and warm.

His gaze wandered the small rotunda, taking in the relics and artwork. One banner, in particular, caught his eye, and he broke his silence. "What's this?"

"It's the Baku," she told him. "The devourer of nightmares."

"According to the Japanese?"

She shrugged. "According to Troy."

A shadow flickered through his eyes, blue fading to slate.

Aislen walked barefoot across the tatami mats and stood beside him. "I owe you an apology, Raziel," she said quietly, placing her hand on his shoulder.

He flinched at the contact—a jolt ran through both of them, the alchemy of their energies intermingling, crackling with static. She realized it was the first time she had reached for him, the first time she'd closed the distance. It felt different, urgent, electric.

He stared at her coolly. "For what?" He knew for what. He just wasn't going to admit that she'd hurt him.

"For thinking that you'd kill Mathis... back at the house. I immediately jumped to that conclusion. Even after what you had said about helping him. After everything you've done for me the past two days. I should have known better."

The shield slipped away from his eyes, and his face softened. He nodded, accepting her apology, then looked back at the dancing chimera on the banner. "Maybe he could devour this nightmare for us."

"We could try." She gave a faint smile. "But I don't think it works that way."

"Belief is half the challenge, so they say."

"What? And I wake up in my bed, and it was all a bad dream?"

"Sure. Why not?"

She looked up at him, searching his face. "Do you believe that, Raziel?"

He contemplated the banner, then shook his head. "No. I don't."

"Me neither," she whispered. She let her hand fall from his back, but he caught it, folding it into his own, anchoring her to him.

"We can make this work, Aislen. We can turn this situation to our advantage."

"How?" she asked, lost. "How do we make this work? Go back in time? To a day where I never dreamed?"

He actually considered it, frowned, then shook his head. "No."

But she *did* think about it. What if she Time Walked? Rewound to the night of her dream? She could create a disruption and wake herself before she ever crossed into The Stratum... before she trespassed into *Demesne*. She could be the Baku. She could devour the nightmare at its source.

Raziel reached up, caught her face in his other hand, forcing her to meet his eyes. "Don't even think about it." His voice was hard, final.

"But why not?" She fought him. "It would solve all our problems, wouldn't it? I could just go back to my old, ordinary life... hide in the distortion of the railroad tracks... go to school... work. My mom would be safe."

Raze's eyes darkened. "If it didn't happen that night, Aislen, it could have happened the next. And if you didn't develop these skills you have today, you wouldn't survive the next time. Sigmund Lange would still be out there. Troy would still be in play, still posing as the hero. You'd be even more vulnerable."

She pressed, desperate. "But you could have *your* life back, Raziel. I wouldn't have come along and ruined it."

His jaw tightened, and his eyes narrowed, burning with something fierce. "I don't want that life back, Aislen." The words were low, weighted. "We would have crossed paths eventually. If I hadn't met you then, it might have been a thousand times worse for you—and your mother." There was pain in his voice now, a deep, honest ache.

"If you hadn't been in *Demesne* that day..." He stopped, his voice smoky, his eyes glimmering. "Then you wouldn't be here now." He brushed his thumb softly along her cheek, trailing it down her throat. A current shot through her, lighting up every nerve, every cell.

"I wouldn't trade that day for this." He bent down, caught her lips with his, and kissed her. This time, it was real. Deep, open, blazing. Nothing left to hide. The room ignited with white heat.

He pulled away, but not far. "Come away with me, Aislen." His voice was a husky whisper against her mouth. "Let's do what your mother asked. Let's run. Together. I can keep you safe. I can take care of you." Both hands framed her face, his gaze boring into her. "I love you."

Aislen could taste the words on her tongue, sweet and wild and dizzying. All the inner conflict burned away, replaced by something vast and certain. Raziel claimed her mouth again, this time hungry. The visceral charge between them made the room quake with energy.

He drew his hands down her arms, pulled her close. The demand in his body matched the need in hers. She let herself fall forward, into his arms, surrendering. He slipped one arm around her waist, and his other hand tangled into her loose curls. Pulling her head to the side, he dropped his head, letting his mouth taste down the curve of her neck. She arched into him, sensation blazing through her, hungry, desperate. A part of her wanted to be ashamed for how badly she wanted him, but it was a very small part now, made infinitesimal by the fact that he wanted her just as much... maybe more.

He slowly savored her throat as he moved back up to her ear. The ragged sigh of his breath against her ear sent another scorching tremor down her spine.

"Let me feel you, Aislen," he whispered, his voice raw and husky. "Let me feel who you really are. Just this once."

Aislen understood, and she let go. She let all of the energies she'd been masking herself with fall away, not only the facades she'd been hiding in the past two days, but all the camouflage she'd been hiding behind her whole life. She dropped them all, exposing the barest essence of herself, inviting him in entirely. The space around them went ultraviolet.

He groaned, mouth finding hers, drinking her in. This time, she answered him, reaching her arms around his neck and pulling herself into his arms. The cool mercury of him wrapped around her, gently caressing every part of her at once, coaxing, stroking, teasing.

Her body responded. All the crooked and folded places of her being unfurled, blooming like a lotus, opening to him in every way. He pressed on, the low vibration of him pushing through every last barrier as he penetrated the center of her etheric being.

Quicksilver into a violet sea.

For a heartbeat that might have been forever, they existed as one current. Somewhere deep inside, something marked the moment, as if the universe had taken note.

∞

AFTERWARD, in the dark, Raze held her, listening to the slow, even breath of her sleep. He marveled at her. The miracle of Aislen Walker.

She had dismantled him, remade him, down to the last particle of his being—and he would not change a thing. What he'd always denied, fearing it would make him weaker, had made him unbreakable.

All his life, he'd told himself that control and power were strength. That building walls, sealing himself off, made him invulnerable. Emotions were weakness; love was destruction.

Yet love alone had shattered the walls and unleashed a force he could never have imagined.

Aislen had saved him. Raziel, who never believed in any god, who trusted nothing but himself, now found it impossible to believe there wasn't something out there that meant for them to find each other. Something that had decided he was worthy of her.

He looked down at her beside him, memorizing every detail of her, bare skin gleaming like silver in the moonlight, hair radiant across the pillow, face serene for the first time since he'd known her. He resisted the urge to kiss her, to start again from the beginning. There would be other chances.

He looked up at the skylights, through the fractured panes to the starlight burning beyond them. A thousand possible futures sparkled overhead. If they could survive this, if fate would only spare them a little more time, maybe one of those futures could still belong to them. With Aislen beside him, he knew that they could find one.

He wished he could stop time here—hold back whatever

waited at the edge of sunrise. He gathered her close, matched the soft rhythm of her breath, each inhale and exhale echoing in his chest, lulling him downward, downward, deeper, letting sleep swallow him whole before the dawn could reach them.

— • —

HYMN TO RESONANCE
Madness ~ Muse

— • —

THIRTY-NINE

AISLEN DRIFTED ACROSS THE NIGHT, buoyed by a weightless happiness, a fulfillment so complete it shimmered through her bones. The connection with Raziel had left her humming, every cell radiant with the pulse of rightness. She floated, wrapped in velvet blackness, gazing at the stars as they spread above her—constellations telling a story, whispering how everything had always been leading here.

She watched as the stars moved, slowly, like a ticking clock, keeping time like the constellations do. Only they were moving *backward*, not forward. Rewinding faster and faster until the stars folded in on themselves, opening a counter-clockwise vortex that twisted the whole sky before her eyes.

Her pulse quickened. This wasn't some wandering dream. This was a chance—maybe the only one—to set things right. If she could find the beginning, maybe she could undo the nightmare before it ever started.

She entered the vortex, tumbling through a tunnel of spinning dark and light, until she was spat out, breathless, into another night sky. This one was so still, so familiar, and as she hovered over her house, she knew immediately where—*and when*—she was.

She'd traveled here before with her father, and something in the weight of the darkness made her sense him nearby. She steered herself toward her mother's window, slipping through the cracked pane like memory.

Peaceful in sleep, haloed in the hush of the room. Aislen ached to run to her, to shake her awake, to whisper love and warnings and all the things she'd never said—but she remembered: this was only a Viewing, a vision, a place she could not touch. She could only watch.

She glanced around, the echo of her father's presence growing stronger, but the room was empty. She pulled herself toward her own bedroom, hoping he might be there. Her room was empty except for her own form sleeping on the bed.

It was strange, uncanny, to see her own form like this: peaceful, untouched by loss or fear. She looked almost unrecognizable. It could have been years, not days, since she had slept so soundly.

Aislen eyed the clock on the nightstand: 3:00.

The distinct memory hit her, the sharp recollection of waking up at 3:33.

This was the night—the night it all began.

Her sleeping self was about to have a dream.

Dreams didn't last long, she remembered. Seconds, or maybe forty-five minutes at most. She studied her own face, the subtle smile on her lips. Not yet, she thought. The dream hadn't arrived.

Her heart pitched. Now. This was her chance. She could stop it all now—shatter the clock, slam the door, make enough noise to break the spell. Maybe she could save her mother, save herself.

But she thought of Raziel. He would appear in that dream. If she woke herself up, they would never meet. The thought hollowed her out. She could not bear it.

Yet there must be purpose in this moment. She was here for a reason.

Her sleeping body breathed in sharply. Her eyes began to move under the lids. There wasn't much time; the dream was about to begin.

Aislen made her choice and dove in. Doing what she'd done with Thomas, she folded herself into her own consciousness and followed the dream's current into The Stratum.

Aislen recognized the landscape instantly: empty desert, desolate sky, no horizon. Only this time, Aislen saw her dream-self, barefoot and lost in a nightgown, spinning in bewilderment. So exposed, so out of place in the forbidden terrain.

Her dream-self didn't see her. Frightened eyes flickered past, searching for meaning. Aislen thought to reach out, to comfort herself, but the words stilled on her tongue.

On cue, the ground began to tremble, and the sky morphed. The atmosphere became visible with particles and atoms, dancing and rearranging themselves, evolving into something different. Aislen knew what was coming—but it was as terrifying now as the first time. Maybe more so, because memory had sharpened the edges.

Buildings assembled out of nothingness. This time, Aislen could sense the order behind the chaos: the city of *Demesne* birthing itself into place. She felt Raziel's presence in every line and angle. It exuded and pulsed with creative energy, the energy she clearly recognized as the person he had been then. But underneath, she could sense the latent energy of who he had become—a current waiting its time.

Her dream-self began to walk, leaving prints in the ashen dust. Aislen followed. She watched as she spotted herself in the broken glass, walked toward it, looked at her reflection, and tried to figure out who she was.

"Aislen," her dream-self whispered. "My name is Aislen Walker."

The vibration of her voice sent a ripple into the ethers. Aislen watched the disturbance travel, absorbed by the grid—a change radiating through the reality, an echo of her presence. She was supposed to be here. It was always meant to be.

Then, another rupture. The hologram fissured, and Preston, her father, emerged.

Aislen's breath left her. He saw her, only a few feet away, his smile flickering at the edge of being. He belonged here, too.

She watched as her dream-self studied her reflection, fingers touching the dimple in her chin.

Watched as Preston knelt beside her and whispered, "I love your little butt-chin, Buttercup."

Both Aislens felt the jolt: for the dreamer, a key unlocking the past; for the watcher, the certainty that her father was orchestrating this moment.

He straightened, pulled away from her dream-self, and looked at *her*. A thought sharp as a beam of light echoed in her mind: *Read the letter, Aislen.* Then he stepped back into the grid, the portal sealing behind him.

Aislen reeled—watched as her dream-self did the same in an effort to make sense of it all. She knew now that they both were supposed to be here. They both belonged here, but for what? Was she supposed to leave—to read the letter right now?

Before she could decide, footsteps rang out. Both selves heard it: dream-Aislen dove for cover behind a car. Aislen herself froze, torn between the instinct to hide and the impossible gravity of Raziel's approach.

Dream-Aislen sprang into action, hiding herself behind a car. Aislen froze.

Would he see her? Would he feel her, sense the truth? She tried to move, but the pull of him was inescapable. Already her world was veering into a new orbit, one she could not resist or break.

She saw the four of them: Raziel at the lead with Blake and two holographic drones.

Raziel raised his fist, and the whole group halted, dropped into a defensive, crouched, predatory readiness. He scanned the street, already aware of her presence before following her footprints.

He lifted his visor, and Aislen's heart stuttered. Of course. Their meeting here was the fulcrum of everything that followed. If not for this, he would never become the man he was today, the man she was in love with.

The emotion rose up, fierce and terrible. She loved him, even knowing what he was about to do; she loved him as he was and as he would become. Everything that was about to happen had to happen—for him, for her, for change.

Raziel prowled toward the car, tracking her path. At the end of the street, a new shimmer appeared in the grid: Scott Parrish showing up in what he thought was only a dangerous game. Oblivious that it was a deadly one.

Aislen's heart hammered. Now, Aislen thought. She could jump out of the dream and wake herself. Maybe enough had happened to ensure Raziel would still come to her.

But again, she stopped. If she left, Blake would kill his father—and if her dream-self wasn't here, Blake would succeed in killing himself. She couldn't do it. There must be another way.

Scott's approach distracted Raziel; the visor snapped down, the weapon raised. The whole team dropped to their knees, guns trained on Parrish.

Blake dropped his weapon, lips parting for a reply.

"Blake. Carry on," Raziel intoned, a frequency in the command that was deep and hypnotic.

Blake nodded once.

Scott Parrish turned his fury on Raziel. "I don't know who you think you are, to assume you have more power over Blake than I do. You have some fucking nerve! I demand that you let him leave here with me and never contact him again."

"That isn't going to happen," Raziel replied, in a tone Aislen recognized; uncaring, apathetic, and in control.

Aislen felt the shape of what was coming, saw in a flash how she could intervene.

She hurled herself into the group, appearing at Blake's side.

"Then I will be forced to report you to the authorities," Parrish threatened.

Raziel didn't even blink. "Blake. Carry on."

Blake's hand moved; he drew the gun, sighted the barrel between his father's eyes.

You can miss, Aislen whispered to him, sending the suggestion in the same tonal frequency as Raziel's orders.

No, I can't, came the reply. But it wasn't Blake's voice.

It was Sigmund Lange's.

Cold shock tore through her. Blake's face twisted in a smile that wasn't his. Pain spiked through her skull as Sigmund pressed in, cruel and precise.

Time stopped.

Oh, Poppet. Pain lanced behind her eyes, a migraine made of static. The pressure built until the inside of her skull felt like it might split apart under his frequency. *It is such a pleasure to know you are here. I have so many plans for you, you have no idea.*

Aislen gathered her energy, amplified it, and slammed it into Sigmund—a burst so powerful it threw him from her mind and knocked Blake off-balance. His wrist snapped sideways as the gun fired.

Time snapped back to motion, and Aislen was ripped from the Viewing just as the bullet met its target.

FORTY

THE GRID TORE apart like paper, and Aislen was yanked out of the Viewing—out of her own past—like a hooked fish. She didn't see where the bullet went. She only heard a blood-curdling scream as it smashed into its target. She felt sick to her stomach from the vertigo of her uncontrollable free fall and the sick twist of dread.

All she could think of was Raziel. That she might have changed the course of the bullet so that it hit him instead filled her with agonizing grief.

Her descent gained speed, and the darkness grew thick and murky. Maybe the bullet had hit *her*, her dream-self, hiding behind the car. Maybe she had altered the course of her own life, and this was what death was like.

Had she just undone her own life, or Raziel's?

Had she ripped the thread that held them together?"

A deafening roar filled her ears, a crushing din of black noise with the high-pitched whine of a tape rewinding. The sound wasn't just in her head—it was time itself convulsing, grinding backward through her neurons. Memories of the past week were being overwritten by the new reality she'd just created. Her bones felt like they were turning inside out, marrow twisting with the pull of reverse time.

She fought back, pushing against the uncompromising current that clawed through her mind, erasing futures, unmaking choices, deleting her from her own history.

She grabbed hold of her last moment of cognizance: of Raziel above her, wrapped around her, within her. The heat that had consumed her as they moved together. The sight of his piercing blue eyes locked with hers, the taste of his lips, skin, and sweat, the sound of his voice when he whispered, "I love you, Aislen Walker," as they ascended together into a dazzling array of color and light.

Aislen battled the darkness in a tug of war for the memory, but the darkness knew a weak spot. She had never said "I love you" back. She had given herself to him body, heart, soul... but had withheld those three words. Raziel would never know how she felt about him.

"Please!" she screamed at the vicious void. "I'm sorry! I know I shouldn't have disrupted time! But please just let me keep this one memory!"

The void dropped her. She landed hard on something cold and craggy. Moisture sprayed her face. The crashing noise remained, though it was diminished. The blackness that blinded her lifted, and she was standing on the jagged black outcropping of hardened lava rocks, stretching out into an endless expanse of sea. It churned violently, a cauldron, deep and uninviting. The sky was the angry void, hovering over her, prepared to devour her at any moment.

Loneliness overwhelmed her. She was drowning in it as if it were the ocean swallowing her whole. She might as well jump into the tempestuous waves and let them relieve her of this misery. Life was not worth living this way. She wailed a primal scream, a final revolt. But the wind and the waves ate it up as their own.

Suddenly, warmth coiled around her like an embrace—his embrace—his arms shielding her from the cold. In this space of death, she realized she had known this presence forever. He had been there throughout time, always protecting, always loving, a twin flame that made her feel whole.

She could feel him now behind her, his resonant energy undeniable. She turned to face him, to say the words "I love you, too," so he would know and never forget.

But he wasn't there. Behind her, only rock, the cliff's teeth grinning back.

Aislen had lost him. The void in the sky evaporated, taking away her last memory.

∞

AISLEN STARTLED, opening her eyes into pitch blackness yet again. A different stormy sky was above her now, flashing with lightning and rolling with thunder. It roiled within the circular glass portal of a skylight. She was in the temple, lying naked and exposed on the tatami mat. The negative ions of the storm caressed her skin, prickling her with a chill, but a warmth radiated beside her and blanketed her with a protective heat. She turned her head to see the back of a naked man beside her.

She was in the temple, but it was different. She and Raziel had arrived on a clear night, not a stormy one, and the shrine was dark now, not glowing with the candlelight they had made love to. She looked at the back of the man next to her, wondering if it was Raziel or someone else.

She had woken up in the dream temple before... on a stormy day... with Troy. Was this that day again? She thought of what Raziel had said could happen if she altered the past. That she might still think of Troy as the hero.

Was that what had happened? Had she killed Raziel? Had she changed her life and lost something that had become invaluable to her?

Aislen was afraid to look, afraid to see who she was lying next to, but realized she still had all her memories: of Raziel, Troy, Sigmund, San Francisco... all of them. Maybe she hadn't changed the course of reality after all.

She quietly sat up so as not to disturb the sleeping man. She carefully moved around to the front of him and waited for her eyes to adjust so she could see his face. It was Raziel.

Her knees went weak with relief. He was here. She hadn't killed him. And she hadn't died, either. She looked around at the floor of the temple, strewn with all their clothes that they had ripped off in a fit of passion. That had happened, too.

She looked toward the door where their shoes were still in the places that they left them, and the backpack was still sitting next to his shoes. They were still together and on the run.

Did he still love her? Like he'd said? Had she changed that? Aislen felt a chill wash over her as a gust of wind blew through the cracks of the door. She reached over and grabbed Raziel's sweatshirt off the floor and slipped it on. Her pockets were full.

She reached into her left pocket and pulled out a letter: a sealed envelope with "Aislen" written on the front in her father's handwriting. But she'd had two. Her mother's letter wasn't there. And she could have sworn she had put them both in her right pocket.

Oh no, what did I change?

In the distance, she heard the faint cry of an approaching

train being carried toward her on the wind. *Read the letter, now!* She could hear her father's voice within its wail.

She moved under the skylight, carefully opened the envelope, and unfolded the letter.

DEAREST AISLEN,

I was hoping this day would never come. I was hoping my premonitions could be avoided. But each one has fallen into place up to this point, and like dominoes, I know that the rest will follow as designed.

Sometimes we make choices that can lead us to a different reality. And sometimes our choices make no difference.

Fate can be more powerful than Free Will when she wants to be.

And Destiny is a command directive.

Raziel has a destiny.

And you have a destiny as well, Aislen.

Unfortunately, they are independent of each other.

I have seen the future. If my visions are correct, you will alter it somewhat... but Fate and Destiny will not be denied.

If Raziel goes to Australia with you, he dies.

If you run away with him, he still dies... and many more people will die as well: your mother, Blake Parrish, Robert Mathis, and eventually, you.

I'm sorry, Buttercup, you didn't alter that.

I cannot guide you in the choice you make, but there are some things we must do on our own, and no one can save us.

Always remember...

Love travels a straight line.

It is the only constant. And it is eternal.

Forever,

Dad

AISLEN LOOKED up from the letter toward Raziel sleeping soundly beside her. Her heart broke at the thought of not being with him, but shattered at the thought of him dying because of her. Aislen wanted to wake him; wake him and tell him how deeply she has come to love him, wake him and have him tell her that he truly loves her. She reached out to touch his face, but something heavy fell out of the other sweatshirt pocket.

She looked down at the mat. Two dolls looked up at her. She had left the effigies behind when they ran from the warehouse in San Francisco.

But here they were, in a different reality.

And one of them had changed—changed in a way that told her exactly what she must do.

Her path would split from his.

She quietly moved next to Raziel, absorbing the heat of him, the intoxicating current still humming between them. She pressed her lips to his hair, breathing him in.

"If I didn't tell you before," she whispered into his sleep, "I love you, Raziel."

The wind outside rose like a train, carrying her father's words.

Love travels a straight line.

GLISSANDO

Into Dust ~ Mazzy Star

FORTY-ONE

A PIERCING howl wailed against his ear, reaching down into the depths of his delta wave state. Raze had cycled himself down to 1 hertz to recover—mind and body—for the long journey ahead with Aislen.

The wail penetrated again, demanding consciousness immediately. Maybe Aislen was having another nightmare, he thought, as he tried to cycle up the ladder. It wasn't easy to come out of such a deep sleep space and gather your five senses back. He only allowed himself to go into Delta because he knew they were safe. If Sigmund and Troy were headed to Australia now, Infinium wouldn't be able to track his new signature frequency. Their current pool of talent wasn't that advanced.

Raziel continued swimming up from the depths... 2 hertz... 3 hertz... 4. Static wrinkled through his brain, a tremor shaking his neural lattice—what he imagined a stroke might feel like. He dropped back down, treading consciousness at 3 hertz. He felt a sizzling thread of it zap into his hippocampus, and from delta watched as the memory of

Demesne and the killing of Scott Parrish glitched into a different memory.

Instead of a bullet penetrating Parrish's skull, it slammed into his shoulder; not a lethal blow. Scott bellowed in agony, falling backward to the ground, writhing in the ash.

A woman's horrified scream rose from behind the car, and Aislen stood up. Blake yelled out from the left, "Dad!"

None of this was how it really went down.

Raze felt the sharp voltage squirm through his memory banks. He ran to Scott Parrish, placed a hand on his head to send an option-lock frequency into his brain, to erase his neural pattern and push him out of *Demesne*. Then he ran to Blake, grabbed hold of his skull, and deresonated him as well.

Then he turned to Aislen. She was standing in a night-gown, covered in ash. Raziel felt the connection even in the new memory; recognized the danger she presented to him in an instant. The electric worm in his brain manipulated his memory centers, trying to change the story he knew, the one where he deresonated her, into a new story. This was a Raziel who wouldn't take the risk of feeling emotions; he lifted his gun, not to de-rez Aislen but to *kill* her.

Raze dove down—down, down, down—into the cold depths of consciousness, coming to a screeching halt at .2 hertz. He hovered there, on the precipice of death, shutting down all other brain activity, denying the memory-seeking charge access to any more of his memories.

He realized in that moment that Aislen had gone back to that night, and she'd changed the timeline somehow.

Raziel lingered in low delta until he was sure he could manage the ascent, keeping his past memories intact while absorbing whatever new memories the shifted timeline had created. He prepared himself to face the truth: that he had killed Aislen Walker and would wake up in his own bed back in San Francisco, overcome with grief that he had killed the woman he loved.

The howling on the surface intensified, and Raze could feel his physical body shaking. It was time to face the present and whatever it was in the now. He slowly scaled the frequencies, clinging to the one rope of memory he couldn't bear to lose: Aislen in his arms in the candlelight and the afterglow.

The howl grew louder; a deep rumble vibrated through his flesh and bones. He held onto Aislen as other memories snapped into place. The trembling increased, like a powerful earthquake. It felt like the walls of his room were going to disintegrate.

As he forced himself up into Alpha, a new memory came into his head.

It was her voice, clear and embedded with emotion.

"If I didn't tell you before, I love you, Raziel."

His breath hitched, sharp as a static snap. The words weren't sound but current, racing through his nerves until his skin prickled with heat.

It was Aislen, imprinting the thought as well as the feeling into his head as he slept. He could feel her presence all around him as his pulse slammed in his chest—slow at first, then double-timed, hammering against his ribs as his body pushed into Beta.

He was awake—in the temple—tatami mats cool beneath him, incense ghosts lingering in the damp air. The faint rattle of shoji screens answered the storm outside.

Raziel searched the darkness for Aislen as his eyes adjusted, but she wasn't there. He looked to the door. Her shoes were gone, along with the backpack.

Had she ever been there?

Raziel felt the mat around him in the darkness for any trace of her energy having been next to him, any proof that she wasn't only alive in another reality, or just in his memories.

His hands found something. Actually, two things. He lifted them up.

The dolls.

The Aislen doll, still all in black.

But the Raziel doll *had* changed. Naked. Painted entirely white. Feathered wings on his back.

The Night We Met ~ Lord Huron

FORTY-TWO

AISLEN WAS FLYING AGAIN. Only this time in a plane, through a real sky, and wide awake. She gazed out the window of the small jet. Gigantic puffs of pure white clouds drifted lazily by. From up here, they looked edible, like meringues floating on a plate of pristine Tiffany blue. It was understandable why sages throughout history depicted the sky as heaven. From this height, the world felt holy and dangerously easy to linger in.

Below: ochre, rust, and blotches of green that almost looked black from up here, a hard-edged opposite to the perfection above. The view looked exactly like the map her father had drawn as a child. It looked exactly like The Stratum. It looked like Hell.

She slammed the window shade down, hard, as the plane kept leaping forward, eating up hours and latitude at five hundred miles an hour, shoving her toward the future.

She didn't bother shifting frequencies anymore. Why should she? Everyone knew where she was headed. Sigmund knew—or was betting on it. Raziel knew, except she'd left him, taken the money, left him stranded. Infinium and The 8? They only knew she existed. Any frequency they found of her would be that of a girl she'd left behind days ago. Aislen had changed. No one really knew her now. Aislen wondered if she even knew herself anymore.

The amulet purred against her sternum, a constant undertone the way jet engines were—there but ignored. It had watched her unravel, helped when it chose, and stayed silent when she chose violence. It never complained once, never warned her to stop, just let her continue down this destructive path alone.

Except once, when she'd almost gone to San Francisco Airport. The amulet's opinion had jolted through her, a full stop. No. It sent her to San Jose, and then went dead silent again until Los Angeles.

Aislen had no idea where she was supposed to go in Australia. All she knew was that the continent was massive, and finding her mother would be like finding a needle in a haystack. The map her father had given her was useless—a child's picture, not a plan. To Aislen, it was art. Only Raziel could read it, could turn it into directions. She had been counting on him to get them there.

The memory of the dolls in the temple—of Raziel as an angel, naked and winged—flashed through her like a verdict. It read as an omen, a warning of the cost: that he might die with her at his side. Leaving him was a brutal kindness. She'd done it to save him.

At LAX, she bought travel clothes, a new bag, a travel atlas. In the bathroom stall, she hovered the amulet over the map, pleading with it. It had no interest in the obvious, pointed to Brisbane, not Sydney, then hushed for nearly a day, content to wait. Only when she arrived in Brisbane did it guide her to Alice Springs before drifting into its usual, indifferent purr. The hum should have been reassuring. It was anything but.

She lifted it off her chest and held it in her palm. It looked the same as it had days ago when she'd awoken from her time walk to Sigmund's house, in which she had watched him murder Astrid. Five stones dead black, four lit up so fiercely it almost hurt to look. Sapphire, diamond, amethyst, and in the middle—the impossible fire of the center gemstone, with colors that couldn't be of this earth.

The pendant hadn't changed one bit, even though she'd changed the timeline. That was something. If the stones mapped what she'd lost, then her actions in *Demesne* hadn't cost her anyone else. Her mother was still alive, and she could still save her. And even though she had left him behind, Raziel was still alive. If she did this right, she could save her mother and find her way back to him.

Aislen pulled out the new map that she bought in Brisbane. This one had more details of the region. Australia was huge. It was the size of America with a fraction of the people. Towns spread out like specks in a void.

She hovered the amulet over Alice Springs, got a trill of certainty.

As she followed the main highway north, away from the airport and toward the city. The amulet sparked in her fingertips. No.

She circled, methodical, until the pendant vibrated again and led her south, then west, the song growing stronger as the road stretched on.

Uluru.

Her father's purple crayon was a dot on the map. The amethyst on the pendant matched it.

It would be a long drive, five to six hours, but she still had time on her great-grandfather's clock. Whether a week to him meant five days or seven, whether it was by the calendar or the watch, he would wait. He needed her. And there would be no deal, no compromise. He would let her mother go, or nothing.

Aislen checked the watch on her wrist. Raziel's watch. It vibrated with the same promise as the amulet, but unlike the amulet, the watch brought her comfort. It kept her steady, reminded her what she was capable of, why she was fighting.

He'd taught her everything. About control, about how survival meant controlling yourself. About love and how nothing else could power justice or fairness. And about turning all your strengths into weapons.

She'd need it all, every bit, for what was coming.

The jet engines dropped to a growling bass; the plane began its descent into Australia's Red Centre. As soon as the wheels hit earth, she'd rent a four-wheel drive, load up on supplies, steal a gun, find Sigmund Lange, and blow his fucking brains out.

The amulet scorched her palm, sudden and vicious.

Oh! You care? You got something to say about that? Well, fuck you!

Rage burned in her like spilled gasoline. She pressed her nails into the pendant until metal bit skin, watched the other passengers shifting uneasily, made sure her voice was quiet so only she could hear the animal inside.

She had been used. She had been violated. She had been imprisoned. Every choice stolen. Every future twisted against her. Not Raziel's fault—all Sigmund. Him, his schemes, his monstrous plans, the menace to everyone she cared about.

And her father? She hated him, too, for ever pulling her into this deplorable reality. He'd awoken her. If not for him, The Stratum would have faded like any other nightmare. And the amulet? It wasn't any better. It hadn't protected her. It only sang when it wanted to and only led her further and further down this road, a road that only led to ruin.

She tore the chain free. The pendant skittered across her palm—hot as a coal—and she shoved it, still sparking, into Raziel's backpack. The clasp snapped shut with a small, cold click.

Fuck Fate. Fuck Destiny. She was done with all of it. She would destroy Sigmund Lange, every piece and echo of him, if it was the last thing she did.

❦

FIGHT SONG
Unbreakable ~ Fireflight

❦

FORTY-THREE

RED DUST, green scrub. Horizon in every direction, empty and endless. The copper-cast sun hung behind a haze of rust, broiling, flattening everything beneath it. This place made The Stratum feel like Disneyland.

The clerk at the rental car company insisted that Aislen not leave right away.

"You won't be makin' it to Uluru before dark," he'd said, voice somewhere between warning and resignation. "Don't be drivin' those roads at night. Roos, cattle, even camels—they come out after dark. They'll take that roo bar in a heartbeat. Do yourself a favour, 'avago early in the mornin'. She'll be right."

Aislen smiled, pocketed the keys, and turned her back on him. She headed south, straight down the Stuart Highway. The emptiness hit instantly, vast and untouched as if humanity had never come this way. No houses, no stations, no people at all—a blank, sun-blasted sweep. For an hour, she drove and saw no one. The only kangaroos appeared as carcasses on the shoulder, reminders, warnings. Heat pressed in through the glass; the AM radio sputtered static, offering no company. At last, a roadhouse appeared, brittle and improbable. She filled up, grabbed supplies, and tried not to wilt under the owner's gaze.

He was grizzled, unimpressed. "Ya on a walkabout alone there, Yank?"

She bristled. She didn't need this, not after everything. If he knew where she'd been, he'd know she could handle the Outback. She dropped a shadow of Raziel's dark energy into the space between them, just enough to make herself clear.

Back off.

He got it; shrugged, hands up. "Eh, 'ave it your way then."

He offered a room, went through the routine lecture about night driving. She passed. Cooler driving now, she told herself. The faster she found her mother, the better. She pulled the amulet out of her bag and checked her map with it. It had calmed down and seemed to be fine with her pushing south, even though the sun began its slow fall.

Halfway to the next roadhouse, Aislen regretted her decision. As soon as the sun touched the horizon, a mob of roos appeared, big as men and just as reckless. No cartoon charm, no gentle hopping: these were wild, unpredictable, crash-test nightmares. They eyed Aislen's car as if they were judging whether or not to play chicken. She slowed, inching along, more afraid of crashing and surviving than of any sudden death. Out here, stranded, broken down, there would be no one. Nothing.

And then the sun vanished. The night here was not ordinary darkness. It was absolute, primordial. No moon, no glow from distant towns; only the electric teeth of her headlights, fighting and losing against the pitch.

Thankfully, the next roadhouse was only a short distance away, and she pulled into the lot with a tremendous sigh of relief. Next time, she'd listen to the locals.

She took a room, then slipped to the tavern for food and to

collect local gossip—and to find a gun. She wouldn't get her mother away from Sigmund and Troy without some firepower. A bar in the Outback would be the likeliest place.

Not wanting any more scrutiny from the locals or other travelers, Aislen read the vibe of the room before stepping inside. It was a stale mixture of the Old West meets apocalypse, tin roof, battered wood, air thick with isolation and suspicion. Aislen charged her space to match so she could blend in without anyone noticing. Just another shadow at the edge of the night.

She picked a corner table, sat with her back to the wall, and watched. There were travelers and a few locals. This was probably the only watering hole for another hundred miles. She scanned the walls, looking for a gun rack. In America, there'd be a gun rack behind the bar, clear as day. But not here. It wasn't going to be that easy.

Aislen remembered how Raziel had taught her to find her passport: close her eyes, reach for it, let it reveal itself. It wasn't magic; it was technique, practiced until reflex. She did it now, picturing the weapon she wanted.

A handgun would be best, but out here, probably rare, useless. A shotgun would be more cumbersome, but it was probably something a local would have. She conjured its shape and heft, how it would sound, and let the thought go, allowing the signature to wander the sparse crowd.

Two sparks leapt out. One: a heavyset man, VB cans lined up on the bar. The other: an older woman with a silver ponytail. Both matched the pulse of the shotgun.

Aislen tuned into the woman's frequency first and saw a shotgun—loaded, beside her bed. She traced the woman's frequency to find where she lived, her mind seeing a homestead five miles down the road. Aislen could take her if it came to a fight, but the risk was sharp; ten miles round trip, in the dark, through roo country, could end her.

She slid to the man's frequency. Saw the shotgun, locked in a cabinet by the door. She tracked his energy and saw that he lived nearby, on the outpost property. Judging by the empties on the bar, he'd be slow to notice if anything changed. Less risk. She fixed his resonance in her mind and slipped out the back before anyone could notice. If she did it now, she could get back before he got home.

Using his energy as a compass, Aislen followed it toward the far edge of the property. She ran, letting his energy guide her down the dirt path for half a mile. His place: a battered modular trailer. There were no lights on, but just in case, she raised her left hand to the house like she'd watched Raziel do and felt for any other signatures inside, like a wife he'd left at home or a child in bed. Nothing. But something outside, on the porch, flickered in the field.

It felt her too and charged. Barreling out of the gloom, breath huffing before its body showed—a pit bull. Unchained. Aislen wrapped herself tight in the man's frequency. The dog stopped, head cocking, tail wagging, trying to make sense of her. She didn't look or smell like his master. Aislen increased the intensity, holding the man's frequency like a leash, and the dog fell into heel beside her, following her to the back door.

Tentatively, she tried the door handle. It was unlocked. Of course! No one needed locks out here. She stepped in, found the narrow gun cabinet exactly where she'd seen it in her mind. No time to marvel. She opened the cabinet, grabbed the shot-gun, jammed a pocket full of shells, and slipped back out, retracing her steps.

The dog followed, happy for the company, tail high. At the edge of the property, she stopped. *Stay,* she told it, and the animal slunk back to the porch, disappointed.

Aislen broke into a sprint the last stretch, not stopping till she was back in her room. She tossed the shotgun and ammo onto the bed, heart hammering. She'd just broken into a stranger's house. Stolen a weapon. She tried to wrap her head around it, but the facts were undeniable: she was out here, in this wild, still-untamed country, doing things she would never have imagined.

What was she turning into? She didn't like the answer. Her moral compass felt off. But her mother was everything. The rest had to wait.

Tomorrow was the day. She'd kept her mind off it, boxed it away so fear wouldn't cloud her senses. She'd let herself think about it in the morning, when she was closer to the rendezvous point. Then she would stop, tune into her mother, and follow her signal line to where Sigmund and Troy had her. She would find her mother. And kill Sigmund Lange.

She stepped outside, needing air. The sky caught her. She stared up—and it was as if the world had cracked open, flooding overhead with a billion points of light. The Milky Way cut the night in half, thick and bright, a river of stars she'd only ever seen in pictures. Here, now, it was real. It made her feel small, but alive.

She wandered to a clearing and lay down, letting the field of stars settle over her. Just like the dream: the constellations circling, indifferent and unstoppable, marking time. Nothing would slow the turning.

She finally allowed her mind to wander, to the one thing she had blocked out, out of necessity. Raziel. He was out there, under the same sky. She let herself remember the energy of him: the brush of his hand, the way his frequency had tangled with hers, fused until she didn't know where one ended and the other began. The power of it infused her soul. The love she carried for him burned in the core of her.

She understood him now—how and why he became who he was. He'd done it for survival, for protection. Maybe it had taken over, maybe the power had seduced him, but he'd tamed it. Used it for her. Helped her become this: someone ready to save and protect the ones she loved: her mother and Raziel.

He was probably angry with her right now for leaving. But as much as she needed him, wanted him—she would never forgive herself if he died because of her.

She allowed her gaze to wander across the firmament. A billion stars, each a different celestial soul. What were the odds that she and Raziel would have ever found each other naturally? None. It took all this. It took this nightmare to bring them together.

Far off, a million light-years away, Aislen found one particular star—a wild, living thing, flaring in a multitude of colors, like the center stone in her amulet. She blinked, and suddenly the amulet pattern appeared in the sky as clearly as if she were holding it in her hand.

Their very own constellation. Fate and Destiny.

Tomorrow, she promised herself. *I will end it. Finish this, and come back to this guiding light—back to Raziel.*

FORTY-FOUR

I SMELL LIKE BACON, was his first thought as he started waking up.

Jesus Christ, how many days had it been since he'd showered? Two? Three? And running around Sabine's house chasing phantoms didn't do his body odor any favors. He really needed to get it under control pronto—he had things to take care of today, like filing a missing person's report and putting out an APB.

But the bed. Oh, the bed was a revelation. Familiar, cradling, the worn sheets and the way the mattress yielded in just the right spot—it was as if his own shape had been carved into it, a hollow of exhaustion and need. It felt better than any night of sleep he could remember, a kind of bliss that pooled in his bones, settling them after years of unrest.

Another whiff of pork, more powerful than before. It was too much; he needed to part ways with the bed and hit the shower.

Reluctantly, Mathis rolled over and forced himself upright, bracing for pain or protest. After the night he'd had—a full-throttle heart incident, his pulse battling through chaos, then the manic chase and fist fight with a ghost—he expected his body to punish him. But it didn't. He felt spectacular, every limb charged, every cell humming with life. He felt better than he had in years, maybe ever.

But why was he naked?

He never slept naked.

Mathis looked down, expecting to find the rumpled hospital gown, but found his jeans, his favorite karaoke shirt, and his tightie-whities instead, discarded as if he'd torn them off in a hurry. He wasn't wearing those yesterday.

Mathis squinted his eyes at the other shape lying next to the clothes.

A black bra.

Mathis didn't wear black bras.

His brain felt like it was short-circuiting. He looked around to make sure he was in his own room, in his own house, and hadn't stumbled into a stranger's house by accident in the night.

No... there was his chair, his dresser, his hallway, every detail known and mapped. But something had shifted—something was moving through it.

He heard a faint sizzling sound and smelled eggs. It was coming from down the hall. A flicker of static ran across his skin.

Someone was in his house!

His throat went dry. Mathis slipped on his jeans, rough denim against bare skin. The sensation was strange, uncomfortable, but he'd worn worse in stakeouts and standoffs. He crept down the hall, each step measured, the hush of anticipation in the air. Beyond the edge of the wall, a woman's voice hummed softly, threading through the metallic clatter of utensils. He eased himself around the corner.

And there she was: a woman in his kitchen, haloed in early

light and the shimmer of frying oil. Her hair was long, falling down her back like a crimson waterfall. She wore his t-shirt... and nothing else. The hem stopped just short of the curve of her perfect ass. He could not mistake it; there was no ambiguity, no doubt. He'd recognize that ass anywhere.

She turned around and spotted him staring at her from around the corner with his mouth gaping wide in shock and awe. She smiled.

"Good morning, Robert. I made breakfast... just how you like it," Sabine said.

His breath stuttered; the world narrowed to the sound of her saying his name.

He understood, all at once, with the clarity of someone stepping into sunlight: he had died.

And this was heaven.

NEW MEASURE / TIME SHIFT
Love Is Alive ~ Gary Wright

CRESCENDO

Killing Moon ~ Roman Remains

FORTY-FIVE

THE RED ROCK rose out of the desert in front of her as the sun's early rays blazed over her shoulder. At first, just a small button on the flat landscape, it swelled into a colossal wonder as she drew closer on her trek west. In the first light, the silhouettes and colors that played across it were magical. Aislen could not deny the resonant pull; she could feel it in her bones. It was like a heartbeat, a pulse that throbbed persistently across the landscape, beckoning her closer. It felt like the whole of Earth's frequency originated here and radiated out. The closer she got, the stronger it pulled.

But even as the rock loomed, she knew Sigmund would never bring her mother here. Not with tourists crawling all over it. Too risky, even for him. Still, Uluru was on the map. A place to begin. Now that she was here, however, she felt lost. Sigmund could be anywhere in these wilds with her mother, and there was only one way for Aislen to figure it out.

Veering off the paved road, she followed rough dirt tracks until the grasslands opened into a hidden clearing and killed the engine. She fished out the amulet and the map, not in the mood to listen to the pendant bicker when, in her core, she knew what had to be done.

Aislen rolled the map out on her lap and hovered the amulet over the center. Letting it drift over the lines and landmarks, she waited for the amulet's frequency to align with Uluru. It reverberated resolutely in the space where the amethyst stone was set. Once she had her bearings, she dragged the amulet to the spot that lined up with her current location. Instantly, the amulet's frequency shifted, attuning to her—a hum that matched the diamond, both on the map and in her hand.

Without meaning to, she'd stopped in the very patch her father had drawn all those years before. He'd seen it. He'd known she would end up here.

Aislen tuned her focus, dialing into her mother's energy, pulling up the signature from her own memories. She braced for the amulet's pull, thinking it would drag her to the varicolored stone on the map.

Nothing. The amulet went dead.

Her chest locked; panic flared. *Was her mother already gone?*

The amulet seared her fingertips. *No.*

She started over, realigning the stone above Uluru. The hum sprang back, strong as ever. She traced it to where she sat. Again, it clicked into alignment. She reached for her mother's vibration once more, and again the amulet went silent.

Dread landed in her belly, a brutal blow.

She isn't here, she thought. The amulet purred to life.

I shouldn't have come. The amulet died.

"Fuuuuuuuck!" The scream ripped out of her as she hurled the amulet and threw herself out of the car. She stormed through the baked red sand, head back, unleashing a primal scream into the morning heat.

Sigmund didn't have her mother. It was a change she had made in her Time Walk—the only thing that had driven her to this goddamn place, and her mother wasn't even here.

Relief should've come. It meant her mother was safe, probably at home, worried about where her daughter had disappeared to. But instead, it left her more shaken, set her nerves jangling.

She wasn't just lost in the desert. She was lost in the broken machinery of time. The old sequence of events was gone, but she'd been acting on those memories. Not on what had been overwritten. She didn't even know what had been overwritten. A five-day gap in history, and the whole shape of the world had changed underneath her feet.

Aislen screamed out again until her throat burned as hot as the blazing sky. She was raw with fury, splashing from Sigmund to her father to Raziel, a tide of rage for anyone who had twisted her reality. But most of all, for herself. Stupid. Blind. Playing a game she didn't know the rules to. She was meant to stay a small-town girl, insulated in a bubble of obliviousness. She wasn't meant for this life.

She collapsed in the dirt, sobbing, letting the tears burn down her face into the red grit. She let every drop of weakness and stupidity drain out of her. This would be the last time she'd cry. This would be the last time she would be played. There would be hell to pay for the misery she'd been put through. Starting with Sigmund Lange.

Behind her, gravel crunched. Tires, slow and steady, moving up the track. Of course! If her father had mapped her here, someone else was about to arrive. This wasn't just about her collapse; he hadn't drawn a map for that. She pulled herself up, wiped the tears away, and returned to the truck. The shotgun came up easy in her hands, as did the racking of a shell into the chamber.

Whoever was coming to meet her right now had picked the wrong time. She wasn't going down without a fight.

Dust twisted across the plain, an ochre twister closing fast. As it braked to a halt behind her car, Aislen leveled the shotgun, aimed for the windshield, finger ready on the trigger. As she braced for the kick of the gun, the driver's door jerked open.

Raziel vaulted out.

He sprinted toward her, catching her just as her knees broke, and pulled her hard into his arms. The relief was blinding. She sobbed against his chest, clinging to him, realizing how much she'd needed this, needed him. He held her, kissed the top of her head, breath shuddering with emotion.

"God damn it, woman!" His voice was gritty. "I never thought I would see you again."

"I'm so sorry, Raziel." She fastened her grip, letting herself anchor in his arms, knowing now that he wasn't just important, he was everything.

She tipped her face up, confessing in a rush. "I changed time—changed it bad. I woke up, and everything was different. Then I found my dad's note, and it said you shouldn't come with me... that if you did you would die. And the dolls were different. You weren't in a suit anymore. You were an angel, all white, with wings."

Raziel pressed her head to his lips, sealing her forehead with a kiss. "I know. I saw them. And I saw how history was shifting as I woke up. So I knew what had happened. I gathered all my hidden resources, followed the map already in my head, and I traced your resonance here."

There was no judgment. No anger. No "I told you so." Just Raziel, holding her, like she'd never left him at the temple, never abandoned him.

His thumb lingered at the fine hair behind her ear, and the simple, reverent way he memorized that small place told her everything—she mattered to him in a way that reshaped the world.

She met his eyes again. "My mom isn't here. She didn't fall for it."

He nodded. "I know. She's with Sgt. Mathis. She's safe."

A fresh wave of relief made her lightheaded. "What else?"

"Mathis never had the game, never entered *Demesne*, never got blasted. And Scott Parrish is alive. You knocked the trajectory off; it hit him in the shoulder, not the head. So Blake still has his father."

"Oh my God. That's... that's amazing." She could barely breathe. Her change had made things better. The risk had been worth it.

"So I didn't need to leave," she said, stunned. "I never needed to come here at all."

Raziel's eyes went dark. "No, you did. Your father saw how this timeline would go, Aislen. He knew you'd change it. That's why he drew the map."

He let her go and went to her truck. He came back with the map and amulet, slipped the amulet back around her neck, and pressed it to her chest. "Keep this on. You're going to need it."

She looked down at the pendant, then back to him, not understanding.

He spread the map between them. "You need to get to this spot." He tapped the glittering patch that matched the varicolored gem on her pendant. "Your dad will meet you there, take you someplace safe."

"Why? If I fixed everything, why do I still have to go?"

Raziel's gaze softened, but there was a death-row gravity behind it. "Because you didn't fix everything, Aislen." He brushed her hair out of her eyes and traced the contours of her cheek. Aislen had a distinct feeling that he was memorizing her face. "The 8 still know you exist. In this timeline, *Troy* got to them first. And he's been ordered to hunt you down. Hunt *us* down."

"Because I told him about the dream?"

Raziel shook his head, "No. Because Lange did."

Aislen sucked in her breath. Raziel pressed on. "Before you ever clocked in at work, Lange told Troy and pulled him straight into it. Troy ran straight to Grant and The 8. In this timeline, I was on the run that same day. Hunting you. To kill you, for wrecking my life. But it was never supposed to play out that way. You and I are destiny, too."

Another red cyclone appeared on the distant horizon, moving steadily toward them. Aislen felt an intense shudder of fear turn in her stomach.

Aislen felt fear coil in her stomach.

Raziel was all certainty now. "You need to go, Aislen. Go to the place on the map. Your dad will come for you there. But you need to leave, now. I'll take care of this."

She looked at the oncoming storm, then back at him. "Come with me! We can go together."

Raziel shook his head. "No, I can't. That is not my path."

"Why wouldn't it be your path? If you and I are 'destiny'? That doesn't make sense."

"Our destiny was for me to protect you, get you to the point where you could protect yourself. You're there, Aislen. It's time for you to go."

He shoved the map into her hands. Pain wracked his face, but he was determined.

"But you can still do that! Protect me until I get there!"

He glanced over his shoulder—the dust devil was closing. He turned back.

"Aislen, please listen to me. There's no time. I have to end this—handle it once and for all. If it works, I need to find my way back into *Demesne*. In this timeline, I never destroyed it.

It's still up and running, still a threat. I can't live with that. Not after everything I've seen."

The 4x4 was almost on them now. She could see the silhouette through the haze.

Raziel caught her face, eyes boring into hers. "If I make it, I will find you. I swear. If I don't, you need to know: I love you. I always have." He kissed her, hard. An overpowering voltage coursed between them and through her, welding his energy with hers so she couldn't ever forget.

Then Raziel charged his space with a frigid vengeance and shoved her toward her truck.

"Go now, Aislen!" he shouted, turning to face the threat barreling down on them.

The black four-wheel drive skidded to a stop, kicking up grit. The door swung open. Troy Kellen stepped out, draped in head-to-toe black, a shadow's echo of Raziel's own past—a Control Operative reborn as an assassin, power-pistol slung loose at his side.

Troy leveled the gun at Raziel. Barrel thick and long, polished steel catching the sun, a blue laser slicing out to mark Raziel's forehead.

"Stand aside, Raziel. She is coming with us."

Aislen, please go now! Raziel's voice lashed through her.

She edged toward her car.

"Don't you dare, Aislen," Troy sang out. "I will blow his fucking brains out if you move." Troy grinned at Raziel. "How does it feel to be powerless now, Raziel? Good, right?"

Aislen, it doesn't matter. Get in the car and go!

Troy turned his smile on her—a monster's delight. "Stay still," Troy said. "This thing melts people—try anything, and he's gone."

Aislen froze.

Troy's passenger door swung open. A figure slid out.

"Now, now, Troy, let's not go scaring her. We catch more flies with honey." It was Sigmund Lange's voice, but it was Blake who strode into view, swaggering like a man who owned the ground he walked on, Sigmund's dead-white eyes in his face.

Blake grinned at her, real slow. *Hello, Poppet. How I have missed you.*

Her knees nearly gave; cold swept over her. She staggered two paces back, and a glacial, phantom hand clamped onto her shoulder, locking her in place.

Steady, darling, Sigmund's voice snaked through her mind. *This won't take long. You've made this too easy. One Time Walk too many. You finally changed something in my favor.*

Tendrils of his energy stabbed into her brain, following the pathways he'd already carved.

Now be a good girl and let... me... IN!

Aislen's entire neural network turned to ice, edges blackening. But this time, she had her own reserves, and she drew them in, coalesced every atom of it into herself. Before Sigmund's energy could snuff her out, she exploded it like a bomb in her brain. The blast not only ejected Sigmund from her skull, it knocked Blake's body off its feet thirty feet away and sent a cold gust spinning through the desert.

Sigmund righted himself fast, howling with laughter, mad and exultant. "Beautiful, Ashlyn! Look at you! A fucking masterpiece. I am going to savor every minute using your body for my pleasure!"

The cold hand was back at her crown, winding through her hair. *I will have you, Poppet. I made you. I'll get you, one way or another—even if it's the hard way.*

The ghostly grip slid down to her throat, crushing her windpipe. At the same time, Blake's body hit the ground, and he started gasping for air.

Sigmund was strangling them both.

I'm not going anywhere without taking someone with me. I will kill you both. But I am pretty sure your lover will resuscitate you, put you back together, no matter whose soul is inside.

The hand squeezed tighter; Aislen could barely gasp for breath. She rallied, pooled her energy together again, grabbing some of Raziel's energy as well, and shoved Sigmund out once again. As she gasped for air, she watched Blake's body jerk up from the sand, then slam down hard, pinned to the earth as Sigmund choked the life out of him. Blake's neck bulged, veins standing out, skin blue.

Aislen, are you really going to let this boy die in the desert? Is that who you have become? Sigmund taunted her.

Blake's real voice came out, the thin wail of a child through the collapsing larynx of his throat. "Help me, please!"

Aislen, don't do it, Raze pleaded in her other ear. *Don't let him have you! Let Sigmund Lange die with Blake.*

Troy laughed, watching the show unfold.

Aislen looked from Raziel to Blake, who was fading fast. Sigmund was right; she couldn't let a child be murdered over her.

All right! STOP! she shouted at Sigmund. *I'll make you a deal.*

Blake stopped choking, but his face was forced sideways, still implanted in the dirt, looking at Aislen, his eyes milky white.

"Go ahead, I'm listening," the possessed Blake said from the ground.

Aislen, please, Raziel begged.

Aislen blocked Raziel out, closed every channel.

I'll let you in, she told Sigmund. *But on my conditions.*

"Still listening," Blake's body said.

Let Blake and Raziel go.

"That's it?" Sigmund rasped, incredulous.

"That's it," Aislen said.

Blake's body sprang up off the ground, landing on both feet. "Deal!"

Immediately, Sigmund was at her skull, but this time, Aislen let him in. The cold flooded her, filled every cell, and she felt Sigmund's raw excitement as he poured into her, unadulterated glee as he flooded her mind and body, filling her with his essence.

Aislen looked at Raziel one last time, hoping he understood, hoping he forgave her. She saw Blake's small body collapse as Sigmund's energy drained out, the eyes turning blue at last. Then Blake's face turned to Troy.

"Kill him," Sigmund spat from Blake's mouth as his body crumpled to the dirt.

Troy smiled at Raziel. "My pleasure."

And a shot cracked across the desert.

FORTY-SIX

AISLEN'S BODY COLLAPSED, boneless, onto the red earth, arms and legs bent at strange angles. Blake lay face down nearby, cheek crushed against the grit and sand, unmoving except for a tremor of breath. Troy sprawled on his back, eyes wide to the sky, his chest a ragged wound that pumped thick blood into the ground, turning the dust black and oily beneath him.

The desert dust rose like a halo, clinging to their clothes and the thin sound of the world.

Raziel was the only one left standing.

In her last moment of consciousness, Aislen had shot Troy in the chest with the shotgun, sacrificing herself for Raziel. And now, Raziel wanted to die. He looked down at her body, torn. He wanted to run to her, lift her from the earth, and force her soul back behind her eyes.

But that was pointless. What she'd done could never be undone. She had let Sigmund in. Not by accident, not by force. By permission. She had known what she was doing. Consent opened the door, and once inside, only the host body's death would throw him out.

Raziel would not be the one to kill her body, even if she wasn't the one possessing it.

Aislen was lost to him now.

He felt the fury building up in his bones, the urge to incinerate this entire hellish landscape, to burn the Red Centre to glass and salt, to rip out the sky—but this wasn't his world, his domain. It belonged to Sigmund Lange now.

Blake moaned and shifted, rolling onto one side, then pushing himself upright with slow, uncertain hands. His own life-force pulsed through his body fully again. His eyes found Raziel, squinting through a haze of pain and confusion.

"Hello, Mr. Raziel. Am I dead now?"

Raziel shook his head, voice gentle, almost absent. "No, Blake. You're not. But you have a decision to make. You can come with me, but I don't know where we will end up or if we'll ever be able to come back. Or stay here and take your chances with..." He couldn't say her name. He looked at the broken shape of her, then back to Blake.

"She's Ichiban now. And you're still useful to him. He'll want to use you for whatever he has planned, or keep you as a backup, just in case. If you choose to go with him, you run the first chance you get. Scream at an airport, run to someone, and tell them you've been kidnapped, whatever it takes. Get back to your family. Your dad will be waiting for you at home."

Blake looked at Aislen's crumpled body. "She saved my dad."

Raziel followed his gaze, watching the faint rise and fall of her chest as Sigmund Lange took his first breaths through her lungs. His heart shattered into a million pieces. "Yes, she did. She saved all of us."

Her body groaned, limbs jerking, spasms working through

her muscles as Sigmund's frequency took hold, hijacking each nerve ending. Aislen had to be in there somewhere, just enough to keep the body alive for Sigmund, but she would have no say in what happened next. No control. Raziel couldn't bear to watch the rest of the process—the slow, awful overwriting of every last thing that was Aislen.

He turned from her, found Blake's eyes.

"Do you want to come with me?" Raziel asked, voice raw.

Blake looked at him, back at Aislen's twitching body, then back at Raziel, chin set. "I want to see my dad."

Raziel nodded. There were no good options. Running into the unknown with Raziel wasn't any kinder than staying with Ichiban, but at least Blake had chosen it for himself.

"You are going to be okay, Blake. Just remember who you really are. Don't let them take that away, not ever. "I did terrible things..." He swallowed. "And I am sorry. For all of it."

Raziel walked over and crouched beside Aislen's body. The seizing had gotten worse; soon, Sigmund would crush down whatever spark she had left, shrinking her to a flicker. Raziel bent at the level of her face and pressed his lips softly to her forehead, one last benediction, a breathless goodbye. He reached out with whatever energy he had left and whispered to the lingering ember inside her:

I will always love you, Aislen. Nothing ever changes that.

He straightened, picked up the map that lay in the dirt beside her shotgun, and turned away just as the last convulsion locked her limbs and the new presence fully claimed her.

Without looking back, Raziel climbed into his four-wheel drive and steered into the empty horizon and the barren unknown.

FORTY-SEVEN

AISLEN CLAWED her way through the numb dark, deep inside herself, where Sigmund Lange's glacial force battered her. He lashed through her with freezing violence, and every time, Aislen hit him back, burning him with currents as white-hot as the desert sun outside her crumpled body. He whipped his energy through every crack of her being, and she didn't yield; she flared, she fought, she threw up barricades wherever he tried to press further in.

Sigmund wanted her logic centers—to seize her from the inside and reroute her at the source. She electrocuted his attempts, surging volts through the tangled places he tried to occupy. But he was relentless.

When brute force failed him, he detonated his frequency into a scatterbomb—a million Sigmund fragments embedding into every cell, every synapse, every strand of her like a virus coded to reconstruct itself. He knew he would splinter. But he knew, too, that she would never get all of him out; eventually, if she slacked her grip, he'd reassemble himself and come back.

She could feel her flesh and bones tremble against the

surface of the earth as deep inside her body, Sigmund Lange's putrid soul bore itself into her biology. If she didn't do something, he would win, and she would lose herself forever.

So she watched his strategy, considered it, and went one step further. If he could infiltrate, atom by atom, she could do the same. But she saw the trap: if she simply pushed him out, if she exorcised him in a supernova, he would just take flight, find another host. Maybe even land in Blake. She wasn't going to let that happen.

Sigmund was right about one thing. He had made her. She was he product of his own years of tinkering and torture, every experiment and manipulation. But he had underestimated what it would cost him. Because Aislen's rage was bigger than anything he could muster. His evil was old, but her fury was fresh.

Instead of detonating her energy and ejecting him, Aislen summoned an undertow, black and endless, and let it rip. The dark gravity well hooked Sigmund's splintered pieces and reeled them in. She sucked his frequency deep. And as his consciousness caught on, as he felt himself being dragged into her, he screamed.

She could hear him wail as he was pulled into the vortex of her energy. As he flailed against it, Aislen flagellated him with every ounce of fury she had, lassoing him with hot cords of voltage and reeling him in.

Sigmund shrieked, begging for mercy, but Aislen wouldn't let up beating the living shit out of him until her revenge was satisfied. If he was going to be inside her, he was going to be her bitch.

His voltage started to wane, worn down by the power of Aislen Walker. As his energy submitted, Aislen gathered all the remnant strands of his frequency, flattened them out, then carefully began folding him up into a little box like origami. Once she had him contained, she shoved him down into the abyss, somewhere in the recesses of her reptilian brain.

She could feel residual slivers of Sigmund wriggling in the hidden crevasses of her. She would have to deal with that later. She needed to refocus her energy on her body before it died from a lack of life force. Aislen would never be rid of him: Sigmund was a part of her now—until the day she died. But she would do everything in her power to contain him, except when she needed him. She was going to use this motherfucker for all he was worth.

Once she had him where she wanted him, she allowed herself to unfold again, back into her body, her rightful vehicle. As she started surfacing into consciousness, she could hear Raziel's voice in the distance.

I will always love you, Aislen. Nothing ever changes that.

Good to know, she thought to herself. She hoped it was true. Because she was counting on that. Someday she would need him.

Aislen hydrated her cells with her essences again, feeling her flesh and bones and cells in a way she had never felt them before. Her whole body tingled with energy. She could feel it radiating, vibrant with life. How funny. That sensation had always been there, but it had become white noise with familiarity. She vowed she was never going to forget what life felt like again.

She opened her eyes into the blazing sunlight and took a deep breath of the scorching air. It felt like nectar, this breath, this oxygen, full of grit and dust and perfection. When she settled back into her skin, her limbs trembled, and sweat cooled on her brow; victory had teeth in it.

She slowly pushed herself up and saw Blake kneeling on the ground a few feet away from her. He looked petrified.

"Hello, Blake," she said, her own voice coming out of her mouth.

Relief washed over his face, and it looked like he had just taken his own first breath, too.

"Hello, Ashlyn," Blake said.

"My name is Aislen," she said. "Sigmund didn't know who I am."

Blake smiled. "Good. Hello, Aislen."

Aislen got up off the ground and walked over to Blake. Troy's lifeless body lay in the dirt, a shitbag in a black suit, in a black pool of blood. Aislen felt no remorse. She would never feel remorse again. Because she had plans. And there would be more bodies.

She turned and looked down the long, dirt road. The barest thread of dust rose up in a column against blue sky; Raziel on the run.

"I don't think he wanted to leave," Blake said quietly from beside her.

"I know," she said, watching the dust cloud extinguish on the horizon. "But it's destiny."

GOSPEL OF A TIME WALKER

Dig Down ~ Muse

RAZIEL DROVE through the Outback for three days. If he'd taken the main highway, it might have only taken him one, but he couldn't risk taking the roads where any of The 8's mercenaries could find him. The 8 wouldn't rely solely on Troy to assassinate him. They would have deployed their sleeper cells in the area, just in case.

There were millions of people around the world on standby, ready to do their bidding at the flip of a switch. Cultivated through *Demesne*, the media, and frequency manipulation, they could be turned on and activated with the single intention of hunting and destroying Raziel Tanis.

Blind, preprogrammed sheeple who thought they were their own independent individuals but who were really sleeping Manchurian candidates. Legions of them existed, completely unaware of the powers that held their strings.

Raziel shifted frequencies every five minutes but stopped using humans. There were too few out here. A human frequency would stand out; even if it wasn't his, it would be suspect. Instead, he took on the surrounding landscape. At first scan, there wasn't a lot of diversity to choose from, a rock or a shrub, a roo or a lizard. But the more he tuned in, the more intricacies he found, and he could blend in with spiders, a camel, a dingo, a mineral, or any different genus of plant life.

If he wasn't careful, the Outback could have bitten him, sucked him up into its endless mirage and miles and miles of cloned shrubs. At times, he thought that maybe he was really just caught up in a computer simulation. Maybe he'd never made it out of *Demesne* or The Stratum. Maybe this was all just a dream. He would have loved to wake up in The Womb right now and start the week over. But then he would run out of gas, be forced to get out and stretch his legs, and remind himself he was of the living.

Thankfully, he'd packed enough gas, food, and, most importantly, water to survive this trek. Even though he'd hoped he wouldn't have had to take it. He'd thought he would have been dead, killed while protecting Aislen, and she would have been the one making this journey. But the further he drove, the more he realized that she was never meant for this journey. He was.

Raziel had Preston's map. Though he didn't have the amulet to guide him with its constant resonance, he had an atlas that he'd bought at the airport. He'd matched the two up as he filled the tank with gas and rested on his first night. Uluru was the purple spiral on the drawing. Where he found Aislen was the diamond in the middle of nowhere. The place he was headed was in the midst of the MacDonnell Ranges, the strangest mountain range he had ever seen.

On the atlas map, the mountain range consisted of two parallel ridges with a large meteoric crater in the middle. To Raziel's eye, it resembled the Eye of Horus, with the ridges forming the outer eye socket and the crater forming the iris.

Most people saw the Eye of Horus as an Egyptian symbol

of protection and good health. Raziel understood it as something more. It was a map of its own: a map of human consciousness, a map that, when followed, took one to the portal that allowed consciousness to travel out of its three-dimensional limitations of the brain into the realities and infinite worlds beyond comprehension.

Preston Reed, at five years old, had mapped the natural pineal gland of the earth, something humans had tried to recreate with pyramids and temples across the globe, always forgetting it was right inside their brains all along. This would be the last place Reed actually went. Raziel hoped he would find him there, hoped he could beg his forgiveness for failing his daughter and would help him find his own way to cope.

Raziel was taking the long way, but the exact spot was only 600 kilometers northeast of where he'd left Aislen and Blake.

Sigmund and Blake, he reminded himself. She wasn't Aislen anymore. He had to remember that. He didn't know what to consider her. Was she even a person anymore? Or did the monster who possessed her completely extinguish her? Raziel tried not to think about it. The pain was too raw, and it clouded what limited capabilities he had right now. The only way he could justify leaving her behind, the only way he could live with himself, was by remembering that Aislen no longer existed.

He focused on the road ahead. He was almost there. He could not afford to get sidetracked by his grief. Night was falling fast, and if he didn't get there soon, he'd be lost.

Raziel saw movement on the horizon. He squinted, trying to see through the wet emotion in his eyes and the evening summer radiating off the rusted earth. But there was nothing there. Outback fever was setting in, and his imagination was being fueled by dehydration.

No. There it was again, bigger now and moving toward him.

Raziel stopped the car and got out, trying to get his awareness straight. He closed his eyes and took a deep breath, then opened them again. Still, something moved toward him. He watched as the phantom continued approaching. It wasn't until it was a hundred yards away that Raziel could make out what it was.

A man. He was nearly naked, a pattern of white dots and yellow streaks painted on skin black as night. He looked like a night sky, filled with stars and meteors, and blended into the landscape around him like he was actually a part of it, an ancient mediary between the heavens and the earth.

Raziel reached out to him, feeling for a frequency. Was he friend or foe? But there wasn't one. He was as still and silent as a void.

Cool trick, Raziel thought.

The man spoke. Raziel couldn't understand what he was saying. There were no words in the midst of the clicks, clucks, and buzzes that emitted from the man's mouth. It sounded like pure vibration, not language. He could feel it in his chest, but could not decipher it in his brain.

Raziel shook his head. "I don't understand."

The man gave him a look, one that Raziel *could* read: a look that said something like, "Come on now, yes, you do."

The man walked up to Raziel and put his palm on his chest, then spoke again.

We've been waiting for you, Raziel. You are right in time. The man handed him a hollowed-out gourd of water. *Follow me.*

They walked in silence for another hour along the sandy, dried-up riverbed that snaked through a range of plateaus.

Raziel hadn't brought anything with him from the car, and by the time he realized it, night had fallen completely. He could only see his guide by following the stars painted on his body.

They trekked off the riverbed pathway and into a grassland clearing. Embedded in the earth they walked across was a crop circle: rings within rings, concentric circles nested deeper and deeper within each other, arranged side by side in an array of sacred geometry. They looked like Raziel's original structure outline for programming *Demesne*: six Octaves, one nested within the other. In 3D, they would look like a stepladder as you moved up through the Octaves until you reached The Stratum. Here, his outline of the gaming system was scorched into the earth, not just one but hundreds, maybe thousands, side by side.

They crossed the meadow of worlds and into a thicket of trees. The ghosted gum trees were white beings all their own, blinding sentries in the darkness. He walked through them feeling as though they were watching him with eyes more ancient than humanity.

It was then he realized the gourd he was drinking from was not filled with water. His vision began to swim. Reality began to morph. The ghosted trees appeared to part before them, clearing a path before him and his guide, opening into another glade.

A wall of black granite rose up in front of them 200 feet high, stretching a long distance to the north and south. In the center of the towering wall was an entirely unnatural indent: a perfect rectangle 100 feet tall and 50 feet wide, a solid rock doorway that led a few yards into another solid rock wall. The surreal stone portal was in no way man-made. Primitive man would not have had the means to create such a seamless and enormous carving. Even with machinery, it would have been impossible to engineer such a trench.

Lined up in front of the black rock wall was another block-ade...this one of men. Each one was black as midnight, and each was painted like Raziel's guide, a galaxy all their own. They stood in a half-circle facing him, like The 8, yet a hundred strong. Together, they fanned out across the darkness like a galaxy.

Raziel felt light-headed but reached out his energy to feel for their intent. Like the guide, they were empty: no judgment, no demands, no frequency.

Each of them stood beside a lit torch staked into the ground to ward off the night.

His guide directed him to a cushion in the middle of the semicircle.

Please, sit, the guide said.

Raziel grew uncomfortable. Was this some type of judg-ment day? Was he about to be a human sacrifice? He looked at his guide, the wall of men behind him, and the wall of moun-tain behind them. If he wanted to run, the only way out was back through the ghosted forest and into the sea of wilderness. Even if he made it, he wouldn't survive.

Raziel sighed. If this was his final judgment, so be it. After everything Raziel had done in his life, he deserved whatever was coming. He sat down.

Another man came forward carrying a bowl and knelt before him, extending it toward Raziel.

Eat this, he communicated. His face was shiny and cheru-bic. It radiated joy as if serving Raziel his last meal was an honor.

Raziel realized he was starving and took the bowl. He sniffed it. It smelled disgusting, a mixture of sulfur and acetone. It had to be poison. He pushed it back, but the man just smiled.

It's okay. Eat. He nodded his head and somehow made Raziel believe it was actually all right.

Fuck it, he thought to himself. He had nothing to lose. If it was poison and painful... again, he deserved it.

He scooped his fingers into the warm mash and swallowed as much as he could in one bite. It tasted as bad as it smelled, and his stomach tried to revolt. But he pushed it back down into his gut. He was already in this deep. He wasn't getting out. He might as well go this way rather than face death any other way.

A didgeridoo began to play. A droning and warbling bass snaked in and circled through the crowd, spiraling its way toward Raziel. He felt it tickle his skin first, the hairs on his body standing up on end. It encircled his head, causing him to swoon...or maybe that was the poison, or possibly a combination of both.

The melody caressed down his spine, relaxing him instantly, and then unexpectedly slammed into his body with a powerful punch. The drone pulsed through his inner core with purpose, on its very own search and destroy mission. Raziel felt his stomach lurch violently, and he crumpled into a ball in the dirt.

The wood trumpet warbled lower, and Raziel could feel it twisting through his guts. He curled into the fetal position, trying to protect himself, but it was no use. The sound started finding pieces of him that he had long forgotten.

His dad was dredged up first: all the times they had played together, throwing a ball, riding a bike, raking leaves in the yard. Then the drone found his mother; her sadness, her grief washing through him like it was his own. Raziel felt her sorrow, felt the love for a son that she had grown within her body, given life to, and lost forever. Raziel felt a longing of his own in return, for her unconditional adoration. It was a yearning he'd buried so deep he'd obliterated it.

Each spiral of the drone dug deeper into his body, through

his guts, his memories, his soul. It churned up his darkest pain, grabbed hold of it, and pulled it back up to the surface for him to feel.

Raziel felt himself as a five-year-old boy again, being ostracized by his peers because he was different, brutally bullied, and crushed by loneliness.

He felt his adolescence come to the surface, the angsty, lost soul who started converting the energy of pain and suffering into anger, a shift that felt better. Later, when he converted anger into rage, lashing out and hurting people, it felt even better than just being mad. As the instrument drew these memories to the surface, Raziel felt how his rage became an addiction, a beast all its own that soothed him, but needed fed.

The drone punched in deeper, reminding Raziel just how he had fed his beast: punishing humanity through his work at Infinium. Raziel had blood on his hands, and the instrument wouldn't let him forget it. Every face was pulled up from the past, every victim, and they stared him down until he acknowledged his wicked actions.

Raziel began to weep uncontrollably. It was the only way he could purge the pain and release the emotions that were tormenting him. He lifted his head, searching for the player of this torture device. He spotted him off to the side, another ancient man, all black and stars, with long white hair that dangled to the ground. He wanted to cry out for mercy, but noticed a second man sitting beside the first, holding another hollowed log, only bigger. He looked Raziel in the eye and smiled ever so slightly before raising the instrument to his lips.

Raziel shook his head. *Please no.*

His plea was ignored. A deeper bass burst from the instrument, piercing Raziel, this time right through the heart.

Aislen.

It was a whisper in the wind, and she bloomed in his mind

in a kaleidoscope of the senses. The green of her eyes and their bursts of gold, her face as she looked up at him as they became one. The scent of her, and her taste on his tongue. Her energy intertwined with his, aligned with his own for what he could feel was eternity. He never knew. She was always meant to be his, supposed to be a part of him.

A third instrument added its voice to the serenade. It reached in, seized Aislen's frequency, and began pulling it away from him. Like a pied piper, it enchanted her energy to let go, coaxing it to untangle from all the spaces, unweaving it from his heart, and severing it from his soul.

Raziel tried to fight it, tried to hold on to her, but the other instruments and their deeper vibrations held him down with a powerful force. Helpless, he felt her energy being unwoven from his being, like a vibrant thread being pulled from a tapestry. He writhed in agony. At last, he couldn't take it anymore, and he cried out, arms outstretched to the sky, a primal scream as his very soul was laid to waste. He collapsed on the ground, spent.

The music shifted, and the crowd surrounding him began clapping. They stamped their feet on the earth as they closed in on him, creating a vibration beneath his body, urging him to rise. He found himself sitting up, almost levitated by their combined efforts. The stars of them began to move and dance in a circle around him. The earth felt like it was moving, turning on its axis with them. The veil of reality shifted and warped.

Raziel felt hands on him, taking off his shirt. He was broken and couldn't bring himself to fight. His pants were removed, and soon he stood completely naked in the night. The air was not cold; Raziel felt one with it. He no longer felt his body, the boundaries of his form having melted away. He could not tell where he began or ended.

The guide suddenly appeared and placed his fingers upon Raziel's face, and began to chant. He sang a song about the sky and its people, about creation and First Man. Raziel felt more hands upon him, spreading warmth across his skin. He glanced down at his arms and saw they were painting him with warm, pure white clay. Their fingers pressed along his back, and Raziel knew they were covering it with white feathers.

This has been foretold, the ancient guide sang to his people. *This was the way of the World Walkers.*

The crowd opened up, parting before Raziel and surrounding him from behind, all chanting in unison now.

The guide pulled Raziel forward, reached one finger up, and touched the center of his forehead.

"This is not a dream."

White light cut through the rock wall before Raziel, a portal opening in the black granite. The tribe's singing swelled in awe and celebration.

"It's time for you to go," the guide said as he stepped aside.

Raziel began walking toward the doorway of white light, propelled forward by the song at his back, his feet lifted by the woodwinds. As he drew nearer, the light became blinding, its heat searing. The atoms in his body began to irradiate. His skin felt like it was ripping apart. Yet an ever-pervading peace descended upon him, and he moved into the doorway. All remaining burdens dropped away, and an utterly beautiful feeling of connection took his breath away.

Raziel saw sparks flying, shooting stars exploding away from him in all directions. A billion light particles that were once a part of himself blew apart as Raziel deresonated into bliss.

In a blink, the billion particles of his self collided back together, and he floated blindly, cradled in a droning hum.

"Gamma 42," a voice, oddly precise, said from somewhere in the diminishing whiteout.

Raziel started lifting into an upright position, and a shadowy figure moved toward him. But it wasn't the ancient one coming to guide him.

"Hello, Raziel," Preston Reed said. "I'm glad you made it. We have a lot of work to do."

GOSPEL OF A WORLD WALKER

Run ~ Snow Patrol

CLOSING CREDITS

Levels ~ Avencii

ACKNOWLEDGMENTS

To all the Dream Walkers who patiently waited to become Time Walkers; the time is now.

First readers, Kelsea Overstreet, Rick Posey, Kim Anderson, Phyllis Hoffman, Renea Dawes, your notes, questions, insights, and support help shape these novels and are priceless to me.

My daughters Kelsea and Mattéa Overstreet. I keep pursuing my dreams so you will keep pursuing yours.

Mom. Life with you was complicated. But everything I am, began with you. My drive to create, find passion in life, and do whatever I fucking want... that came from you. You better be tearing it up beyond the Veil.

To everyone who ever underestimated me—you fueled the fire.

ABOUT THE AUTHOR

Shannan Sinclair is a retired 911 dispatcher, who brings grit, dark humor, and emotional intensity to her characters, weaving stories that explore the edges of consciousness, time, and love.

When she isn't writing about—or traveling in—alternate dimensions, Shannan is developing *Second Spring*, a contemporary romance about reinvention and finding love in midlife.

She lives in California's Central Valley with her family, two cats, and a very opinionated French Bulldog. When not at her desk, you can usually find her line dancing, roller skating, or chasing sunsets.

You can connect with her at:

www.ShannanSinclair.com and on social media
IG:@SoulSideOutOfficial
TikTok: @SoulSideOut and @DreamWalkerFiles.

ALSO BY SHANNAN SINCLAIR